Jack of Clubs

BARBARA METZGER

A SIGNET ECLIPSE BOOK

SIGNET ECLIPSE
Published by New American Library, a division of
Penguin Group (USA) Inc., 375 Hudson Street,
New York, New York 10014, USA
Penguin Group (Canada), 90 Eglinton Avenue East, Suite 700, Toronto,
Ontario M4P 2Y3, Canada (a division of Pearson Penguin Canada Inc.)
Penguin Books Ltd., 80 Strand, London WC2R 0RL, England
Penguin Ireland, 25 St. Stephen's Green, Dublin 2,
Ireland (a division of Penguin Books Ltd.)
Penguin Group (Australia), 250 Camberwell Road, Camberwell, Victoria 3124,
Australia (a division of Pearson Australia Group Pty. Ltd.)
Penguin Books India Pvt. Ltd., 11 Community Centre, Panchsheel Park,
New Delhi - 110 017, India
Penguin Group (NZ), cnr Airborne and Rosedale Roads, Albany,
Auckland 1310, New Zealand (a division of Pearson New Zealand Ltd.)
Penguin Books (South Africa) (Pty.) Ltd., 24 Sturdee Avenue,
Rosebank, Johannesburg 2196, South Africa

Penguin Books Ltd., Registered Offices:
80 Strand, London WC2R 0RL, England

First published by Signet Eclipse, an imprint of New American Library,
a division of Penguin Group (USA) Inc.

First Printing, March 2006
10 9 8 7 6 5 4 3 2 1

To the Irish rover who broke my heart
for the last time.

CHAPTER ONE

1815

The Honorable Jonathan Endicott, or Captain Jack as he was known, was finally home from the wars. So what?

Six years of war had been hell, terrifying and tedious in turn. Peace was simply boring. The first peace, the false lull between the Corsican's exile and his return, had been a pageant. Jack had thrown himself into the festivities with the same fervor he'd ridden into pitched battles, with his heart leading the way. Wine, women, and who cared what song they were playing if he could hold a sweet-smelling lady in his arms?

Jack's older brother had even traveled to the Peace Congress with his bride to reunite their small family, making the celebrations more joyous yet. Everyone knew Ace had to take a wife, for he was Alexander

Chalfont Endicott, Earl of Carde, with a succession to ensure, the poor blighter.

If Jack had thought about it, he would have guessed Ace would hide behind his spectacles, studying the field of possibilities, researching their pedigrees, examining each filly for temperament and soundness before making his choice of countess. He was that meticulous and logical about everything else and always had been. Who would have thought he'd fall arse over Adam's apple for skinny little Nelly Sloane, their deceased stepmother's young cousin? Why, Ace had helped Jack put frogs in Nelly's bed, although he had drawn the line at snakes down her back.

Of course Nelly, who insisted upon Nell now that she was Lady Carde, was not little, skinny or merely someone's poor relation. She was all grown up, gorgeous in looks and giving in nature, great of heart. In other words, Nelly was everything Jack would have wished for in a wife—for his brother. The best of brothers, Ace had been Jack's anchor since they were orphaned as boys. He deserved nothing less than the perfect bride, his own true love.

The love Ace and Nell shared glistened more than all the jewels at all the balls in Vienna, and softened the hardest hearts, turned to stone by years of war. Some day Jack would find a woman like that—after he had waltzed and wined and wooed his way through the ranks of warm and willing womanhood.

Vienna had been as glowing and glorious as a springtime rainbow, but it had been as fleeting.

The current victory celebrations in London were a travesty, abhorrent to Jack. The country should have been in mourning for all the men they had lost, for all the blood shed at Waterloo. Instead they were holding fireworks and festivals in the streets of London, sparing no expense while the returning veterans were begging in the alleys.

Jack took part in as few of the events, public or private, as possible. He sold his commission as soon as he could, refused a position at the war office despite the promise of a knighthood, and burned his uniform. He locked his pistols away, vowing never to kill another man, and gave his sword as a belated christening gift to his brother and Nell's firstborn son, Jason, named after the previous earl, Jack and Alex's father.

Jack was six and twenty, home to stay, his life ahead of him. So what was he going to do with it?

"You are always welcome here," Alex said when Jack traveled to Carde Hall in Northampshire. Nell was breeding again, and feeling too ill to travel to London. They had begged him to come to Cardington to visit. Or to stay, making his home with them. Jack thought he'd sooner rejoin the army than sit by while his brother and sister-in-law made sheep's eyes at each other and cooed over their young son. How many times could even a doting uncle chuck a babe under the chin—under the four chins the little dumpling seemed to have—before going cross-eyed? And with another brat—baby—on the way, Jack would feel like a trespasser, a voyeur, if he did not go batty from boredom.

"You could take over some of the duties of the earldom," Ace proposed, while Jack pondered how soon he could make his departure. "Act as overseer for me. I hate to leave Nell and the baby to travel to all the properties and holdings. Appearing in Parliament is duty enough."

"I know nothing of crops and cows. And wish to know less."

"Then you could handle some of the financial affairs."

Jack used a word he should never have uttered in front of a gently bred female. "My apologies, Nell. I have been too long out of polite society."

Nell nodded graciously, turning back to embroidering tiny roses on a tiny white gown for the daughter she hoped to have this time.

"But we both know I have no head for investments. I let you handle my own accounts, don't I? By the way, thank you for making my inheritance grow, far more than I could have hoped. The only numbers I am good with is gambling odds."

"You have the wit, just not the patience. As always." Alex wiped his spectacles while he considered his sibling's future. Jack was taller, broader, far more muscular than Alex was, but he was still his little brother. They shared the same dark hair, although Jack's was curlier and cut longer. They had the same brown eyes, but Jack's vision needed no glasses. Unfortunately, they had the same nose. Lucky Jack had his broken, more than once, it seemed, so the Endicott eagle beak was not as prominent. Alex said a silent prayer skyward for his future daughter's feminine features, then turned his attention back to Jack.

Alex wanted his restless brother here, safe, but he knew the decision was not his to make. "You do have that piece of farmland in Kent from our mother," he reminded Jack.

"What, I should sit back and watch the turnips grow?"

Alex's gaze traveled to his wife's burgeoning belly. "There are worse things."

Not for Jack, there were not.

"Then go back to London and take up the high life. Your bank account can stand the expense, and the estate can afford the rest."

"What, I should live on my brother's largesse? What do you take me for?"

"A hero, that's what," Alex promptly replied, and Jack felt his cheeks grow warm, knowing his brother believed it.

"Go on, I just did my job like everyone else."

"And the country owes you for it. You deserve a life of leisure."

"What, become a Bond Street beau on the strut? Set up a racing stable and a mistress—sorry, Nell— and attend all the balls? Then go on drinking and gambling through the night so I can sleep through the day? Fuss with my clothes and flirt with the debutantes? What kind of life is that?"

"One many men pursue," Nell said, "or wish they could."

Jack shuddered. "I do not."

Alex was not finished. "What of politics? You could have the seat for Cardington in the Commons."

Jack grimaced. "The war could have been over years ago if the pettifoggers had stayed out of it."

"The law?"

"I have broken more than my fair share. Do you recall the night we—"

Alex cleared his throat.

"Right. Not the law. Or the church, before you mention that. If my prayers had been answered, Bonaparte would have been trounced two years ago."

"What about travel, now that the Continent is safe? Although I would hate to see you so far away again."

Jack frowned at the glass of brandy in his hand. "I have heard enough foreign languages to last a lifetime. Your heir's babble is the only tongue I want to hear, other than the King's English. We are working on 'Uncle Jack,' although 'nuh-nuh' seems the best we can manage."

Nell tried to hide her smile. Her brilliant son used his one word to call for his nursemaid, his breakfast, and his favorite blanket. "Didn't you always want to own a string of race horses?" she asked now, recalling how the young Jack and his pony had been inseparable. Her husband smiled at her as if she'd made an outstanding suggestion, but Jack shook his head.

"I have spent six years of my life on the back of a horse. That's enough."

The only sound in the room was the crackling of the fire in the hearth as they all tried to think of ideas for Jack's civilian life. Nell thought he should find a nice girl and settle down, but she was too wise to say so. Alex had heard that advice too often himself to think of offering it to his brother. When the time came, Jack would know it. Until then . . .

"You need a quest, like a knight errant," Alex offered.

"Do not harp on that knighthood business again, brother. I told you I was not interested in any title. I never wanted yours, and I surely do not want one granted in return for your paying another of Prinny's debts."

Alex held up his hand. "I truly meant a knight of old, damsels in distress, sworn oaths and chivalry, the tales we used to read as boys."

"Speaking of damsels in distress, what news is there of the search for our half sister?"

Nell excused herself. She could not bear to hear the conversation about Lottie, her cousin Lizbeth's child, not when her own older brother had been behind the little girl's disappearance fifteen years ago. Phelan Sloane had hired someone to stop the coach, in a misguided attempt to keep his beloved Lizbeth from leaving their home. He had been too obsessed with Lizbeth to acknowledge her eagerness to return to her own husband, the former Earl of Carde, father to Alex and Jack. The carriage had gone over a cliff, however, killing the young countess and the servants. Little Charlotte was never seen again, but Phelan had bankrupted his estate and stolen from Alex's to pay his hireling blood money to keep her alive. Or so they all hoped.

The old earl had died of a lung congestion and a broken heart. The kidnapper, Dennis Godfrey, was long dead, and Phelan was kept in a secluded inn where he could not harm anyone else, or himself. Nell could only pray for him, and for Lottie.

After she left and the two men had resumed their seats, Alex said, "We have not discovered much since I wrote to you last. We found that Dennis Godfrey's sister suddenly had a child no one knew about. She had been a seamstress who occasionally worked at Drury Lane, but she left London less than a fortnight after Lottie went missing. No one knows where she went or what name she used. Actors are an unsteady lot at best, their careers not long-lived, and the theater itself has undergone several transformations. After all these years, few people there even recall Molly Godfrey. She must have picked up Phelan's money at the bank, but no one there can describe her, and the funds have not been withdrawn in three years now."

Jack took a sip of his drink. "I have a mind to find Lottie."

"What, because you are at loose ends?"

"No, because I promised our father that I would never stop looking for her."

"Jack, you were eleven years old!"

"And you were fourteen, but you have not given up."

"No, and that is why I have two Bow Street Runners in my employ looking for traces of Molly Godfrey everywhere. We fear she has died or left the country. What makes you think you could discover more than they can?"

Jack smiled, showing a dimple in one cheek. "Because they have to obey the laws they are sworn to uphold; I do not. And, remember, I am used to giving orders and being obeyed."

"That's rubbish. Actors and dressmakers and the like are not going to salute when you walk by. They will not talk about one of their own kind, not to an officer or a gentleman. You'd be wasting your time."

"I have nothing but time. And who says I am a gentleman, anyway?"

"You were born and bred one. You cannot be anything else."

"Odd, all of our nannies called me Spawn of Satan and the Devil's Cub. The men under my command never worried what title my father held, not when they were following me into bloody battle. No, you are the gentleman, Ace, raised to be just what you are, a pillar of the community, a conscientious, compassionate upholder of the values this country needs and respects."

"Bah, you make me sound dull."

"Sometimes I envied you that respectable dullness, waiting to be ambushed in the Peninsula. Not that I would have chosen any other course but the army, but it changed me from a tame little member of polite society."

Alex laughed. "You were never tame, brother. The army was the only place for your hey-go-mad escapades. But you are older and hopefully wiser."

"Ah, but I am far more useless. I was the spare, the dispensable second son. Now you have an heir of your own, with another on the way, perhaps."

"I pray this one is a girl, for Nell's sake. As you

said, second sons can be the very devil." Alex raised his glass. "To little girls."

Jack lifted his. "Like Lottie."

Alex knew there would be no dissuading his brother from whatever route he chose. "What will you do, then?"

"Why, I believe I shall become one of that shadow class where information can be bought and sold, where a man is judged by his wits, not the height of his neckcloth or the length of his pedigree. I shall go London, of course, where everything has its price, even the women. Especially the women. That is where pretty young women come to make their fortunes. More than that?" He shrugged broad shoulders. "Who knows?"

"I pray Nell never does. She'll have my head on a platter for not urging you into a respectable career and a chance to meet respectable young ladies. You do know, don't you, that your actions might set you beyond the pale of what is acceptable in polite society, even for a second son? You will always be welcome at Carde Hall, of course, but be sure what you want before you slam other doors in your own face. You might never again be invited to those balls you disdain now, or the gentlemen's clubs."

Jack raised his glass again. "So what?"

Nell and Alex were better off not knowing Jack's plans, he decided. Big brother had always been a worrier, and poor Nell was scarcely recovered from her own brother's shame. They would not be in London anyway, not with the new babe imminent, so Jack could set the town on its stiff-rumped rear if he wanted. He wanted.

He wanted to establish the flashiest, most fashionable gaming house in the city. As he'd told Alex, he did have a head for gambling odds and the pasteboards. He intended to bring in the wealthy swells, and he intended to hire the prettiest females he could find to serve them. The money he made—and he figured it would be considerable—would go toward feeding hungry soldiers and their families, and to finding Lottie.

Baby Charlotte would be eighteen years old by now. She had never had the upbringing or the education or the advantages of an earl's daughter, the life to which she was entitled. She had never been presented at court. Hell, she might never have been presented to anyone but pig farmers. For all Jack knew, she was wed to a tailor, in bed with an actor, or dead.

Anything was possible, but Jack was counting on gambling, wasn't he? If Lottie had grown to anything like the promise she had shown as a toddler, all blond ringlets and big blue eyes, she had grown into a comely young woman. If she resembled her stunning mother, whom Jack remembered fondly, or her beautiful cousin, his new sister-in-law, she was a diamond of the first water. She was not going to be a seamstress like the woman who had stolen her. Not if Jack knew the way of the world.

With Molly Godfrey gone—a reasonable assumption since the support money had not been withdrawn—Lottie would be on her own. She must not remember her true heritage or she would have found Alex long since. So what would a beautiful young female of no family, no fortune, and a modicum of ambition do? She would come to London, of course. And not to work in the dark backroom of some dressmaking shop, not if she was an Endicott. Pride had to flow in Lottie's veins, whether she knew it or not.

The odds were long, but Jack was used to losing

causes. He had been on the wrong side of too many battles to count, even when the British were declared victorious. He'd won his way through, and led his men as best he was able . . . with that same Endicott pride.

The idea of his own baby sister entering a dark, dank gaming den with scoundrels and cheats and cigar smoke was abhorrent, so his establishment would be elegant, refined, in good taste, and expensive.

The women dealers would be decorative, not debased. He was not about to promote prostitution, not when his own kin might be forced to sell herself to the highest bidder. No gentlemen other than himself were to be permitted above stairs in the private living quarters of the house he found, nor would he take money from the girls' outside activities. Those were none of his business, literally, as long as his employees dealt an honest hand. His income would come from the losers, not the ladies.

Jack wanted information, not a guiltier conscience than he already had. So he paid the girls a higher share, hoping to keep them from other positions—on their backs. Soon he had more applicants for the jobs than he could possibly use. Why not? He was offering decent wages and clean conditions. If half the women were more interested in dallying with the handsome boss than dealing the cards, well, that was a mere fringe benefit.

Jack was having a wonderful time, refurbishing the house he had found on the edges of Mayfair and filling it with treasures that had been missing in his life living with the army. The objets d'art were not shabby, either.

On every wall and hall was a portrait of Lizbeth, some softened to make her look eighteen, some more like Nell, who had painted half of them from memory of her cousin and what she imagined Lottie to look like now. Signs were posted beneath them, seeking information about a missing child, an earl's daughter, now grown to womanhood. The reward was substantial. The results were phenomenal.

Now Jack had even more young—and not so young—women on his doorstep, looking for work or a long-lost legacy. He had to hire helpers and assistants to sift through the claims, and set up a separate entrance to the club for applicants and informants. The word was out on the street, everywhere that women, or their greedy menfolk, gathered to talk. If anyone knew of Lady Charlotte Endicott, missing for fifteen years, they would come to Jack's club.

Not unexpectedly, Jack's promised reward yielded hordes of pretenders, prevaricators, and implausible blondes. He even had one lad in a yellow wig claim to be Charlotte. So he and his helpers devised a series of tests that only Lottie could pass and questions only she could answer, if the missing girl had any remembrance of her earliest childhood. The charlatans kept guessing, and the gamblers in London had a new game to wager on.

The gaming house was going to be a success, Jack could feel it in his bones. And yet . . . And yet he could not like the idea of hiring his own sister by accident or, worse, taking her to his bed. He could either stop sleeping with the pretty girls or he could hire only raven-haired women or redheads.

So he renamed Lottie's Club The Red and the Black. The blondes and brunettes—on the chance that Lottie's fair hair had darkened—could come to the office to be inspected for blue eyes and uncertain backgrounds, to be quizzed about their doll's name and their first pony's, but neither could deal at the tables.

The new name, the mysterious search, Jack's connection to a noble family, his status as war hero, and his growing reputation as a connoisseur of women all combined to give the club the perfect cachet. The casino was crowded, the money rolled in, informants multiplied. Jack was a success. His efforts at finding his missing sister were less so, but a soldier, and a gambler, lived on hope.

CHAPTER TWO

First fire, then flood, then plague—a severe congestion, at least. What was next, frogs?

No, it was a toad who answered Allie's fifth rap on the door of Lord and Lady Hildebrand's London town house. He was short and squat and the color of something that lived under a rock. He had the manners of a mud-dweller, too.

"Whadda y'want, then? Can't y'see the knocker's off the blasted door?" The dirty lout in his leather apron tried to slam that same door in Allie's face.

She was taller than he was, and stronger than she looked. Besides, she was desperate. Allie stuck her foot in the door, then shoved in one of the valises she carried. She had spent the past five years drumming letters and learning into recalcitrant little girls. No mere lackey was going to defeat her now. Heavens, she had survived a week of traveling with Miss Harriet Hildebrand. She could face anything.

The youngest instructress at Mrs. Semple's School

for Girls, Allie had been given the unenviable task of delivering the Hildebrands' granddaughter to London after a fire destroyed the school. She had also been given a woefully inadequate purse to cover the expenses. First they had been left stranded at the posting house when Harriet ran off while Allie was using the necessary. The private coach they hired next was bogged down by rain, after which Harriet developed a cough and a fever because the impossible child *would* play in the puddles. The delays had consumed the money Mrs. Semple had allotted, and more of Allie's own purse than she could afford. Who knew how long she would be out of work, with Mrs. Semple deciding to emigrate to Canada rather than rebuild the school?

Now she was tired and hungry and anxious about her future. She was irritable, with the beginnings of a chill herself. Oh, no, she was not going to be denied handing the cause of all her problems—except the flood, perhaps; she was not certain about the fire—over to her family. With a firm grasp on the eight-year-old's skinny wrist, Allie pushed her way into the elegant foyer.

"I am Miss Allison Silver, formerly of Mrs. Semple's School for Girls, and I am escorting Miss Harriet Hildebrand to her grandparents, as Mrs. Semple's letter stated. Please notify Lord Hildebrand that we have arrived."

The man scratched his armpit, then pointed a dirty finger to the hall table, where a stack of mail overflowed the silver tray placed there. Some cards had fallen to the floor, showing ominous black bands on their edges. Allie's throat went dry, and not from the incipient illness.

"The viscount's gone'n stuck 'is spoon in the wall."

"He's dead?" Allie looked at Harriet, who was playing with the canes in a brass urn in the corner of the entryway, waving one around like a sword. Allie almost felt sorry for the poor girl, until Harriet started decapitating the faded silk blooms in a large floral arrangement.

"Stop that," Allie ordered, coughing at the dust raised.

The servant stopped scratching his armpit, at least. " 'At's what I said, ain't it?"

"Then please tell Lady Hildebrand that her granddaughter has arrived."

"The old lady got sent to Bath two months ago, onct 'is lordship took sick. Fer 'er health, they said."

Allie was wondering how much coach fare to Bath might be, when the man went on: "More like 'er mind went, I reckon, 'cause they put the old bat in a belfry tower. You know, a crazy house. Didn't know 'er own name anymore, they said. Sure as hell ain't gonna know any red-haired brat."

The red-haired brat had finished with the flowers and was batting the mail across the room with the cane. The servant did not seem to mind. Allie did. "Stop that, I said."

Harriet stuck her tongue out at Allie. "You can't make me. This is my house, and I do not have to listen to you anymore."

"No, it ain't. Place's been sold. Right out from under the heir. The viscount shipped 'is first son off to India years ago, after the bloke killed someone. Couldn't keep the title from 'im, but old man Hildebrand left everything else to charity."

"Surely he made provision for Harriet, Miss Hildebrand, that is. Her father was his second son, a respectable soldier."

The servant shrugged. "None of my business. I'm here to finish the packing, is all, afore the new owners take over." He turned to leave, to go back into the cold, dark interior of the house.

"But what are we to do?" Allie asked, more of herself and the angels who watched out for orphans and out-of-work schoolteachers.

The man smiled, but not in any friendly manner, showing spaces for three missing teeth. "You're the one with all the book learnin'. You figure it out."

For yet another of Allie's precious coins, the dirty dastard deigned to give her the Hildebrands' solicitor's address. He ought to know Mr. Burquist's direction, since the solicitor was paying him.

If the Hildebrand man-of-affairs was paying that oaf, he could pay Allie, too. And make arrangements for Miss Harriet.

Mr. Burquist felt otherwise. He tapped a folder on his desk. "Ah, no, Miss, ah, Silver. I am not empowered to release any funds from the estate. Only Lady Hildebrand's trustees are permitted to make withdrawals for her care."

"And those trustees are . . . ?"

Mr. Burquist consulted a different folder beneath the first one. "My lady's trustees . . . Ah, yes, her doctors in Bath. And I doubt they would take on Miss Harriet, if a hospital could be considered the proper environment for a young girl. I did hear mention that her ladyship never recovered from the brat—That is, from the brief visit from Miss Harriet last Christmas."

"Very well, if not Lady Hildebrand or her doctors, surely some other provision was made for her granddaughter, before the rest of the money was dispersed?"

Mr. Burquist looked insulted, as if Allie had found fault with his legal or moral decisions. "Of course," he bristled, nostrils flaring. "Her dowry is invested in the Funds, making a handsome return under my management, if I say so myself."

"She is eight years old." And destroying the man's outer office and entire filing system while they spoke, if Allie had to guess. Allie was not inclined to save the man's records, not when he was giving her such a headache. "Miss Harriet does not need a dowry. She needs a home, a place to stay, people to care for her, an education."

Burquist smiled in satisfaction. "And that was why Mrs. Semple was paid her tuition for the next ten years, and extra to keep the child over holidays."

And that was why Mrs. Semple was moving to Canada, Allie supposed. With the money, without the headache. Ignoring the noises from the outer office and Mr. Burquist's obvious impatience to have her gone, Allie rubbed at her temples, trying to think. "Surely there must be somewhere the child can stay until another school is found for her. The viscount's country seat? That would have been part of the entail, so the new Lord Hildebrand must own it. Harriet can wait there with the servants until her uncle returns from India and makes other provisions for her. He is coming back to England now that he has come into the title, is he not? I heard about the alleged murder, but now that he is elevated to the peerage, his name is bound to be cleared."

"The barristers are working on that unfortunate matter even as we speak." Mr. Burquist opened yet another file. "And the new viscount will be sailing on the ship *Speculation*, arriving in England with the spring."

"Excellent. Miss Harriet can spend the winter at her family's estate. If you would be so good as to give me the direction, and carriage fare, which I am certain his lordship will approve, we shall be out of your hair in the blink of an eye."

Mr. Burquist blinked at the loud thud coming from the other room, but he shook his head. "I do not think that would be a good idea, not at all."

"What, that the child should not reside at her ancestral estate, or that I should not accompany her there? I assure you, if you wish to take on the responsibility for her safe delivery, I shall be happy to leave her to your—"

"No, no! I am sure you are doing an excellent job of looking after the young lady." Burquist winced at another thud. "But I cannot think that her father, Captain Hildebrand, would have wanted his daughter residing under his brother's roof."

"Would he rather have her out on the street?" Allie wanted to toss a few of the man's folders on the floor herself. "She has nowhere else to go!"

The solicitor lowered his voice and leaned across his desk, closer to Allie's ear. "But, you see, the woman the current viscount was accused of murdering was Captain Hildebrand's wife, Miss Harriet's mother."

"Good grief!" Allie had never once fainted. Now seemed a good time to learn how. Except that Mr. Burquist might toss the glass of water on his desk at her, and she was already chilled to the bone. Or he might call for Harriet. The last time Allie had fallen asleep before the child, she had woken up with her braid tied to the bedpost.

The solicitor appeared to take pity on her, for he said, "You seem like a mature, well-educated lady. Perhaps your family . . . ?"

If Allie had a kind, loving family, she would not be escorting a miserable, misbehaving little monster halfway across England. Or looking for another low-paying, pitiful position. She would be sipping tea and reading a novel, her weary feet resting on a footstool. She shook her aching head. "No, my parents are both deceased."

Her own lack of other supportive relatives was not the issue. Harriet's was.

"What about her mother's family?" Allie asked, grasping at straws.

Now the solicitor shook his head. "They never answered my letters."

They must have heard of Harriet, then, Allie thought.

"Irish," the solicitor added, as if that explained their reluctance to claim Captain Hildebrand's daughter.

Allie could not drag Harriet all the way to Ireland, even if she had the funds or the energy, not without a guaranteed welcome at the end of the journey. "What about you, sir? You seem to be taking commendable care of Harriet's inheritance, so you might as well have the rest of the responsibility. That is, the joy of having a daughter. All the better if you already have children, for Harriet would have playmates."

Allie did not know if the lawyer had ever fainted before either, but he seemed on the verge of it now. She eyed the glass of water, just in case.

"A bachelor," he gasped. "No wife. No children. No. Dear lord, no."

"Then I suggest you think of an alternative, unless you wish us to sleep in your outer office. I have no other choices."

Whether the latest crash from the other room or the thought of having two females sleeping there convinced him, Mr. Burquist frantically riffled through the files on his desk. "Something, there was something . . ." he muttered as he tossed papers aside. "Ah, here it is! Captain Hildebrand's will. I urged him to make one out when he first took his commission. A soldier's life being uncertain, you know."

Allie sat on the edge of her seat. "And he named a guardian for his daughter, in case his parents predeceased him?"

"Oh, Miss Harriet was not born yet. But he never made another will, to my knowledge."

Allie sat back, disappointed. What good were the late officer's last wishes?

Burquist had placed a pair of spectacles on his nose, though, and was trying to read a messy scrawl on a yellowed page. If Captain Hildebrand had penned those cat scratches, Allie could see whence Harriet inherited her scholarly aptitude, or lack thereof. She prayed the child had inherited something else.

"Hildebrand sent it from Portugal when he was a mere lieutenant, but the document was witnessed, so it should hold up in court." Burquist adjusted his spectacles. "Yes! He leaves his horse and his sword and his worldly goods, et cetera, to his good friend, the Honorable Jonathan Endicott."

Allie was afraid to hope. "Do you think that Harriet counts as 'et cetera'?"

"Definitely!" Burquist smiled. "If ever I saw an other, Miss Harriet is it."

"But the will was written so long ago, Mr. Endicott might have died or moved. And he might not want Miss Hildebrand."

"No one wants— That is, he has no choice. The best part is that he is right here, in town. Brother to the Earl of Carde, don't you know. Young Endicott became a fellow officer of Captain Hildebrand's and distinguished himself in the war. He was considered quite the hero, in fact. The newspapers were full of his name."

A brave hero, a loyal friend with noble and wealthy

connections, just minutes away—what more could Allie wish for Harriet? Allie was so pleased, thinking that such a fine gentleman was bound to be an excellent guardian and bound to repay her for expenses, that she missed Mr. Burquist's last words.

He was shaking his head as he mumbled, "The scandal pages are still full of his name."

Allie was halfway out the door. "How nice."

So relieved was the solicitor to have a solution, and to have them gone, that he pretended not to notice the fleet of paper boats, erstwhile deeds and declamations, sailing across his reception room carpet. So guilt-stricken was he that he hailed a hackney carriage, gave the driver directions, and even paid the man himself.

How nice.

"I won. I told you they did not want me."

"Nonsense. Your grandmother is ill and the poor viscount died. I suppose you should be wearing black gloves, at the least. Your new guardian will have to see about that."

"Mrs. Simple did not see the need."

"That is Mrs. *Semple*, as you well know, not Simple." And the woman had turned out to be as wily as any fox. "Perhaps if Captain Endicott has a wife she will know what is most proper for a very young lady in mourning."

And perhaps this paragon, wed to a noble officer, would keep Allie on as Harriet's governess, at least until Allie could find a more satisfactory position. Minding red-rumped monkeys might be more satisfactory, but Allie could not be fussy, not with her savings dwindling so fast. As they left the narrow roads of the more commercial districts and headed toward Mayfair and wider avenues, with small parks dotted here and there, Allie tried not to think of what she would do if Mrs. Endicott already had a governess. She busied herself with looking out at the passing scenery instead of inward, at her doubts and fears.

Tomorrow would come soon enough, willy-nilly. Today she could appreciate that the air was clearer in this neighborhood too, less thick and sooty. She still found London's atmosphere difficult to breathe, or else she truly was catching Harriet's cold. The sooner they reached their destination, the better. Surely Captain Endicott would let her stay the night, no matter how many nursemaids and tutors he already employed. One of the country's fine, brave officers, born to the nobility, could not be less than gracious.

"I bet he doesn't want me either."

Allie did not pretend to misunderstand. The gentleman might not know of Harriet's very existence. He certainly could not know that she would be arriving on his doorstep, bags and baggage, or what had not been lost in the fire, at any rate. Even more certainly, heavens be praised, he could not know what a headache Harriet was.

"Of course he will want you, his own good friend's daughter," Allie said to bolster both of their confidences. In the confines of the carriage, she tried to tidy up her charge's appearance. "He is a gentleman of the first stare, and you must not embarrass him."

There was nothing to be done about the bedraggled pinafore, the muddied shoes, or the missing bonnet, the dripping nose, and torn gloves. Allie did manage to get her own comb through Harriet's snarled red hair and tied it with her own hair ribbon in a semblance of order, and used her own handkerchief to dab at a strawberry jam stain on Harriet's cheek from breakfast. She would worry about her own appearance next. It was Harriet who had to make the best first impression. The second impression was bound to be worse.

"And you absolutely must comport yourself like a lady," she stated, looking Harriet in the eye to make sure she understood.

"I do not see why. He won't want me either."

"He will if you are prettily behaved and show him what a bright, obedient child you are." Allie almost choked on the falsehoods, but had to try. "Captain Endicott will come to love you."

"Want to bet?"

Betting was abhorrent, of course, morally indefensible and more reprehensible when a child was involved. "How much?"

"You already owe me five thousand pounds. Double or nothing?"

Since they had been wagering imaginary sums for the entire journey, Allie agreed. Mrs. Semple might have palpitations at Mrs. Silver's method of discipline and sense of decorum, but the schoolmistress had not volunteered to accompany Harriet Hildebrand to her relatives. Allie was doing the best she could.

Unfortunately, she could not do much with her own travel-worn appearance, for the carriage stopped before she could repin her hair or retie her hat's bow under her chin. She crammed the bonnet back on her head, her hair stuffed underneath, and looked at their destination.

The house was not as imposing as some they had passed on their way through Mayfair, but it was substantial, well-kept, and welcoming. Allie's spirits lifted. "You see? A true gentleman's residence. Captain Endicott will do the right, honorable thing."

Oddly, the house had two front doors, one red and one black. The coachman looked at Allie, as if asking where he should place their valises. "In the middle, I suppose," she directed, finding a coin in her reticule to repay the man's efforts. He tipped his hat and went back to the carriage.

"Which door?" Allie asked as the hired coach pulled away. "You choose."

Harriet studied the large house with its trimmed front hedges and gleaming windows. "No matter. We won't be staying."

The afternoon light was fading. The night would be cold. They had nowhere else to go, and little funds to get there. "Do not bet on that, my girl. We are staying."

CHAPTER THREE

Allie chose the red door, to match Harriet's hair (and red nose).

A very large, very angry man answered Allie's knock. Harriet scurried behind her. "Can't any of you widgeons read?" the man yelled, pointing to a sign above the door before he shut it in their faces.

GUESTS, it read.

"What an odd way to welcome company," Allie said, studying the sign as if it could answer the questions in her aching head.

"I told you he didn't want me," Harriet whispered. "I won."

"Nonsense. That coarse fellow cannot be Captain Endicott," Allie reassured her, hoping she spoke the truth. The man was weathered, whiskered, and rude, not the respectable young officer she had been picturing in her hopeful mind. Only a well-tailored, well-mannered gentleman ought to live in such a quietly

elegant residence, according to Allie's sense of fitness.
"Perhaps that was the butler."

Not even an eight-year-old would believe that. But-
lers were the starchiest creatures in the kingdom. They
did not have wads of tobacco in their mouths or musta-
chios, and they did not open the door with their sleeves
rolled up to show thick, hairy forearms with tattoos.

"Maybe he's a pirate come to kidnap the captain
and hold him for ransom. We ought to call for the
Watch."

Allie had to grab the back of Harriet's cloak to keep
her from heading back to the street. Instead she led her
across the well-tended yard to the other, black-painted
door. That one had a sign that read INTERVIEWS.

"How peculiar. I would have thought the servants'
entrance was around back."

"We're not servants, are we?"

Well, Allie might be considered one. She was an
employee, at any rate, or hoped to be. Lord Hildebrand's grandchild, however, was not applying for a
menial's position, only a daughter's. Allie supposed
Harriet might have to prove her identity before Captain Endicott accepted her as his ward, but an interview? Allie might be in dire straits, but she still had
her pride . . . for Harriet's sake, of course. She raised
her chin and tugged the girl back to the red door.
Harriet scuffed her feet, leaving tracks in the mani-
cured grass.

This time when the rough chap answered the door,
Allie was ready. Before he could shout at them, she
announced, "I am Miss Allison Silver and this is Miss
Harriet Hildebrand. We are calling on Captain Endicott on a personal matter." She pointed at the sign
above his head. "Guests."

He was staring at their bags and boxes, then at the
ruined lawn, ready to loose a tirade, it seemed. Instead

he loosed a stream of tobacco juice, missing Allie's feet by inches. "You got some brass, lady."

Allie did not know whether to say thank you or be insulted. The doorkeeper had not stood aside for them to enter, so she chose icy hauteur. "The captain will not be happy you kept us waiting out in the dank air."

"Cap'n'll be less happy iffen I let you in." He leaned forward until Allie could smell onions on his breath. She took a step back, despite her vow not to be intimidated. "It's the eyes," he said. "And the hair."

She had tried to tidy her hair, but her eyes? Allie took another step away from the demented doorman. "Perhaps we shall try the other door after all."

"Won't do you no good," the man told her, spitting another stream of foul brown liquid near Allie's shoes. "You ain't got blue eyes, and you ain't got blond hair. Nor red nor black hair, for that matter." He switched his gaze to Harriet. "An' the cap'n keeps a decent house. He wouldn't hire any moppet, not even a red-head. Fact is, he'll be deuced furious you thought to bring her along."

Bring her along? Where was Allie supposed to leave Harriet, with the solicitor?

The doorkeep was shaking his head. "Revolting, that's what it is. Now go on with you afore I get mad. Take your skinny chick and find some other nest to foul. We don't want your dirt here."

Allie did not think he meant their shoes. "Come, Harriet, we shall try the other door. Perhaps they are more hospitable there." She picked up one of her suitcases. "And we will inform Captain Endicott of his surly staff."

Harriet was already hefting her bag and "accidentally" knocked the doorman in the shin with its brass corner. "At least I do not have to write my name on my arm in order to remember it," she said, loudly enough for the man to hear.

Allie pulled her away. "I do not think the man's name is Snake, dear. And I do not think it wise to antagonize a member of one's own household."

"I'm not staying. You'll see. Double or nothing."

"You are staying," Allie said firmly, knocking on the other door. It swung open at her rap.

Maybe Harriet would not be staying, after all.

This entry was a long, narrow room, with wooden benches along both sides. The benches seemed filled with . . . Well, Allie did not use such words, and perhaps young women in London dressed differently from those in the country, wearing lower necklines, tighter bodices, and face paint.

Allie did not think so. Neither did Harriet, whose mouth was hanging open. "They look like . . ."

Allie clapped her hand over the child's mouth. She took a deep breath, ignoring the smell of liberal amounts of inexpensive perfume and less amounts of soap and water. Under the unwelcome odors was the blessed scent of fresh paint. ". . . Applicants for housemaids," she completed the girl's sentence. "The captain must have moved in recently and is renovating and hiring his staff."

He must be a bachelor, for no agency would send such . . . colorful females to be interviewed for positions. Allie did not think any proper female's lips could be so red, although she was aware her own cheeks must be pink by now, and not just with the fever. Perhaps they all had a contagion. But there went her hopes of any Mrs. Captain Endicott keeping her on as governess. An unmarried man would send Harriet to some school, or to his family.

A desk was positioned at the far end of the room, with a gentleman sitting behind it. He had sandy-colored hair, a neatly tied neckcloth, and a pleasant, although tired-looking, expression on his face as he spoke to one of the women.

Allie sat Harriet down on an empty stretch of the bench near the door, as far from any of the other women as possible, their baggage around her. "Stay there while I announce us to the captain."

She headed toward the opposite end of the room and the desk, not looking at the hard-faced women to either side of her. Then one of them called out, "Here now, where do you think you're goin', missy? You can wait in the queue like the rest of us."

"There is a line?"

"That's right. First come, first served. You're after Darla, over there." A dark-haired woman pointed to a plump redhead sitting near the entrance door, across from Harriet.

"I beg your pardon. You are all here to see Captain Endicott?"

"Cap'n Jack, that's right," the black-haired woman said. "Iffen we get past the bloke at the desk. You'd think he was guarding the pearly gates the way he acts."

Even as she spoke, a young woman with improbably yellow hair turned from the desk and trudged down the length of the room, her head lowered, her feet dragging.

"Too bad, ducks," a different redhead called out to her, while the man at the desk sighed and said, "Next."

Another fair-haired woman stepped up to the desk and he smiled at her.

"You mean that is not Captain Endicott?" Allie asked, disappointed, for the man looked kindly and polite.

"Nah, that's Mr. Downs, Jack's assistant. He does all the work while the cap'n plays."

Allie glanced again at the women on the benches. "He . . . plays?"

The female with black hair poked her neighbor. "Her highness wants to know if Cap'n Jack plays."

The neighbor grinned and said, "That's part of the interview, once you get past Mr. Downs."

Allie could not help her gasp. "He . . . dallies with the staff?"

Both women laughed out loud. The first one winked and said, "Only if you're lucky, luv. Only if you are lucky. But not blondes or brunettes, so you won't get to find out."

The other woman looked at Harriet. "And your chit's got red hair, but she's far too young. Cap'n Jack don't play with dollies."

Allie was not sure of the women's meaning. She was sure, however, that this was no proper place for Harriet. Or for her.

Gone was her dream of a considerate, sober gentleman who would accept his responsibilities and provide a loving household for an orphaned girl . . . and her governess. The officer must be a depraved rake, a London libertine, the worst sort of swine.

Oh, dear.

She walked back toward Harriet, who was carving her initials into the bench with a hat pin one of the women must have dropped.

"Do not do that!" Allie said, sitting down and wishing she could shut her eyes and have this nightmare fade away. She'd be back at Mrs. Semple's, correcting French conjugations and reminding her students to sit up straight. No, if she was going to have pleasant dreams, she would imagine herself back in Suffolk at Papa's side while he read a book to her. Instead, the scratch of the pin on the wood kept her right here, in purgatory with painted women.

"Stop, I said!"

"Why? We're not staying anyway. I heard the women. I'm too young and you're not pretty enough."

"That was not what they said. And we—you—are staying. The captain is your legal guardian unless someone else steps forward. He has to make provision for you." Allie hoped so, anyway.

The carrottop from across the way came and sat next to Allie. She was pretty in a soft, rounded way, and had the first friendly smile Allie had seen in London. Allie ignored the expanse of bosom billowing over the other woman's gown and smiled back.

"How do, miss. I'm Darla Danforth. I used to be Dora Dawes, but Darla sounds a lot better, don't it?"

Allie bit her lip before she corrected the young woman's grammar out of habit. "I am, ah, pleased to meet you, Miss Dawes. Or Danforth. I am Miss Allison Silver, and this is my charge, Miss Harriet Hildebrand. Harriet, practice your curtsy."

Harriet gave her a sullen look but stood and bobbed awkwardly before slumping back onto the bench. Her manners were lacking, her posture was atrocious, but, Allie noted, her first *H* on the bench was perfectly formed. At least those months at Mrs. Semple's were not an entire waste.

Darla smiled. "How sweet. But you are new here, aren't you?"

How could she tell? Just because Allie was sitting next to a pile of suitcases, her traveling gown was stained and wrinkled, and her hair was trailing in witch's locks from under her bonnet's brim? Or because she was appalled to be in the room with so many fast women? "You might say so," she admitted.

"Then let me give you a couple of hints, dearie. You'll need them, 'cause you're too old."

Allie sat up straighter, wondering at the woman's mental state.

"And your hair is a mite dark for blond."

It was almost brown, but had golden highlights when it was clean and shining.

"And your eyes ain't quite blue."

They were gray, mostly, unless Allie wore her best gown, a light blue silk that had been lost in the fire.

"But you walk and talk like a lady, so you might get by Mr. Downs. You have to remember your brothers' names are Jonathan and Alexander."

"I do not have any brothers."

Darla clucked her tongue in frustration. "I'm trying to help you here, miss. That's what you've got to answer if you want to get in to talk with Cap'n Jack. You can't remember the name of your doll or your first pony."

"I never had a pony."

Darla went on as if Allie had not spoken: "And you barely recall your parents."

Allie stiffened her spine, if possible. "My mother died when I was young but I recall my father perfectly. He was the most learned gentleman of my experience, headmaster of his own academy. I would never dishonor his memory by saying otherwise."

Darla shook her head. "If you ain't going to try to pass for Lottie, then what are you doing here?"

"Lottie?"

Darla pointed to a painting on the wall, one Allie had barely noticed in her shocked survey of the room's occupants. A young lady—obviously a lady by the jewels at her neck, the fine mansion at her back, and the dignity of her pose—stared back at her from the gilded frame. She had hair so light it might have been a sunbeam, and eyes so blue they could have been painted from a summer sky. She was the most beautiful woman Allie had ever seen, and a total stranger.

"Now I know you ain't been in London long. Everyone knows about the captain's half sister what went missing fifteen years ago. They made the painting from her mother's portrait and her cousin's, ones that hang in the public rooms where everyone and his uncle can see them. The earl's family's been looking for her for all these years, and Cap'n Jack's offering a king's ransom to find her. That's what all the blondes are here for, claiming to be Lady Charlotte Endicott."

Darla tipped her head to a newcomer, a true, pale-skinned blonde this time, who was dressed in fashionable black mourning, if not the finest-quality fabrics. They could not see the young lady's eye color under an exquisite wide-brimmed and veiled black bonnet, but they could see that she was nervous, clutching her reticule and biting her lip.

"Your turn is after Miss Silver here, miss," Darla called out to her. "She won't be long, neither, so you might get in afore they shut down the line at five o'clock. The next interview day is next Tuesday."

The younger woman nodded, but stood, staring at the picture that may or may not look like the missing heiress.

Allie nudged Harriet with her elbow, to stop her from defacing her guardian's furniture, and told Darla, "We know nothing about a missing girl, and need to speak to Captain Endicott on a entirely different matter."

"Oh?" Darla asked, looking at the luggage that surrounded Allie and Harriet, obviously wishing for an explanation.

Allie did not feel she could discuss the situation with anyone but Captain Endicott, so she said, "It is a private matter, I am afraid."

Now Darla was even more curious, her green eyes

opened wide as her imagination took wing. "Well, you'll have to tell it to Mr. Downs or you won't get in. Those are the rules." She stood up, heading for her place on the opposite bench, closer to the desk now that another woman had left while they were talking. "Good luck to you, then."

"And to you," Allie said, wondering if Darla would think it lucky to be employed in this house, or why all the redheads and raven-haired women were here if they could not claim to be the missing young lady. Before she could ask, another female entered the waiting room, a beautiful redhead this time.

Her flame-colored tresses were piled on the top of her head, and one dyed-green feather was fixed there, to trail down her porcelain cheek. She wore a green velvet gown that hugged every curve of her body. There were a great many lush curves.

She ignored the women on the benches, curled her lip at Harriet, who curled hers right back, and sailed past Darla without a nod. Instead of taking her place at the end of Darla's bench, however, she glided down the length of the room, nodded toward Mr. Downs, and sailed through the door behind him.

"She has weasels around her neck!" Harriet exclaimed before the door could shut. A few of the other women laughed.

"Dead ones, " Allie whispered, trying not to show her own distaste. "A fur tippet." Then she leaned toward Darla and asked, "That is not Mrs. Endicott, is it?" Such a cold woman would not want Harriet around, or Allie.

"Cap'n Jack married?" One of the women slapped her knee.

Another gave a snicker. "Don't she wish, though."

Darla stepped back closer to Allie, glaring at the door where the Diamond had disappeared.

"That's Mademoiselle Rochelle Poitier, who's as French as I am. She's nobbut Rachel Potts, putting on airs now that she's become the captain's—"

Allie clapped her hands over Harriet's ears. She was all too aware of what place a woman like Rochelle Poitier held in a rake's life. Harriet was too young to understand. Or so Allie prayed.

Once more her prayers went unanswered.

"Ow! If she's his mistress, will she be my mother?"

Now Allie put her hand over Harriet's mouth before any of the women could overhear. Harriet bit her, but not hard. "Will she?" she asked when Allie pulled her hand away.

"No. Gentlemen, especially not the sons of earls, do not marry their, ah . . ."

"Ladybirds?"

Allie could accept that, barely. "Their ladybirds. And they do not discuss such things as, ah, ladybirds, with gently bred females, especially not young girls. So do not let him think you are a rag-mannered guttersnipe, speaking of matters of which you should have no knowledge." Captain Endicott might blame Mrs. Semple for the child's precociousness, and Allie by association. "Remember, we need to make a good impression." She tried to fix Harriet's hair ribbon—her hair ribbon—again.

"Then maybe you ought to unbutton your collar and pinch your cheeks and puff out your chest. Although I don't suppose you have much to puff out. Not like Darla and the rest."

Allie wondered if she ought to speak to Captain Endicott herself, without Harriet. Happily, as one woman after another went up to the desk, some to leave, some to pass through the portals to the next test, Harriet fell asleep, leaning against Allie. Allie did not have the heart to awaken her, nor the desire. So when newcomers entered the room, she simply said, "I am after Darla," and stayed in her place at the bench. After what seemed like hours, only Darla was ahead of her.

The plump redhead must have passed the first test, for she turned and waved to Allie, grinning. Allie stood up before Mr. Downs could call "Next," and gently laid Harriet's head down on the bench, cushioned by Allie's cape.

"Will you keep an eye on her?" she asked the young blond woman who was after her on the line, the one who wore such a pretty black bonnet.

The girl nodded.

"Thank you. Oh, and your brothers' names are Jonathan and Alexander, you do not remember your first pony's name, or anything about your family."

The woman bit her lip again, and nodded again.

Just as Allie was about to take the seat in front of Mr. Downs's desk, a clock started chiming.

"Five o'clock," he said, sounding relieved. "No more—"

"No more after me," Allie insisted, quickly lowering herself onto the cushioned chair and placing both hands firmly on its wooden arms, indicating that Mr. Downs would need brute force, and a lot of it, to dislodge her. "My name is Allison Silver, and I am not leaving until I speak with Captain Endicott. And no, I am not here to seek a housemaid's position or to claim any long-lost legacy."

The man, who appeared to be about Allie's age of five and twenty, shook his head. "You are not his type for anything else."

"And you, sir, are offensive. You do not know what my business is with your employer and yet you assume the worst."

Downs squared his shoulders. He recognized a determined female, and a well-bred one at that. No light-skirt by her dress, no common wench by her accent, Miss Silver was an enigma. Downs did not like riddles. He hardly liked women anymore, after the past few harrowing days. "You are not with that Women's Decency Society, are you?"

"No, but I might join if I do not get to see Captain Endicott soon."

"Perhaps if you told me your business." He looked toward the end of the room where the other women were filing out. He saw Harriet asleep at the end of the bench and luggage. He frowned. "That and the child's. You have five minutes. But I warn you, I've heard all the stories before."

Downs steepled his fingers and leaned back in his chair wearily. He tipped the front legs backward and checked his watch.

Allie had five minutes. She only needed two.

Then she needed another one to help the man off the floor and right his chair.

CHAPTER FOUR

"Deuce take it, Downs, you know better than to burst in here like this. And it's after five. Go home and get your dinner. We have a busy night ahead."

Downs averted his eyes from his employer, who was already busy. But his message was too urgent. "A, a lady," he sputtered, pointing toward the waiting room. "And a little girl. Red hair. Yours."

For the second time in minutes, a rump reached the floor. This time it was a well-rounded derriere as Jack jumped to his feet, dumping Rochelle Poitier to the ground. "The hell, you say!"

"She says it, not me!"

"Who, by Harry?"

"Miss Allison Silver."

"That's all right then. I never heard of the lady." Jack sat back down, ignoring the indignant protests as Rochelle realized her feather was broken, to say nothing of the mood and Jack's amorous intentions. He was pouring a glass of brandy from a decanter on his desk. One glass. "Send her away."

"Not until you hear me out," came a voice from the doorway.

Someone growled, but Jack could not be certain whether it was Rochelle or his old dog, Joker.

A slim woman of medium height was standing in the doorway, her hands in fists. She was past her first blush of youth, but not long past, Jack knowledgeably estimated, although her appearance was calculated to give the impression of rigid, righteous maturity. She wore a shapeless gray frock that covered every inch of skin, and an uglier bonnet, sadly limp. Mostly scraped back under the wretched hat, her hair was a nondescript color halfway between blond and brown, and her face was pale and pinched-looking. Everything about her bespoke untouchability, an old maid by choice. Which was a pity, for the woman did have magnificent eyes, Jack could not help noticing, storm-cloud gray, with glimmers of fair-weather blue.

She cleared her throat, making him aware of his rude inspection, and then she tapped her foot, like one of his nannies used to do. That's what Miss Silver reminded him of, a dour, disapproving governess. Which also reminded him that he was a gentleman, by birth if not by trade. He stood and fastened the buttons on his white marcella waistcoat, wishing his jacket was not draped on a chair across the room.

"I did not hear your knock, Miss, ah, Silver," he said, trying to shift the blame and the rudeness.

"But I heard something fall, so came to your assistance."

She had a husky voice, one that did not fit her looks. That voice belonged to a sultry siren, not a sour spinster. Then she cleared her throat again and coughed.

She was not a seductress; she was sick. The sooner he got her out of here, the better.

"I do not believe I have ever met you, Miss Silver."

He expected her to try to claim some forgotten incident while he was at university or home on leave, or at a drunken house party. He supposed he might have fathered a child some time in his youth, although his big brother had pummeled the dangers and the disgrace into his head often enough.

He did not for an instant suppose he had lain with Miss Silver. Not a stiff-backed, slight, and unshapely female who wore her virtue the way Rochelle wore her furs. He much preferred his women ripe and ready, full-bodied and free of pesky morals.

Miss Silver appeared full of indignation as she said, "No, I have never had the pleasure."

Now Downs coughed, but Jack did not think Miss Silver meant any double entendre. He doubted the woman had an innuendo in her. And yet Miss Silver had a child.

He spoke the thought out loud. "And yet Downs mentioned a child."

Color flared in her cheeks at the mention of her daughter. She looked almost pretty, Jack thought, and he felt sorry for a woman in her unfortunate situation. Still, she was not going to pin some other chap's sins on his shoulders. Jack had enough of his own.

One was tugging on his sleeve. "C'mon, then, Jacko. You promised me dinner, you did."

Suddenly Rochelle sounded common and coarse. Jack felt himself embarrassed, and decided to be angry at Miss Silver for the uncomfortable feeling. She was the one who had walked into his club of her own free will, dash it. Why should he be ashamed of his way of life? And who was she to look so pure when the proof of her own fall from grace was sitting in his waiting room?

He looked down his formidable nose, which never ceased to intimidate his junior officers, and spoke in his coldest voice. "Forgive me, Miss Silver, but I do have other commitments, as you can see. And since we have never met, I do not suppose that we have anything to say to each other."

She met his stare without flinching, only raising her slightly pointed chin. "Would you prefer to speak to the solicitor?"

Lud, he'd dragged the Endicott name through enough mud by opening a gambling parlor. Playing his own games with the lady dealers had been fun after the deprivations of wartime, but had added fuel to the raging gossip fires. He had even taken on a mistress to stop some of the rumors that he was an insatiable satyr. Rochelle was not nearly as much entertainment, but Jack's name had not been in the scandal columns in at least three days. His big brother ought to be happy that Jack was settling on one woman, instead of one every night. Hell, his brother the earl ought to be happy Jack was no drain on the family estate, and neither were his inamoratas.

A breach-of-promise suit or whatever Miss Silver was threatening was bound to make headlines. His brother would not be happy, no matter who had to settle the accounts, but Ace would recover. He would grumble and lecture, and pay whatever it took to keep Jack from prison or penury. Jack worried more about his lovely sister-in-law, though, heavy with child and still fretful of the skeletons in her own family's closet. Nell did not need another scandal in her dish.

"Very well, Miss Silver, speak your piece."

"In private, if you please."

He did not please, nor did Rochelle. She pulled on

his arm, leaving creases on his sleeve. Miss Silver blushed again at the brazen display of familiarity and possession. Good grief, how had she borne a child if her sensibilities were so easily shaken? Hell, how had she *made* a child?

Truth be told, Jack was not enamored of Rochelle's grasping ways either, not her clinging nor her carping for more of his time, more of his money. Besides, he was not willing to air more of his dirty linen in public. Downs had served with him in Belgium and was as loyal as they came. Rochelle's fidelity was for sale to the highest bidder. She was not even faithful to her own name, so what should she care about his? "Would you wait outside, Rochelle? This will not take long."

"What, you mean to listen to some gentry mort's lies? That's the oldest trick in the books, Jacko, claiming some brat needs your blessings and your blunt. You're too downy a cove to fall for that faradiddle, so come on, love. I'm hungry."

Miss Silver did not try to refute Rochelle's accusations. She did not retreat, either, which the soldier in Jack could not help admiring.

"Downs," he said, "will you be so good as to escort Mademoiselle Poitier to dinner? I made early reservations at the Grand Hotel."

Downs looked as if he'd rather go back to the front, facing French cannons. He gulped and nodded, holding out his arm. Rochelle did not accept it. A lowly clerk? A mere former lieutenant? A cripple with a limp? She walked past him, the broken feather tickling her nose, and dog hairs showing on the back of her gown from her encounter with the carpet.

Jack could hear her angry footsteps—and Downs's halting gait hurrying to keep up—all through the waiting room. The outer door slammed. He winced, knowing he would be paying for that later.

"Very well, Miss Silver, you have cost me a dinner and a pleasant companion. Now what is this private matter? And it had better be good, or I will call the Watch and have you taken off to jail, I swear I will. What is this about a child?"

The child had been awakened by the slamming door. Now she stood in the entrance to Jack's office rubbing her eyes, dragging a lady's cloak behind her. "I told you we were not staying," she said.

Miss Silver muttered something incomprehensible, and possibly blasphemous, under her breath, but made the introductions. "Captain Endicott, may I present Miss Harriet Hildebrand, your ward."

"Hildebrand, you say? Nelson Hildebrand of Northampshire? Damn if she is not his butter stamp with that curly red mop and that space between her front tee—My ward?"

"Captain Hildebrand named you as Miss Hildebrand's guardian," Allie lied. It was growing dark. This was not entirely the non sequitur it sounded. She was willing to do nearly anything to have this settled before night fell. If she was out in the streets, alone, she wanted to see where she was going.

Jack sank back onto his seat, belatedly remembering to offer the opposing chair to Miss Silver. "No, he must have meant my brother, the earl. We all grew up together, but Ace was always the respectable, responsible one of us."

"You are Jonathan Endicott?"

Jack heard his name reverberate like a death knell. "It's only till Hildebrand comes back from the army, right?"

Miss Silver shook her head and lowered her eyes. "He is not coming back. I am sorry."

"He was a good man," Jack said. "I will miss him." Then he remembered hearing the stories about Hildebrand's wife and brother. Who hadn't heard them? "Gads, the poor poppet."

The poor poppet had sat down on the floor next to the dog, an old hound of some sort that had gone back to sleep near the fire after his one feeble effort at protecting his household.

"Do not bother the dog," Miss Silver called.

"Oh, old Joker is as gentle as a kitten. He would never hurt a little girl."

"I was not worried about the little girl," Miss Silver murmured. Then she proceeded to explain about Lord and Lady Hildebrand, Mrs. Semple and the school—without mentioning the suspicious nature of the fire that had burned down the place—and the solicitor.

"You say Hildebrand named me in his will?"

"I saw it with my own eyes. You can see for yourself at Mr. Burquist's office tomorrow. That is, on Monday, tomorrow being Sunday."

Jack had not taken his gaze off the child in the corner. "Good grief, he must have been foxed."

Miss Silver did not disagree.

Jack sighed. He looked longingly at the brandy decanter, knowing he could not drink alone in front of the lady. "May I offer you some refreshment?"

"Tea would be lovely. And milk and some toast for Harriet. We missed our midday meal."

She looked like she had missed more than a few meals, and the child—Gads, there was a child in his office!—was skin and bones. Hildebrand had been a beanpole, though, so perhaps she had inherited his physique too, along with the red curls.

Miss Silver coughed again.

"Oh, yes, refreshments." Milk? Toast? This was a gaming club, not a lady's drawing room! Where the deuce was he supposed to get nursery fare? Jack stepped out to the hall, the one that led to the public rooms, not the applicants' waiting room, and bellowed for Sergeant Calloway.

Miss Silver winced, but Jack did not apologize. When Calloway arrived, Jack's former batman and current majordomo looked as if he was ready to fend off an ambush, single-handedly. Jack told him to fetch tea, cold meats, bread and cheese, and milk.

Calloway's mouth was hanging open, seeing the brat and the biddy in his boss's office. He would have swallowed his wad of tobacco if he had not spit it out at the captain's call.

"You're goin' to feed them?"

"I am not going to devour them for dinner, so yes, I have invited Miss Silver and Miss Hildebrand to share a meal with me."

Calloway kept staring. Miss Silver nodded as if she were the queen, and the halfling stuck her tongue out at him.

"Milk, Sergeant. Tea, food, you know. I keep an expensive chef in the kitchen. Surely he can provide us a light repast while we decide what to do."

"What to do? I says run 'em off like we did the Frogs."

Oh, how Jack wished he could. Before he could say anything, Miss Hildebrand piped up. "I would like chocolate, please," she said in a sweet little voice, "Mr. Snake."

Miss Silver started coughing. Jack looked at Snake—Calloway—pleadingly.

"Right, Cap'n, tea and chocolate. An' another bottle of brandy."

That was why Jack kept a former convict on his payroll. The man understood his needs. After Calloway left, Jack turned back to Miss Silver. "While we are waiting, why do you not tell me your part in this?"

"My part? My last duty as an instructress at Mrs.

Semple's School was to deliver Harriet to her grand-parents. I do not wish to sound mercenary, but the funds given me for the journey were insufficient, so—"

Jack brushed that off. What were a few coins in the face of catastrophe? "I shall reimburse you, of course. But what were your plans?"

"I fear you have not been listening, sir. I admit I was hoping to be asked to stay on as governess with Lord and Lady Hildebrand until I could find another position or they found another school for Harriet, but that was all."

"You came to London with no position and no place to go?"

"I had no choice." She stood, and bent to reclaim her cloak from where Harriet had dressed the old dog in it. "I think I will leave you now, though, now that I have fulfilled my commission. You and Harriet need some time to grow accustomed to each other, and as you pointed out, I have to find a place to stay."

"You are going to leave? Like hell! That is, not without supper. And not without a plan for Miss Harriet's future. I do not know anything about little girls!"

Allie sat back down. She was hungry, and her throat was sore. Tea sounded heavenly. So did Captain Endicott's desire for her to stay with Harriet. She would not have to go off on her own in the city this very night, thank goodness.

Relieved at the schoolmistress's silent acquiescence, Jack continued his inquiry. "Very well, let us think. Have you anywhere you might take Harriet? Family? Friends in town?"

"None."

"Then perhaps another of her schoolmates would invite Harriet to spend some time with her family?"

"Harriet had no friends at school. That is, no particular friends." Before he could ask about that, Allie hurried to say, "Mr. Burquist, the Hildebrands' man of affairs, suggested your family might take in Harriet."

"Yes, Nell would take in any number of foundlings. She even kept a pet goose because she could not see it eaten. That is not the point. Nell and my brother are not in London. The family town house is being renovated, so I cannot even send you there with the servants."

"We could go to . . . Northamptonshire, did you say?"

"Yes, but Nell is increasing and having a difficult pregnancy. Not as difficult as my brother is having, I understand. I cannot send them company at a time like that."

Allie could understand. "Of course not. Harriet would be underfoot."

"And they wouldn't want me," Harriet added from the corner, where she was pouring out the contents of Jack's decanter for the dog to lap off the floor. "Not with babies of their own. I don't like babies anyway. I like your dog, though."

"He's a good old—What the deuce are you doing, feeding him my most expensive brandy?"

Miss Silver quickly asked, "Why could we not stay here? It is not what I might wish, being a bachelor's residence, but you will find another school for Harriet in short order and I shall find a new position. Your home seems ample for a single gentleman."

"Stay here? A child? For a night or two, perhaps, but I had a hard enough time getting the proper licenses as is."

"Licenses?"

"You know, to run a dice table and a roulette wheel. I had to grease a hundred palms before I could open. The magistrates would close the place down in a flash if they saw Harriet here. They frown on children in gaming parlors."

"Roulette?"

"Yes, a game with a wheel and a tiny ball that men with tiny brains watch endlessly. They are paying my bills."

Her voice was growing fainter. "This is a . . . gaming house? Not your home?"

"Well, it is that, too. I saw no reason to take separate rooms when there was space here. And now I do not have to leave near dawn to find my own bed when the club finally shuts its doors."

"A club?"

"Well, it is technically an exclusive gentlemen's club, with membership by subscription, but in actuality anyone with the fee can join." Jack proudly added, "We already have a great number of members. The Red and the Black will be a great success."

She barely whispered, "The doors?"

"I thought that was a clever touch. So you see why we have to find somewhere else for Harriet to stay permanently. I would rent a little cottage for you, but I am below hatches at this moment. I sank everything I had into the club and I am not seeing any profit yet. Tonight is our first big event. I invited General We— Where are you going?"

Miss Silver was on her feet again. Good manners dictated Jack also stand.

"Anywhere. I cannot stay here. Surely you can see that."

"I can see that you cannot desert me like a rat leaving a sinking ship. How the deuce am I to care for the chit tonight? What do I know about putting her to bed? For that matter, I have to be down in the club all night. I cannot caretake a—Deuce take it, that is my new coat from Weston she is dressing the dog in! You cannot leave!"

"I must! I have to think of my reputation, my references. I will never find another position if I spend a night under the roof of a gambling den."

"Of course you will. Nell can write you new references. She's a regular Trojan. Who knows, she might have a girl this time and need the services of a governess."

"In five years! For now she is in childbed, and I have to make my own bed. Good grief, not with your fancy pieces. Now I understand about all the women. This place is no better than a brothel!"

"Now hold, Miss Silver. The girls—the young ladies—are dealers, nothing else. Gentlemen like to look at pretty women when they are out on the town. The ladies deal and serve drinks. I am not running a bordello."

"What of Miss Poitier? Or should I say Mademoiselle? I should not even be speaking of women such as she!"

"Rochelle does not live here. She has rooms of her own. I don't suppose . . ." At the schoolmarm's gasp he said, "No, I thought not."

"You considered that I would stay in the same house as your mistress?"

Now Miss Silver's husky voice was loud enough to be heard in Hampshire! "Ssh. Remember the child."

The child had tired of dressing the dog and was looking at some of the picture books on Jack's shelves. Pictures of—"Thunderation, put that book back!"

Harriet looked up at him. "You don't have to marry your ladybird if you don't want. I don't mind not having a mother, you know."

Jack turned to Miss Silver. "Good grief, you cannot leave me with her!"

"I cannot stay."

Jack was ready to pull his hair out, or pull his pistol out to threaten her into staying. No, he had locked the guns away. Oh, lord, what was he going to do? Beg, he supposed. First he asked, "Where will you go?"

"A hotel, I suppose."

"A single woman with no companion? They will slam the door in your face."

"That would not be the first time today. An inn will do, then."

"A single woman without protection? You would not be safe. No, you absolutely have to stay here for the night. I insist."

"But you have no right to insist about anything. I do not work for you."

"I hereby hire you."

"Impossible."

"I'll hold my breath if you go," Harriet warned.

Now why had Jack not thought of that?

Miss Silver ignored the child, pulling on her cloak after brushing dog hairs off it.

"Great gods, she is turning purple. Do something!"

"Why? She will faint before she dies. You will have to get used to such manipulations. Tears will be next, I believe."

Jack already had a mistress to enact him scenes; he did not need an eight-year-old with a flair for the dramatic. "I am begging you, Miss Silver, please do not leave. Give me one night. That's all I ask, one night. Tomorrow we will come up with a plan, I know we will. Something respectable, above board, that even the highest sticklers cannot find fault with. There is always that inn where they stashed Nell's brother. No, he is insane, you cannot stay there." Jack realized he was babbling. Harriet had his quizzing glass from his coat pocket and was—"Not the French playing cards!" He snatched the cards and the magnifying glass away from Harriet and looked at Miss Silver beseechingly. "Please."

Allie looked out the window. All daylight was gone and the street lamps had not been lit. Outside was dark and empty and cold and lonely. She'd be lost in a minute if she could not find a hackney to take her—where? Inside, she could hear the man Calloway clumping down the hall, the smell of hot chocolate preceding him.

Then she sneezed.

CHAPTER FIVE

"Aha!" the captain shouted. "You are not well. That does it. You cannot go out in the rainy night, heaven knows where, with no escort. I cannot take you myself, not with the club about to open for the evening, and I cannot spare Calloway or Downs. I swear you will be safe here. No gentlemen but I are permitted in the private rooms upstairs. The girls—the ladies—will be below, serving, so the place will be quiet and restful, and they sleep on the attic floor above anyway."

He tried to adjust his neck cloth, to give weight to the propriety of his offer. A disheveled gentleman did not bode well for discretion, he realized. "In fact, I can have Calloway bring your dinner tray there, yours and Miss Harriet's, right now, before anyone is about. That way no one will see you at all. The guests never need to know of your existence, and the girls—the ladies—will not, either. There will be no talk, and no encounters that might embarrass you, I swear. You can have the best bedroom and . . . and a bath." He knew he was grasping at straws and did not care. "I'll carry the hot water myself. No, I won't come anywhere near your rooms. I'll send a maid, one of my soldier's widows who is closemouthed and sensible. Please stay?"

A sweet little voice chimed in his ear: "Offer her double her wages."

Jack smiled at Harriet. Perhaps the urchin was not so bad after all. "I will double what Mrs. Semple paid you for accompanying Harriet if you stay the night."

Allie was torn. The extra money would be a blessing, but this was a gambling parlor, and worse. "What of Miss Poitier?"

"What, I should pay her double—No, of course not. She will not be back, I promise. I'll give her her congé tonight. She will never cross your path again."

"What's a con jay?" Harriet asked. "Is it anything like a woodland jay, and is that where she got the green feather?"

Allie ignored her, but the captain said, "I'll triple your fee."

"One night, other accommodations in the morning?"

He nodded.

"Very well." Allie turned to Harriet, pretending not to hear Captain Endicott's sigh of relief. "We are staying after all, both of us. So I win the bet. You owe me twenty thousand pounds."

The gentleman was about to raise his glass in a toast to their agreement and his salvation. At her words, though, he said, "Aha!" again. "So you are a gambling woman after all, Miss Silver, despite your righteous indignation."

"No, it's just a game."

"For twenty thousand pounds? That's one hell of a game for someone who disapproves of wagering so much she'd rather sleep with the fleas at an inn than on clean sheets here."

"You should not say 'hell' in front of a child."

"Or in front of a lady. My apologies. You see how much I have to learn about being a proper guardian? I need you, Miss Silver." The smile he flashed her would have melted an iceberg, much less one old maid's resolve.

"It is pretend money anyway, silly," Harriet interrupted, lifting the captain's fob watch out of his coat by its chain.

He took back his prized timepiece, a present from his father. "Oh, then you are not an heiress? Too bad, I was counting on your fortune to pay my tailor's bills," he teased. "Perhaps I should send you to an inn after all, if you are going to be such an expensive proposition. Overpaid governesses, extra meals, more coal for your fireplaces. I suppose you are going to want new shoes eventually too."

Harriet looked at her scuffed and thin-soled slippers. "If you send us away will you give us a con jay too? I'd rather have your dog."

"The dog stays. So do you." He opened the door for Calloway, but told the older man, "Take the tray upstairs to the guest suite. The ladies are staying."

"Here?" The dishes rattled.

"No, at Kensington Palace. Miss Harriet Hildebrand appears to be my ward, at least until I speak with some solicitor on Monday morning. And Miss Silver is my own silver lining. Unless you would like to help Miss Harriet brush her hair and her teeth and say her prayers and who knows what else?"

Harriet knew. "Read a story. Or you could tell me one. I like pirates and highwaymen and Red Indians."

Calloway was bowing to Allie as best he could with a tray in his hands. "This way, ma'am."

As Captain Endicott had predicted, they saw no one on the trek up the stairs and down the carpeted halls. Calloway opened the door to a sitting room and adjoining bedchamber that were freshly painted and tastefully decorated, with no red satin sheets or mirrors above the bed, thank goodness. The bed was large enough for half the girls at Mrs. Semple's School, so Allie would not be kept awake by Harriet's tossing and turning again. The sitting room would get the morning sun, but the bedroom faced the rear of the house, so she would not even be bothered by carriages arriving and leaving. She could even pretend she was in a gentleman's residence instead of a gambling den if she tried hard enough.

The food was excellent, and far more elaborate than Allie expected for a hastily gathered snack. Of course the chef had thought he was feeding the owner of the establishment, too, obviously a hearty eater. There was enough for three or four or ten, with enough variety that Harriet found something she favored, once she had scraped the sauce off the veal and the breading off the chicken. The tea was hot and heavenly to Allie's sore throat and aching head, and Harriet declared her chocolate sweetened perfectly. She ate two servings of pudding, prattling on about her new guardian, his house, his dog, his library that was far more interesting and informative than the one at Mrs. Semple's School.

"What do you think I should call him?" she asked Allie between bites. "He's not really my papa, and not even an uncle."

Allie put down her fork. "I think Captain Endicott is fine for now, since everyone still seems to be calling him by his army rank. And say 'sir.' Do not forget to show him respect, for he is being very kind."

"Cap'n Jack sounds better."

"It sounds overly familiar. As you say, you are not related. I do not want you to be disappointed, Harriet, but you must remember that we might not be staying. I am not, and I doubt if the captain will keep you here on his own." When the child's lower lip started quivering, Allie went on: "He is not really fixed to be a father, you know. And his way of life is truly not suitable for a child. Why, he stays up all night and likely sleeps during the day, not wanting any noise or playing in the house. He knows nothing of raising a little girl, and his, ah, associates are not proper company for Viscount Hildebrand's granddaughter. We were a shock to him, you saw that, so do not get your hopes pinned on the captain. But I am certain he will find you a loving family and a real house, perhaps in the country where you can play outdoors and learn to ride."

A tear fell down Harriet's sticky cheek.

"And a dog of your own," Allie promised, making perjurers of those poor people who would have Harriet left on their doorstep within the week, if Allie guessed the captain's intentions correctly.

"But I like it here!"

"You will like it there, too, wherever 'there' is."

Harriet wiped her nose on the back of her sleeve. If Allie's appetite had not left before, it did now. She handed over her last clean handkerchief. "He would not send you somewhere hateful."

"But I like Cap'n Jack!" Harriet wailed, throwing herself into Allie's arms, not playacting for effect, but truly upset.

"Yes, I like him too."

That was the trouble. The man was wondrously handsome in a rugged way, broad-shouldered and fit. Allie could not help noticing all that while he was in his shirt sleeves, which he should not have been, of course, in the presence of a lady. His stomach was flat, his thighs were well-muscled like the cavalry officer he had been, and his face was still tanned from being outdoors. He had a lopsided smile to match his crooked nose, and his neckcloth had been awry too, to match his skewed morals. He was in dishabille because he had been in debauchery—in the daylight!

Allie patted Harriet's back, knowing the child was tired, overwrought, and halfway smitten with the man who had let her take the dog upstairs into the bedroom. Joker was a large, lazy, smelly dog, Allie could not help noticing, who was eating everything on the tray that Harriet had not.

"Do not let the dog have chicken bones," she told Harriet now, distracting her. "He might choke, and then the captain will be angry."

Harriet jumped down and offered Joker Allie's last biscuit instead. At least she was not crying anymore.

Allie wished she did not feel like weeping herself.

Harriet's guardian was polite when he remembered to be, and kind. He had accepted his responsibility for Harriet on the instant he recognized her as his friend's daughter, and was intending, Allie knew in her heart, to do the best for the orphaned child. He was courteous to Allie, a mere schoolteacher, and he was generous.

Her first hopes had been correct: Captain Endicott was a fine gentleman. But he was a gambler and a womanizer, too. Heaven help her, Allie no more belonged in his house than she belonged on a barge. Why, she should not even know such a person! Mrs. Semple would have cat fits if such a man came within a mile of her school or her senior girls. Then again, if the captain smiled at her, crinkling his eyes the way he did, inviting her to share his jokes, Mrs. Semple would titter and bat her eyelashes at him.

Allie was not in danger of tittering or batting. She was in danger of destroying her reputation, without one ounce of enjoyment to show for it. Not that she would find pleasure in flirting with a libertine or listening to his silver tongue. Of course not.

Her good name was about all she had. With no connections, no property, no income, and no dowry, Allie had to make her own way in the world. She well knew that a woman with a poor reputation had equally poor prospects. She had found her niche at Mrs. Semple's School, enjoying using her mind, imparting her knowledge to others, finding friends among the staff, satisfaction in her work. Now she was chancing it all, the independence and the future.

She should have insisted on leaving. The captain would have found her a hackney, and might have given her the directions of decent lodgings, plus her wages. Allie had been afraid, though, and was angry at herself for her cowardice. London was vast and dirty and dangerous, and Allie had never truly been on her own before. She had gone from Papa's house to Mrs. Semple's School. She found terror in being without funds, without a position, without a plan. Her dreads multiplied in the dark, like lice.

Allie supposed a hero like Captain Endicott would laugh at her lack of backbone and bravery. He had thrown off his family expectations and gone into trade, and not an acceptable business like banking or shipping, either. Allie half admired the captain for that, although she could not respect his choices. He was a self-made man, though, like Papa, who had started his own successful school.

She missed her father still, and could understand Harriet's clinging to the first likely replacement for her own. But Harriet was a child. Allie was not.

She should have gone, before she tasted the luxury here. She might miss her father and the security she had known at the school, but she did not miss the narrow room at Mrs. Semple's she shared with the next junior instructor, Miss Wolfe, who snored. Now she had well-cooked, ample food, the hearths burning warmly, and someone to serve her. No one had looked after Allie, her clothes, or her person, since she was Harriet's age and her mother had been alive.

When they were finished eating, a maid of middle years came in. She curtsied politely, said her name was Mary Crandall, and instantly led Harriet to the bedroom to help unpack their few belongings. She took their dirty clothes to be laundered, their shoes to be polished, and said a bath was being brought up, as soon as miss was ready.

Allie had never known such luxury, not even at Papa's house. Here the soaps were scented, the towels were heated, the water had not been used by anyone else first. As she scrubbed her hair, determined to stay in the copper tub until her toes turned white and shriveled, Allie thought that such opulence was far more seductive than any raffish, lopsided smile.

Who was she fooling?

The captain was the hero of every female's fantasies, and he made Allie feel emotions she never knew she had, or had forgotten. She was five and twenty, no dewy miss to be infatuated with a handsome face and a virile form, and yet she was thinking of him while in her bath, naked, washing herself. Goodness, he no more belonged in her waking dreams than he belonged in her bed!

And she had accepted his money. Heavens, he

might think she was open to other suggestions. She should have left.

He had been right, though, to convince her to stay. She had been feeling light-headed and hungry, and she needed the extra coins. It was dark, Harriet would have been all alone . . . and Allie had been afraid. Besides, no one needed to know where she was. Tomorrow she could try the placement agencies if the captain did not find a separate residence for them. No, that would never do, either. If he set up an establishment in London, people would assume the worst. They would decide Allie was under the protection of a rakish bachelor, which would be nothing less than the truth, albeit the innocent truth. They would assume she was his next Rochelle. Perhaps she should change her name to Allyne d'Argent? Allie stifled a nervous giggle, making sure the maid was busy with Harriet in the other room.

She'd had too much wine. Calloway had said it would help her stuffed head. Instead the wine, along with the warmth of the bath, was helping her think licentious thoughts. Allie stepped out of the tub and dried herself briskly, shaking off unwanted images with the bath water. She reminded herself that when Captain Endicott sent Harriet off to school, the governess would be left homeless and jobless again, but this time with the references of the owner of The Red and the Black, a gambling casino, not a polite academy for girls. The thought of applying for a position with a rake's recommendation in hand left her colder than the night air before she lowered a clean flannel night gown over her head. Mary had produced it from somewhere, thank heavens, for Allie's own still smelled of smoke from the fire at Mrs. Semple's.

No matter the comforts here, Allie knew she should have gone. Nothing good could come from being at

The Red and the Black but a decent dinner and clean hair. There was no way the captain could make her employment by him respectable, and many ways he could make it ruinous.

Of course, she thought as she got into bed beside Harriet, the one thing she did not have to worry about was her virtue. Captain Jack might be a womanizer, but he was not interested in her as anything but a nanny. She was safe from seduction, at least. The realization did not make Allie happy.

Knowing that in the morning she had to leave the comfort of this soft-as-eiderdown bed forever did not make her happy, either.

Her thoughts were dismal, and the dog snored louder than Miss Wolfe. And Harriet tossed and turned so often that Allie could not sleep despite the wine and her exhaustion. Having that nice maid bring her a lavender-soaked cloth for her aching head, now that made her happy.

She eventually drifted into slumber, not thinking of tomorrow, not thinking of Captain Endicott or Harriet or any of the day's events. They would all be gone soon, like a bad dream.

But, oh, that lopsided smile was hard to forget.

CHAPTER SIX

Damn, a daughter!

What the devil was Jack Endicott, late of His Majesty's Army and currently a knight of the baize table, going to do with a daughter? Harriet was not even his daughter, by George, or by Nelson Hildebrand. Jack had been kicked by a horse with less dire effects. Hell, he had been shot by the French and survived better than he thought he would survive the hell-babe and the broomstick, as Calloway called the pair upstairs. Pinafores and plaits and priggish schoolmistresses? Old Hildebrand must be laughing in his grave, wherever that was.

Jack was not laughing. He did paste a smile on his face, though, as he greeted the club's patrons that evening. Tonight was too important for The Red and the Black's survival for Jack to worry about his own.

He had sent invitations to everyone he could think of: peers, politicians, business potentates, and half-pay officers, anyone with deep pockets and a proclivity for gambling. If they came, if they subscribed, if they enjoyed themselves and found The Red and the Black a comfortable, honest venue where they could bring their sweethearts if not their spouses, Jack would see a profit. They would tell their friends, the tables would be filled, money would roll into his dangerously empty coffers. What had started as a chance to thumb his nose at polite society had turned into a matter of pride, a drive to succeed.

Jack was not a mere retired soldier, not a mere second son. He was no man's pensioner and no man's lackey. He'd had to use his brother's blunt to pay the informants for clues about Lottie. Soon he'd be spending his own income on the search. Lottie was his sister, his promise to keep, too.

So he could not afford for anything to go wrong tonight. At least nothing more than what had already gone so desperately out of kilter.

First the place had been invaded by foreigners, a prickly virgin and a thigh-high orphan being as alien to Jack as a Hottentot. Then his *belle du nuit* had turned belligerent because he'd broken their dinner engagement. If she was mad now, Jack trembled to think how Rochelle would be later, when he broke off their affair. He would not have his mistress and his ward under the same roof—not even if Miss Silver would have permitted it.

Maybe he would wait for tomorrow to tell Rochelle that their relationship was at an end, though. Valor extending only so far, he would tell her in the park, Jack decided, where she could do less damage to the chandeliers and crystal glasses and the carefree ambiance he had strived so hard to achieve. She was already pouting, not looking half as decorative or being half as charming to the patrons, which was her purpose in being at the club. Her purpose elsewhere could be filled by any number of less demanding, less temperamental females.

Jack could not help thinking that Miss Silver's looks had improved when she was angry. The self-righteous teacher had turned vibrant, challenging, her gray eyes shooting sparks of blue fire. Rochelle, for all her vivid coloring, simply looked sullen. He would be glad to see the last of her. And of Miss Silver too, of course.

The captain stopped thinking about what waited upstairs or what would be waiting in the park tomorrow. Tonight Jack was king of all he surveyed.

He straightened his intricate, snowy neckcloth, touched the diamond stickpin for luck, smiled, and strolled around his realm.

He patted backs, filled glasses, consoled losers, and congratulated winners. He beckoned for fresh decks and full bottles, found seats for new arrivals, and introduced nabobs to noblemen, officers to ordinary chaps. He flirted with the ladies, not with any serious intent, but enough to make their escorts jealous. A man whose mind was on his ladybird was a fool whose mind was not on his cards. Jack would not take advantage of green boys or drunks or men with nothing left to wager. Everyone else was fair game.

The house always won. Tonight it was going to win more.

As he made the rounds of the tables, keeping a steady watch on his domain, Jack chatted with old friends and new customers.

"Have you heard anything about that sister of yours?" a bald gentleman in a puce waistcoat asked him, pointing to the portrait of Lottie's mother that was across the room, above a reward notice.

"Not yet, but I have heard a lot of sad stories."

The man's shiny pate glistened in the candlelight as he shook his head. "Bound to be a million orphans with amnesia, when a fortune is at stake. I'd wager every blue-eyed blonde in England lands on your doorstep sooner or later, ready to call you brother."

"Greedy and dishonest, every female, what?" Lord Harkness put in. "Can't trust a one of them, can you?" he asked, his arm around a slender redhead, while his wife, to Jack's certain knowledge, was home nursing Harkness's sick mother.

Jack did not try to defend womanhood, although he might have used his paragon of a sister-in-law as an example. Harkness had not come to a gambling parlor for a sermon. He'd come to satisfy his greed and flaunt his dishonesty.

Jack smiled and moved on, wondering about Miss Silver. She'd taken his money at the expense of her scruples, but did that make her grasping, or simply needy? He doubted if anything else about her could be bought, not her loyalty, not her honor. Not that he was interested in anything else but her care for Harriet, of course.

And he should not be thinking about Miss Prunes and Prisms while he was patrolling his parlor. He should be watching to make sure everything ran smoothly and the money kept flowing in.

He whispered to one of the vingt-et-un dealers to discourage a young baronet whose pockets were known to be let. Jack was not a bank, extending credit; nor did he want any bankruptcies or suicides on his conscience. He peeled one of the serving girls off a colonel's lap. Jack was no procurer, either. Pretty lasses in low-cut gowns were enough distraction for his purpose. He wanted the gents to put their money on his tables, not down those same low-cut necklines.

He thought of Miss Silver upstairs—Again! Drat, the woman stuck in his mind like a burr!—with her collar buttoned to her chin. Her skin might have been purple, for all a fellow got to see of it, and her chest might be as flat as his own. Not that he cared, of course. It was just that the connoisseur in him hated to see such a confounded ugly waste. The woman could be pretty, he thought, if she were dressed properly. She ought to be gowned in sapphire or silver to make the most of her glorious eyes, not the dull gray thing she had worn. And the fabrics ought to be light and lacy, emphasizing her fine bones. Her hair would need to be trimmed so that shorter curls framed her face, softening the severe lines until she added a few pounds. And she would have to smile. He detested giggles, but a warm, tender smile could make a man melt. Nothing made a woman more attractive to a chap than thinking that he had brought a smile to her lips, that she was enjoying his company.

Not that Jack would ever get to see the schoolteacher smile, except when he paid her the bonus, perhaps.

Not that he cared.

He had a great many more important things to do than imagining that pattern card of propriety in elegant gowns . . . or out of them. He had a club to run, by Jupiter. Setting the priggish female firmly in the back of his mind, for the tenth time, it seemed, he continued his rounds. When he reached the far end of the room, he ducked through the service doors and checked on the wine stocks and the kitchens. A late supper would be set out in a smaller parlor, but other delicacies would be taken around on trays.

Everything was in order. It ought to be, for what he was paying the chef. Jack sampled a lobster patty before backing through the service doors to resume his watchful perambulation.

At the table closest to the kitchens, he noticed a scrap of white fabric on the floor. A napkin, most likely, he thought, dropped by one of the card players, or a towel one of the waitresses had used to wipe up a wine spill. Either way, it offended Jack. His casino was a reflection on him now, and he would not appear less than pristine. He bent to pick up the cloth, reached down, and touched a foot. A tiny foot. A bare foot. A misbegotten, misdirected, meddlesome foot. A where-the-devil-was-Miss-Silver-when-he-needed-her foot. It was under a white flannel nightgown, like a foot of surrender. A flag, that was.

Luckily the gamblers at the table were busy placing their bets, so they did not hear the squeak from the foot's owner, or the curse from the club's owner.

Jack stood up and thought furiously for a moment. Harriet could not stay there, of course, and she could not be seen. He'd be in trouble with the licensing officials. Worse, he'd be a laughingstock. Worse still, his club would lose all claims to sophistication, exclusivity and elegance. A child underfoot? A fellow might as well stay at home by his own fireside playing jackstraws with Junior.

Just then a serving girl came out of the kitchen with a tray of filled wineglasses. Jack had hired the new girl on Downs's recommendation because she was young and cheerful, rounded and rosy-cheeked under her freckles. She was just what Jack decided the club needed to offset the brittle beauties like Rochelle he had already hired. The girl's hair was more orange than red, but she would fit in, in the dark. Besides, Downs liked her, and the man was too serious by half. The captain's capable assistant deserved a bit of liveliness in his life, too.

Jack stepped in front of the young woman so his back was to the room, and stopped her progress by lifting one of the glasses off her tray. "Darla, is it?"

"Or Dora, sir. I ain't used to answering to the other yet."

"Yes, well, Darla or Dora, I wish you to create a diversion."

He might have asked her to create the Taj Mahal the way she gaped at him.

"Come now, Dolly, you are a bright young woman. I would not have employed you otherwise. Go over toward the front door where Mr. Downs is greeting the new patrons and make a scene. Nothing like crying fire, mind you, for I do not want to empty the place. I just wish everyone to look in that direction."

She was looking at him as if he'd sprouted another head, or devil's horns on this one. "Mr. Downs, he said as how I was supposed to act like a lady."

"Yes, but right now I need you to act like I am paying your wages. Which I shall raise if you do as I ask instead of arguing." He put a guinea on her tray to ensure cooperation, whether she understood her role or not.

"A scene, he wants," she muttered as she walked away. "But not a riot. And they said as how this position was an easy one."

Jack positioned himself behind one of the cardplayers, within easy reach of The Foot. He waited. Darla seemed to be arguing with Downs, although no one appeared to notice except Jack. She'd put her tray down, except for one glass. Now she looked over at her employer. Jack raised both hands, palms up. Up, more, louder.

So Darla tossed the contents of the glass into Downs's face, shouting, "How dare you touch me like that, you swine! I ain't that kind of girl." She raised her voice to a screech. "And I'm going to tell Cap'n Jack you pinched me, see if I don't."

That had everyone's attention, all right, calling out bawdy comments. Poor Downs had gone as pale as a ghost. "But I . . . That is, I wouldn't . . ."

"What, are you going to deny it when me bum is black and blue, you miserable maggot? Cap'n Jack said this were an honest bit of work, and I believed him. *He* is a gentleman!"

The ladies were applauding; the gents were laughing and turning back to their wagers.

Darla had missed her calling to the stage; Jack had not missed his chance.

He had stooped down, scooped up Harriet, and swooped her away through the service entry without a soul noticing. He dropped her to her feet, her bare feet, as if she were a bag of stinging nettles. If she had been, she would have shriveled under his scrutiny. His soldiers would have been quaking. But not Harriet. Oh, no. She just looked up at him with wide, innocent eyes.

Innocent? Hell. Things were going well in the club, so Jack had a moment to interrogate the infant and perhaps put the fear of God, or the fear of her guardian, into her. "What the devil were you doing under that table? Or in the gaming rooms at all, for that matter? And where is Miss Silver?"

"Sleeping, of course."

"Of course."

"But I had a nap, so I was not tired. I put Miss Silver's bonnet on Joker, but then he ran away, down the stairs. I came looking for him."

Jack could not blame the poor old hound for trying to hide, the hat was that ugly. Before he could expound on how one crime did not excuse another, Harriet was going on: "She will beat me if I do not get her bonnet back."

Jack did not for an instant believe that Miss Silver

would strike a child. If she ever had, perhaps this brat would not be so plaguesome now. "You have caused me so much trouble I am tempted to beat you myself. Did you think of that?"

"Oh, you would never do that. You are a gentleman. Darla just said so, and so did Miss Silver."

"She did?" He was surprised the teacher accorded him that much respect. He was also surprised how much her respect gladdened him. "That is, being a gentleman has nothing to do with it. You are not acting like a lady, creeping about in your nightclothes, so I am not constrained by proper manners either. I thought I made it clear that you were never to enter the public rooms. You could get me shut down. Unless you are an heiress after all, which I intend to investigate come Monday morning, we need the income from this place. And why do you not have any slippers?"

Her toes were curled on the bare floor. "They burned up in the fire."

He sighed. "You had better be an heiress, then, for I can see that you are going to be deuced expensive."

"But I can save you a lot of money."

He tallied the cost of a new bonnet for the teacher, new slippers, maybe a new dog. "I do not see how, brat. You cannot work at the tables for at least another eight years." Not that Jack would let an old friend and fellow officer's daughter deal cards at a gaming parlor. He turned to go back into the club.

"The cheater would have cost you more."

That had him turned around so fast the breeze stirred Harriet's white night gown. "Cheater?"

She nodded. "One of the men at the table was playing crooked."

"You are nothing but a little girl. How could you know?"

"I know enough to understand he was not supposed

to have an ace tucked in his boot top." She held up the card.

"Hell. Sorry, I should not have said that in front of you." But hell and damnation, a Captain Sharp could destroy everything Jack had built. His reputation for running an honest table was more important than the quality of his wine or the friendliness of his pretty dealers. If a man could not count on fair play, he might as well take his money to a diving ken in Seven Dials. At least there he'd *know* he was going to be robbed.

"Which man?" He held his hand out for the card.

Instead, Harriet wiped her nose on the back of her nightgown sleeve. Jack handed over his handkerchief. She mopped her nose, then held the cloth out to him.

Jack stepped back. "No, you keep it. Which man?"

"What will you give me?"

"I'll give you a birching if you do not tell me!"

Harriet sniffed, jutting her jaw out, holding the ace to her skinny chest.

"That's blackmail!"

She sniffed again.

"And blow your nose, for heaven's sake. All right. What do you want, a new doll to dress instead of my poor dog?"

"I want to stay here."

"In the hall to the kitchen? You'll be trampled and cold. What, are you hungry? I can have some sandwiches sent upstairs."

"No, I want to stay here, in this house, with you."

"No, you don't. You want to go to live with a nice family, or go to a school in the country."

"Where everyone will point to me and whisper about my mother. Where I'll be no one's favorite, only a charity girl."

"Nonsense. I expect to be paying your expenses

until I find some poor fool to wed you. That is not charity."

Harriet did not hand over the ace, nor did she take her green-eyed gaze off him.

Were females born knowing how to twist a man into knots? "Very well. For a bit. Then we will see how things work out. That's fair, isn't it?"

"What about Miss Silver?"

Lud, what would he do with this conniving little cub without a bear leader? "I will invite her to stay, but I make no promises. She is a highly moral woman, and she does not approve of me or my club. An offer to raise her salary is the best I can do. And that is my best offer to you, brat. If you wait any longer the game will be over and my customers might discover they have been gulled on their own."

"I saw seagulls once. Is it the same? I did not see any in the other room."

"No! Forget about seagulls. Which man?"

"The one with the high-topped boots, of course."

Damn, he should have gone back and looked for himself, instead of bargaining with the devil's own granddaughter. "There may be more than one man at the table in boots. Which seat did he have?"

"With his back to the door."

Excellent. Now all he needed was Darla, and another diversion.

The poor girl had tears in her eyes when he told her, after she'd done exclaiming over Miss Harriet, out of bed and in her bare feet. "But that Mr. Downs is such a nice man."

"Yes, and I shall raise his salary, too." Lud, what this night was going to cost him, Jack worried, as he put another two guineas on Darla's tray. "Now go."

This time Darla cracked poor Downs over the head with her tray, a great resounding smack that could be heard in the rear of the room, where Jack was standing behind Sir Jethro Stevens's chair. Jack placed his hand firmly on the baronet's padded shoulder when everyone turned to look toward the altercation.

"The game is over," Jack whispered in the older, thinner man's ear while his gaming partners were laying side bets on the outcome of the contretemps, or if Downs would survive the night. "You have an urgent message to go home."

"Impossible. No one lives in my rooms but me. No one wants me there, or knows I am here."

"I know you are here and I do not want you, either." Jack showed the ace in his other hand. "Now get up and leave quietly, leaving the money on the table, or I shall drag you into the kitchen and hand you to my chef. The man's a genius with a carving knife. Then, if anything is left, I shall let Calloway show you what I think of ivory tuners in my club. You do recall Calloway, don't you? He's the large gentleman outside the door, the one who looks like a cutthroat. Which is what he was, before they let him choose the army instead of Australia. Oh, and then it will be my turn. I do hate to get my hands dirty, but in your case I might make an ex—"

"Excuse me, gentlemen," Stevens said, rising. "Urgent message from home, don't you know. Have to leave." He tossed his cards, including the extra ace, onto the table, mixing them into the unused cards and the coins and the vouchers resting there. "Sorry. The game's not over, so divide the ante as you will."

"What about your winnings?" one of the others asked.

"Sir Jethro has kindly donated his winnings to the Widows and Orphans Fund." Jack had his hand on the baronet's shoulder, squeezing. "Isn't that right?" He spoke loudly, thinking he might shame some of the other gamesters into a bit of charity while he was cleaning house.

Sir Jethro looked ill, but he nodded. "Perhaps another evening," he told his former victims.

"Not in my club. Not in London," the captain said softly as he escorted the now sweating baronet from the room. Jack had a smile on his face for the other players to see. "Or you are a dead man."

So was Jack, when he had to tell Rochelle she was leaving and Miss Silver was staying.

CHAPTER SEVEN

Allie could not breathe. She was febrile, fevered, and felt as if a weight pressed on her chest, another on her feet. Oh, no, she was too ill with Harriet's contagion to go to church. Mrs. Semple would be furious. Matron would have to escort the younger girls herself.

Then Allie remembered she was not at the school. She was in London, at a sinkhole of depravity. Instead of little girls with pleasing manners, the women here worked at pleasing men, one way or another. Did they even go to church?

Allie groaned. She was too sick to go to services, and she was staying in a gambling establishment. The Good Lord would have to forgive her for both. Then she remembered Harriet and groaned again.

She struggled for breath, for the energy to open her eyes. When she got them open, she screamed. The weight on her chest was brown and hairy and licked her chin. The dog was lying on top of her, panting, and it was wearing a lace-edged nightcap. A familiar lace-edged nightcap. Allie got one of her hands out of the covers and touched her head, which was bare. Her hair was in a tangle, for she had gone to bed with it damp, thinking her cap would keep her curls manageable. She screamed again: "Harriet!"

That was the weight on her legs. "Oh, good, you are awake."

Allie pushed the dog aside and took a deep breath. Maybe she would live through the day after all. The room was bright with morning light, and her head seemed clear.

"We are staying."

Maybe Allie would not want to live through the day if it meant arguing with Harriet. "We talked about this last night. You should not raise your hopes."

"But Cap'n Jack said so."

He would not know what it meant to make a promise to a child, or how a few words could be construed as a vow. He would not have to console an angry, disappointed child. Allie would.

"I am sure he did not mean—"

"And he'll raise your salary triple if you stay, he said."

"No, he could not have."

"Want to bet? A thousand pounds says he offers double at least."

Allie could not imagine how or when Harriet had such a conversation with her guardian. "I am glad Captain Endicott seems to have taken a liking to you, enough that he wishes you to stay with him, but I cannot."

"He might offer more if I pretend to cry."

"Money does not matter. It cannot repair a damaged reputation. Your guardian is not a man with whom an unwed female should associate."

"Darla likes him fine."

Goodness, she did not wish to discuss with an eight-year-old child the difference between a woman who took money to educate minds and one who took money to entertain men, or why Harriet should not be speaking with Darla. "Liking him does not matter either." Not that Allie did, despite admiring his bravery, not in battle, but in forging his own path and following it. She did not respect his route, however, and she did not trust a man who would make those disreputable choices. Besides, Captain Endicott and his bravery, bad choices, and beguiling smile were nothing to her, nothing but something to avoid.

"But he will buy you a new bonnet."

"I could never accept such a personal gift from a man who— What happened to my old bonnet?"

Harriet jumped off the bed, Joker following. "Mary is bringing breakfast to the sitting room. Hurry to get dressed or it will be cold. I am starving!" She skipped out of the room. The old dog lumbered after her, still wearing Allie's nightcap, half-covering his eyes.

If Allie could not get to church, she could still say a prayer. Allie prayed for patience. And deliverance. She found hot water in the washbasin, which was a treat after Mrs. Semple's, where one nearly had to break the ice on one's water pitcher in the mornings. She also found that her two packed gowns, all that remained of her once modest, now meager wardrobe, had been sponged and pressed. They hardly smelled of the fire or soot at all anymore.

Allie picked the brown wool, since the dark blue's cuffs were less frayed. That gown would be more suitable for calling on placement agencies and academies on Monday morning. She could not apply for a position without a bonnet, however, so after brushing most of the knots out of her hair, she went to find Harriet.

She would finish the brushing after breakfast, and coil the long mane into a proper bun at the back of her neck. For now her hair was clean, which felt so good she swung her head from side to side, just to feel the hair's weight and smell the fine soap that had been provided with her bath.

Someone had braided Harriet's red curls, she saw when she reached the sitting room, and tied the braids with ribbons. The child's stockings were clean, and her white pinafore was freshly ironed. If she had not been eating bacon with her fingers, one might have assumed she was a cherished, wellborn, well-mannered child. Allie sent another prayer skyward. Maybe someday that would be the truth.

Once again the cook had sent enough food for half of Mrs. Semple's students. Allie chose a sweet roll and tea. Just as she was about to bring the cup to her lips, someone rapped on the door.

"Come in," she said, thinking it was the maid, Mary.

It was not.

Once again, Allie was hot and weak and could not breathe. No, she was cold and stiff, and could not breathe. Captain Endicott walked into the room and stole all the air out of it. Yesterday he had been disordered, half his clothes missing, his hair mussed. Today he was nearly perfect, from the tips of his shining shoes to the gleaming dark curls on his head. What was in between was a figment of a tailor's fantasies— and a maiden's. In formfitting trousers and narrow blue Bath superfine coat, he was all tight muscle and broad chest, with no fat and no affectations. He did not pose or preen like a London dandy, or walk with a mincing gait. The captain could have been in the country, or still with the cavalry, so natural was his air of confidence, his casual grace, his sinewy stride.

He was taller than she had remembered, and far better looking. No wonder the women adored him.

What saved him from being too good-looking, too much the beau ideal, was his nose. It was definitely crooked and flattened at one point, likely where someone's fist had smashed into it. The irregularity, the asymmetry, saved Captain Endicott from being a masterpiece of manliness. Now he was simply intensely appealing. That hint of vulnerability, that imperfection, took him off a pedestal, back to where a woman could throw herself into his embrace, beg to be held by those strong arms, rub her soft body against his hardness. She could do none of those things if he was the consummate image of virility, an idol to be worshipped from afar. Now he was just a run-of-the-mill hero.

No wonder the women adored him. Or had she come to that conclusion already? He not only stole her breath, he stole her wits. He smiled at her then, and Allie could not recall what she disliked about him.

"You look a hundred percent better without that old-maid bonnet," he said by way of greeting.

Now Allie remembered what she did not like about her host. He was a flirt and a womanizer, a gambler and a gouger. Yes, he was devotedly looking for his sister, and yes, he had kindly hired former soldiers, but he was improper. A gentleman did not comment on a lady's marital state, nor did he question her taste.

"Good morning to you, sir," Allie said in quelling tones, the ones she used to bring her young students back to order.

He grinned at her and gestured to the overladen table. "Might I join you?"

How could Allie refuse him when it was his table, his food? She nodded.

Jack sank into the chair, relieved his knees had not given out. Gads, the woman was a beauty! He could have fallen over from the shock. That hair alone made her one of the most attractive women he had ever seen, long and flowing in darken golden waves like honey down her back, over her shoulders, half hiding the ugly brown sack she wore. After a good night's sleep she did not appear as pale and drawn, either, but had a clear, glowing complexion, all rosy from her wash. Her eyes were more blue than gray this morning, and her lips were full. Heaven help him.

But then those lips pursed in disapproval as she said, " I thought you promised not to enter these rooms."

Ah, there was the Miss Silver of yesterday, the prim schoolmistress. Now he could stop looking at her and eat his breakfast.

"Yes," he said, "but no one is around to see me, and how else was I to invite you to attend church with me this morning?"

"You go to church? That is, I had not expected—"

"You had been thinking that I followed some pagan religion, worshiping Mammon and sacrificing virgins?"

Allie cursed her pale skin for the blush she could feel creeping across her cheeks. Just because he was a knave was no reason to be impolite. "I had not considered that you would arise so early, after a night of . . . of managing your enterprise."

He brushed that aside, filling a plate with eggs and ham and kidneys and kippers. "I need little sleep. I need more of God's grace to make a go of this business. So will you attend with me, you and Harriet, of course?"

Harriet was eating, feeding scraps to the dog, and watching the two adults eagerly. "We should thank the Lord for saving us from the fire and finding us such a nice place to live."

"We can thank Him in our prayers every night, and beg his forgiveness for our trespasses." Allie still was not sure about that fire, or her bonnet. She was sure, though, that it was not a good idea to go anywhere with the devilishly handsome former officer. "I thought we had agreed that arrangements were to be made today for other accommodations."

The captain looked at Harriet, who smiled at him, dripping jam down her chin. "I had second thoughts about that. I think you and Harriet should stay here for awhile, even after I speak to the solicitor Monday morning. I should get to know my ward, don't you think, so I know what is in her best interests? Church is a good place to start."

"But I thought it was understood, sir, that I could not stay here. No one was to know I was in residence at your club. My reputation would be destroyed at the hint of such an association with The Red and the Black, which would be obvious if I attended services with you. Furthermore, aside from the nature of the club, an unwed woman cannot be seen accompanied by a single gentleman."

"I think you care over much for your reputation, but no one needs know where you are staying, just that I am escorting my ward and her governess. We will not attend the service at St. George's, anyway, where the *ton* congregates, just a small chapel nearby where the parishioners are not likely to be hiring your services or gossiping about you."

"I think you do not know your neighbors if you believe they will not take note of the comings and goings of such an exotic establishment."

"Ah, but my neighbors are a tea-trading business

and an apothecary. Both are closed on Sundays. Besides, you shall not be alone with a rake and a rogue, as you seem to fear. Do not try to deny your thoughts, ma'am, because your blushes give you away. Mrs. Crandall shall accompany us as your very respectable chaperone."

"Mrs. Mary Crandall, the maid? You must know that a maid does not satisfy the proper conventions."

"Not for a debutante, no."

What he was saying was that Allie had no claims to the airs of a young lady, despite whatever status her birth might have endowed. She was past the age of marriage now, and part of the working class. She toiled for her bread the same as the seamstress and the scullery maid. Unlike theirs, however, Allie's employment depended on her reputation, which the captain did not seem to understand or wish to consider. Of course not. He had Harriet; ergo, he needed a governess.

He was going on: "Besides, Mary is no longer merely a maid. Due to a generous contribution to the Widows and Orphans Fund, she has her pension, one the government did not see fit to grant. Now my former first sergeant's wife is a lady of leisure. She chooses to stay here, however, until her sister returns from Ireland in the spring. We will find you another maid."

"See?" Harriet asked, her mouth full of toast and jam. "Cap'n Jack thinks of everything."

He had not thought that he himself was the problem, not her lack of chaperone, though. A proper governess could walk with a gentleman. But was Captain Endicott a gentleman? "No, thank you," she told him now. "Although I appreciate your efforts, I must think of my career."

"Fustian. My sister-in-law can fix any silly blot in

your copybook caused by being seen with me. What is the point of being a countess if you cannot influence everyone else? And my brother supports any number of schools. He can secure you a position at one of them. Besides, no one knows you in town, so no one can sully your good name."

"I cannot like it."

Harriet turned to Jack, jam on her chin. "I told you she wouldn't go. You owe me ten pounds. Twenty if she leaves altogether."

He was not admitting defeat. "But it is Sunday, Miss Silver, and the sun is shining for once. The placement agencies are closed, the schools will not be interviewing new teachers. Where would you go?"

Allie still had no idea. She thought she might go with the captain to Mr. Burquist's office in the morning and ask him to recommend a suitable lodging house or an employment office. That would mean staying here another night, if the captain was not inclined to find separate lodgings for her and Harriet.

"Would you stay inside the entire day?" he was asking, taking for granted that she would remain at The Red and the Black.

Allie could easily have gone back to bed and slept until Monday morning. The sunshine was tempting, though, and so were the golden lights dancing in his brown eyes. Too tempting. "Why?"

"Why do I wish you to accompany me and Harriet to church? Frankly, I am terrified of the brat."

Harriet giggled. "Snake says Cap'n Jack is not afraid of anything, ever."

"That is Calloway, imp, and he is grateful for his job, so he exaggerates. Now take Joker out into the rear garden. After all you have fed him, he needs the exercise." He turned toward Allie. "It is not much, but it is walled in. And wipe your chin."

Allie lifted her napkin to her chin before she realized he meant Harriet, not her. Harriet scrubbed her face with the cloth without needing a second reminder, made a decent curtsey without needing the first reminder, and left.

"How did you do that? Make her listen to you?"

"I promised to show her my pistols if she behaved. She is a bloodthirsty little savage, isn't she?" he asked, but Allie detected a note of fondness beneath the gruff words. She must have missed a great deal while she slept.

"Why?" she asked again, encompassing a hundred questions.

He picked the ones he wished to answer. "Why bargain with the brat? The same reason you did, because life is easier that way. Or why do I need you along? The last should be obvious, if I have to bribe my ward to obey."

He did not need Allie at all, and they both knew it. Harriet already listened to him better than she had ever heeded anyone at Mrs. Semple's. And anyone could teach the child her letters; perhaps Mrs. Crandall could do it. She seemed a quiet, competent woman. The dealers could teach Harriet to add, even if no higher than vingt-et-un. But Allie's staying was not the immediate question. Harriet's was.

"No, why did you tell her she could remain with you?" Allie asked, taking a last sip of her tea. "She will have her heart broken when you send her away. She will not understand, and will not easily trust you again."

Jack was not going to admit that he had been blackmailed by an infant. "She does not like school. The other children are unkind to her."

"Of course they are. Who would be kind to a fellow student who put spiders in one's bed?" Allie set her napkin on the table, finished with her meal. The captain refilled his plate, to her amazement. "Did you like school?" she asked him.

"When I was there and not sent down for some offense or other. But I had my older brother watching out for me. He was born a viscount, then succeeded to the earldom at the age of fourteen, so no one offended him, or me by association. He had the power of authority even as a lad, and became a deadly shot later. He's still handy with his fives, except when he has to remove his spectacles."

"Do you not think Harriet should attend school, meet girls her own age and station? Not that your employees are not decent women." She hoped they were, anyway. And hoped she did not sound too much of a snob. "But are they proper companions for Lord Hildebrand's granddaughter? Do you truly think Harriet belongs here?"

"I think she has lost her entire family, and she is lonely and afraid. Lud, when our stepmother passed away, and then our father soon after, I could not bear to let Ace out of my sight. My brother, Alexander, that is, who was nothing more than a boy himself, poor blighter, with a runny-nosed rapscallion stuck to him like glue. Harriet has no big brother to make her feel safe, no parents to adore her, no grandparents to spoil her. The poor mite needs a home more than she needs schooling or social graces or more snubs from wealthier, better-born brats."

Allie felt sympathy for the little boy left with no one but his big brother, although she knew there would be trustees and old family retainers to look after the wealthy aristocratic orphans, but the captain was wrong. "But this is not a home! That is my point. It is a habitat for wastrels, pleasure seekers, here-and-thereians."

"It is a polite gaming parlor," he corrected her. "But you are right, it is not a suitable dwelling for a child. In another month or so my brother's town house should be ready. By then we should be firmly in the black, besides. I could purchase a small place, perhaps in Kensington where property is not so dear, and live apart from the club. Downs can manage on his own when I am not here. Harriet would need a proper governess, of course, to show her how to go on like a lady. She already respects you and wishes you to stay."

Allie shook her head, sending the long golden hair shimmering around her. "I am certain the agencies can supply an older woman, one whose age protects her from slander. I am not quite in my dotage."

Jack clutched his fork so he would not be tempted to smooth the wavy tresses back, away from the plates on the table, away from her face, letting it run through his fingers, letting it smooth his skin, stir his senses more than—He choked on a bit of toast. Lud, what was he thinking? When he could speak again, he said, "You are not in your dotage, Miss Silver, but neither am I an old goat, forcing myself on my female employees." At least he never had been, before.

"I never said you were . . . goatish, just that people will talk."

"People always talk. Let them."

"That is easy for you to say. You have your family to fall back on, any number of skills you can use to earn a living. You could be a farmer. You could go back to the army if the club failed."

"Never."

"Then another business. If your brother has so many schools in his keeping, he must have a position for you. Training his horses, overseeing his lands, caring for his hounds, for heaven's sake. Gossip cannot hurt you. That is why you can afford to be so cavalier about it. Life is different for a woman on her own, no matter how unfair that is. The world is different for a female without family or funds, and it is far crueler."

"But no one will know you are here or who you are, I swear! Other than my own staff, who know better than to chat with outsiders, that is. You could change your name like half the women do."

Allie stood, and so he stood also, showing that he did have the manners, at least, of a gentleman. That was not enough for her. "I am sorry, Captain Endicott. I am proud of my name and wish to stay proud of it. You are the hero, the one who is afraid of nothing. I am not half as brave. Nor am I a gambler."

CHAPTER EIGHT

Allie went to church after all. How could she preach propriety if she did not follow the simplest rules of righteous behavior? She had to set a good example for Harriet, and she had to ask for guidance.

She did not go alone with Captain Endicott and Harriet, of course, who did not count as a chaperone. That she would have refused outright. Instead they were accompanied by a group of The Red and the Black's residents. Dressed in their Sunday best, they looked like any other folks walking to church, not hardened gamesters and ladies of ill repute.

Mrs. Mary Crandall, who had confessed she could not read and thus would not be a fitting governess, nevertheless held Harriet's hand and told her stories about the Spanish campaign.

That was not what Allie might have considered appropriate for a Sunday lesson, but Harriet was not pestering Snake—Mr. Calloway, that was—who walked ahead with his massive arms crossed against his barrel chest, his mustachio neatly combed. He had recently threatened to carve Harriet into horse feathers if she did not stop asking to see his tattoo again.

Two dark-haired women followed Calloway. Allie did not know them, but they smiled prettily, and had no face paint this morning, so she smiled back, admiring their bonnets. Her own had been mended by Mrs. Crandall, although she was no longer a maid. She liked to keep busy, the older woman had said, pinning a cluster of silk violets to the bonnet's brim to hide where the dog had pawed on it to get the wretched thing off his head. Mary pinned another cluster of silk flowers onto Allie's cloak, which had been sponged and dried, so the mud and travel dust were gone.

"I like to see pretty things after all the ugliness of war," Mary told her, so Allie could not refuse the gift of the flowers and the woman's efforts. She did feel a great deal better this morning anyway, clean and rested, well-fed, with Captain Endicott's extra coins in her purse. Maybe she was prettier, too. Nothing to compare to the women of The Red and the Black, of course, but Captain Endicott had smiled at her when she finally agreed to attend church with him. With them.

He, of course, looked magnificent. He walked at Allie's side, matching his strides to her shorter steps, speaking politely of the weather, the political news, the buildings they passed. Nothing about him or his conversation could offend, which was, in a way, more offensive to Allie. The man was a gambler and a shabster. Why could he not be a total cad so she could hate him entirely?

To keep from noticing the laugh lines at his eyes, the curving smile at his lips, or the way the morning light brought a golden warmth to his brown curls,

Allie kept her attention on the couple directly ahead of her.

Darla and Mr. Downs were arguing. He wore a sticking plaster on his head and she wore a scrap of ecru lace, tied in a saucy bow near her left cheek. The captain's assistant did not look at the girl, and Darla could not seem to look at anything but him.

"I said I was sorry," Darla was saying, loudly enough that Allie could not help but overhear. "And I was only following Cap'n Jack's orders."

"I know. He told me. If you'd asked me before going off half-cocked, I could have caused a ruckus at the door, without putting on a raree-show for the customers."

"I didn't mean to hit you so hard."

Allie looked over at Captain Endicott. "She hit him?" she whispered.

He held his finger to his lips. "Ssh. They have to settle this themselves."

Downs was feeling his head and the sticking plaster there. "I've had worse."

"And I know the cap'n gave you a bonus."

Downs nodded. "For being wounded in the line of duty, he said."

Allie looked at the captain, but he just smiled and patted her hand, slowing their pace so the other couple was a bit farther ahead, despite Downs's limp.

Allie could still hear them, though. Darla was prodding Downs with her parasol and saying, "So what has your garters tied in granny knots? Seems to me we helped the boss and got paid for it. We choused the cheat, and made sure no one saw the brat."

The brat? Harriet? Allie walked faster, to make sure she did not miss a word. The captain was smiling beside her, enjoying the walk and the morning and the bickering couple ahead of them.

Darla poked Downs with her parasol again. "So why are you acting like I am the worm in your bushel basket of apples? Cap'n Jack says I helped saved the club."

"Because you made me look the fool, that's why!" Downs said, taking the weapon from her and tucking it under his own arm. "All the patrons were laughing at me, and the staff, too."

"Oh, who cares about them?"

"I do! I have to face them again tomorrow night and listen to all the jokes."

"What, that a short little carrottop bashed you for getting familiar?"

"That the prettiest girl in the place rejected my advances."

Darla stopped walking. "You think I'm pretty?"

Downs kept going. "I used to."

Darla hurried to catch up. "But you didn't make any advances. That was just the diversion the cap'n wanted."

"I know that, but no one else does! They think I am some pitiful, crippled blighter who can't win a girl on his own."

"A'course you can. Any female in the club'd be proud to walk out on your arm. I'm here, ain't I?"

"Hah. He's most likely paying you again. I'm the captain's charity case, and everyone knows it."

"They know you half run the place for him, and do his hiring and firing, too."

"I hire the women. He gets to flirt with them. Not that I would want to or anything, of course."

Darla ignored his disclaimer. "Then we'll show 'em tomorrow night."

"Show them what?"

"That you won my heart. Not my favors, mind, 'cause I still ain't that kind of girl. But if I smile at you, and bring you a glass of wine, and whisper in your ear and, you know, rub up against you a little, then no one will laugh."

"They'll be jealous as hell."

"You really think I'm pretty? Not too short and plump?"

"You're a regular Pocket Venus. That's what the swells call a little goddess, you know."

Darla seemed to stand taller and expand her chest. "Then we'll put on another show for the customers tomorrow, right?"

"Just pretend?"

Allie could not hear any answer, but she thought she saw Darla wink at the former soldier. He stood taller, too.

When they reached the chapel, a stone building tucked behind a row of shops, Allie demanded an explanation. Jack let the others file into the pews first, then gave it.

Harriet in the gaming rooms? A cardsharp? A shouting match, with flying serving trays, over a supposed seduction? Good grief, The Red and the Black was no place for a child! Or for a respectable schoolteacher. Surely Captain Endicott could see that.

He only said they would talk about it later.

Later, though, after the service, of which Allie heard not a word, except his rich baritone singing the hymns, he would not discuss another home for Harriet.

"I promised," was all he said. "And that incident last night is already forgotten. No one noticed anything."

Except Harriet, of course, who was busy recounting her adventure to Calloway and Mrs. Crandall, and anyone else who would listen when they stopped for refreshment at a coffee shop on the way home. To hear Harriet tell it, the captain had the courage of a

lion, the strength of an elephant, the cunning of a
tiger. "Can we go to the menagerie this afternoon,
Cap'n Jack?"

Before her guardian could answer, Downs spoke up,
reminding everyone of Darla's brilliant role in foiling
the would-be felon. It seemed he had been struck by
more than the serving tray.

After coffee and meat pie, they went home to fetch
Joker for a run in the park. The two dark-haired dealers went back to their attic rooms to rest after their
long night yesterday, and Calloway decided to check
every deck of cards for shaved edges and marked
backs, every pair of dice for extra weights inside. Allie
would have stayed behind too, looking at old newspapers for notices of positions available. Harriet was already holding the dog's lead, though. As long as
Captain Endicott was paying her wages, Allie had no
honorable choice but to earn her salary. And the sun
was still shining, besides. Time enough for the employment ads tomorrow, when the newspapers would have
new listings.

No one had asked Joker if he wanted a jaunt in the
fresh air. He dragged behind Harriet until they
reached Green Park. Then he rolled in the browning
grass, ate a crust of bread someone had thrown for
the birds, and crawled under the bench where Mrs.
Crandall was taking out her knitting. He sprawled
there, ignoring the squirrels.

Harriet ran, though, laughed and chased leaves as
they fell, and brought pretty ones back to show her
Cap'n Jack. Allie did not think she had ever seen the
girl so merry, not since the time Mrs. Semple had
discovered a mouse in her chamber pot. Harriet
skipped down the paths, and Allie could not help but
worry that her pupil was growing too happy in a situation that could not last. The captain seemed amused,

but how long before he decided he'd rather have a pretty woman on his arm? What would happen to Harriet then?

Some of the sunshine dimmed for Allie, and she tugged her cloak closer.

"Are you cold, Miss Silver?"

Allie shook her head, but put more distance between herself and the captain. She must not let herself grow used to having a caring, courteous, handsome gentleman at her side either.

While Allie was thinking, Mr. Downs and Darla had taken a different path. Harriet was far ahead, kicking acorns off the walkway. Allie and Captain Endicott were as good as alone, or as bad. This was just what Allie had feared, or one of the things, anyway.

As if reading her mind, Captain Endicott waved his arm in a circle. "No one is here but a few nannies and their charges, the occasional poet, and a single drunk, asleep on a bench. You see? This is not Hyde Park, where the beau monde meets to shred reputations and arrange marriages. There is no one here to care that every punctilious rule of polite behavior is not met. There is no one here to frown in disapproval that the sensible Miss Silver is enjoying herself for once. Smile, ma'am, for life is too short not to enjoy days like this."

The captain was right: No one could see her but the squirrels. Allie would have one more night in a comfortable bed, another day of fine meals, one afternoon of not worrying about tomorrow. The club was closed, besides, so she had no fear of encountering would-be employers or inebriated gamblers. Her host was acting like a perfect gentleman, not a rakehell, and Harriet was acting like a little girl, not a house-wrecker. Allie would enjoy this day.

She held her face up to the sun and smiled.

The captain smiled back, then paused at a bench where they could sit and watch Harriet talking to the dairy maids who tended the small herd of cows, selling milk to the park visitors.

Harriet ran back, and Captain Endicott tossed her a coin, after asking if Miss Silver wanted a glass.

Allie was content to sit and listen to the birds and the cows and the girls' chatter.

"You could take your bonnet off, you know. I won't tell." The captain was holding his own hat in his hand. "Be daring."

No. That was too daring. According to Mrs. Semple, once one rule was relaxed, the others fell like raindrops. If a woman loosened her stays, she would loosen her scruples. Bend her posture, bend her moral backbone, too. If a girl smiled at a handsome stranger, Mrs. Semple warned, she would throw herself into his arms next, begging for his kisses. After kisses . . . Well, everyone knew what came after kisses.

Everyone but Allie, it seemed.

Oh, she knew the mechanics of the physical act. She was five and twenty, after all, and well-read. But she could not imagine a woman losing herself in a man's embrace so that she forgot her principles, lost her reservations—and then lost her virtue.

Mrs. Semple would have apoplexy if Allie removed her bonnet. She would have dismissed her on the instant, thinking her a bad influence on the senior girls. Bother Mrs. Semple. Allie was not about to toss her bonnet over the windmill, merely over her back. She was not going to accost the captain, casting herself against his broad chest, weaving her fingers through his wavy hair, feathering caresses on his smooth-shaven cheeks, breathing in the clean, spicy scent of him.

"Are you warm now, Miss Silver?" he was asking, concerned at her quickened breaths.

"Fine. I am perfectly comfortable. I shall keep my bonnet on, however."

After the park, they returned to the club for an early dinner. Harriet would never go hungry at The Red and the Black, it seemed. The captain was a large man who needed a quantity of food to keep him content.

Meals were too uncertain in the army, Mr. Downs explained when Allie questioned another lavish meal, with the supply wagons leagues away, if there were any supplies for the men at all. Soldiers and officers alike had learned to value regular meals and full bellies.

Captain Endicott did not believe in skimping on his staff, either, unlike many employers. He might not be able to pay them as much as he wished, but he could feed them as well as he ate himself. Dinner was served in the staff dining room, near the kitchens below stairs.

Allie could have insisted on a tray for her and Harriet up in their sitting room. She could have insulted Mr. Downs, Darla, Mrs. Crandall, and the others, too, besides disturbing someone's dinner to wait on them. Harriet was already asking the chef about dessert, and Captain Endicott was wiping the milk mustache off her lips. This would be Harriet's new family, Allie supposed, dealers and demimondaines, and dinner with the staff would be routine. Heavens, her guardian might have run a chimney-sweeping business, mightn't he? This was better, wasn't it?

One more broken rule was not going to matter to Allie's future, so she permitted the captain to lead her into the long room. He placed her beside him at the head of the plank table, with Harriet next to her, and Mr. Downs across. Darla popped into the chair next to him, and glared at a redhead who tried to lean across the table toward Downs, revealing more of her bosom than a request for the salt warranted.

Allie kept her eyes on the food, not on the females at the other end of the table. Her host kept her and Harriet entertained with stories of his own childhood, his brother, and their various pets. He also explained about his missing half sister, and why the family believed she might be alive.

So fascinating was the story of how the two brothers had never given up hope, but had traced the child to her kidnapper's sister, that Allie forgot about the coarse accents and the casual manners at the other end of the table. The captain told how Molly Godfrey had not withdrawn funds from the blackmailer's account in three years, and how scores of Bow Street Runners and hired detectives were out looking for where she might have lived and under what name.

"As soon as the club is on sounder footing, I intend to scour every dressmaking establishment in London," Captain Endicott continued, "because we know Molly was a seamstress. She might have taught her adopted daughter, who would now need to earn her own living, if Lottie is not wed or settled in some small town, sewing flour sacks for the grist mill. I have hope. It is long odds, I know, but if my half sister is in London, I will find her. If she is in the countryside somewhere, the hired investigators will find her. We will have her back, I swear."

And he would, Allie believed. Captain Endicott could do anything he set his mind to, except run a proper household befitting an earl's brother.

Calloway had produced a fiddle, and a few of the younger women were dancing. They taught Harriet some of the steps, while others sang the words to the popular tunes. The captain and Mr. Downs raised their own voices, and soon the dining hall was filled with song and laughter. The chef danced with Mrs. Crandall, and the captain partnered Harriet and the buxom redhead. Allie refused to dance, but she did sing along when she knew the chorus. The smile Captain Endicott gave her was sweeter than the syllabub.

Later, when most of the staff had retired or gone out for the evening—Allie did not want to know where—the captain took out a book and started to read aloud. Mrs. Semple had done the same on a Sunday evening, reading sermons and improving works to her captive audience.

To Allie's shock, and everyone else's delight, the captain had chosen a lurid, purple-covered, gothic tale of dark castles, hidden treasures, evil barons, and daring rescues. Mrs. Semple considered such works the devil's handicraft, and would have burned the thing instantly. The women hung on his every word, and Harriet's eyes were wide as saucers. Even the men, Downs and Calloway and the chef, pretending to be savoring their ale, listened attentively. So did Allie, sighing over the poor damsel's plight, sighing louder over the dashing hero.

When Captain Endicott closed the book, everyone groaned. His throat was tired, he explained.

"Miss Silver can read some tomorrow night," Harriet insisted, "so you will not wear out your voice."

But tomorrow night the casino would be open, and Allie would be gone. No one wanted to ruin the child's pleasure, though, so they all nodded and smiled and helped put away the glasses and dishes.

"Wasn't this the best day ever?" Harriet asked Allie when she would have led her upstairs to bed, far past her usual bedtime.

To Allie's surprise, it had been. "I cannot remember a nicer time."

Harriet yawned and asked, "Don't you think so too, Cap'n Jack?"

"One of the happiest I can recall," he answered without hesitation. "Thanks to you and Miss Silver."

Someone was not quite as happy with the day, however.

Rochelle Poitier stormed into the room, cursing that no one had answered her knock at the front door.

"It's Cap'n Jack's ladybird," one of the dealers whispered to another, as they hurried out of the dining hall. "And she looks fit to pluck a few feathers."

Harriet tugged on Allie's hand instead of following her away from the coming tempest. "If she's his ladybird, does that mean Cap'n Jack is a gentlemanbird?"

CHAPTER NINE

Oh, hell, Rochelle.

Jack remembered, too late, that he was supposed to take her to the park this afternoon. Not Green Park, either, but Hyde Park, where she could be seen in his curricle, in her furs and finery. He was supposed to take her to dinner to make up for the missed engagement yesterday. He was also supposed to bring her a final gift and a fare-thee-well. Mostly he was supposed to keep her away from Miss Silver.

Instead he had spent his day trying to make the schoolteacher smile. She was not smiling now. She was trying to drag Harriet out of the dining hall, as if Rochelle carried some dread contagion. In the old maid's opinion, she likely did: leprosy, lung fever, light skirts.

"How can you tell the girl birds from the boy birds anyway?" Harriet was asking, to avoid leaving the room while such an interesting encounter was taking place.

"Not now, brat," Jack said, positive such a discussion was Miss Silver's job, not his. It could not be her duty, though, if she did not stay.

He had tried all day to change her mind about leaving. He had thought the task might be impossible and hardly worth the effort, until he'd seen her with her honey-colored curls down in the morning. Who would have thought the starchy spinster had come-hither hair? Lud, with that fiery mane, she had to have some flame in her soul, some spark that would let her take a chance.

Money would not work on the prickly female, nor promises. So Jack had tried to show her how decent his odd household could be, how comfortable, how good for Harriet. Surely she could see that the poor poppet was having far more fun than she would at any stuffy school or with some unfeeling strangers paid to foster her.

Whatever ground he had gained, however, was trampled under Rochelle's satin slippers. If a barque of frailty could sail into the house unannounced, Miss Silver's pursed lips seemed to be saying, the governess would be leaving port. He'd be lucky if he waited until the next morning.

The worst of it was, she was right. Rochelle was no fit company for a child, unless he wanted Harriet to grow up thinking of her body as merchandise and men as meal tickets. Damn, he had been a guardian for little more than a day. Was he destroying the child's morals?

Miss Silver was not giving Harriet the right role model either, though, holding virtue as a shield against the world. Harriet was no prim and prissy miss, and he would not want her to be browbeaten into one. He despised those paragons of proper behavior who were afraid to contradict a gentleman, afraid to laugh out loud, afraid to wear bright colors, lest they lose their vouchers to Almack's. Harriet deserved better.

Maybe they would be better off without Miss Silver after all. Jack looked at her glaring at him. Then he looked at Rochelle, glaring at the governess. Both were defending their means of support, but that was where the similarity ended. The courtesan was guarding her territory. The schoolteacher was guarding her reputation. The contrast between the two women's motives was as vast as the differences in their appearances.

Rochelle wore an ermine cape, her scarlet hair piled high, her pink silk gown cut low. She wore diamonds at her wrist and rubies at her throat.

Miss Silver wore a dark, shabby sack of a gown, an ugly bun behind her neck, and a watch pinned to her flat chest.

Rochelle was like a bright fireworks display; the governess was an unlit candle, straight but cold and pale.

And Jack was a jackass. He wished he could flee the room the way Downs and Calloway did, herding the others ahead of them, except for Harriet and her duenna. Damn, was it just two days ago when all he had to worry about was making money? Now Jack was responsible for a chit and a chillingly respectable female. Then, he'd been thinking himself quite the man about town, with a full-time mistress and anytime maids. He'd had no one to please but himself and his desires.

A man about town? Now he felt like a molester, robbing Harriet's innocence, giving a decent woman a disgust of him. His brother would be disappointed, his sister-in-law appalled. He was ashamed of himself, and he was angry at Miss Silver for the unfamiliar feeling. Just because she was a prig and a prude did not mean he had to live like a saint. Did it?

He was about to get rid of all of them, sending Harriet and the governess to their chaste beds and sending Rochelle to perdition with a bank draft, when Harriet looked at the furious intruder. She twirled one of her red curls around her finger and said, "Maybe she did not like the bird you gave her, Uncle Jack. You know, that con jay."

Rochelle snarled, her painted fingernails curled like talons.

"Stubble it, brat!" Jack said, wishing Harriet had not picked this of all times to claim him as a relative.

Miss Silver looked angrier, if possible. She pulled Harriet further toward the exit door. "There is no call to shout at the child."

Of course there was. If not for Hildebrand's heiress, Jack would not be in this damnable coil. If not for her, he would not need a blasted governess, and he would not be floundering for a way to avoid the social solecism of letting his convenient converse with a lady.

Not that they were precisely conversing. Rochelle was sneering at Miss Silver. "What, couldn't you convince Jack that he'd fathered your bastard?"

Miss Silver gasped and tried to hide Harriet's bright head in her skirts.

"She called him uncle, not papa. So your ruse did not work. Why are you still here, then? Jack is not swimming in lard, if that is your ambition, and you are anything but his type. So try your tricks on some other swell. Maybe his high-nosed brother will pay you to keep another scandal from his precious wife."

"Rochelle, you do not understand. And I would appreciate it if you would leave my family out of this conversation."

"Oh, I understand, all right. Some cheap slut scrubs her face, dresses like a vicar's daughter, and throws herself on your mercy. You, gullible fool that you are, let her and the brat chouse you out of what little blunt you have. Meanwhile I have been waiting for this stupid club to turn a profit so you can treat me the way you promised. And now that it is close to being a success, you don't have time for me? Well, Rochelle Poitier is not going to leave quietly, not to have some dreary soiled dove feather her nest instead of me."

"She's not soiled. Miss Silver had a bath yesterday." Harriet pulled out of Allie's hold and stood face to face, or face to fur wrap, anyway.

Jack grasped the child's arm and pulled her away, shoving her back toward Miss Silver and the door, hoping they would leave. Then he faced his former mistress, wondering at his onetime infatuation. "Rochelle, that is not the way of it at all. We can still go to dinner and discuss this calmly."

Rochelle crossed her arms over her chest, drawing attention to that bounty. Perhaps that explained his once-smitten state.

She tapped her foot on the floor. "I am not going anywhere while that woman is here, sinking her hooks into you. You swore that *I* would be hostess at the club. I would be the toast of London and have a carriage of my own."

Lud, had he been promising with his private parts while his brain went begging? He could not have pledged so much, not even if he'd been foxed. Her breasts were not all that entrancing. They were too large and pendulous, now that he thought about it, utterly udderlike, in fact. He might have promised a carriage, though. Finding the money for that was a problem for another day. Getting rid of Rochelle before Miss Silver swooned or Harriet heard more than an eight-year-old ought was more immediate. "I do not believe we had a formal agreement," he said now in a lower, more private tone of voice. "Such arrangements as we had are ephemeral at best. You of all people should know that."

"What's a furimal?" Harriet asked, ignoring his efforts. "And will she kill that and wear it, too?"

"Dash it, Harriet, go to bed. No, wait. Rochelle, I should like you to meet"—he was not liking it, not at all; the girls who dealt at his tables were one thing, but Harriet simply should not know women like his former mistress—"my ward, Miss Harriet Hildebrand. And her governess."

Harriet would recover from the introduction. Miss Silver might not, so Jack purposely did not use her name. He could protect that much, if not her maidenly sensibilities. He could not look at her without seeing condemnation in her eyes, so he looked at his prior paramour instead. Damn, what had he seen in the flamboyant redhead? The answer was immediate and obvious. He'd seen the dasher's flagrantly sexual style and succumbed, dash it.

Rochelle snorted, giving the lie to any ladylike pretensions she might have had. "Your ward? What am I, then, your cousin? That is a Banbury tale if I ever heard one. People might swallow your gammon about looking for your lost sister because the reward money is tempting and the search brings curious people to the club, but no one will believe this latest hog slop. I never took you for such a fool as to think they could. Think on it, Jacko. No gentleman would trust you with a wellborn babe, and no proper governess stays at a gaming parlor. So you will never pass the skinny little guttersnipe off as a lady, no matter how many highfliers you dress in nun's habits."

Before Harriet could ask how high those flyers

could soar, Allie set the girl behind her. She raised her chin, squared her shoulders, looked daggers at Jack, then said, "Now do you see why I wanted to leave?"

Hell, he wanted to leave. "Nonsense. Miss Poitier was on her way out, weren't you, Rochelle?"

But Allie was not finished. She faced the other woman, who was beautiful, fashionably dressed, and poised, everything Allie was not. She was taller, too, and likely had her money invested in gems and the Funds. Allie's was in her reticule. No matter. Right was on Allie's side. "I agree with you, Miss Poitier," she said, taking care to keep her voice well modulated, not shrieking like a fishwife the way she was tempted, "that this is no fit place for a genteel girl or a respectable governess. I have been trying to convince the captain of that very thing. However, while we are here, in this house, the residence becomes no place for lax morals or lewd talk."

"Hoity-toity, miss. What, did you take acting lessons afore you turned to blackmail? Too bad you couldn't make a go of it in the theater, what with a brat hanging on your skirts that way."

Allie released her grip on Harriet's shoulder, setting the girl away from her but smoothing a red curl off her forehead. "On behalf of my pupil, I must take umbrage at your insults. Miss Hildebrand is the daughter of a valiant fallen army officer and the granddaughter of a viscount. She is not a waif from the streets of London, nor a would-be actress. In fact, she would not be here at all if there had been an acceptable alternative."

"Amen to that," Jack muttered.

Three pairs of eyes sent daggers his way.

Allie went on: "And just as Captain Endicott does not wish you to discuss his family, I do not wish you to slander mine or my good name. My father was not a vicar; he was a highly respected Latin scholar and academy instructor. My mother's father is the Marquess of Montford. I am no actress, no extortionist, and no man's mistress. I am a schoolteacher, an educator, and an independent woman, whether you choose to believe it or not. I am proud of my father's name and my own name, Miss Poitier, or Miss Potts, as it were." She took a deep breath. "I am Allison Silver, a lady born and bred, and I shall remain a lady, no matter my circumstances. Is that understood?"

Jack cursed, but Allie ignored him. She'd spoken her piece out of pride, yes, for Rochelle's sake. She was no conniver, set to capture a rakehell for herself or win his coins. But she had spoken for the captain's sake, too. Maybe now he would understand why her reputation was so important to her, why her pride mattered. She was not bachelor fare, not another of his flirts, not another Rochelle Poitier. She was a woman with morals, with a heritage nearly as dignified as his own, albeit with some shaky limbs on her family tree. She worked for a living, but in a more respectable trade than Captain Endicott had chosen—and in one far more respectable than Miss Poitier pursued. Miss Allison Silver was a lady, by heaven!

Rochelle slammed the door on her way out.

Harriet was jumping up and down. "Is your grandfather really a marquess? Mine was only a viscount."

"Yes, but Lord Montford never recognized my parents' marriage. Do not tell Miss Poitier that, of course."

"You spiked her guns, all right! Good show, Miss Silver. I'll wager a hundred pounds we never see her again."

Allie was not so sure, and not sure it mattered. If not Rochelle, Captain Endicott would have another woman to fill her place, to warm his bed. Allie looked at him to see if he was angry that she had sent his lover to the roundabout.

He was cursing, softly, thank goodness.

"If I overstepped my authority, I apologize. Perhaps I should not have let on that I knew her real name."

Jack stopped swearing long enough to say, "No, you were pushed past endurance. I should be the one to apologize, after promising that you would not be accosted by any, ah, birds of paradise. And no, brat, I am not going to describe one of those rare birds for you. Is it not past your bedtime anyway?"

Harriet poured herself another glass of lemonade, stalling.

The captain poured himself a glass of wine, simmering. Then he went back to blasphemy, but in French, Spanish, and Portuguese, because there were ladies present. "Ladies," Allie heard him mutter, as if it were a curse word.

"You are angry. I am sorry, but you must see what an impossible situation this is. I could not let her think me a . . . a woman like her."

"No one would think you were one of the frail sisterhood, by Harry," he snapped at her, making Allie feel even more stale and spinsterish. "But did you have to recite your blasted pedigree? It is not her name that concerns me. Yours does."

"Ah, I see what has you in such a taking. A poor governess does not matter; the granddaughter of a peer does. Now that you finally realize I am a respectable woman, you are afraid I will expect you to do the honorable thing to restore my reputation."

"Great gods! Do you mean I should marry you?"

"You are the one who placed me in this untenable situation, aren't you?"

The glass slipped out of his hand to fall to the floor.

Harriet was laughing and dancing a jig. "We can be a real family!"

"No, we cannot," Allie firmly stated. "For no marriage will take place. And you need not panic, Captain. I will not make any such demand on your person. Nor will any of my maternal relations come breathing fire and carrying a special license or a blunderbuss. My grandfather does not acknowledge me, not that an honest woman should require a male to defend her virtue."

Jack was picking up the glass shards before Harriet, or his dog, could skip through them. He looked up from his kneeling position, wondering if he truly was supposed to propose while he was at her feet. Lud, he felt like lapping the wine from the floor! "I never threatened your virtue."

"Only my good name and my livelihood. But never fear, you are safe."

He started breathing again. "Do you promise? That is, I take it that you do not wish to marry me?"

"What, a gambler? A man who has a hundred women? A gentleman who turned his back on his dignity to become a dealer in others' misfortunes and misspent hours? No, sir. I would not wish to marry a man I could not respect, even were I shunned by all society, not just the highest tiers that rejected me and my mother ages ago. My father worked for a living, like you, but his family had no title like yours, so he was deemed unacceptable. I will only wed as fine a gentleman as he was."

"Even if that means you remain unmarried?"

"Far better to stay single than be shackled to a man I cannot admire. What little I own would belong to him. Every choice I have would be his to make. My very life, body and soul would belong to him. So thank you, sir, for the offer you never wished to tender, and for not making it."

Miss Silver did not want to marry him. Now why didn't that make Jack feel better? He'd think about it later. For now he was still upset that she had been so outspoken in front of Rochelle.

"But why are you upset I gave my name if you are not afraid I might claim to be compromised? Is it because you finally see that you have to make other provisions for Harriet, away from The Red and the Black? She cannot grow up among your, ah, female friends if she is ever to make a suitable match herself."

"I do not want to be married either," Harriet put in. "Not if some man will take my money. You still owe me ten pounds, Uncle Jack."

"Your wedding is a decade away and we will worry about it then." Jack found a fresh glass and poured himself more wine, after Allie declined a drink. "Nell will know how to smooth the way," he told her, "no matter what irregularities in Harriet's upbringing. Lud knows the Hildebrand name carries its own burdens."

"Then you are annoyed because at last you see that I truly cannot stay on here and you shall have to make other arrangements for Harriet's care."

"No, Miss Silver, I am neither upset nor annoyed about you and Harriet staying here. I am not feeling guilty about your circumstances, your highly vaunted heritage, or your honorable reputation. I am not even insulted that you find me so despicable you would shrivel as a spinster before taking my hand in marriage. No, what bothers me is that after harping on your good name for endless hours, you blurt it out to Rochelle Poitier."

"But she cannot know any prospective employers.

It is not as though I was counting on her as a character reference."

"And I do not suppose you were counting on her living above the offices of the biggest scandal pages in London, either."

CHAPTER TEN

Some words were like rocks. Tossed into a still pool, they could make ripples. Thrown against a window, they could break the pane of glass. Slammed against someone's head, they could addle his wits, or worse.

The word *marry* sat atop the gaming parlor that night like a boulder, waiting to decide which way to roll.

Allie was not worried about Miss Poitier or Rochelle's downstairs neighbors. Captain Endicott would send the woman a check in the morning and the mercenary female would be satisfied. She would go on to her next protector and forget about Miss Silver's claims to gentility. Besides, who cared about one stray governess and her long-severed connections? No, it was the idea of marrying that kept Allie awake that night, that and Harriet's restless slumber on their shared bed.

Marry. Once the word was spoken, Allie could not get it out of her mind. She had put such hopes and dreams aside ages ago, or so she thought. She was five and twenty, poor and plain. Allie had become resigned to her spinsterhood, because railing against fate was a waste of her time.

Marry. Gracious, the word itself was seductive, wrapping her in a haze of possibilities: a husband, a family, perhaps children of her own to love, not spoiled, silly schoolgirls. A home of her own, without worrying over where she was to put her head the next day or the next year. Someone else to share the worry about finances and finding money for the future. Someone else to help carry her burdens and her suitcases. Someone else to share her thoughts—and her bed.

The smelly dog was sharing it now, and Harriet, of course. Allie left the bed when the girl kicked the covers off, kicking Allie in the shin at the same time. The dog snored louder.

Crossing the room by the light of the last embers in the fireplace, Allie opened the draperies and looked out the window at the quiet London night, with the fog muting the gas lamps' glow. Allie was as alone as ever, but her thoughts were so warm she did not feel the chill of the floor, even with her feet bare.

Marrying meant sharing one's body, too. Allie had never thought much about that, either, until she met Captain Jonathan Endicott. Jack. Not that she wanted to marry the owner of the gambling den, of course. Her earlier words were entirely true. He was not what she could admire in a gentleman, much less a husband. Except.

Except he had the kindest smile. And he looked at her as if she were really there, not a piece of furniture, as the parents of the students considered her, or another pesky employee. His very size and strength and gentleness made her feel . . . womanly. He made her wish her breasts were bigger and her hair were smoother. Or red, because he seemed to prefer redheads. He made her think of what else a man and woman shared when they wed, besides a name and a house. He made her want to know about love, and lovemaking.

He would know how to touch a woman, know how to make a spinster's dead senses come alive under his expert tutelage. Why, Allie could feel her breasts—insignificant as they were compared to Rochelle's—pucker at the very thought of his touch, his kiss, his warmth and wetness. No, that was the cold, Allie told herself, trying very hard not to imagine him in his nightshirt, or out of it, holding her closely, stroking her softly, loving her.

He did not love her.

He might not even like her. Allie got back into bed. She got under the covers, where she tried to hide from the cold of that truth, after shoving the dog off. Jack wanted her—as a nursemaid for his ward, nothing else. No, she would not entrap him into a marriage of convenience, her services as a nanny in exchange for the restoration of her reputation. That would be a bad bargain for both of them and bring nothing but years of misery. Besides, it was outright extortion to force a gentleman to wed against his will. Allie was no coldhearted huntress. She was just cold, so she dragged a blanket back from Harriet's side of the bed, where the dog had already jumped up again. Allie told herself to go to sleep and stop thinking of Captain Endicott.

He might be everything a woman could want in a lover. He was nothing she could want in a husband.

Harriet was so excited she could not sleep, especially when Miss Silver got up and then stole the blankets. Maybe Miss Silver was excited, too, thinking about marrying Uncle Jack. She would not have to work anymore, or dress like a servant in a stark household. She could take Harriet to Astley's Amphitheatre and the menagerie and the waxworks without worrying over money or classes or stuffy old rules. Maybe Uncle Jack would come, too.

Oh, how wondrous it would be! A family of her own who would not ship her away. A room of her own where she could hide her slingshot and her snail collection. A dog of her own—Well, she was willing to share Joker with Uncle Jack until she could convince her guardian to get her a new pet, one who did not snore. And she would listen to Miss Silver's lessons, to prove she did not need schooling at some awful place far away. She would be as good as gold, and they would love her forever and ever.

She pulled Joker under the covers so he did not sound as loud.

Marry Miss Silver? Jack would sooner go back to the army. What, had he lived through Waterloo only to die a more painful death here in England? Hell, he would not even have the hope of a quick demise. Marriage was forever and ever. And marrying meant being faithful. It did to Jack, anyway.

He'd never gone back on an oath yet and he did not intend to start with "I do" when he did not. How could he face his mother in Heaven knowing he had forsaken his vows? He could not, no more than he could face his father in the afterlife without trying his damnedest to find Lottie after swearing to do so in this one. Even his blasted family motto said it: *Ever true.* He and his brother had pricked their fingers and mixed their blood in a pledge to their family's honor.

Great gods, how could he face his sweet sister-in-law or look into Harriet's innocent eyes if he was unfaithful to the one person to whom he owed unconditional loyalty? He could not. He'd be true to his bride, whoever she was.

But Miss Silver?

No more affairs, no more flirts. No more redheads or ebony-locked beauties with long legs and luscious lips. No more women, ever, except Miss starched and straitlaced Silver? Saints preserve him!

Jack could not sleep for the nightmare of his waking thoughts.

His brother, Alex, had the title and the responsibility for carrying the earldom into eternity. Jack was free, deuce take it, and meant to stay that way. He'd served his country; he'd fulfilled his obligations. He owed no man money and he was trying his damnedest to satisfy his promise to his father to find Lottie. Now he'd taken on Hildebrand's brat. Did he have to take on a ball and chain, too?

He had not compromised the woman. By George, he'd know it if he had. He'd sleep better, too. No, Miss Silver was as pure and priggish as she was when she barged through his office door. He was the one whose life was turned arsy-varsy, making compromises, dismissing his mistress, having no pretty thing cooing in his bed. Hell, he did not even have his own dog snoring on the rug. They'd stolen Joker, besides his peace of mind.

No, he was not guilty of any crime, and he would not pay the penalty.

Of course, he would not let the woman leave alone to face an even more uncertain future now. Who knew what could happen to a female of decent birth on the streets of London? Jack did, and vowed Miss Silver would not be subject to insult or worse. He'd have to make sure she found a respectable position if she refused to stay at The Red and the Black, someplace where the master of the house minded his manners and the sons were too young to threaten a defenseless female.

Jack pounded his pillow at the very idea. If any lust-filled libertine looked at Miss Silver, he'd pound the scoundrel, too. Then he remembered that no man got to see Miss Silver with her hair down, thank goodness. She'd be safe. So was his pillow, as he relaxed back on the bed.

With his thoughts turned from mayhem, he mused on whether he was the first man, after her father, naturally, to be so blessed by the sight of those glorious honey-colored waves. He hoped so, almost jealously guarding the image in his mind.

He used to think his stepmother's hair was the ideal for a woman: straight and silky, so pale a blond as to be nearly white. Alex's wife Nell's hair was as lovely, with a bit more color, streaked from the sun. Redheads had always fascinated him with the hint of fire, and black hair on a woman was as seductive as nighttime itself. But Miss Silver's hair, ah. Just ah. Or maybe oh, that such vibrant, soul-stirring color could belong to such a stick.

He sighed at the waste. But she kept it hidden, the whole long, thick, wavy dark gold mass of it, which was good. No man would be tempted to run his fingers through it, spread it out on his pillow, let it cascade over his chest in an amber waterfall. Oh, hell, now he would never get to sleep.

But he could stop worrying about Miss Silver's next employer. She would be safe with her hair scraped back and her figure—if she had one—swathed in her dark ugly gowns. Of course, if any man looked—really looked—at her intelligent blue-flecked gray eyes, he might be tempted to see what hid behind the stiff exterior. He might be interested to see what she looked like if she wore a smile instead of her habitual scowl. And if he were a gambler, he just might lay odds she was a beauty under the schoolmistress mien.

Damn, almost every man he knew was a gambler.

Miss Silver definitely needed his protection to see that she did not land in a worse fix. She might think a gaming parlor run by a womanizer, patronized by philanderers, and populated with Paphians was a catastrophe. Which only showed how little the woman knew of the real world.

She'd just have to stay here.

The solicitor was expecting them Monday morning, even before he received Captain Endicott's message. Mr. Burquist met them in his outer office, where the files were now all locked and guarded by his assistant.

"Welcome," he said, "and what a pleasure it is to see such a nice little fam—" Then he realized he was about to have his next words stuffed back down his throat by an imposing gentleman with a pugilist's battered nose and a slim lady with steel in her eyes. "A nice little familiar face," he concluded, looking at Harriet, whose handiwork had caused him hours of work and overtime wages for his secretary. Lord Finsterer's deed was still missing, with the tenants due to move in tomorrow. He covered his dread with a tight smile at the governess and the gambler. "Quite."

With a bit more enthusiasm, after the captain handed Mrs. Crandall a few coins to take the child out for a treat, he bowed them into his inner office.

Once his guests—they were not precisely clients—had been seated, Burquist handed Captain Endicott his fellow officer's last will. Then he straightened his folders and his waistcoat, and waited. The questions flew like darts at his head.

"This scribbled bit of nonsense is what landed a child on my doorstep?"

"There was no choice."

"Did you know he ran a gambling parlor?"

"There was no choice."

"Did you know she was Montford's granddaughter?"

"Unacknowledged, and there—"

"I know. There was no choice. Do you realize you have placed both of us in an awkward position? And if you say you had no choice, I shall put the rest of Hildebrand's bequests, his guns and his sword, to good use, I swear."

Burquist could well imagine the large, bellicose former officer resorting to violence. Endicott was a gentleman, however. It was Miss Silver, toying with the penknife on Burquist's desk, who had him truly worried. Women were an uncertain entity at best.

He held up both hands. "I did the best for the child that I could. The Hildebrands, after all, were my patrons. I have already written to Lady Hildebrand's trustees to see if they can release funds for Miss Harriet's education, since the sum already paid seems to have disappeared." He looked at Allie as if she had been the one to abscond with the fees. "And as soon as the new Lord Hildebrand returns to England, I am certain he shall make other arrangements."

"The man is a murderer," Jack said. "He cannot have Harriet."

"My thinking precisely, good sir."

"And there were no other relatives, no other neighbors or friends of Captain Hildebrand's?"

Burquist shrugged. "No one is anxious to pursue a connection to the scandal, or to a supposed killer. No one wrote to me asking to take Miss Harriet into their homes."

Jack did not think he wanted to give the moppet away, anyway. She had crept into his heart, freckles and all, and he had made that foolish bargain. "Yes, well, see what you can do about getting her an inheritance. I would be satisfied with whatever they give, for I am not plump in the pocket at this moment and girls are deuced expensive, in my experience."

They all knew his experience was with females far older than Harriet, but no one disagreed. Burquist scratched out a notation on a fresh sheet of paper. Miss Silver still held the penknife, so he used a worn quill, which dripped ink.

Her voice dripped venom. "I am not satisfied. I feel that I have been used and abused. Thrown to the lions and then ignored. You do realize, Mr. Burquist, that my livelihood depends on my reputation, that no one will hire a fallen woman to instruct their daughters?"

He nodded, unhappily.

"Yet you sent me and an innocent babe"—even Allie had to choke on the last words—"into a den of iniquity."

"Here now," Jack said, taking offense. "It is a refined gambling parlor, not a Seven Dials crib."

Both Mr. Burquist and Allie ignored him. The solicitor told her, "As I explained, there was no choice."

"Of course there was. You could have found us a hotel room and written to the captain to call on us there. You could have released a small sum from the new Lord Hildebrand's estate. Lord knows he owes Harriet something if he truly killed her mother. You could have done any number of things I was too weary to demand. For heaven's sake, you could have let us sleep on the floor here until you found another solution."

Mr. Burquist started trembling at the very idea of leaving Miss Harriet loose in his office for a minute.

But now Jack was truly insulted. "Dash it, you had the finest room in the house, decent meals, Mrs. Crandall to help you."

"It was still a gambling parlor, you thickheaded oaf!"

Mr. Burquist gasped, and Allie clapped her hand over her mouth.

Jack grinned, happy to get his own back after the slurs on his elegant enterprise. "Ah, the lady is not all politeness and propriety after all. Good for you, Miss Silver. Now maybe you can loosen your stays, let down your hair, and enjoy what life has offered."

Allie turned three shades of pink. Mr. Burquist turned four.

"Do you see what your lack of foresight has subjected me to?" Allie demanded of the older man. "Loosen my stays, indeed. And what shall I say if a prospective employer asks where I have spent the last few nights in London? I shall blame you, sir, if I do not find a new position, and I shall camp on your doorstep until I do!"

Mr. Burquist drew out a clean sheet of paper and hurriedly scrawled the directions of three respectable placement agencies that he knew. Allie took the page, but she was still angry. "What could you have been thinking, sir?"

Jack leaned forward, curious himself. Hildebrand's will was tenuous at best, not mentioning any daughter. The family had to have a small holding somewhere Harriet could have lived in comfort, Miss Silver at her side. Burquist had not even tried to find another alternative. Jack could not blame Miss Silver for being angry. And he could not blame himself for noticing how charming she looked with the bright color in her cheeks.

"I . . . I thought this the easiest, quickest, entirely

legal solution to the dilemma. And hopeless old romantic that I am, I was hoping that the pair of you might make a match. An earl's brother, a marquess's granddaughter, what could be more fitting?"

Now Allie wished she had loosened her stays, so she could breathe. She took a quick glance at the captain and saw that he was gasping like a landed fish, too. But Mr. Burquist was not finished.

"With such a suitable connection, perhaps Lord Montford would relent and dower his daughter's only child. And then you, Captain Endicott, could retire from your unfortunate foray into trade."

Except Burquist had not considered that Jack liked his trade. And that Allie would not have accepted a groat from her grandfather. Both were shaking their heads.

"You would have had a ready-made family in Miss Harriet," the solicitor continued, although his voice lost some of its confidence as he debated whether Harriet was a boon or a black mark against any marriage. "And both of you are intelligent, educated, and well-born. You have a great deal in common."

Jack had been raised in luxury, tempered in the army. Allie was a scholar's child grown into a poorer educator. He sought his sister and his pleasure. She longed for a secure position and a pension.

The only thing they had in common at this moment was an urge to strangle the solicitor.

CHAPTER ELEVEN

"**D**on't go!" Harriet wailed.

Or was that Jack? Lord, what was he going to do with the brat without Miss Silver? He had a club to run, not a nursery!

Mary Crandall had stayed behind at the solicitor's office to ask about investing her new pension. And the schoolmistress, the expert on little girls, was insisting on going to the employment agencies on Burquist's list.

A promised raise did not change her mind, nor did begging. The begging came from Harriet, of course.

"Fine, we will take you in my carriage." Jack thought that was a reasonable offer, saving her the hackney fare and saving him from worrying about her being accosted on the streets.

"What, and will you and Harriet stand outside the agencies' doors so the proprietors can ask about the handsome gentleman waiting for me?"

She thought he was handsome? "We could wait around the corner."

"But if I am sent on an interview, that might take hours, and I know you are anxious to reopen the club this afternoon. And Harriet, if you are going to pretend to cry, at least wipe your nose with a cloth, not your sleeve."

Harriet was crying? "Downs can open the club."

"Nonsense. I shall take a hackney and have the driver wait for me." She bent to dab at Harriet's face with her own handkerchief. "Hush, silly."

She thought he was silly? No, she was talking to the brat.

"I'll be back to get my bags if I am fortunate enough to secure a position. But you shall have your uncle Jack and the dog, and all the new friends you have made at Captain Endicott's house, Darla and Snake and Mr. Downs. Mrs. Crandall will look after you, and you will hardly notice I am gone."

Harriet's tears fell faster; her cries grew louder.

Jack grew desperate. "I'll bet you can't guess how tall a giraffe is, snippet. They have one at the Royal Menagerie."

Suddenly there were no tears, no cries, just avarice. "How much if I guess right?"

So Jack and Harriet went to the zoo at the Tower. Allie went to the first agency on her list.

They only placed older women as governesses, she was told. Younger ladies were too flighty, too liable to run off with tutors or dancing masters. Their patrons could not be hiring new staff every other month. And no, they did not list academy positions. Daughters of the finest families were schooled at home until reaching a certain age, *n'est ce-pas*?

The second agency was a bit more encouraging about Allie's references and experience. Unfortunately, no one was looking for a governess at this moment. Nannies, wet nurses, and nursery maids were always in demand. Hired chaperones could name their price, but those had to be ladies of distinction with entrée to the polite world. Miss Silver did not claim any noble connections, did she?

None that would claim her in return. Allie asked about schools.

This agency was not as elitist. One of the educational institutions they represented, however, was in need of an instructor in music, not Allie's forte. Another seminary required a teacher conversant with classical tongues. Allie was fluent in four languages, all still being spoken. Could she teach watercolors?

As well as she could teach Latin or Greek.

Ah, well. The proprietress of the agency was certain something would turn up soon for a well-read young woman of excellent diction and ladylike bearing. As soon as she had a new position listed she would send a message. Where did Miss Silver say she was staying here in London?

Allie would have to call again in a week.

The third agency had actual jobs.

Lord X needed a governess for his five daughters. The last one had jumped in the Thames just last week. The Duchess of Y required an ugly instructress, because her husband was wont to harass the pretty ones. A country squire was looking for an attractive governess, but the agency was not able to confirm that he had any daughters at all. Mr. Z of the East India Company wished an English lady to educate his daughters, in India, however. A widow sought a governess, if she could cook and sew and clean at the same time. A knight's twin daughters needed supervision, but the knight also needed to pay the previous employees their back wages. And on. The reason this agency had listings was that no sensible woman would accept any of the positions, or stay in them.

Schools? Oh, yes, there were academic vacancies in Yorkshire and Cornwall, with no guarantee of employment after traveling to either place for an interview. A charity institution was hiring a matron, but at near charity wages. A private lunatic asylum wished someone to read to the inmates. Calmer, the Bedlamites might not bludgeon another guard. And on.

The driver of Allie's hired hackney carriage knew of a nearby school for girls, so they tried there next. The children appeared meek and mannered, their eyes on the floor. The two instructors Allie glimpsed kept glancing over their shoulders. The halls were spotless and silent. She was glad the choleric-looking schoolmaster declared that no openings were available.

The coach driver swore he knew of four more placement agencies, bonnified ones that did not lure innocent misses into prostitution with promises of legitimate work.

Gracious, Allie had not known such possibilities existed! She vowed to carry a weapon of some sort tomorrow, a kitchen knife if she could find nothing better. For now, though, the day was nearly over. Allie had waited in enough cold, bare reception rooms on hard wooden seats to last until morning. She was worried about Harriet, too. Actually, she was more worried about Captain Endicott and The Red and the Black than Harriet, so she gave the club's address.

"Are you sure, miss?" the driver asked, scratching his head. The young lady had spent the day seeking an honest piece of work, which that location was not about to offer.

"I know, I know," Allie wearily replied. "But take me there anyway. I am too tired to go anywhere but home."

Home? The Red and the Black? Was she really thinking of a gambling parlor as home? Goodness, Allie thought, taking her bonnet off her aching head for the first time since early morning, she had better find a new position quickly.

Harriet gave her a warm, sticky welcome.

"But this does not mean I am staying, you know," Allie reminded her. "I shall read all the newspapers tonight and answer any likely advertisements tomorrow."

Harriet was too excited to have Allie back to worry about tomorrow, and she was too eager to tell about her wondrous day.

"We went to the menagerie, and the giraffe was not as big as a house, so I owe Uncle Jack a shilling. But the baboon threw my strawberry ice at Uncle Jack, so maybe I owe him more, for a new shirt and neck cloth. And the lion looked sad, so I gave him Uncle Jack's ice while he was wiping his hair, and then the guard made us leave. So we went to a jewelry shop, only it was for trading, not buying. Uncle Jack gave the man his pistols and the man gave him a pearl necklace. And now I know what a bird of paradise looks like!"

"That's nice, dear. Remember to add it to your list of—a bird of paradise?"

"It's ladies like Miss Poitier, that's what the man at the store said. With bright plumes and big—"

"That's enough, brat. Let Miss Silver enjoy her tea."

Captain Endicott's welcome was warmer, in relief, if not quite as sticky, since he had already bathed. His hair was still wet but his neck cloth was tied in an elegant knot, and his dark blue coat hugged his broad shoulders. His white satin waistcoat had gold embroidered stripes of varied width, reflecting the golden glints in his brown eyes. He looked even more inviting to Allie than her cup of hot tea and plate of biscuits, except for the frown lines on his forehead.

Jack was worn to a nub, with an entire night of hosting his paying guests ahead of him, and half of the dawn hours, too. At least he did not have to go trace the governess's new employers and change their minds. For now, he was happy enough to give Harriet into Miss Silver's care, and go destroy every newspaper in London.

"You are back at last! No luck finding a position? Ah, that is too bad. Here is Harriet. Did you know she can hold her breath for an eternity? Isn't her new locket lovely? I am off to see about my own business. I have spent far too long away from the management of the club as is, doing your job."

Allie set down her teacup. "But it is not my job, Captain. We agreed I would stay on until more suitable arrangements could be made. I am trying to make those arrangements myself, since you seem reluctant to do so."

Reluctant? After a day in Harriet's company, Jack was ready to chain Miss Silver to the doorknob.

"But you will look after her tonight?" he asked, desperation tinging his voice, his hand disordering the freshly combed curls on his head.

"Unless you wish me to seek an inn? I supposed I could stay here until I found a new job, but if you'd rather . . ."

"No! That is, you must stay here as long as you need to. Save your coins and all that. Another day or two will not affect your reputation one whit more, as long as you stay out of the common rooms below stairs. Your supper will be served here, and anything you need. Please stay," he added out of honesty. "There is no one else to look after the brat."

"What about Mrs. Crandall? Was she no help to you?"

"Mr. Burquist suggested she look into running a boarding house, so they spent the afternoon viewing prospective properties. I thought that if she found a place, perhaps you and Harriet could—"

"No! You said I could live here with you, Papa Jack! Remember, so I wouldn't tell that nice man from the newspaper that Miss Silver was staying here, too?"

"Papa Jack? The newspaper?"

"It was nothing," Jack answered. "And now Mrs. Crandall is lying down with a cloth over her forehead, after Harriet threw a ta— that is, after taking the dear child to the park. Now I really have to be off. Yes, I think I hear the first customers arriving already. Good evening, Miss Silver. We will discuss the future in the morning. Or the afternoon."

He was anxious to leave, to make sure everything was in order at the club. Harriet and Miss Silver did look comfortable in their sitting room, though, surrounded by books and pastries and his dog. A warm fire and a footstool were appealing after the day he'd had, but Jack had a business to run. And why should he be thinking of cozy evenings by the hearth? He liked his entrepreneurship, liked making a success out of his own efforts, and liked the convivial nights spent with other choice spirits. A Captain Sharp of a child and a bluestocking biddy were not Jack's idea of pleasant companions.

Still, he was seeing the club in a different light tonight, through the eyes of innocence. The women he had handpicked as dealers and waitresses suddenly looked tawdry. Their red hair and ebony locks appeared too flamboyant, their bounteous breasts too exposed. He would not want Harriet associating with his former playmates. Lud, he could imagine Miss Silver's outrage, and her blushes.

The gentlemen were not much better. Many of the

players were friends or acquaintances of Jack's. He'd gone drinking and wenching with half of them, and won money from most of the others. Tonight he noticed the feral glints in their eyes, smelled the sweat of nerves, saw the wine-reddened veins in their faces, felt their rabid concentration on the turn of a card or the toss of the dice.

A night's gambling, win or lose, was worth more to them than time with their wives and children or tending to their estates. Most of them thought a governess was fair prey to their lustful pursuit. One or two were reputed to think little girls were, too.

Even the furnishings that he was so proud of displeased Jack tonight. The floor coverings were already showing stains from spilled drinks and burns from cigars. The crystal chandeliers held a film of gray from the air, and the portraits of Lizbeth and Lottie were barely visible through the blanket of smoke.

That was another thing that bothered Jack: The search for his half sister was suffering from his lack of attention. The investigation was supposed to be the reason for the club's existence, to make people aware of the reward, to ferret out any information from the sporting class and the frail sisterhood. So far he had learned little. Worse, while he'd been having ices at Gunter's and measuring giraffes, the interview room had been overflowing with possible leads.

Downs was competent, but he had been left in charge of the club, the staff, and the prospects, with too much else to do. Besides, his mind was on Darla, not on a girl who might have been dead for over a decade. And when, for once, he had something interesting to report, Jack was not there to hear it.

A young woman had come this afternoon, it seemed, a particularly attractive one with blue eyes and pale, almost white hair. According to Darla, she

had come to The Red and the Black once before, the
day Harriet and Miss Silver had arrived, but had been
turned away before speaking to anyone. Darla recalled
the female because of her looks and her fashionable
black attire. French, Darla thought, or designed by
a master.

This time Downs had spoken with her. She did not
give her name and seemed more interested in asking
about the missing girl than volunteering information.
She was uncertain about her own parentage and
thought she might make inquiries, was all she said.

Downs told Jack that he put the usual questions to
her and she knew the brothers' names. Of course she
did. Everyone with a Debrett's knew Jonathan and
Alexander; every female who entered the long receiving room was clued by the others to say Jack and
Alex, or Ace.

As usual, the young woman did not recall anything
of an accident or an earl. Both were public knowledge
she could have discovered if she was trying to win the
reward and the inheritance. The most significant part
of the interview, however, was Downs's query about
her pony's name. Half the women pretending to be
Charlotte said they could not remember. The other
half guessed: Crumpet, Thumper, Strawberry. This
dark-clad woman, this beautiful, fashionably gowned
female, said she did not remember having a pony, not
that she did not recall its name.

Charlotte was to be given her first mount when she
returned with Lizbeth from the north. Lord Carde
meant it for a surprise. Jack believed old Trey was
still eating his shaggy head off at Carde Hall, waiting
for the little girl to come ride him. Perhaps Alex's
children could learn on his broad back instead.

The blonde could not stay to wait for Jack's return,
nor could she promise to come back. Her plans were

uncertain, she'd told Downs, with a catch in her voice, and she might have to leave London in a hurry. Coming here was just a whim anyway, she'd said, but she had reached out to touch Lizbeth's portrait.

The closest clue to Charlotte so far had gone, seemingly troubled, without leaving a hint of her whereabouts, while Jack was minding a midget Machiavelli.

So, no, he was not enjoying himself, although everyone else in the club appeared to be. They all laughed about mice when he kept looking under the tables to make sure Harriet was not lurking there, and they all made ribald comments when he rushed toward a fair-haired woman in an elegant rose velvet gown. That female turned out to be Lord Havelock's paramour, his bailiff's daughter, and not even a natural blonde, up close. Jack handed her a stack of chips to wager in apology. She tried to rub her velvet skirts against him, in appreciation, which rankled Lord Havelock into leaving in a temper. So Jack's abstraction was costing him customers too, damn it.

His play was also suffering. Instead of recalling the discards, Jack recalled Miss Silver's sigh as she sank back against the cushioned chair and sipped her hot tea. Instead of calculating odds, he was calculating what it would take to make her sigh in satiated contentment, and not for a cup of tea. More than he was worth, he figured. More than he was willing to give, too. Deuce take it, the woman had stolen his sleep, demolished his day, and now she was destroying his devil-may-care attitude.

He put another stack of chips on the table. It was his club and his money. He won even if he lost, didn't he?

Allie, meanwhile, was not content with her day, or her night, either. Harriet was fast asleep and not toss-

ing and turning for once, but Allie was wide awake.
If she strained her ears, she could hear the sounds of
laughter and the clinking of glasses. The clients of the
club were enjoying themselves, sharing a gaiety that
Allie had never known in her life. She shared her bed
with a hellion and a hound.

Granted, the patrons downstairs enjoyed a shallow
merriment, induced by spirits, the spin of a wheel,
seduction. Allie told herself that she was being foolish
to be jealous of their illicit affairs, their outrageous
wagers, the headaches they would suffer in the morning, the bills they could not pay. She told herself all
that, but she still envied Jack and his patrons their fun.

Life was not about fun for people like Allison Silver. Life was about duty and responsibility and respect. It was about earning a living and doing the best
at her chosen vocation. An abiding contentment, the
satisfaction of seeing her girls turn into worthy women,
that was more important than an evening's revels,
wasn't it?

But a woman could keep her head on her shoulders
and still let her thoughts drift to the clouds. Just once,
Allie could dream of pretty clothes and pretty compli-
ments, champagne toasts and midnight suppers. She
might as well add in a waltz, although The Red and
the Black did not offer music, for that would detract
from the wagering and thus the club's and Jack's income. It was her dream, wasn't it?

A waltz it was, soft and slow, silk skirts flowing as
she floated in a man's arms. She laughed with joy,
dancing on air, beguiled by her partner's rapturous
gaze on her, prim and plain Miss Silver, schoolmistress. So what if her partner was tall and broad, with
the erect bearing of a former officer, and the laughing
brown eyes and lopsided smile of a scamp?

It was only a dream.

CHAPTER TWELVE

"What do you mean, you do not get the newspapers? You had them yesterday. I saw them at breakfast."

"I cancelled the subscriptions, to save money, you know. And yesterday's issues have been disposed of."

"Disposed of? You throw old papers in the trash?" She clucked her tongue. "Your household could have used them for kindling and for wrapping and in a hundred other ways to save money instead of wasting it. Then you might have afforded to keep up with the news of the world."

Jack winced at the shrill sound of Miss Silver's lecture. He had barely gone to bed when Calloway woke him, hours before he would normally have arisen after such a late night. He was not up and about for the pleasure of seeing the schoolmistress with her hair scraped back to an inch of its honeyed life or her shape hidden under another of her dreary gowns. Or was this the same dark, dull gown he had seen yesterday? They were all equally as offensive to Jack's sense of style. The world news could not have been as gloomy as the governess, or his mood.

No, Jack was out of bed with the birds—noisy, pesky, roof-fouling fools that they were—because he had so much to accomplish. He had to intercept the newspaper deliveries, for one thing, and burn the pages, even before reading them. Then he had to make a list of respectable agencies that could be counted on *not* to offer Miss Silver a position, not if his carefully worded notes reached them first. And then he had to beg the woman to take Harriet along with her.

"What, drag the poor child to sit in drafty offices while I wait for an interview?" Allie asked, after she thanked him for making her a list of new placement agencies to try. She had to admit, to herself, of course, that she was nervous about entering an unknown building after the driver's warnings yesterday. Captain Endicott might be misguided, but he truly was a gentleman, she was convinced, after he insisted she take his carriage on her quest. "That is very kind of you."

Kind? Jack was almost out of coins, paying messengers to deliver his notes, including gratuities for the agencies to compensate for their time and trouble. He'd also had to pay James Coachman extra to stop at no other employment services but those on Jack's list. For the promise of an even more handsome tip, the driver was to see that Miss Silver did not purchase a newspaper, ask any nannies in the park if they knew of likely families, or leave her references at noble houses. James was to claim that the horses were ailing or something if she insisted on traveling beyond Mayfair. Mostly, he was to bring Miss Silver back in the same unharmed, unmolested, unemployed state she left in, unattractively. Jack would double the tip for tending to Harriet as well as the horses while Miss

Silver conducted her business, which was bound to be brief.

"Harriet won't mind waiting in the coach, will you, snippet?"

Harriet was practicing tying neck cloths around Joker's neck with one of Jack's discarded cravats. Of course the starched linen had not been discarded before Harriet got to it.

"But I shall mind," Miss Silver replied. "I will not be able to concentrate on making the proper impression if I have to worry about her alone in the carriage. Besides, people might get the wrong notion, that I am going to ask to bring Miss Hildebrand along to my next position, or that I am cheating her guardians by seeking new employment when it is not my day off."

Which was exactly what she was doing, Jack thought, except that he was not actually paying Miss Silver. She would not accept any money but what they had first agreed on, for her expenses on the trip to London and the first two nights. Her tending to Harriet was in exchange, she said, for her meals and a place to sleep. Jack still felt cheated. His lifeline was drifting away and he was drowning while the heartless wench watched. Honey-haired females should not be cruel.

He tried to appeal to the woman's compassionate side, if she had one. "But the poor little sprig will be bored here." They both knew that a bored Harriet was a catastrophe waiting to happen. "And she will miss you. Anyone can see how fond the dear child is of you."

Anyone could see that was Miss Silver's bonnet on Joker again.

Allie snatched her hat back before the old hound could leave another bite mark on the brim. "Harriet is fonder of you, sir. Every other word out of her mouth is Papa Jack this and Papa Jack that."

Jack almost preened, until he remembered that Harriet had no father to compare him to, no other male in her life. "But I will not have time to devote to her today. I intend to stay close to the club in case a certain blond woman comes by again. No," he added at the dark look Miss Silver sent his way. "This one truly might have news about the search for my sister."

Allie dismissed his excuses. "I have left schoolwork for Harriet to complete. When she does, then Mrs. Crandall can take her to the park again."

Mrs. Crandall refused to have anything to do with the hoyden, after fishing her out of the Serpentine, stopping her from "rescuing" an organ-grinder's monkey, and apologizing to every gentleman whose top hat fell to the chit's slingshot. The widow was calling on the bachelor Mr. Burquist again today, thinking of more than a boarding house, it appeared. A tenant for life was more like it.

"You have no one but yourself to blame," Allie was saying. "If you had found a place for us, a respectable situation in a lady's household, we would both be out of your way. You could visit Harriet whenever you wished, Harriet would have suitable surroundings, and I could enjoy accepting your stipend to teach her. Anywhere but here."

"Yes, so you have mentioned, more than once." Jack was not his best in the morning, and this was not the best of mornings. His mouth tasted as if he'd swallowed the newspaper ashes, and his eyes burned from their smoke.

Miss Silver had no sympathy. "Well, you were the one who let an eight-year-old wheedle you into a devil's bargain."

"I told you, I have no respectable female acquaintances nearby that I can call on for a favor." Not after opening a gaming parlor, he didn't. "And I cannot impose on my sister-in-law in her delicate condition."

Allie stood to leave, forcing Jack to come to his feet. "Then we have nothing further to discuss. Good day, Captain Endicott, and thank you again for the loan of your coach and driver. I hope to return for my bags and my farewell to Harriet this afternoon after I secure a post."

Fine, he had a day before he had to resort to kidnapping a keeper for his ward. Meantime, Calloway could instruct Harriet on polishing silver; Downs could explain how to pick bottles from the wine cellar; Darla could teach her how to deal vingt-et-un; and Cook could show her how to roll pastry dough.

Lud knew this was not what Miss Silver had in mind for the girl's daily lessons. Which went to prove that she should not have gone off on her own without Harriet. A day of domestic chores was not what Nelson Hildebrand might have wanted for his daughter, either, but Hildebrand had not left the brat to Alex, the wealthy, respectable Earl of Carde, as he should have, or made other provision. Being passed from servant to stranger was deuced well not what Jack wished for any child under his care, but it was the best he could do today.

He would be too busy to watch the chit practice her penmanship or total her sums. He had to pen notes to his brother and sister-in-law, then total his own sums to see what he could afford in the way of a house for Harriet. And for Miss Silver. He looked at poor Joker, thinking he could not afford to have one without the other.

Allie could afford to relax. London was not half as frightening in the daylight, for one thing. People were polite for the most part, and Allie was never in danger of becoming lost, now that she'd found a guidebook under the seat of Captain Endicott's coach. She was becoming accustomed to the noise and the speed of traffic, the thick air, and the unpleasant odors. Knowing she had a place to rest her head if her search proved unsuccessful made her more confident. Knowing she had money for hired coaches if James went home lent her the courage to argue with the grizzled driver.

She was having a hard time making James leave her off any distance from the agencies on Captain Endicott's list. Whoever heard of a governess arriving for an interview in a private coach? Heavens, people would wonder what she was doing to deserve such particular treatment.

But James Coachman was another former soldier under the captain's command. He followed orders, but only when they came from his superior officer, not a slip of a girl. Besides, he had daughters, he told her. He wouldn't want any of his own chicks, all safely married with babes of their own now, wandering alone on the streets of London, not even in the daytime or in these respectable neighborhoods. A young lady could never be too careful, he warned.

Allie refused to get back into the carriage after her first stop, however, unless James promised to leave her at the corners. Short of leaving Cap'n Jack's horses, which James would sell one of his own daughters rather than doing, he had no choice.

The distance between Allie's destination and her conveyance made no difference. The first placement office had no positions available, although they did have a roomful of hopeful applicants clutching advertisements from the London journals that said otherwise. Perhaps the other neatly dressed, reserved women were looking for employment as companions or ladies' secretaries. Allie could do either, she supposed, but when it was Allie's turn, the proprietor of the agency smiled and said her references were not appropriate. The gentleman wished Allie good fortune, with another, more knowing smile.

The next establishment on the captain's list was run by two women of a certain age. They listened to Allie's name, looked at her references, and shook their matching gray heads. They had various openings for which she might have applied, they sincerely regretted, but, no, they could not send her for any interviews today. Most likely not tomorrow, either. But she was sure to be successful, and they hoped she remembered them then.

The third placement service was run by an attractive woman in black bombazine. She was also polite, but curt. Miss Silver was five and twenty and unwed? Educated but impoverished? She could do better than working for some cit in London. If she played her cards right, the woman said, slyly laying her finger alongside her nose, she might land in clover.

How odd.

One of the applicants at the last office, a successful one, it seemed, had left her unneeded newspaper clipping of employment opportunities behind, so Allie directed James to try another place. Day and Day was already circled.

"What do you mean, James, you cannot drive me there? Oh, I am sorry. I must have kept you from your other chores. Very well, I have my guidebook and can continue on my own."

"Cap'n Jack'll have my head an' you go off alone. I was to take you to the three places an' nowheres else."

"But I did not have as much as an interview for a position at any of them."

James shrugged, holding the door open for her to get into the carriage. "Not my fault you ain't what they're lookin' for."

Allie reread the advertisements. "But I am, precisely what they say here. Not the ones seeking music instructors, of course, but otherwise my credentials equal anything required in these notices."

"Then you can send a letter. That's the ticket. Why waste your time and tire out the horses for nothing?"

Her future was not nothing. The horses were well-bred beauties, their coats gleaming. They were not the least tired, from standing or walking while they waited. She eyed James with suspicion. "I thought you were to help me find a post."

The coachman spit over the side of the front wheel. "Not by half," he muttered. Louder, he said, "But you've had no luck today, miss. Every gambler knows when to wait for his luck to change."

"But I am depending on my skill, my experience, and my own education, not luck. Not everything in life is about gambling."

James's livelihood was. "Please, miss, let's go home."

"What, after three failures?" She discounted yesterday's lack of success. The places recommended by Solicitor Burquist might not have been very busy operations. "I have not begun to be discouraged."

So James drove her, as slowly and by as roundabout routes as he could devise, afraid she'd call for the Watch or leap out of the carriage if he headed back toward The Red and the Black, where he was afraid to face his employer anyway, for disobeying orders.

Mr. Day of the Day and Day Agency declared every position filled.

Miss Smythe of Select Services sniffed and nearly slammed the door in Allie's face as soon as she gave her name.

Herr Gottlieb declared, "Ve don't vant your sort here."

"They must hire only foreigners," Allie told James before saying she would walk across the street toward the next address.

She fared no better there, or the next, or the next.

After two more she was finally discouraged. After five she was livid. The clerks were rude, scornful, sneering. Half of them would not read her references. The other half would not let her sit in front of their desks.

"No, we have no openings for your kind."

"We do not hire women like you."

"How dare you think we would place you in a decent home?"

"Go back to the gutter where you belong."

London was not friendly, after all.

James pulled at his ear, in confusion. "And those weren't even the ones Cap'n Jack wrote to."

"What was that?"

"Can we go home now, miss?"

"There is one more position listed, at a Lord Bainbridge's home."

"You can't be calling on any lord, miss, not without an appointment."

"The advertisement says Lady Bainbridge is calling for interested applicants to come for interviews all afternoon."

Lady Bainbridge called Allie bachelor fare.

Allie marched through the black door of the club and strode down the long length of the receiving room to the desk at the far end. Captain Endicott was sitting there studying his ledgers, looking despondent, his hair mussed, his neckcloth limp. Obviously he had not found his sister or the funds he needed. Allie did not care. She slammed the page of newspaper advertisements on the desk.

He looked up at her and smiled. "What, no job?"

She poked a finger at the page, unfortunately poking a hole in her worn gloves, which made her more furious. "They know."

He was still smiling. "What do they know?"

"They know that I have been staying here, under the roof of a gaming casino, with a known libertine."

Jack slammed shut his accounts book. "What? I never wrote anything about your immediate situation, only that the Earl of Carde was planning on engaging your estimable services in the near future."

Now it was her turn to ask, "What?"

"Well, I could not very well put my own name on the notes, could I? And it is true. Ace would hire you in an instant, if this new baby turns out to be a girl. And I did write to tell him about it."

"Let me understand this. You wrote notes to my prospective employers, forging your own brother's name?"

"Well, I could copy his signature if I had to. Did it for years, in school. But this time I signed my own initials, as his secretary. Earls don't bother with their own correspondence, you know. And no one cares about the secretary's name."

"But why?"

"How else was I to make you unsuitable for a position? I hinted that you'd be leaving too soon to bother with another bit of employment. I know that was underhanded, but I really need you. Harriet—"

"You wrote to every agency in London?"

There had not been time. "Only three. The ones on the list I gave you."

So that was what all the sly grins were about. Allie was so angry her hands were shaking. She put them flat on the desktop so he could not see, although now the other worn spots on her gloves were more visible, so she bent her fingers into fists. "You resorted to prevarication and misrepresentation, merely to keep me from leaving?"

"You should be complimented."

"When they nearly called me your whore to my face?"

Now the captain was on his feet, outraged. "Who said such a thing? I will call him out!" Jack forgot all about his vow never to duel.

"They know, I say." She pounded on the desk. "The ones who did not outright label me your doxy pulled their skirts aside or shut the door in my face. I am ruined!"

"Lud, Rochelle must have spoken to her landlord after all. I never had a chance to read the papers this morning before I burn—"

"Aha! You did not even throw the newspaper away as you said. You are a pernicious liar and an unprincipled cheat and a vile villain."

"But I never tried to seduce you."

"And that is supposed to make me feel better?"

He stopped wondering who to kill first. "You'd rather I tried?"

"Of course not, you clunch! I'd rather you had let me stay at an inn the way I wanted. I'd rather I had never met you!"

Now he stopped wondering how he would go about seducing a poker-backed prig in a pique. He might be a gambler, but he never bet on such long odds. "Well, you did come to my house, and you did meet me. Still, things cannot be as bad as all that. Let me fetch you a pot of tea. No, I do not dare show my face in the kitchen while Cook is there. Calloway can— No, he went to visit his mother this afternoon."

"Snake, that is, Mr. Calloway has a mother?"

"He does this afternoon. And Downs is resting. Or drafting his resignation, I could not tell which, through his whimpering." He came around the side of the desk, holding out his hand. "Come, let us go to the tea shop and discuss this as rational adults."

"What about Harriet?"

"Harriet is neither adult nor rational. Why would anyone grease a roulette wheel with Darla's face cream?"

"Where is she?"

"Harriet and Joker are in the rear garden. One of them is chained."

CHAPTER THIRTEEN

"'A little bird told this reporter,'" Jack started to read from the scandal sheet in front of him.

"What kind of bird?" Harriet asked. "Does it say?"

Jack and Allie had taken pity on those big sad eyes—of the dog—and taken Harriet along with them to the tea shop. Jack had ordered a plate of assorted cakes and creams, deciding that Miss Silver needed something sweet to relieve her day. She was too thin, besides. And he did enjoy his jam tarts, none of which, he understood, were to be forthcoming this day from his own kitchens.

Jack pushed the plate closer to Harriet so she would eat and be quiet.

"A young person does not speak unless addressed by her elders, Harriet. You know that, dear," Allie absently lectured, turning the pages of the newspaper she had in front of her, searching for an *on dit* column. Without looking up, she dutifully added, "And do use your napkin, not your sleeve."

"I bet it was a parrot. Or a mynah bird. Maybe a raven," Harriet muttered around a mouthful of macaroon.

" 'A little bird told this reporter,' " Jack began again, waiting for an interruption. When none came, he continued, " 'that the notorious Mr. JE, formerly of His Majesty's victorious army and formerly welcomed into the highest ranks accorded his brother's esteemed title, has exceeded even his previously outrageous conduct.' "

Allie put down the newspaper and wrapped her cold fingers around her cup of tea. "Oh, dear, it is not just me they have slandered."

" 'The little bird' "— Jack raised his eyebrow, again daring Harriet to interrupt, but she was chewing on a slice of lemon cream cake—" 'was shocked, dear readers, shocked to learn that the erstwhile gentleman and present-day proprietor of a gaming parlor had installed his love child in that same lavish lair for the foolish gambler.' "

Harriet leaned over and kissed Jack's cheek, leaving a sticky smear. "Thank you, Papa Jack. I love you, too."

Jack cleared his throat, not meeting Allie's eyes. He went back to reading aloud: " 'What could be worse? I shall tell you, faithful listener. The child's mother, the child's unwed mother, by her own admission, resides there also, although the wench denies parenthood. Of course she does, my friends. The disgraceful female, according to the little bird, is the disavowed granddaughter of the Marquess of M—d. Miss Silver is here for the gold, my dears, nothing else.' "

The nearly empty confectionary shop was silent except for Harriet's loud gulping of her lemonade. A single gentleman sat at one table, studiously not reading the book he held. A pair of clerks at another table did not bother to pretend not to overhear. Allie thought even the waiter must be listening, for he stood against the wall, frowning in disapproval. She wished they had not gone out in public. She wished she were not with one of the most easily recognizable gentlemen in all of England. She wished she had worn a veil.

She wished she never had to show her face outdoors again.

Jack wished he had something stronger than tea in front of him, but he swallowed the hot drink and tried to sound optimistic. "This twattle is not so bad. I admit it might damage your chances of employment for the immediate future, but you already have a job, so that is not a worry."

Allie almost choked on her own sip of tea. "Not a worry?"

Harriet was beaming. "Now you'll have to stay with us."

Allie repeated, "Not a worry?"

"That's right. No one will believe the cork-brained column. I might have fallen far from the social graces, but no one will believe I would install my former paramour and her illegitimate child at my house. This particular scandal sheet is known to mislead readers and distort the truth."

Allie had finally found the right page in the newspaper she'd been leafing through. "The writer of this gossip column for this newspaper seems to believe it." She read him the same story, verbatim except for the little bird's chirping.

Jack went on as if Miss Silver was not looking at him with ice-cold horror in her gray eyes, as if a fierce winter snowstorm was gathering there. Maybe hot tea was better than brandy after all to relieve the chill.

"Well," he said, "some worse scandal will occur tomorrow and people will forget." He held up one hand before she could protest. "We will make them forget. And we will make this first gabble-grinder recant the story Rochelle fed him. The others will have to follow."

"Can you do that?" Allie asked, seeing a glimmer of hope in his confidence that he could move mountains if he wished.

Jack nodded. "I will send Burquist with the legal documents tomorrow, proving that Harriet is, that is, *was*, Captain Nelson Hildebrand's daughter. We will dig up a picture of him at his parent's home if we have to, to show their similar looks."

"Which will succeed in stirring up another old scandal for the public's insatiable appetite." Allie gestured toward Harriet, who was licking her fingers after eating a custard tart, speaking of insatiable appetites.

The child could eat and listen at the same time. "About my uncle being a murderer? I don't mind, Miss Silver, truly. Everyone always finds out sooner or later anyway."

Jack nodded his approval of Harriet's commonsense acceptance of the facts. "And people will have sympathy for the brat." He corrected himself: "The child. They will see that Harriet had nowhere else to go."

"Which exonerates you from the charge of paternity, but does nothing for my reputation."

"Well, no one will think you are Harriet's mother, because if they recall the murder, they will also recall that she was the victim. That is something."

That was very little, Allie knew, when people wanted to believe the worst.

Jack refilled her cup with tea and pushed the almost empty plate of pastries closer to her, encouragingly. "We'll all go together to the scandal sheet's office and make them print a retraction. They'll instantly see you are nothing but a schoolteacher." No one could mistake the dowdy female for a dasher, he firmly believed, especially if she wore her dark gowns, shabby cloak, limp bonnet, and darned gloves. Not even a blind man could believe Miss Silver was one of Mad Jack's mistresses. For once his own reputation as an admirer of beautiful women would stand him in good stead. He could not relieve her worries by explaining she was too plain, naturally, so he said, "Your accent, your bearing, everything about you bespeaks the lady of education and intelligence."

Allie was not convinced. No one at the personnel agencies had seemed to recognize her honorable qualities, not under the dirt this article had tossed at her.

"We'll show them your references from Mrs. Semple's school and tell them about your father being a noted scholar and educator. The reporter will have to print a revision or I will threaten the paper with a lawsuit. This"—he tapped the first offending article—"is outright slander, untruth piled on innuendo."

"But what if the reporter claims that he had the facts from a reliable source?"

"Trust me, the publishers will not want to offend the Earl of Carde, and Ace will be grievously offended. My brother does not like the family name dragged through the mud like this."

"But your brother is fixed in the country. Why should this writer care about the truth when his lies help sell the newspaper?"

"Never fear, he will care enough to write a new story. It is simple, actually. If he does not, I will break every bone in his body."

Allie could not blame Captain Endicott for the mess, not entirely. She was the one who had let her pride and her temper boast of her connections, and she was the one who had insisted that Miss Poitier be dismissed for being unfit for polite company, if Harriet could be considered polite, wiping lemonade off her lips with the tablecloth. Rochelle's presence did not suit Allie's notions or her delicate sensibilities, so Miss Poitier had been ousted from her lucrative and lush livelihood, on Allie's say-so.

She was not the one, however, whose name was fodder for the gossip columns, or who knew jealous, ill-natured women willing to take their revenge in print.

Allie had stayed at The Red and the Black despite her misgivings, but the captain owned the wretched place. Why could he not have been a true scion of nobility who lived in a grand house with innumerable old aunts and in-laws? He could have wasted his income wagering instead of making his living off other cabbage-headed cardsharps. He might have been respectable.

But then he might be respectably married.

Allie did not want to consider why that idea was as repellent as a worm. If the captain had a wife, Allie would still have a reputation, a job, and a future. The word *wife*, though, wriggled in her mind and left her feeling queasy. No, the stomach pangs were because she had been too upset to eat any of the pastries, or dinner later.

Allie could not face the other women in the communal dining hall. They all knew the truth of the matter and thought the whole newspaper article was a big joke on their Cap'n Jack, being saddled with a daughter he did not beget and a woman he did not bed. Of course they laughed, the dealers and demimondaines the club employed, for they had no good names to lose. Something precious had been stolen from Allie, though, and she was heartsick about it, as if she had lost her father's watch or her mother's wedding ring.

She could not sit at the table and listen to Captain Endicott's ensemble chatting about their gentlemen friends or how much they hoped to earn this evening.

She did not want to see the concerned look on the captain's face, either. He said he could make the newspaper recant, but he did not appear his usual assured self when she fretted that a retraction would have no effect. They both knew that a nail hammered into a board left a mark, even when the nail was removed.

So what was Allie going to do?

She could still leave. She *should* still leave, take her hoarded coins and book passage on a coach leaving London. She should go as far from the gossip as she could travel, and as far from silver-tongued rakes with winning ways that lost a woman's reputation and virtue, too.

She could go to Bath, where the invalids might need someone to chaperone their nieces, or to Manchester, where the manufacturing magnates wanted their daughters to learn the manners of a lady. But she did not know anyone in either place—in *any* place—who could offer her lodgings or work. If residents of the outlying districts received the London journals, Allie's name would have reached there long before she ever could. She would have used up her funds on the fare and food, and eventually spend the rest on lodgings, without ever finding a position.

The thought was enough to turn anyone's stomach, especially a woman who had been turned out of the only home she had ever known on her father's death. Bereft, bewildered that her beloved parent had not made better provision for her, Allie had been terrified. She was terrified again.

And then there was Harriet. How could Allie abandon the poor little chick?

Easily, most times, and with a clear conscience. But

other times, like now, the child was as sweet as spun sugar. She had taken dinner with the staff, who were now preparing for the club's evening opening and a night of work. With everyone too busy for her, Harriet had come upstairs, bringing a plate full of pudding for later. She was trying her best to be quiet, since she knew Allie did not feel well and was upset. For once Harriet was a perfect angel, sitting at the dressing table painting.

Painting? Allie pulled the lavender-soaked cloth from her forehead and leaped off the bed, nearly tripping over the dog on her way to snatch the rouge and lip color and powder and a tiny pot of something dark out of her charge's hands. "You wash your face this instant, young lady!" Allie ordered, reaching for the cloth she'd discarded. "This is a bit of muslin," she said, waving it in front of Harriet, who looked like a miniature Covent Garden corner convenient. "You are not!"

Without waiting for Harriet to take the cloth, Allie started scrubbing at the girl's face, rubbing hard enough to erase the face paint, if not Harriet's freckles. "Where did you get this . . . this devil's dyestuff anyway?" she asked over the girl's howls.

The dog started howling too, but subsided when Allie threatened him with the wet towel.

"I won it from Miss Solange. She's the pretty black-haired lady."

Half the women who worked for Captain Endicott were raven-haired, and every one of them was pretty, so that was no help, not that it mattered. Harriet should not be talking to women who painted their faces, much less be gambling with them. Mrs. Semple would be apoplectic . . . all the way to her new home with Harriet's money. Stealing was one thing; gambling was another. "What do you mean, you won it? You were not playing dice with her, were you, or wagering over cards?"

"No. She bet I could not eat five portions of Cook's eel in aspic at dinner. But I could."

"Ech." Telling the girl not to make bets when her guardian owned a gaming parlor seemed like a waste of time. So did ordering her not to speak with her dinner companions on the principle that only fast women used face paint. Those were the only companions the child was likely to have here. Allie consoled herself by saying, "You are too young for cosmetics, and too pretty to need any."

"Then you can borrow them, if you want."

Why, because she was old and plain? Allie scrubbed harder.

"Want to hear about the rest of my day?" Harriet asked when Allie was done, the girl's cheeks as red as her hair.

"Not if it is about eels or eyelash blackening." In fact, after her own day, Allie thought Harriet's adventures might be a welcome relief. Lessons, a walk in the park, tossing sticks for the dog in the rear garden—these were normal, proper activities for a young girl, except for the dog, Allie supposed, never having had one of the creatures. Harriet needed the routine of a school day, and so did Allie.

School had never been like this.

First Harriet had helped Cook make meat pies for lunch, but Harriet ate half the pie dough and fed Joker half the meat. The chef had started throwing pots and pans, so Harriet had started stuffing his raspberry tarts in her mouth and pockets as she ran.

Then she had helped Snake shine the captain's boots. He used champagne. Harriet drank some.

Mr. Downs was decanting wine from the cellars to serve tonight. He had to taste it, of course. Harriet did too, of course.

One of the dealers was packing to leave, so Harriet was sent to help. She was given a box of bonbons in return. "Do you think they put love nests up in trees?"

Allie did not answer. "Go on, dear. What did you do next? Your mathematics lesson?"

In a way. Another of the dealers sent Harriet with a coin next door for a bottle of cologne, and the apothecary gave Harriet a sack of licorice drops.

Then Papa Jack told Darla and Mr. Downs to take Harriet away after the roulette wheel was so nicely greased, and they bought her a lemon ice. Mr. Downs let her eat his so he could hold Darla's hand under the table.

Then Papa Jack bought her a bag of horehound drops from next door to show he wasn't mad anymore.

And Mrs. Crandall came home with a jar of pigs' knuckles to share.

"I don't feel so good, Miss Silver."

"Neither do I, dear." How could she leave a child alone in this place?

But Harriet really did not feel well. She moaned and groaned for hours and was even more restless than usual in the bed they shared. Then she was truly sick. In the bed they shared.

Chapter Fourteen

Allie knew where the linen cupboard was, thank goodness, and the water closet. She did not have to call to anyone for help, then wonder if anyone would come. Captain Endicott and his employees were all busy downstairs performing their duties at the club. Allie's duty was looking after Harriet.

The child fell asleep eventually, only to awaken an hour later. This time Allie was ready with a basin and clean cloths. She was not truly worried that Harriet had contracted some foul and fatal disease, only that she did not cast up her own accounts while the impossible child emptied her stomach.

She did not dare to go to sleep when Harriet dozed off, so she sat reading by candlelight in her robe, listening for sounds of distress or someone passing by in the corridor. She had left the sitting room door open so she could hear if anyone walked down the hall, Captain Endicott or one of the others, to send for a pot of tea or a restorative for Harriet. Allie was not about to go below herself, to chance meeting one of the gamesters, not even using the service steps. Libertines always lurked in dark stairwells, in novels anyway. Even if she were not accosted, being seen anywhere near the gaming rooms would put paid to any hopes of redeeming her reputation. At least in the guest room Allie was out of sight and, hopefully, out of mind.

Twelve o'clock and all she heard were whimpers from Harriet, snores from the dog, and sounds of merriment from below. With the door ajar, the noise from the club was louder than she expected. Perhaps the casino rooms were more crowded than before, as people came to see the latest scandal for themselves. Maybe they were hoping for a glimpse of Jack Endicott's bastard, or the whore who bore her. Flaunting an illicit affair and its outcome did not seem beneath the captain's dignity. Was anything?

Well, Allie had more self-respect than that. She was not going to add fuel to the fire of public opinion by putting one toe out the bedroom door. Her good name might have gone up in the conflagration, but her pride was merely singed around the edges.

This had to be the longest night Allie could recall, though. Harriet never slept longer than an hour, and stayed sick and fretful for an hour between naps. She cried out for a cold drink, a warm brick, the dog, Papa Jack, and comfort. She swore to be a good girl forever after if Allie made her feel better. She would even give back the miniatures of Miss Silver's parents that Allie thought had been lost at Mrs. Semple's School. And she would not save her pennies to get a tattoo like Snake's. She'd donate all her coins to the Widows and Orphans Fund, if she lived long enough.

"Don't let me die, Allie, please!"

"Silly goose, no one dies of overeating." At least

Allie hoped not, because Harriet was looking as pale as a redheaded ghost, lying limply in the bed. "But maybe you will have learned your—"

Now Harriet was snoring.

Two in the morning and all was not well, not upstairs, at any rate. The club must be earning money, for the noises from below continued. Captain Endicott might know how to run a profitable gaming establishment, but he had to be the world's worst guardian, judging from Harriet's condition.

Three in the morning and Allie was exhausted. She must have drowsed herself, for she had not heard the patrons leaving or Jack coming upstairs, yet the club seemed quiet, with no high-pitched laughter from the so-called hostesses. The serious gamesters might still be present, however, concentrating on their cards, too rapt in their wagers for idle chatter. They were courting Lady Luck instead of the pretty girls who were either on the top floor in their own beds, or elsewhere, in someone else's.

Four of the clock and Allie could not think of anything else but whether Jack had brought one of the females up to his own rooms, just across the corridor from where his ward lay suffering. The devil take him and his doxy.

Everyone had to have gone home by five, hadn't they? The hardiest gambler needed to sleep sometime. And Harriet needed some nourishment. Broth or sweetened tea, perhaps a slice of toast to settle her stomach, or peppermint drops, if there were any on Cook's shelves. Allie needed tea and sustenance herself if she was going to keep awake and on with her vigil.

She put on her shoes and pulled her cloak over her nightrail, just in case anyone still lingered. She hoped Calloway might be up, thinking one of his gory stories might entertain Harriet while Allie made the tea. Even Mr. Downs or Darla could stay with the sick child for a few minutes while Allie rested in the sitting room. The others could all sleep late in the morning. Allie had to see a man about a scandal.

She would not ask Jack to keep Harriet company. He did not belong in Allie's rooms, especially if he had another woman's scent clinging to him.

Of course if he were in his office, adding his receipts, alone . . .

Allie checked there, via the deserted service stairwell, shielding her candle. No one was stirring at all. She could not resist peeking into the public rooms, just to make certain no one was there to surprise her, she told herself.

Her candle's light could not reach into the far corners of the large room, with tables scattered throughout. Some chairs were overturned, others leaned drunkenly against the walls. Pasteboard cards and scoring papers and soiled napkins and empty glasses were everywhere. She knew the cleaning staff came in the morning, but now the place looked disheveled and debauched. She thought she smelled the scent of desperation in the air, plus other even less wholesome odors. A feeling of doom hid in the corners.

Allie shivered. She had obviously been reading too many of those damsel and dungeon novels herself.

The staff dining hall was dark and bare, with a single oil lamp left burning on the side table. She hurried to the kitchen, where she could find what she needed and return to Harriet and the security of their bedroom.

In contrast to the public rooms, everything in the kitchen was tidy, every pot hanging from its hook, every mixing bowl and platter washed and dried. No one was about, but the scullery maid would be up soon to relight the fires and start the day's bread.

Allie lit a new candle and headed toward the pantry to see if anything on the shelves might help poor Harriet's digestion before the apothecary opened in the morning.

She was coughing, though, and her eyes were itching. She was not merely tired, Allie realized, she was inhaling smoke, more than lingered in the card rooms. The air there had been heavy, but this was nearly unbreathable. Her father had loved his pipe and tobacco, and some of his scholar friends had indulged in the occasional cigar. This smelled different.

Allie went back to the kitchen and checked to see that the enclosed stove's fire was banked, the ovens empty. Nothing was left burning, no pots were simmering. The ever-present tea kettle was cold to her touch.

Then she started to feel the heat, seemingly coming from the rear door. She touched the door handle, then jumped back, cradling her stinging palm. She had to see, though, so she wrapped her other hand in a fold of her cloak and opened the door—to find a pile of rags and rubble on fire!

As she tried to kick the burning mound apart and stamp on the smouldering pieces, her first thought was that the fire had to have been deliberately started there. Cook would never have tossed garbage, much less the burning embers, right outside the back door. Her second thought was that Harriet could not have done this because she was too sick and had never left their bedroom. Harriet! She was upstairs asleep, as were Captain Endicott and the women. They would never smell the smoke or feel the heat. And while the rags under Allie's feet had burned themselves out, flames were climbing up the wooden door frame to the back side of the house.

Remembering the nightmare of the fire at Mrs. Semple's School, Allie grabbed up the full kettle from the stove and tossed its contents on the fire. Then she found the pump and a bucket used for carrying water and filled that. Too slow! She could not pump hard enough, or fast enough, and the fire was spreading. Now the flames were higher than she could reach, with no hope of putting them out.

She could not do this on her own. But no one came to her screams. She grabbed another pot from its hook, and a lid, and started banging them together, in between pumping and carrying and shouting and stamping on flying embers. Mr. Downs and Calloway and the cook slept somewhere below. Surely they would hear and come help.

"Fire!" She yelled until she was hoarse, the smoke filling her lungs, tears clouding her sight. She could barely lift the pump handle now, with every muscle burning, her arms quivering. She pulled off her cloak and soaked it in the bucket, then spread that over the first part of the fire, dampening that, at least.

Then she heard someone cursing behind her, the sweetest, most vile words she had ever heard. A bare arm with a snake tattoo took her bucket, and more voices called out for someone to man the pump, someone to fetch a ladder, someone to call for the Watch.

"My beautiful kitchen!"

"Keep pumping, you clunch. The Fire Insurance Company won't get here for hours."

Downs sent Darla—who had obviously not been asleep upstairs in her narrow attic bed—to check the front of the house, in case the arsonist had tried to make more damage. Darla tried to pull together the back of her evening gown as she ran.

Downs pushed Allie out of the way. "Go on, miss, we'll take over. Go wake the others."

Allie ran for the stairs, where the air was fresher, thank goodness. She took a deep, cleansing breath before yelling, "Fire! Fire! Wake up! Fire!"

Jack was already headed down, pulling a shirt over his bare chest, not bothering to tuck it into his breeches.

"How bad?" he demanded, grabbing her arms before she could crash into him.

"Not terrible," she gasped, "if the men can stop it soon."

"Get Harriet!" he yelled as he rushed past.

Harriet was on the far side of the house, away from the fire. So Allie ran up to the top floor first, yelling, banging her fist on all the doors as she went by. "Wake up! Get out. Fire! Tell the others."

Then she went back down to her own floor, panting for air, not because of the smoke but because she had almost reached the limit of her strength. Even with her lungs close to bursting and every muscle in her arms protesting, somehow she managed to get Harriet off the high bed. She wrapped the child in a blanket and half-dragged, half-carried her down the wider front stairs toward the front door, away from the fire. Joker led the way, barking.

Then strong arms took her limp burden from her. "Great gods, is she . . . ?"

Allie shook her head. "Just ill. That's how I discovered the fire. I was trying to find her a restorative."

"Thank heaven!" Jack said, carrying Harriet toward the front casino room, where the chandelier had been relighted. "We think the house is safe enough to stay inside now. And it is too cold outdoors, unless it proves necessary to evacuate."

He carefully placed Harriet on a leather armchair,

tucking the blanket more firmly around her. "Poor little puss." Then he gently touched Allie's cheek with the back of his hand. "And brave little governess." Then he was gone, back to make sure the zealous firefighters did not destroy the rear of the house trying to save it.

Someone handed Allie a blessed glass of water. She drank it and sank onto a chair next to Harriet, looking around while she caught her breath. The dealers sat huddled in their thin night clothes at the tables, some weeping, some hugging each other while Downs tried to make sure everyone was accounted for. Allie heard it in a daze.

"Susan? She's with her lover."

"Jane's out at Kensington with Sir Mortimer."

"Mary? Mrs. Crandall?"

"Oh, she's housekeeping for that lawyer bloke."

They all laughed, relieved that they could. Then they cheered when Cap'n Jack returned with two bottles of wine and the news that the fire was entirely out, with no one hurt, not much damage.

When everyone had a glass, he raised his in a toast, to Allie. "The bravest, most clever woman in England!"

Allie blushed. "No, I was terrified."

"But you did not run away or fall down in a faint or start crying."

One of the dealers stopped sniveling on the instant.

"We could all have died in our beds, without Miss Silver," Jack told the others, who stood and cheered, to her further embarrassment. Then everyone was hugging Allie and kissing her and patting her back. Cook gave a dirty look toward Harriet, where she was sleeping on the chair, but came to kiss Allie's hand for saving his beautiful kitchen.

Allie winced, and Jack immediately grabbed her

hand and turned it up, to see blisters already formed on her palm. Allie did not know whether they were from the hot doorknob or from the bucket's handle, but they hurt like the devil, now that she had time to think about it.

Jack poured another few drops of brandy into her glass and sent Calloway next door for the apothecary.

"But it is so early," Allie protested.

"And his shop would have been the next to catch on fire if you had not been there, and been so brave."

By the time the apothecary had come, put salve on both Allie's hands, and wrapped them in clean bandages, Cook was feeding sandwiches to the firefighters from the insurance company. The women were flirting with them, and Jack was consulting with a serious-looking young man in a red waistcoat.

He brought the man over toward Allie and introduced him as Mr. Geoffrey Rourke, a Bow Street Runner. Mr. Rourke was the officer hired by the Endicott family to head the legal investigation into their half sister's disappearance, Jack explained. "I sent for him to help with this mess as well. Would you mind answering his questions?"

Allie would not, of course. The sips of brandy and a plate of cold chicken had revived her somewhat, and the pain in her hands would have kept her awake anyway. Besides, she needed to wait for someone to carry Harriet upstairs for her.

So she described what she had found and why she was in the kitchens, with a glance toward the sleeping child. She told how she had not seen or heard anyone else on the main level of the club.

Downs and Calloway had come to listen to her narrative too, and Jack had his hand on the back of her seat, just inches from her neck. Allie knew her night-robe kept her more covered than her day gowns, but she was still aware of his closeness, and her dishabille. He had thrown on a Prussian blue coat, but wore no waistcoat or cravat, and his hair was tousled, curls falling onto his forehead. He smelled of smoke and brandy and some spiced cologne. For the first time in hours, it seemed, she felt safe.

Calloway had his coat on too, but without a shirt under it. His thick muscles and softer, hairier belly rippled in fury as he described what he would do to the varlet who had started the fire.

"I'd bet it was that dirty dish Sir Jethro Stevens," he said now, "what you threw out of the club t'other night for cheating."

The Runner wrote down the name. "Anyone else give you trouble recently, Captain?" he asked. "Anyone lose a big bundle at the tables, who might think he wouldn't have to pay if the place burned down?"

"We do not take vouchers here. No one leaves without paying their debts. If they owe their fellow gamblers money, that is between the gentlemen, but it is nothing to do with the club."

"What about Rochelle?" Downs asked. "She was as mad as a wet hen when you turned her off."

The Runner raised an eyebrow.

"That's Rachel Potts, who fancies herself Rochelle Poitier," Darla put in, "Cap'n Jack's mistress afore Miss Silver got here."

After writing the woman's name and direction, the Runner looked more closely at Allie in her plain flannel robe and unadorned virginal night gown, with her hair in a single long braid.

"But Rochelle took her revenge by spreading slander in the gossip columns," Jack quickly stated, seeing the speculation in the Bow Street man's eyes, "defaming our Miss Silver, who is my ward's governess, nothing more."

The Runner did not write that down, but he duly noted the steel edge to his employer's voice.

"I cannot see Rochelle coming to start a fire before dawn, either," Jack went on. "She was never one for early rising, or getting her hands dirty."

"She might have hired a bully boy," Calloway said, already savoring what he would do to the hired torch man.

"Anyone else?" Rourke asked.

They all looked at each other, then shook their heads. The Red and the Black was a popular spot, and Jack was a popular host. They had never been busier, which must mean customers enjoyed the club.

The Runner flipped through the pages of his Occurrence book, checking to see that he had missed nothing. "Well, it might have something to do with Lady Charlotte's disappearance, then."

"A child who disappeared fifteen years ago?" Jack asked, disbelieving the connection.

"Crimes were committed. Serious crimes. We know the man who caused the coach accident is dead, but he might have had helpers. Someone stole the heiress, and that someone could still hang. Mayhaps that person doesn't like your asking so many questions, or raising the reward money so high. This might have been a warning, like, telling you to back off the investigation."

"Never. If the club burns down I will open another and another after that, until I have the answers to my questions."

The Runner nodded, but looked around, at Harriet, Miss Silver, the pretty girls, and the loyal men. All of them would be in jeopardy, too.

"I'll hire night watchmen and more guards," Jack declared. "But I will not shut the club and I will not quit looking for my sister."

Allie tried to clap, but her hands hurt too much. "Good for you, Captain."

The Runner closed his book. "Well, there is always the possibility that the fire was set by a reformer, someone who just wanted to close down your club. There are those who do not approve of gambling at all, gaming parlors especially."

Jack's hands closed on Allie's shoulders. "Ah, but the one who disapproves most is the one who put out the fire."

The Runner stared at Allie again, making her cheeks turn warm—or was that the feel of the captain's touch? No, it must be the brandy.

Officer Rourke seemed to be done, and Harriet was stirring, so Allie said, "We really ought to be going to bed." She hurried to add, "Harriet and I. In the room we share. Upstairs."

Rourke put his pencil in his pocket. "Right, and I'll have another look around the place, talk to the neighbors to see if they heard anything suspicious, that kind of thing. Good day, Captain. I'll report back if I find anything. Pleasure to meet you, Miss Silver, even if under such conditions." He bowed and left, and the others drifted away to help with the cleanup or to seek their own beds.

Allie asked Calloway to carry Harriet for her, but Jack said he would do it. Then he said, "I have not properly thanked you, Miss Silver. Allie."

"It was nothing, really. I just acted without thought. Anyone else would have done the same, if not better." She added, "Jack," liking the sound of it on her tongue. Calling him by his first name could be no more improper than conversing in her nightclothes, practically alone except for a sick child and a half-empty bottle of brandy. Not much could be more improper,

Allie thought with a slight giggle. Now that had to be from the brandy, she told herself.

Jack seemed to be feeling the same lightness of spirits, for he grinned at her. "No one could have done better, my girl. You were a true heroine. You saved the club, and might have saved lives."

"Nonsense, Calloway or Cook would have smelled the smoke soon enough."

"But you did it, you, Miss Allison Silver, and I owe you my eternal gratitude." He was so relieved and so happy—and more than a little drunk with brandy and exhaustion—that he picked her up and twirled her around in an exuberant circle. "You are magnificent!" He laughed as she yelped in surprise, and bent to kiss her cheek before setting her back on her feet.

But Allie had turned to reprimand him. First names were one thing; embraces were quite another. Her face turned, his face turned, and instead of kissing her cheek, Jack found his lips were on hers. It was as if by magic, or fate, or sheer luck. It was like nothing either had felt before.

She did not scream, so he did not take his lips away. He added more pressure to the contact between their mouths and held her closer, against his body. Her lips softened under his, and his body hardened next to hers.

Allie told herself this was like the fire: Don't think, just do it. So she did, because she might never be kissed by a rake again, certainly not one who could make her feel so alive and important, not one who could start a fire in her blood with a mere kindling of a kiss. She kissed him back, ignorant despite all her education, but willing to learn, to experiment. Heaven knew how long the lesson in lovemaking might have lasted or how far she might have let his hands wander.

Hers were too clumsy in their bandages to do more than cling to his shoulders. His were pulling apart the braid of her hair, spreading the curls with his fingers down her back.

But then a thin little voice asked, "What about me, Papa Jack? I helped save the club from that cheat, didn't I?"

Allie jumped back, mortified that the child had seen such a display. But Jack smiled and went over to Harriet's chair. He picked her up, blanket and all, and twirled her around, the same way he had Allie. "You are magnificent too, poppet. And I am the luckiest man on earth to have the two of you."

He twirled Harriet again for good measure.

Which might not have been the best thing to do with a sick-to-her-stomach child.

CHAPTER FIFTEEN

•

Great golden gods, he'd kissed Miss Silver! Jack had not meant to, of course, no more than he'd meant to have a bath at dawn. Here he was, though, sitting in a tub of tepid water because there was no time to heat more.

Gads! Kissing the governess ought to have been like kissing his smelly old dog on the lips, only it wasn't. The kiss had been delightful, delicious, and Jack was dying to do it again.

The water in the tub was not cold enough to keep his body from remembering how she had felt in his arms, her unbound breasts against his chest. Who would have thought Miss Silver had breasts? And such soft ones, as soft as her lips under his, as soft as her sweet breath, as soft as those dark golden locks flowing through his fingers. Lud, he was not soft at all!

Jack was astounded, besides aroused. He'd had scores of Rochelle Poitiers, women who were nameless and faceless a month or a week or a day later—

but he had never felt like this. He'd never been so heated, for so long afterward, by a mere kiss. From a mere old maid. He must be losing his mind.

For sure he should be using his time to think of who wanted to destroy him and his club rather than how Miss Silver was destroying his equilibrium. Miss Silver, Allison, Allie. He rolled the names around as he used the washcloth. No, that was his fresh towel, leaving him nothing to dry himself with. His wits had truly gone begging. The woman was truly devastating his carefree life.

Carefree? Now he had a child to care for, a business to run, numerous dependents to safeguard, a charity to finance, a search to pursue, and ends to meet. He also had an uncomfortable urge for an unbeddable woman. Fighting the French was carefree by comparison.

He tried to bring his thoughts, and his throbbing, under control. Who was starting fires at his back door . . . and did he have to marry the woman? He'd already destroyed her reputation, through no fault of his own, and he would have decimated her virtue, stopping through no restraint of his own. No, Jack told himself, he would not have made love to Miss Silver on the craps table. He was still that much the gentleman. At least he would have carried her up to his bedroom.

No, no, no! She would have stopped him, Jack knew. She would have slapped him. The only reason she had not was the brandy, and the moment. The kiss they started by accident was a celebration of life after near death, a confirmation of pleasure after the dread of peril. He'd seen it in the army after battles, when men went crazy with lust for a woman to slake the lust for blood. He was no berserker, though, no madman with no control over his appetites. He would have come to his senses. Or so he prayed.

Or she would have. She'd gone all starry-eyed after one kiss, though. The woman was so ignorant of passion that she might not have protested if his fingers unbuttoned her nightgown, reaching for satiny skin. In her inexperience, she might not have noticed if his hand trailed down her thigh, lifting the flannel. The devil take it, she might have been as bewitched as he was, recklessly sharing in her own seduction, forgetting who she was and where she was.

But in the morning? Hell, he would not want to face Allie Silver after a night of illicit passion when the brandy wore off and her scruples woke up.

For that matter, Jack would not want to face himself in the morning if he'd tumbled the lady in the casino. Or his bedchamber. Or the backyard. He was no despoiler of innocents. Usually just thinking of his missing sister, unprotected by either father or brother, being deflowered by some dirty dish was enough to confirm his code of conduct. Introducing Harriet to his employees was a breach in that code, but it had been unavoidable. Seducing Miss Silver was not unavoidable, despite his body's protests. His principles could easily overcome his prick, couldn't they?

But what, a sneaky, snaky voice hissed in his inner ear, what if the lady wanted to be seduced? What if under those shapeless gowns and prim bonnets was a siren waiting to be stirred? She was not too old to have urges of her own, and who said all spinsters were happy in their untouched state? Miss Silver was an educator. Maybe she wanted to learn more about life for herself. Books could not begin to describe the rapture nor paintings depict the ecstacy of lovemaking. Jack could be the one to teach her.

And then he'd be the one to walk her down the aisle.

Which realization cured his ardent imagination and his arousal at the same time.

Goodness, she'd kissed a rake! Unfortunately, there was nothing whatsoever good about the experience. Oh, it was mind-numbing and toe-tingling and quite the most exciting sensation of Allie Silver's life, but kissing Jack Endicott was so bad as to be sinful.

Allie was not surprised he was proficient at it. A womanizer who could not please women was a contradiction in terms. The captain was practiced and polished and perfectly capable of making a female's legs turn boneless so she had to cling to him or fall on the floor in a puddle of passion. No, his prowess was no surprise. What was, was Allie's own shocking response. She'd kissed him back.

He had not meant to kiss her, she knew. Their lips had met by accident, and he, experienced seducer that he was, had taken advantage of the happenstance. But she had not pulled out of his embrace, had not protested, had not made him stop. She knew she could have ended the intimacy with a word or a gesture, without resorting to a slap or a well-placed knee. She had not. What she'd done was clutch his shoulders, press her body against his, and mew for him to deepen the kiss.

If Jack thought she was a wanton now, Allie could not blame him. She felt like a wanton, panting and perspiring after a mere kiss. Why, just recalling the moment made her heart beat faster and her lungs work harder. And it was only a kiss! To him, it must have been a chance encounter; to her, it was cataclysmic.

The problem—one of the problems—was that she

wanted more, a lot more. Which, of course, was how girls—and mature women who ought to know better—were led down the primrose path. The vicar was not waiting at the end of that path either, only a lifetime of ruin and regret.

So she had to leave.

Allie even had an idea of where to go this time. The lofty grandfather she never knew never missed a session of Parliament. He'd be in London now. Unless he never read the papers or listened to gossip, which Allie doubted, Lord Montford would now know that she was in London, too.

He would take her in rather than leave a stain on his family's escutcheons. He was too proud to do otherwise, she reasoned. She would have to swallow her own pride by going to him, the man who turned his back on his flesh and blood, but a marquess's approval could eradicate any blots on her own copybook. If he accepted her, the rest of the world would have to also.

The marchioness had passed away decades ago, unfortunately, or Allie's grandmother could have been a bigger help than Montford. Women were better at smoothing ruffled feathers and spreading propaganda. Then again, if Allie's grandmother had been alive, in touch with her daughter's family, Allie would not be in this fix now.

It was not as if Allie were asking the marquess for a competence or an allowance. She had no intentions of asking for a dowry, either, or the presentation she never had, in order to find a husband. At her age that would have been ludicrous. After this contretemps, a come-out would have been impossible even for a marquess to manage. No, she wanted nothing more from the man than the respectability of his house, a place to stay until she found another position as far from London and its pitfalls and temptations as possible.

Heaven knew Montford House was enormous enough to have a spare room for her. From her father's tales, the pile could host half the king's army. Allie might even have passed it on her way through London or to the park. She'd find it easily enough.

The marquess's heir, the Earl of Montjoy, was seldom in town, Allie knew. Her mother's brother preferred to stay in the north country and as far away from his domineering father as possible. Allie had never met her uncle, his wife, nor their two sons and a daughter, her cousins. She suffered no loss, her father had always said, since they were ninnyhammers all.

Allie had great hopes, now that she had settled on a solution, that the marquess would take Harriet in, too. Any right-thinking gentleman would understand that a gambling club was no place for a child. The wealthy marquess could easily win at court if he petitioned for guardianship of the orphaned girl. No judge would choose a ramshackle rogue over a trusted member of Parliament, an advisor to kings and princes.

Things might have been different if Jack's brother had been named Harriet's trustee. Lord Carde was said to be a serious, sober gentleman, although rumor had it that he'd once had three fiancées at one time. He was happily wed now, though, with a promising family, far from London.

Allie's grandfather was minutes away. Lord Montford had to take her in, for curiosity's sake, if for no other reason. She was his only daughter's child, and he had to be interested in her appearance at the very least. Allie knew she was curious to meet a man so stubborn he rejected a daughter who married without his blessings, so proud that a gentle scholar was not good enough to sit at his table.

Allie might have inherited her share of that pride,

but she had also been at Mrs. Semple's School for years, beholden to her employer, bound to follow her dictates. So she understood humility, too. She would go to Montford House and introduce herself to the marquess, humbly, courteously, like a lady. Like her mother's daughter.

She would go to Montford House, Allie decided, right after the *London Lookout* printed a retraction.

They did not set out from the club until after two the next afternoon. Harriet woke up near eight, fully recovered and hungry, but after a coddled egg and some toast went back to a restful sleep. So did Allie. Used to making do with little rest, Jack spent the time marshalling forces to protect his property and his people. In a way he was glad, because now he could employ more veterans from his old army unit both as guards and carpenters to repair the damage from the fire and the firemen's axes. They were happy for the work, despite the pittance he could pay, and they were good, loyal men. The club was sadly back in the debit column, but the cost was worth it.

The small party stopped first at Mr. Burquist's office, where he had long, legal-sounding documents ready for them in response to Jack's earlier message. The writs threatened the scandal sheet's publishers, printers, editors, and reporters with dire consequences. The solicitor also provided copies of Harriet's birth records, Hildebrand's so-called will, and Mrs. Crandall to act as Allie's companion in the coach.

Jack rode alongside, in case anyone was watching— or in case Harriet became sick again from the motion of the carriage.

James Coachman knew the way. He ought to, having driven Cap'n Jack to Rochelle Poitier's rooms on enough occasions. Allie tried not to think about that.

Or the kiss. Or how handsome Jack looked mounted on a horse, sitting as effortlessly as a god, if pagan gods rode horses. She would have to look that up . . . when she was not thinking about her grandfather, the newspaper, or the man who had kissed her.

Neither she nor Jack had mentioned anything about last night this morning. They had spoken of the fire, of course, and the extra guards, the inconclusive report from Mr. Rourke at Bow Street, and Mr. Burquist's efficiency. They had not spoken of personal matters, thank goodness. Allie thought she might have expired from embarrassment if he'd apologized, or died of shock if he'd proposed. This way she was merely mortified. Alive, but mortified. Harriet seemed to have forgotten the intimacy, if she'd even noticed it, and the captain was so used to casual affairs that he could ignore it. Allie decided to leave the entire episode in the far reaches of her mind.

Unfortunately, she left his clothes there, too, leaving the image of him half-dressed all too near.

"Are you all right, dearie?" Mrs. Crandall asked when Allie started fanning herself with her bonnet. "You are not coming down with something, are you?"

"Nothing, thank you." Just a touch of moon sickness, from which she would recover as quickly as Harriet had from her bout of indigestion. Allie firmly set her hat back upon her tightly gathered hair, made sure Harriet's ribbons were neatly tied, and stepped out of the carriage without taking the captain's hand when they arrived at the newspaper office.

Two people were visible in the small, cluttered office, a youth in a leather apron with ink-stained fingers, and an older, thinner man with tobacco-stained teeth. Jack approached the older man, a Henry Hapworth, at his desk. Only one chair faced the editor, so they all stood.

"We are here about an article that appeared in your . . . journal yesterday." Jack caught himself before he labeled the *London Lookout* a scandal sheet. That was what it was, of course, barely mentioning any news that was not salacious or startling. The truth was as foreign to the paper's pages as Hindustani would have been.

Jack placed his calling card on the man's desk.

Hapworth read it, then looked toward Allie, Harriet, and Mrs. Crandall, who were crowded into the small area between rolls of newsprint and machinery. "Ah, that article. Very popular, it was. We had to print more copies. And it made us a nice bit of the ready, it did, giving the other rags a shot at the story while it was still fresh."

Jack had wondered how the other gossip columns had the tale at the same time. "You sold the information to other reporters?"

"Gentlemen's arrangement, don't you know."

"*Gentlemen* do not deal in slander," Jack said.

Allie stepped closer, before Jack and the newspaper man could start trading insults. "The story was not true, sir, and we are here to request a retraction."

The editor shuffled papers until he found yesterday's issue. "And you wouldn't happen to be Miss Allison Silver, the Marquess of Montford's unacknowledged granddaughter, would you?"

Allie gave the shallowest of curtsies. "I have not had the pleasure of meeting my grandfather, no, but I am indeed the daughter of his only daughter. I am, or was, also an instructor at Mrs. Semple's School for Girls, where Miss Harriet Hildebrand was late a pupil." She pulled Harriet forward and prodded her into a curtsy, too. "I am now acting as the child's governess until other arrangements can be made."

Jack placed Harriet's baptismal records on the

man's desk. Allie put her references from Mrs. Semple beside them.

The editor, who was also the publisher, reporter, and street-corner hawker of the finished paper, looked at the documents, then at Jack. "You can't believe everything you read."

Jack snorted. "Especially in your newspapers. But you can see for yourself that Miss Silver is no lightskirt. Your story has defamed her reputation, and mine, of course, with your allegations of wrongdoing, to say nothing of casting doubt on the legality of a poor innocent orphan's birth."

The poor innocent orphan was disarranging an entire tray of type that was set for the next day's issue.

"Looks can be deceiving, too," the man insisted. "Shakespeare only used male actors, you know. That didn't make his Juliet a real lady."

Jack held the rest of Burquist's papers under the man's thin nose. "These say you must print a retraction or face legal consequences. Miss Harriet Hildebrand's father died in battle. I am her guardian. Miss Silver is her governess. That is as simple as ABC. Writing a paragraph for tomorrow's paper stating those facts should not be too hard for a clever man like yourself to compose."

"I don't know." Hapworth pretended to think, meanwhile rubbing his thumb and forefinger together. "The next issue is all set. It costs money to make changes."

Allie did not think it wise to mention that changes had already been made. The *London Lookout*'s next issue was looking like a higgledy-piggledy pile on the floor.

Jack, however, asked, "How much will it take to insert the new paragraph?"

"You are not going to pay him to recant his mistruths, are you?" Allie was aghast at the idea. That was paying a perjurer for committing a crime. Next Jack would be offering a reward to the man who started the fire, for not burning the house down.

Jack told her, "It is faster than waiting for the courts to force him. And less expensive. Burquist does not work for free either, you know." He emptied his thin purse. "Ten shillings is all I have. You'll have to take it or leave it and wait for the magistrate to come shut down your paper."

"What, stifle free speech and the right of the press? The government wouldn't dare, not after seeing what the Frenchies did." The shillings disappeared.

"Indecent, that's what it is," Allie said, fuming.

"I agree," Hapworth told her with a grin, showing more of his discolored teeth than she wanted to see. "T'other swell paid me twenty."

"Someone else paid you to print a correction?"

"That's right. His nibs's secretary, anyway."

Allie added a precious shilling from her own pocket. "Who?"

"Why, the Marquess of Montford, of course, your granddad."

Allie smiled, a tightness in her chest easing. Blood was thicker than water, or newsprint ink, after all. She did have family, and she was right to throw herself on their mercy and his lordship's hospitality. She smiled proudly at Jack. "Lord Montford does care about me."

"Aye," Hapworth said. "He cares enough that he paid me to say his granddaughter was dead."

CHAPTER SIXTEEN

"How dare he!"

"What, did you expect the owner of a scandal sheet to be an honorable man? Or to make himself look foolish for free? He is in the business of making money, not giving it away." Jack took Allie's arm and led her back toward the carriage before she could stick her tongue out at Mr. Hapworth, the way Harriet was doing. Curtains were already twitching aside in the neighboring houses. Heaven knew what the onlookers would make of a furious, frumpy female making a scene on the street.

"No, not him. *Him*, the Marquess of Montford. How could my own grandfather pay someone to say I was dead?"

Jack held the carriage door, hoping she would get in before Rochelle spotted them from her window above the printer. He did not need another angry woman on his hands. "To him, you are."

Allie did not get into the coach. "I am not dead!"

"Of course you are not." Although soon more than one gentleman might wish . . . "You are very much alive, and so Hapworth will have to report."

Mrs. Crandall was already seated in the carriage. Harriet was—"Deuce take it, brat, get away from my horse before you get stepped on! He is not used to children."

"Can I ride him?"

"Of course not!"

"I think you should reconsider, Captain," Allie said. "In fact, I think that would be a very good idea. You should take Harriet up in front of you and go to the park. Show how proud you are to have her as your ward. Introduce her to your acquaintances as your fallen friend's daughter. Show the world that there is nothing to be ashamed of in her birth or in your guardianship."

The last time he'd been near to Harriet he'd needed a bath. "Fine, we can all go, in the carriage."

"No, I have other errands," Allie said, walking toward the corner. "If you wish to take the coach, I can find a hackney driver."

"Dash it, you cannot be thinking of going on more job interviews, can you? Wait for the retraction, at least. You will stand a better chance." A pygmy head-hunter stood a better chance of getting a governess position than Miss Silver. "In a few days I should hear from my brother. He or his wife might know of a teaching post for you."

"My errand is not about seeking employment. It is a matter of life and death. Mine. Or Montford's."

Jack mistrusted that murderous look in Miss Silver's eyes. Lord, if she attacked Montford, they would never be free of the scandal, no matter how much money he spent. To his regret, however, the prim and preachy female had turned into a virago right in front of his eyes—and the eyes of anyone watching. "Why do we not get into the coach and discuss this?"

Allie signified her agreement with a jerk of her head, but she went toward the driver's position instead. "James, do you know the location of Montford House?"

"A'course, miss. Everyone does. Right on Grosvenor Square it is."

"Fine, then take me there. Captain, you can follow with your horse or you can ride inside, but I am going to visit my grandfather."

How had he lost control of the situation, to say nothing of his own carriage and driver? Jack was glad to see that Allie had spirit, that the slur from her relations had not left her despondent, but he was sorry to see she was a peagoose. What did she hope to accomplish by confronting Montford except more humiliation, if the man did not physically toss her out? Which of course meant that Jack had to go along to protect her. He followed her into the coach, after tying his horse behind.

"Have you ever seen the man?" he asked Allie.

"No. Why? Does he have two heads?"

"Do you know anything about him?"

"Other than that he is rich, and that his son cannot bear to live with him? No, for my father would not speak ill of the man. But are you trying to frighten me? It will not work. I am going."

Jack did not know Montford except by sight and reputation, but what he knew was not encouraging. With nearly seventy years in his dish, the power of the Crown behind him, and a vast fortune at his fingertips, Montford made his own rules. "The marquess is known to be a . . . formidable presence. It is obvious your grandfather is not a warm, friendly man. So why would you want to meet him? I fear you are wasting your time if you hope he'll welcome you with open arms."

"I am not that big a fool. He never forgave my mother in all these years, so why should he forgive me for living? But he does not have the right to deny my existence. I know I cannot move a boulder. But I can carve my name in it."

"With a knife?" Harriet sat forward, eager to know more. "Are you going to stab him? I have my sling-shot. Papa Jack must have a sword, even if he traded his pistols. We could go home and get it and—"

"No!" they both shouted at once.

Mrs. Crandall was cringing against the leather cushions. She had made it through the wars alive; she did not want to hang for attacking a nobleman now that her future was looking so rosy. "I'll be getting out on the next corner, then."

Allie and Jack both said no again. "I need you with me for propriety's sake," Allie told the older woman. "And you, Captain, will keep an eye on Harriet."

He'd rather face the lion in his den. "I will come with you."

"No, I have to do this myself."

The carriage was slowing. Mrs. Crandall was still protesting, more loudly when she saw the edifice in front of them. "Miss, I don't belong in no marquess's mansion. You'd do better with Cap'n Jack at your back. He was born to this folderol. And he's been in the thick of battle, too."

"You belong wherever you wish to go, Mary. You are brave and loyal, and your husband died so that rich aristocrats like this one can enjoy their advantages over the rest of us. Besides, would you rather take Harriet and her slingshot to the park?"

Mrs. Crandall was at her side in a flash. Jack was

holding Harriet's hand, feeling forlorn. He ought to be leading the charge, not babysitting. He was the knight errant and Allie was the damsel in distress, damn her. Jack Endicott had never let another man fight his battles though, not since his big brother defended him against bullies at school. He could understand that Allie needed to kill her own dragons. He could even admire her for having more bottom than half the raw recruits he'd trained. He only hoped she did not get too badly singed in the confrontation.

"We shall be right across the street if you need reinforcements," he said. "But the coach will stay in front of Montford House in case you need to make a quick retreat."

She gave him a quick smile, only slightly tremulous, and said, "And do not feed the animals."

"We are not going to the zoo— Oh, Harriet. Right."

The butler at Montford House was so stiff he could have been an old-fashioned wig-stand, complete with white powdered sausage curls. He stared over Allie's shoulder and announced that his lordship was not at home.

"Fine, then I shall await his return."

"I regret that his lordship shall not be at home later either, miss."

Allie wondered if the marquess would ever be at home to a young woman without an appointment, especially an unwanted scrap of the family's dirty linen. "I shall take my chances and wait anyway."

"I regret that will be impossible. We cannot entertain company in his lordship's absence."

"I am not asking you to play charades or sing an aria. Now I can wait in one of the many receiving rooms this house must possess, or I can wait in the street, introducing myself to all and sundry who pass by. I did mention that I was Lord Montford's grand-daughter, did I not?"

"This way, miss."

In short order Allie found herself in a magnificent room filled with priceless works of art, relieved that Harriet was not with her. Mrs. Crandall gladly followed the butler to the servants' hall for refreshments, where she would be more comfortable. With the door left ajar, Allie thought she heard furtive footsteps as the household tried to catch a glimpse of the family's Fallen Woman. She did not care. Let them look, for she herself could happily spend the rest of the day here, studying the canvases and sculptures in their niches, the jade figurines in the glass cases.

True to his contrary nature, Montford sent for her before she could admire even one wall of treasures. He'd been home all along, of course.

This time Allie followed the poker-backed butler deeper into the house to a smaller room, a library lined with bookcases. She could have spent days here too, just looking at the titles on the leather-bound volumes. Lord Montford seemed willing to permit her five minutes. Without rising from behind his vast desk, the marquess tossed her a leather purse of coins.

"Here. Take this and get out of London. You are not wanted. Your presence is an offense to us."

Allie caught the heavy pouch in her sore hands rather than let it hit her. Then she took three steps closer to the desk and made a deep, courtly curtsy. When she rose, she set the pouch on the highly polished cherry wood. "Grandfather" was all she said.

The old man turned purple. The color did not complement his steel gray hair or the liver spots on his cheeks. He was a large man, she noted, without an ounce of fat. His hand shook slightly, but he sat erect, staring at Allie as if she were last week's leftover fish course. "I. Am. Not. Your. Grandfather."

Allie remained standing beside the leather armchair he did not invite her to take. She kept her own spine as straight as a broomstick. "Yes, sir, you are. And I am no more happy about that fact than you."

"How dare you come to my house, you insolent wench."

Allie crossed her arms over her chest. She would not let this aged autocrat intimidate her. He might have been a cabinet minister and was obviously an eminent art collector, but he was nothing more than a mean, nasty old man. She might be afraid of London and being alone, but she would not fear a mere misanthrope. "How dare I? How dare you try to declare me dead? I am very much alive, and in London, whether you like it or not."

"Causing another scandal. Just like your mother."

"My mother was a lady. The only scandal she caused was marrying the man she loved, against your wishes. She never, ever, did anything shameful. Nor have I. You are the one who ought to be ashamed of your actions."

The marquess sucked in a breath. "You dare to lecture me?"

"Why not? You are the one who condemned me on the evidence of a notorious scandal sheet, believing your own flesh and blood could sink to such depravity. Illegitimate children, illicit affairs? All lies."

"So you say. There is enough truth in the tale to make you a byword in town. Get out, I say."

Allie stood her ground. "Not until I have had the rest of my say. I might have destroyed my reputation, but you, sir, have destroyed my respect for the nobility. You are the one who was born to wealth and privilege yet has forgotten that with such a legacy comes great responsibility. You have turned your back on those most deserving of your care and consideration, out of foolish pride. You did not do anything to earn your title or fortune. Both were handed to you at birth. Yet you forget that others need to make their own way in this world."

"You would teach me, Marquess of Montford, about noblesse oblige? You are more fool than that father of yours."

"My father was right, that there is little noble about you but your house and possessions. You are an old man who deprived himself of a beautiful, loving daughter. You chose not to know the kind, learned gentleman she married, and you are choosing again to repudiate their only child, your own kin."

"No, you are no kin of mine, I say. Your mother ceased being my family when she took up with that poor scholar. I told her he wanted her money only, but she would not listen. He never got his greedy fingers on a shilling of my blunt."

"My father was so greedy that he gave half his academy's income away in scholarships to needy boys. He housed indigent professors, and he fed hungry students, on his own money, none of yours. My mother gladly wore her old clothes and went without jewels and carriages and servants—what your money could have provided—because she had something far more valuable. But you would not recognize that, would you, my lord, a love that transcends material interests?"

"She could have married the heir to a dukedom, by George!" he said, pounding on the desk, his face gone pale now.

Allie stopped worrying that he would have apoplexy and die on his elegant Aubusson carpet. "And she could have been miserable with him, a man chosen for dynasty-building instead of love. Does that not matter to you, even now? Then I pity you. You never saw how happy your own daughter was, how my parents shared a perfect communion, despite the deprivations."

"Bah! Buried in the country, seeing no one but runny-nosed boys, who else could she commune with? The chickens?"

"At least chickens repay one's affection with eggs. But I suppose you would have been pleased to see my mother wretched with her lordling, waiting for his father to die so she might be a duchess. Affection would mean nothing to you, in light of your ambition. Well, think on this, old man. If you had handed over the dowry promised to my mother, she might have had a finer home with more servants. Who knows but she might have had better medical care than my father could afford. You contributed to the death of your only daughter, Lord Montford, and for that I shall never forgive you."

"Hah! As if I care what a hoity-toity old maid thinks. Blame your father instead, girl, for he kept her in poverty. A decent man would have walked away from my daughter. No, a gentleman would never have approached her in the first place, when they were so ill-matched."

"They met in a bookstore, I was told. And they shared a love for books and learning, until death parted them. Or did you not even know how well suited they were in everything but your foolish social castes? And lack of funds aside, my mother would have had it no other way if they were together. My father sacrificed his own career to found a school. He made a living for them the best way he could."

"The way he is providing for you now?" Montford said with a sneer. "Look at you, a homely spinster with the tongue of an adder and the effrontery of an ape. You do not know the world, and you do not know your place in it." He snapped thick-knuckled, arthritic fingers. "So much for your learned sire. He did not leave you a groat to live on, and he did not leave you with the savvy of a newborn babe. It is no wonder no man will wed you, much less make you his mistress."

"For once you are correct, and I thank you for believing that much. I am no man's mistress, and no man's chattel to be tossed away if I do not follow his rules or obey his foolish dictates."

Montford was on his feet now, leaning on the desk and breathing heavily. "Get out. That is a dictate for you, one that you will obey or I'll have the servants toss you out. I'll send for the Watch, accuse you of trespassing or stealing, anything to see you on a prison ship for Botany Bay. Don't think I can't do it, woman, and keep it out of the gossip columns, too, because I will not let you debase my family name more than you already have. Get out," he repeated, pointing with trembling hand at the door. "Take the money and get out of London. You are willful, just like your mother. You are not even half as pretty as she was, or half as intelligent. At least my daughter had the sense to marry the father of her brat."

Allie picked up the purse—a regrettably heavy one—and tipped it upside down, so coins fell onto the desk, some rolling to the floor. "I would not take a ha'penny from you, no, not even were Harriet Hildebrand my own child and we were starving on the street. I would rather sell my body then than sell my soul to you." She gave the purse one last shake and a last gold coin bounced out, making a pinging sound in the silence. "I shall make do on my own, the same as my parents did, without your help. But know this, old man: I am proud of my name, too. Allison Silver. That is Allison *Montford* Silver. And I am staying here in London. Get used to it, my lord, because you cannot do anything about it."

Outside, Jack was watching Montford House through the park gates. He'd given the guard a bribe to let him and Harriet pass through the private entrance. His brother lived on the opposite side of the square anyway, and Jack told the man he had forgotten to borrow the key. Mention of the Earl of Carde, a coin, and a smile worked as usual, except on Miss Silver.

Damn, he should have gone in with her. Old Montford would make mincemeat of the silly woman. Jack would have followed Allie, despite her wishes, but then he'd be facing the old curmudgeon himself, who had every right to ask his intentions.

Jack did not have intentions, dash it! Not honorable ones, and not dishonorable ones either. He could not afford a wife, even if he wanted one, which he did not. And he could not offer a marquess's granddaughter a slip on the shoulder. Seeing Montford House, knowing that Allie belonged in that world, not his own shadowy milieu, firmed up his resolve. There could be no more lusting after the governess. No more lewd thoughts of the bluestocking without her stockings. No more firmness in his fundaments. He might not be her knight in shining armor, but he would still be a gentleman and leave her a lady, by Jupiter.

So she had to leave. He had to find another solution to the problem, even though it would be breaking his word to Harriet to send her and Miss Silver away. He could not break his own code of honor, though.

Harriet would recover. He would, too, despite the little imp's worming her way into his heart. He was sorry. Harriet was . . . in a tree.

Damnation, what happened to little girls sitting with their samplers and their dolls, learning to pour a proper tea? Miss Silver would have his head if Harriet fell and broke her leg. As it was, the halfling was filthy, her pinafore was ripped, and her hair was full of twigs, like some wild little forest creature. A wood sprite, that's what Hildebrand's brat was, and he would miss her sorely. Almost as sore as his head when she landed on it, coming down. He forgot about the pain when Miss Silver appeared.

"Where to now?" he asked after he had handed Allie and Mrs. Crandall into the carriage.

"I wish to go home."

"Home to . . . wherever you lived before Mrs. Semple's School?" Jack asked, thinking that her grandfather might have made provision for her after all. Jack would have been astounded, but relieved, too, in having his own problem fixed. He did not want to question Allie about her conversation with the marquess until they were alone, however. She was not looking at him, and not noticing that Harriet looked like a street urchin either. At least Allie was not crying, he thought, or bleeding, or running from the authorities.

She stepped into the carriage. "Home to The Red and the Black, of course. Where else?"

CHAPTER SEVENTEEN

.

"Hooray!" Harriet shouted. "I told you the old skint would not help her leave us! You owe me a pony, Papa."

Allie put on her schoolmistress voice. "You will please show respect for your elders, miss, especially my grandfather. And I will have you know that the old skint did offer me a handsome purse to leave you. To leave London, anyway."

Jack had sent his horse home with a groom. He took his seat next to Harriet, across from Allie and Mary Crandall. "But you did not take it," he guessed.

"No, I did not. I am staying."

Mrs. Crandall let out a sigh of relief and Harriet whooped again, until the driver called back, "Everything all right in there, Cap'n?"

"No. That is, yes, everything is fine, James. Drive on. But no, you are not staying, Miss Silver."

Allie had made her mind up. Aggravating Lord Montford into apoplexy was only part of her decision.

"Yes, I am. I realize this is in contradiction to everything I have said before, but I have concluded that I
am needed here."

"It is my club, my house, and my ward. I say no."

"Papa!"

"Hush, Harriet, this is between the captain and myself. Sir?"

Jack took a deep breath, knowing that what he was
about to say would reek of hypocrisy and stink of self-
serving. "I have concluded that your staying at The
Red and the Black is not proper."

He was right. Miss Silver clucked her tongue in a
very governesslike manner. "Now? After all this time?
I have been telling you since the moment I arrived
that my being at The Red and the Black, that Harriet
being there, was not proper."

"Too bad we did not have a wager. I would have
owed you a horse, too."

"Do not be preposterous. You asked me to stay. In
fact you nearly begged me not to leave you alone with
a child you did not know. You offered me a considerable salary and you made concessions." Rochelle Poitier's name remained unspoken, but her dismissal
hung in the air between them, a concession with clout.

"That was then, this is now," Jack insisted.

"Nothing has changed."

"Everything has changed. You are Montford's granddaughter, for one."

"I was born Montford's granddaughter. I am no
more his kin today than I was yesterday. In fact, I am
less, because now I have no wish to acknowledge the
connection either."

Jack ignored her reasoning. "And Hapworth printed
his vile lies."

"He is retracting them in the morning."

"In type so small no one will be able to read it, if

they find the notice in the back of the newspaper where he will bury it."

"But I shall know it is there. You and Harriet already know the truth, as does Mr. Burquist and the staff of the club. Who else matters?"

Jack started tapping his riding crop against his high-topped leather boots. "You used to think that the good opinion of every soul in London mattered, if not the entire British Empire, in case you were applying for a position in India."

"And you yourself taught me how foolish that was, especially since I already have employment. Your very career is an example of living one's life according to one's own self-determination, no one else's."

Jack ignored having his own reasoning tossed back at him when he was trying to argue the opposite case, damn it. "In addition," he went on, as if Miss Silver had not spoken, "Harriet and I are well acquainted now, so I have no qualms about managing her upbringing. She is a perfectly behaved young lady."

Mary Crandall coughed into her hand, but Harriet told him, "Papa, your nose will grow if you keep telling such lies, and your eyes will cross. That is what Mrs. Semple always said, anyway."

"Do be still, Harriet. This is an adult conversation."

"I thought it was about me. Don't I get to help decide if Miss Silver stays, Papa?"

"No. You are too young to understand the entire situation."

Allie understood perfectly. She was not too young. She was simply not old enough to be residing under a gentleman's roof without raising eyebrows. Now that she was known to be of the captain's own social class— the one he was born into, anyway—he could not play so fast and loose with her reputation, not without wedding her. His code of gentlemanly conduct could not let Captain Endicott keep a wellborn woman of marriageable age in bachelor quarters. A poor governess without connections, or a middle-aged one, was a horse of a far different, less socially damning, color. He might not care what that society thought of him, but he cared mightily about staying single.

"Captain," she told him, "you can stop weaving rationale out of moon beams. I do not know whether you are more concerned with my elevated relatives or my lowered reputation, but understand this: I have no expectations. Beyond my salary, that is."

Harriet looked at Jack. "What does she mean, no expectations? Does that mean you won't buy her a horse, too?"

"It means, my dear," Allie told her, not looking at the captain, "that I do not expect him to offer marriage. And if he did, for some rattle-brained reason, I would refuse. I would never wed the owner of a common gambling den."

"The Red and the Black is not common in the least," Jack protested.

"It is top of the trees," Harriet proudly confirmed. "With brand new decks of cards every night and real candles, not tallow."

"Ah, how could a body resist? But no, Harriet, it is still a place where gentlemen come to drink beyond their capabilities, wager beyond their means, and behave beyond the pale with the pretty women. A governess takes whatever position is available. A lady does not, because she has to think of her children's future. Shall her sons grow up to be cardsharps and ivory tuners? Her daughters dealers? That is if her husband did not gamble away their school fees or their very home. Those children would never be received in polite society, never have choices in selecting their own careers or spouses." She turned to face Jack, smiling as if to prove that there was nothing personal in her rejection of an offer that had not been made. "So you see, sir, you are safe."

The riding crop beat faster against his leg. "You still cannot stay."

He was serious. Allie had not believed him to be, before. Now she had to. The smile faded from her lips as she clutched her nearly empty reticule, remembering the coins she had tossed at her grandfather's feet. She had just burned whatever bridge had not already collapsed under her; now her lifeboat was breaking apart. She only hoped no one would notice the catch in her throat as she asked, "Shall you simply toss me out, then?"

"Of course not, damn it. Do not be a widgeon."

"Papa, you are not supposed to curse in front of a lady. And I don't think you are supposed to call her a kind of duck, either. A turtledove, maybe."

"Peageese, both of them," Mary Crandall muttered.

But Allie was smiling again. Jack was still the quixotic gentleman she knew and—liked. She could relax back onto the cushions for the first time since entering the carriage. In fact, her spine felt as if it had not curved since they had stormed Mr. Hapworth's office. She pitied the Montford butler because he must never get to bend.

She pulled Harriet closer to her for a hug. "I bet the captain has a plan."

"Damn—Deuce right, I do. And I thought we were supposed to stop wagering with the infant."

"I am not an infant and I am not going away."

"You have not heard the plan, brat."

Harriet snuggled closer to Allie. "You said I could stay."

"I agreed you could stay for awhile, not forever. Besides, you will not be so very far away."

"Where?" Harriet asked so Allie did not have to.

"At the House of Cards. That is, Carde House. On the other side of Grosvenor Square from Montford House. It is my brother's, of course, but he's the best of good fellows and I should be hearing from him any day. The place is being renovated and refurbished, which is why I did not send you there at first. All of the usual staff has gone to the country with Ace and Nell or are on holiday, so no one is there but the workmen. You shall have to fend for yourselves a bit, I am afraid, because I cannot afford to hire many temporary servants, but you can still take meals with us, or Cook can send supper over to you."

Mrs. Crandall was nodding her approval, and Allie was weighing the possibilities. Harriet still had her brows furrowed. "I don't see what difference it makes."

Jack studied the whip as if it might have become damaged with his restless twitching. "You see, snip, no gentleman would ever invite anyone, ah, less than respectable to his family home. My sister-in-law, Lady Carde, could come to town with her children and I would never ask her to share her town house with a . . ." He fumbled for a word.

Harriet nodded wisely. "Birds do not foul their own nests. That's what Mrs. Semple always said."

"Exactly. So Miss Silver's reputation will not suffer worse than it already has. And Carde House is definitely a better environment for a child."

"But I like the club!"

"And you will like Carde House. There is a real nursery, with a schoolroom and a sitting room filled with toys. Alex might have taken the toy soldiers for his son, but Lottie's dolls are still there, I'd wager."

Harriet brightened at the mention of the soldiers, but frowned again. "Who wants dolls?"

"Most little girls. But there must be a model sailboat or two, spillikins, and shelves of books about pirates and lost princes. You'll like them. If not, we'll see what's in the attics after the exterminators are done."

"Exterminators?" Allie asked in a weak voice. Vermin were worse than vices, in her nightmares.

Jack was not concerned. "Ace never mentioned termites, so I doubt the walls will collapse on your head."

"Mice?" Harriet sat up, pulling away from Allie. "Can I have some? I'll keep them in a cage."

Allie shuddered.

Jack noticed and said, "That does not appear likely. But Carde House has its own stable mews, so we can see about getting you a pony so you can ride in the park. You'll like that."

"By myself?"

"Of course not." Great gods, who knew what trouble Harriet could find on the back of a horse? "Can you even ride?"

Harriet shook her head no. Jack turned to Allie with a raised eyebrow. She had to admit she could not either.

"I'll come visit whenever I can, to give you both riding lessons."

Harriet did not seem convinced.

"Meantime, there is the park right across the street, and the gardens behind the house. There's a fountain and, um, an orangery." He tried to recall what games he and his brother had played. "There used to be an archery target, and a croquet set."

Harriet's bottom lip was jutting out and starting to tremble. "You said."

Oh, lord. "I'll let you take the dog."

"I want a kitten."

Ace would kill him, turning his newly refurbished home into a menagerie. He compromised, or gave in, whichever definition one chose to use. "The cat stays in the stables."

Allie was thinking. "We will need a maid to help with laundry and cooking and baths. I have not had much experience with household chores, but I am willing to learn. I can pay her wages from my salary since I will not have to pay room and board. Without a position, I would have had to take lodgings elsewhere anyway."

"Absolutely not," Jack said. "Harriet is my responsibility, heaven help me, so her comfort is my responsibility also. You are being paid to teach her and be her companion, not to spend your own money."

Allie knew Jack's economic well-being was not in the pink of health. He had pawned his pistols, hadn't he? Yet she also knew gentlemen were prickly about their finances. They were finicky about their pride and their honor, too, so all she said was, "Are you certain?"

"What, that I can afford a housemaid until Alex's staff returns? Of course. And I can have one of the new men sleep there too, to act as man of all work, messenger, majordomo, whatever. I am already paying his salary, so his lodgings make no nevermind."

Allie was relieved. The notion of sleeping alone in a huge empty house at night then dealing with strange workmen during the day was daunting. The captain would never hire anyone untrustworthy, so she and Harriet would be secure. "And Mrs. Crandall? Shall Mary come, too?"

Jack looked at the older woman, a question in his eyes.

"I reckon I might, for a bit. A certain gentleman is thinking he can have a housekeeper and a bed warmer without benefit of clergy. He might see things different iffen I don't dance to his tune so fast. And there won't be any niffy-naffy servants to look down on me, neither. 'Sides, Miss Silver, did you mean what you said about teaching me to read?"

"Of course. Then the gentleman will come to admire you even more."

"So we are agreed?" Jack asked.

"I want a canary."

"Too late, snip. You settled for a kitten in the stable. You could have held out for a parrot, because I'd have bought an aviary just to be rid of you," he teased, ruffling her red curls so Harriet knew he did not mean anything by his words. Then he addressed Allie again, just as the coach pulled to a halt outside The Red and the Black. "I will need a day or two to make the arrangements. I'll have to notify the architect and ensure that at least one wing will be habitable, even if he has to postpone some of the other repairs. There will be workers and noise and paint smells, I am afraid, but at least you will be respectably fixed."

"A few days more will not make a difference, and I would feel happier knowing we had your brother's permission."

"I have told you, Alex is top of the trees. He would demand that you stay at his house, were he here."

Were the earl in town, none of the past week's events would have occurred. But Allie smiled as he handed her down from the carriage, this time taking the hand he offered and not pulling away when he held hers longer than necessary. Her blistered palm did not hurt at all in his.

Harriet was pulling on his coattails. "But you will come to visit, won't you, Papa Jack?"

"Of course I will. I'd miss Joker too much otherwise."

When they reached the red door, Jack told Harriet to take the dog into the rear yard, to explain the move to him. She skipped off, chattering about the squirrels to chase in the park, the whole of Carde House to explore, and the kitten. "You'll learn to like cats," she told the lumbering old hound. "And you won't miss Cap'n Jack at all, 'cause he'll come see us. Every day," she added louder, for the captain's benefit.

Allie touched Jack's arm before going upstairs to her rooms. "Are you certain about this? I mean, no matter how frugally we live, there is still the expense of another whole household. I would be happy to defer my salary until the next quarter."

"What, and have no funds for fripperies and such? Did you think I did not notice that your gloves are darned and you seem to possess three gowns? You are entitled to your wages, every shilling of them. Lud knows no one else would take on the brat. But I shall manage, so do not worry. I still have a few possessions I can punt on tick. Pawn, that is. And I can take a hand in some of the deeper card games. That is how I made enough money to purchase the club, after all."

"But you could lose!"

"Then I would apply to my brother for a loan." His voice took on a bitter edge. "That is not what I wished to do when I set out. I wanted to prove to him, and myself, I suppose, that I could make my own way in the world."

Allie reached out to touch his hand. "I am sorry if you have to go to him for us."

He grasped her hand in his much larger one. "I will be sorry if it comes to that too, but I will be able to pay him back soon enough. More importantly, you will be safe away from here."

Allie tried to ignore the fact that he still held her hand, which was hard to do since her fingers were tingling and growing warm in her glove, despite the bandages. "Safe?" she asked, diverting her thoughts from the unfamiliar feelings. "You cannot think the arsonist had me in mind when he set the fire, do you? I cannot believe Montford would go so far to get rid of an insignificant connection, no matter how undesirable."

"No, the danger is not Montford, and not the fire-starter, although I would love to learn that dastard's identity. But you will be safer at Carde House, safer from me. I suppose I should apologize for the liberties I took last night, but I am not going to. Worse, I cannot promise that it will not happen again. That is why you cannot stay here."

"You . . . want to kiss me again?" It wasn't just a moment's madness, after the fire and the furor?

Jack raised her hand, darned glove, bandages and all, to his lips, but he turned her hand over and found the inch of skin between her glove and her sleeve. He kissed that. "You'll never know how much."

"Me? Not just any woman?"

"You, Miss Allison Montford Silver. I would kiss you until your knees went weak."

They already were.

"And your breath caught in your lungs."

It already was.

"And you let me take your hair down."

His other hand was already reaching to pull out the hairpins.

"And you let me carry you up to my bedchamber."

Allie was already packing for Carde House.

CHAPTER EIGHTEEN

Allie found the housemaid she needed, although she had not been looking for one in the tiny rear yard of the gaming club where she'd gone to find Harriet. Now that she was officially employed as the child's governess, Allie felt she owed it to Captain Endicott to do a better job of watching his ward. Neither Harriet nor the dog was in the small enclosed area, though, but Allie stayed anyway. Her official position could officially start in a few minutes, after she had time to reflect on recent events.

She sat on the hard bench, barely noticing the chill in the air or the straggling weeds in the garden. A spindly rosebush drooped against the rear stone wall, its flowers all gone, its leaves brown and shriveled. Allie did not see it, only a tall, erect, brown-haired man in her mind's eye.

He was doing what he did not wish to do—borrowing his brother's house, perhaps borrowing his brother's money—for her, not Harriet. Harriet was already tainted with scandal by her mother's murder and her uncle's guilt. Even if the new Lord Hildebrand returned from India rich and reformed, Harriet might never be considered fit company for other daughters of the aristocracy. Whether she lived in a casino or a castle was not going to make much difference. And she was too young to care.

But Allie had to care, and now Jack did, too. He was sacrificing himself and his pride so that she could keep a bit of hers. The very thought almost brought tears to Allie's eyes. No, that had to be the cold breeze. She could not cry because someone was kind to her, could she?

The simple fact was that years had gone by since anyone cared enough about Allie to put her best interests ahead of their own. Now the owner of a gaming establishment was doing just that. A hell-raker with a good heart, the gambler was actually gambling on her, a governess! Jack Endicott had to be the nicest man she had ever met. He was also the most practiced libertine, of course, but he was still kind, still caring. Allie could not help being touched.

She could not help the warmth inside her that ignored the frigid temperature outside, either, not when she recalled the tender touch of Jack's lips on her wrist.

If people had seldom noted Allie's existence since her father's death, even fewer had noticed her in a womanly fashion. The French dancing master at Mrs. Semple's had often tried to steal a kiss, and Lady Beatrice's older brother had once pinched her, but schoolmistresses were not generally mistress material.

Now a genuine London womanizer wanted to seduce her, plain Allie Silver. That was what he said, anyway. He'd also said he would not, because he was a gentleman and she was a lady.

Just knowing that Jack considered her a lady raised Allie's temperature two degrees. Knowing that he desired her, that she had not been the only one stirred by their kiss, set her blood to simmering. A man who could have all the Rochelle Poitiers he wanted, wanted her. Allie's bosom might not match Miss Poitier's in plentitude, but, oh, it swelled now. For the first time in her life, discounting the slap she'd given Lady Beatrice's brother, Allie felt the power of a woman. She could attract a man, arouse a man, appeal to a man's senses.

Unfortunately, she also felt, also for the first time, the power and the pull of an attractive male. Why, she nearly forgot her own name when Jack merely kissed her wrist! She might have let Jack seduce her— again—but Mr. Downs had come into the hall to speak about ordering more wine.

Of course Jack was not going to seduce her. He'd dredged up scruples instead. He was sending her away, which was proper and polite . . . and Puritanical. Her own Don Juan had turned into a disappointing Don Won't.

Allie scolded herself for having such unworthy thoughts. She was rescued, her rightful place as a respectable female restored. She was wanted, as a woman but not as a wanton. She ought to be relieved.

So why was she weeping?

The warm tears might be hers, but those sobs were not. Her heart was not broken, Allie told herself, only a bit tattered around the edges, like her cloak. She pulled it closer around her, but the sounds continued. Now she heard a moan intermingled with the sobs, and a muffled prayer for help.

She was obviously not the intended recipient of that plea, but Allie could not ignore the pitiful cry. "Hallo?" she called.

The sounds all ceased.

"Are you in trouble?"

She got no reply.

Allie sat and waited, until she thought she heard a sniffle. She went over to the side of the wall where she thought the sound was coming from, and called again. This time she thought she heard a scuffling, as of something being dragged, or someone creeping farther away. Allie knew she ought to go inside and fetch Calloway or Downs or one of the new guards if Captain Endicott was busy. That's what she would have ordered Harriet to do. But they were all busy, and Jack had already gone to enough trouble on her behalf today. Besides, she might have been imagining the whole thing.

She looked at the garden wall. It was not very high, just a bit taller than she was. Even if she jumped up, she could not look over. The stones, though, were uneven, and easily climbable—for a man in breeches or a monkey or Harriet. Allie told herself she would have been furious with Harriet for doing such a thing, even as she tucked up the skirt of her gown to keep it out of her way.

She would purchase new gloves as soon as she and Harriet were installed in their new house, so Allie did not worry about further tearing these on the rough stones as she climbed. When she was partway up, her right arm securely wrapped over the top stone, she was able to look down. A narrow alley ran between The Red and the Black's stone garden wall and a wooden fence belonging to whatever house backed onto the property. The space between was wide enough for a man or a horse, but not a carriage. A few barrels, a wooden plank, and some rags littered the area. Allie thought this might have been how the arsonist reached the rear door, by climbing over the wall. He might have left the rags and the barrel for another try, but surely the Bow Street Runner would have inspected the alley, wouldn't he?

She decided to ask in the morning instead of checking for herself. Climbing up had not been hard, but climbing over the wall, and then turning to climb down, was beyond her. Besides, what if the stones on the other side were smooth, without hand- and footholds? Then, too, Allie was willing to spend her wages on gloves, but new gowns and a new cloak were too dear if these were ruined in her foolish scramble. And her hands still hurt.

Then the pile of rags moved. And moaned.

Dear heaven, it was a girl. Allie could see long blond hair—or was it red? No, that was blood! She was over the wall and down on the ground without hesitation. She had a skinned knee, a sore ankle from when she landed, and shreds where her gloves had been, but she was fine. The girl was not.

She had a gash on the side of her head, a split lip, an eye that was swollen shut, and tear streaks through the dirt on her cheeks. She was shivering in her thin gown, without a shawl, a pelisse, or a cape of any kind. Allie took her own cloak off and put it over the girl. She could not have been much over seventeen, as far as Allie could tell under the dirt and the blood and the bruises. Good grief, what if this was Jack's sister trying to find him?

She bent down and softly touched the girl's cheek. "I will go for help, dear, but what is your name?"

"Patsy, ma'am, but you best go. Iffen Fedder finds me, he'll beat you, too. I'll leave as soon as I can." Patsy tried to get up, but cried out when she put pressure on her arm.

"No, you stay here. I'll fetch someone."

"No, he'll kill me for sure!"

"This Fedder. Is he your husband? Your brother? Your employer?"

Patsy started to cry again, while Allie held her handkerchief to the wound on the girl's head, trying to stop the bleeding. "No, he's naught but a villain I met when I come to London. He said as how he'd drive me to a friend he had who took in girls fresh from the country and helped them find jobs."

"Oh, no."

Patsy nodded. "I were that green, ma'am. I didn't know no better."

"But you tried to get away?"

"It were awful. He had locks on the doors, him and the old woman." She was sobbing in earnest now, and shaking again.

Allie was shaking herself, not from the cold, but from anger. "Did he force himself on you?" she demanded, ready to skin this Fedder alive if she could get her hands on him.

"That weren't what he wanted. He wanted me to go with other men, for money! I ain't that kind of girl. My mum would kill me! Then Fedder near did, when I bit that first bloke. So I jumped out the window and I run away. He was chasing me, 'til I found this alley. I rolled a barrel acrost the entrance so he wouldn't look here, but he might when he can't find me nowheres else. Please, ma'am, please don't let him find me!"

"He won't, not if I can help it. You'll be safe with me." She thought a moment, then asked, "Do you have brothers or sisters?"

"Three brothers, ma'am, and two little sisters. That's why I come to London, to find a paying job so as to send money home for them. My da got lung fever from the mines and I don't want the boys to go."

Patsy had a family, and it was not Jack's family.

And the girl was used to children. "Would you want to work as a nursemaid and all-around house servant? Help with cooking and cleaning?"

"For an honest wage? I can't think of anything I'd rather do, ma'am."

"Then you are hired. Now all we have to do is smuggle you into the house so no one sees you, give you a few days to heal, and then you shall be ready to go with Miss Hildebrand and me to our new rooms." Allie did not mention the grand style of the new lodgings, lest she frighten the girl worse. "No one will find you there, and even if Fedder does, you will not have to go with him." Jack had promised them a footman to act as guard, so Allie was not promising Jack's personal protection nor the authority of his brother's name and wealth. Not exactly.

She was spending Jack's money, though, and hiring an unknown female for the earl's household. She decided that she would rather introduce Patsy to Jack when the girl was looking, and feeling, more the thing.

First, of course, she had to get Patsy into the house without the Fedder person spotting her. Leading her out of the alley and around the corner to the front of the club would take too long in Patsy's condition, and be too visible. People on the street were bound to notice a battered young female entering The Red and the Black, which notoriety none of them needed. Allie did not think she could climb back up and over the stone wall. Patsy certainly could not. Bother, where was Harriet when she needed a tomboy?

"You'll have to stay here a minute while I go to get help," Allie told the younger woman.

Patsy grasped her hand. "You'll come back?"

"I swear." Unless Jack killed her for bringing another mess into his life.

Allie struggled to move the barrel from the narrow

entryway. Patsy's desperation must have lent the girl strength, she thought, barely budging the obstacle enough for her to squeeze past it. She looked both ways, in case Fedder was still searching. Drat, she ought to have asked what the dastard looked like! A large man in a moleskin jacket was striding down the block in the opposite direction, thank goodness, so Allie hurried toward the front of the gaming club. She tried not to run, not to draw attention to herself, but Fedder, if that was he, would not chase a prim and proper schoolteacher, thinking she was hurrying out of the cold because she had forgotten her cloak.

The red door or the black door? Jack and Downs had gone to the cellars, but that was awhile ago. And the moleskin-wearer had been big. Downs was no weakling, but he did have a limp. She had no idea where the Bow Street Runner was, or the other guards. And Jack—Well, she did not want to bother him right now.

So she rapped on the red guest door, where the biggest, meanest, most intimidating man of her acquaintance ruled. Snake opened the door, glaring. "You know you ain't supposed to use this—"

Allie would have been frightened except for the tiny black kitten in Calloway's huge hand and the basket at his feet.

"Cap'n Jack promised Harriet a cat," he said, trying not to look embarrassed as the kitten dug its claws into his shirt to climb toward his neck. "I knew where the mama cat stashed this one, so I fetched it back. I figure it's worth getting scratched to get rid of the brat. She's off bothering Cook so she don't know yet. It'll be on your head if we don't get any dinner tonight."

"Forget about dinner, Harriet, and the kitten. I need you to come with me."

"I can't leave my place here. You know that, miss."
The kitten had clawed its way to the top of Calloway's
head, so he appeared to be wearing a wig.

"You have to. It's a matter of life and death. And
finding someone to look after Harriet when I cannot."

Calloway handed her the kitten, picked up a short
club he kept by the door for emergencies, and followed her out to the street.

"Oh, no, there is the man in the moleskin coat. If
that is Fedder, we cannot let him see what we are
doing."

"Fedder the Pimp? Did he bother you, miss?" Calloway swung his club from one hand to the other.

"No, not me. But hurry, his back is turned."

When the man headed in the opposite direction,
Allie led Calloway toward the back of the house, telling him about Patsy's narrow escape down the alley.
Calloway moved the heavy barrel with one shove and
followed her to Patsy's side. Then he cursed when he
saw her condition. The girl cowered back against the
stone wall until Allie reassured her that Mr. Snake—
Mr. Calloway—was a friend who was going to help
her into the house.

"I am? Cap'n Jack'll have my hide."

"Well, we cannot leave the poor girl here, can we?"

Calloway handed her his club, which she took awkwardly, juggling it and the kitten, who was loudly protesting. "Hush, you silly thing. You will have Fedder
coming to investigate."

Now Patsy started crying again. "He'll kill me this
time, I know he will!"

Calloway picked her up to shut her up. He tossed
her over his shoulder, making sure most of Patsy, her
hair especially, was covered by Allie's dark cloak. "Go
look, Miss Silver."

Allie peered around the side of the building near

the street. She did not see anyone who looked suspicious. She did not see any of the new guards, either. "I thought we were supposed to have more watchmen," she said, signaling Calloway that the coast was clear.

"That's at night," he said, carrying Patsy as if she weighed as little as the kitten. They came out of the alley and hurried around the corner to the house. Unfortunately, they forgot to move the barrel back.

Fedder had turned around. He saw the opening to the alley, saw a blood-stained handkerchief, and ran back out to the street, just as Allie with the kitten, and Calloway with his burden, ducked into the club.

"Hey," Fedder shouted.

Calloway kicked the door shut behind them. "Can you walk, miss?" he asked Patsy, putting her down. "'Cause I better stay here and discourage the scum just in case he thinks he saw something." He took his club from Allie, who put the kitten in its basket before quickly helping Patsy up the stairs to the rooms she shared with Harriet.

"This is Patsy," she told her charge when Harriet burst into the sitting room. "She is going to be our new maid, and if you tell anyone about her, you cannot keep the kitten Mr. Calloway found for you."

"Snake found me a kitten? Isn't he wonderful?" she yelled on her way back down the stairs before Allie could tell her to bring back hot water and bandages and liniment from Cook's stores.

"He is that," Patsy said, stars in her one eye that wasn't swollen shut.

While Allie helped Patsy into her own spare nightgown and Harriet was introducing the kitten to Joker, Jack was getting ready for an evening of deep play. First he instructed the new guards to keep their eyes open for any suspicious characters.

"What about that scum what's passed out at the corner?"

"Drunk?"

"Not unless he was so foxed he clouted hisself over the head with a lamppost."

"If he's dead, call the Watch. Otherwise drag him out of sight. This is an elegant establishment. We don't want the club patrons seeing anything so ugly."

They would see a lot worse than that later.

The rooms were not quite full, but Jack was sitting at a table, a growing stack of welcome coins and chips in front of him, when there was a commotion at the door. He barely looked up from his hand of cards, concentrating on recalling what had been played. Calloway could handle anything.

But Fedder had come back with reinforcements. The argument grew louder.

"I told you, we don't have no whores here!" Calloway shouted. "This is a private club for gentlemen, not your kind, Fedder. I told you to get out, and iffen you don't, I'll say it again with my fists, again."

"I want the bitch what ran away. Patsy."

Now Jack had to get up. His customers were muttering at the ill-bred interruption. He went to stand beside the larger Calloway, knowing together they were a formidable force. Jack's lip curled at the sight of the scurvy whoremonger with a bandage on his head. "You are costing me money, Fedder, so take your whining elsewhere."

"You are costing me money, too, damn you and your fancy club. That gal is worth plenty. Fresh from the country, pure as the driven snow."

Jack was revolted, and reminded of the thin line between him and slime like Fedder. "We have no girls named Patsy, and we have no cheap doxies. Now get out."

Fedder tried to push past him to see for himself. Jack was not going to let him. He grabbed the moleskin coat. Calloway stepped in front of the brute he'd brought along. "I said your Patsy is not here. If you want to discuss it outside, I would be happy to oblige."

Downs took Calloway's place at the door, but some of the gamblers left their places at the tables and pushed past him, laying odds on the outcome of the coming mill. Jack handed one of them his coat rather than let Fedder's blood stain it. The bastard had ruined his winning game; he was not going to ruin Jack's expensive clothes, too. Jack briefly thought of his vow to abstain from violence against his fellow man. Fedder was no man; he was a parasite, a leech, sucking the blood of helpless young women. Jack thought of his sister's unknown fate, of what could have befallen Miss Silver, or Harriet later. He swung first.

While Calloway held back the other man, Jack swung again. Fedder was no match for the former officer, not without his bully boy.

"Patsy. Is. Not. Here." Each word was punctuated by another blow. Fedder was on the ground. "Now go, and never come back."

The larger thug dragged Fedder away while Jack put his coat back on and the bettors settled their wagers.

"What was that all about, Calloway?" Jack asked as he wrapped his handkerchief around his bleeding knuckles, trying to smile for the customers so they would go back to losing money to the house. "Why would he think we had his Patsy? Everyone knows we don't take on virgins."

"Everyone but Miss Silver, I'd guess."

CHAPTER NINETEEN

"**Y**ou hired a . . . what?"

Jack had left the club, left his winnings, and left all thought of his customers below when he took the stairs two—or three—at a time to Miss Silver's rooms. No matter that a gentleman never called at a lady's bedchamber, much less when the lady ought to be asleep. Jack had left his gentlemanly instincts downstairs too, along with the skin of his knuckles. He pounded on the door with the side of his fist, prepared to break it down if the blasted thing did not open soon.

It did. There was Allie, rubbing her eyes. She'd been asleep on the chaise longue in the sitting room, wrapped in an extra blanket. Harriet was sharing the bed with Patsy, Joker, and the new kitten, which made it too crowded for Allie's comfort. Awakening to a racket at her door, Allie had panicked that there was another fire. She had not bothered to find her robe to cover her nightgown, but she did have a pitcher of water in her hand. Now she blinked, set the pitcher down, and made sure that the neck of her nightgown was properly tied. "What time is it?"

"It is time we had a talk, Miss Straight and Narrow, Miss My Reputation Is My Redemption. What about my reputation, dash it? I am trying to run an elegant, high-toned operation, catering to wealthy gentlemen of impeccable tastes who prize their privacy and my discretion. I have barely scotched yesterday's scandal and now the club will be immersed in another tomorrow."

"I did not—"

"Not? You did not what?" he raged. "You did not involve my genteel gambling parlor with a notorious procurer? You did not hire a tuppenny prostitute to be my ward's nursemaid?"

Allie raised her chin. "No, I hired a young girl who was lied to, practically kidnapped, and nearly forced to commit unspeakable acts against her will. I hired a person who was brave enough to escape her captors, and who is willing to work hard at honest labor. I hired a female who will learn her letters and numbers, to better herself. What is wrong with that?"

"What is wrong is the filth of Fedder littering my doorstep, the headlines that will appear in the scandal pages, and the new enemy I just gained. Devil take it, I used to be considered a charming fellow without a foe in the world, once the French had been defeated. Now I am in a marquess's black books, as well as a double-dealer's and a rejected mistress's. I am the target of an arsonist, and you, my dear Miss Silver, have just made me another antagonist. A pimp, of all things! Could you not have picked another respectable member of society to offend this time? Besides, my brother will likely turn against me when he discovers what kind of female you hired as a housemaid."

"He beat her," was all Allie said.

Jack sighed, his fury spent. "I know. Calloway told me how you climbed the wall to help her."

"What should I have done?"

"You should have let Calloway hire a hackney to drive her somewhere, anywhere but here."

"Is that what you would have done?"

They both knew it was not. Jack ran his fingers through his hair, trying to find a reply that would justify his earlier shouting at her.

"Your hands!" Allie pulled him farther into the room, closer to the lamp. Then she pushed him toward a chair while she ran for the salve Calloway had sent up for Patsy's bruises. She knelt at Jack's feet, rubbing the stuff onto his bloodied knuckles as carefully as she could.

As lightly as he could, Jack touched the long braid she wore, wanting to feel her hair's silky texture, finding it impossible not to. Somehow his free hand turned totally ungovernable and moved to caress her cheek.

"Why did you not come find me?" he asked.

Allie kept her eyes on his battered knuckles, liking the feel of his hand on her cheek, his other hand in hers. How could one be so gentle and one show evidence of such brute force?

"Didn't you trust me?"

"I did not want to lay another burden on your shoulders."

"They are wide enough."

They were wide enough to cushion a woman's head. Allie spread salve on a finger she had already covered. "But you have done so much for us already."

Now Jack tipped her chin up so he could look into her eyes. In the near dark they looked like midnight at sea. "You deserve more, my brave girl."

"More than being woken up and shouted at?"

"Far more."

He bent down and gave what he thought she deserved—or he did, for fighting her battles. The kiss was long and warm and wet, and should have ended ages before it did.

Hell, he thought, it should never have started. But there was the same trouble again, a totally reprehensible, uncontrollable desire for Miss Allison Silver, spinster. What the devil was it about this woman, anyway, that made him want her? Jack asked himself, as he panted with that self-same wanting of her. She was no great beauty, although he thought she might be pretty enough in stylish clothes with her glorious hair combed in a more becoming manner. She was not as experienced as the women he usually preferred, nor was she as buxom. She was not soft and cuddlesome, in bone structure or personality. No, Miss Silver was a prickly, prideful female who was never afraid to disagree with him or to speak her mind.

Right now her body was speaking, leaning toward his while her breathing was as labored as his own. She sighed, a whisper of desire that sent his curiosity to Cairo, his reasoning to Russia. Who cared why he was attracted to this wrong woman when her kisses felt so right?

The angle was awkward, with him in the chair and her on the floor, so he slid off the seat to face her while she knelt, their mouths once more pressing, pulsing, his tongue parting her lips. She accepted his gentle invasion with an *ah* of surprise or delight or satisfaction at finally understanding what kissing was all about. She was a quick learner, letting her own tongue go tentatively exploring.

Now Jack could wrap her in his arms and pull her closer to him, feeling her unbound bosoms against his chest. He was the one to say "Ah" this time.

He'd stop in a minute, of course. Meantime, Allie's

knees must be paining her from kneeling on them so long. Jack gently lowered her to the carpet, cushioned by his arm. Now he could touch those lovely breasts through the flannel of her nightgown, cup them in his hand, rub his fingers against the nipples until they hardened.

They were not half as hard as he was. Lud, he had to stop.

But Allie responded so sweetly, so eagerly, making those little purrs of pleasure. Her hands were busy too, touching his neck, ruffling his hair, tickling his ears, urging him to keep doing what he was doing, or doing more.

One more minute and he would definitely stop kissing her, positively stop stroking her. Right after he spread her hair over her shoulders. But his inner timepiece must have come unwound there on the floor, because her braid was loosened and his hand was raising her nightgown so that he could smooth her ankle, her calf, her thigh, almost to her—

On the floor? He was about to teach the schoolteacher about a woman's pleasure, on the fardling floor? With a child in the next room? Ah, hell!

Jack pulled down the hem of Allie's nightgown and pulled away from the touch of her body, but kept his arm under her head. When she looked at him, questioningly, he said, "I will not dishonor you."

She licked her lip, almost making him forget his principles, yet again. He wanted to lick her lip. He wanted to kiss away the frown line between her eyebrows. He wanted to bury himself in her and forget everything, her innocence, the floor, his scruples, his own name.

"Is that what you were doing?" she asked, still looking uncertain and unhappy, not knowing what to do with her hands. "Dishonoring me?"

He started to reach out to smooth away the pucker, but held his hand back. If he touched her eyebrows, he'd have to touch her eyes and then her ears and her elbows and her entirety. "No, I was making love to you. But it would have come to the same thing, in the end."

"But then I would not be a maiden, and perhaps that would not be completely terrible. Do you know, I am coming to think that being a mistress is perhaps not so bad, with the advantages you have been showing me. After all, my reputation is already destroyed. I could stay here where no one cares about such things, and you could save the expense of another household. Harriet would be thrilled, and Patsy can make friends with the other young women."

"Where she would likely end up in the same career she fought so hard to avoid, and where Harriet would grow up mistaken about a female's proper place in life." Jack was firm. "Besides, you are not mistress material."

Allie sighed, knowing he spoke the truth. His kisses made her dizzy, that was all, momentarily mad. The shame, the self-disgust would come to outweigh the pleasures, no matter the myriad she was imagining. Why, she would be too attainted to act as Harriet's companion. In addition, she would be wretched as Jack's inamorata, waiting for him to tire of her, furiously jealous if he looked at another woman. And, afterward, when he did leave her, she could never go back to being a governess or a schoolteacher. She could never go to another man, either. Whatever pleasure there was, was being with *this* man, being in *his* arms.

Allie sighed again. "You are right. I am not meant to be a mistress. And you are not husband-worthy."

Husband? Allie's head bumped on that godforsaken floor when Jack jumped to his feet. The dog barked.

Harriet called out, "Allie? Are you all right?"

Patsy cried, "Oh, lord, Fedder must have found me!"

Allie rubbed her head as she got to her feet. "I am fine, and there is nothing to worry about." She glared at Jack. "Absolutely nothing. I, ah, dropped the book I was reading, that's all. Now go back to sleep, both of you. It is very late."

Jack tried to straighten his crumpled neck cloth. He kept his voice low as he told her, "I will see about moving you into Carde House tomorrow."

"Will Patsy be safe there?"

"At an earl's house? Even dolts like Fedder know better than to chance offending the nobility. Alex could have him clapped in irons in an instant. Besides, I don't think Fedder will want another dose of my own brand of medicine, or Calloway's. One small maid could not be worth the cost to him. But I will send another guard to accompany the girl when she goes on errands away from the house, to make sure."

"With yet another guard, Harriet will have a regular retinue."

"Good. She will have more people to bedevil."

Allie was thinking of the cost. Jack was thinking of keeping his womenfolk safe. He walked to the door but turned and beckoned her closer, so she could hear his words: "I will never let anyone hurt you. Not even me."

The Prince Regent could transfer his entire entourage to Brighton for the summer with less fanfare, it seemed, than Allie and Harriet could relocate to Carde House the next afternoon.

Nearly all of the inhabitants of The Red and the Black wanted to help them move. Half wanted to make certain the little hellion truly left, and the other half wanted to see the inside of a real earl's residence. They all knew that their Cap'n Jack was an earl's son and an earl's brother, but that was not the same. Even with most of the house undergoing renovation, the furniture in holland covers, and the artwork locked away for safekeeping, a tour of the place was the closest the working women were going to get.

They all agreed the town house was grand, and those brawny carpenters and bonny painters were not bad, either. Perhaps they could come visit sweet little Harriet another time?

They had traveled the distance between the two houses—and the two worlds—in caravan style. Allie, Harriet, Mrs. Crandall, and Patsy rode in Jack's carriage, along with Joker and the kitten. They had dressed Patsy in borrowed plumes, literally and figuratively. With her garbed in a low-cut blouse from one dealer, a red silk skirt from another, and a bonnet with an ostrich plume from a third, no one would recognize Patsy as a chick fresh from the country. The hat's wide brim hid her hair and her face, and the black eye and cut lip. A hired baggage wagon followed, not that any of them had much in the way of possessions. Mrs. Crandall had her husband's army trunk, while Harriet and Allie had their few valises, plus a new basket for the kitten. Patsy had nothing, of course, since she had lost her satchel when she ran from Fedder's place, so the other women generously filled a sack for her with bits of clothing they could spare.

Cook had packed a hamper of food for them and a box of kitchen staples. Calloway had discovered some extra linen, so they would not have to use the earl's monogrammed sheets and towels, and Mr. Downs claimed that no one at The Red and the Black drank ratafia, so he sent three bottles, and one of sherry, which was far more palatable for a lady. He added a bottle of brandy for when Captain Endicott went to visit, in case the earl's cellars were locked tight.

A hackney coach carried the dealers and hostesses from the club, gawking at the wider streets and immense houses of the aristocracy. Another carriage contained the men, with two guards riding on top. Jack rode his horse ahead of the first coach, on the lookout for Fedder or, worse, news reporters.

If anyone followed them, however, they would see that Captain Endicott's ward and her duenna were properly ensconced at one of the most respectable addresses in all of London, with a chaperone and a lady's maid.

They would also see that Jack was not staying. He was not even helping Miss Silver out of the carriage when they arrived. He was holding Harriet's hand, ignoring the governess as if she were nothing but an upper servant, which she was, of course.

He was dying inside, but he was doing the right thing. He'd feel better about it later. He hoped so, anyway.

Since he had not been able to give the workmen at Carde House much notice, he could not complain that the nursery wing was not ready. His sister-in-law cared more about refurbishing the schoolroom and children's chambers than the public rooms, it seemed. Jack did not think Nell cared for London enough to spend much time here, but her brother did reside outside of town, and Alex would have to come up for Parliamentary votes on occasion. The children would come too, naturally. Nell was not the kind of mother to leave her babies behind.

"Very particular, Lady Carde," the foreman explained to Jack. "But with fine taste," he hastily appended, seeing Jack's smile fade at the slight to Nell.

"She married my brother, didn't she?" was all he said, following the man to the guest chambers the workmen had hastily cleared of dust and debris.

Harriet and Allie would share a suite of bedrooms, with a parlor between them. They could use that for lessons, instead of interfering with the construction in the nursery below. Patsy was thrilled with the bed in the small dressing room, since it would be the first time in her life she had not shared a mattress, much less had a whole room to herself. Mrs. Crandall had a room across the hall that almost left her in tears it was so fine, as if she were a real lady.

Seemingly exhausted by the move, Joker collapsed onto Harriet's bed and proceeded to snore while the kitten batted at his tail. Jack did not even bother to mention that the cat, which was still nameless, was supposed to live in the stable. A good officer knew when to stand and fight and when to retreat.

"But no more pets, mind you," he ordered, leaving the women to unpack while he settled the two men he had chosen as footmen and guards.

Some of the workmen were housed in the servants' rooms in the attics, since Alex had sent them from Nell's home and her brother's bankrupt shipyard in Hull. So Jack put Hawkins and Lundy in the butler's apartment near the servants' hall. The earl's majordomo would be more offended than Alex at the men's lack of polish, but they were more of Jack's former soldiers, and he knew they were good men, brave and loyal. They would defend the women against all enemies—and defend his brother's house against Harriet.

Cook had inspected the newly modernized kitchen

while he stored the victuals. He was making clucking noises that sounded envious and expensive to Jack, so the captain hurried the man away and gathered up the women, to the workers' disappointment. He gave his last instructions to Harriet about listening to Miss Silver, learning her lessons, and leaving the hammers and saws alone.

"What about my pony?" she asked, her eyes filling with tears at his good-bye.

Great gods, had he promised her a pony? Jack feared he had.

"Not now, Harriet," Miss Silver scolded. "Captain Endicott has done so much for us. Be grateful for the kitten."

"No, if I promised, I shall find a pony. An Endicott never goes back on his word, you know. 'Ever True,' that's our family motto."

A tear fell. "And then you'll come visit, to teach me how to ride?"

He gulped and nodded.

She sniffed. "And take me and Miss Silver for rides in Hyde Park?"

Zeus, just what he did not want to do. Harriet was clinging to his leg, though, looking like an abandoned puppy. "Of course."

She grinned and skipped off to finish exploring the house.

"Do not pester the workmen!" he called after her. "Then again," he told Allie, who was smiling and shaking her head at how easily he had been manipulated, "maybe one of them will wring her neck and save me the bother. And the expense of a blasted pony."

"If you cannot afford a pony right now, she will have to understand," Allie said, worried for his sake. "And I can wait until next quarter for my salary."

Jack swore, but too low for Allie to hear. Deuce take it, he had more pride than that, to be borrowing from a woman! "No." Jack used his army commander's tone that brooked no opposition. "My expenses are none of your concern. I shall manage."

After all, what did he need a racing curricle for, anyway? They could not all fit on the narrow bench.

CHAPTER TWENTY

Jack went to the stables after seeing Darla and the others back into the coaches for the return to The Red and the Black. Samuel was there, because Samuel was always there. He'd been the assistant stable man in Jack's father's time, and took over as both head groom and driver after the accident that killed the previous earl's wife and the previous coachman. He'd stayed on in London when Alex and Nell went to the country, because Carde Hall had its own stable staff and drivers. Besides, someone had to look after the horses kept in town for emergencies or messages or a hurried visit by the earl or his countess. And old Samuel had an old lady friend in town, too.

Now he slapped his thigh and almost fell off the bale of hay he used as a seat.

"You? A guardian for a girl child? And a prunes and prisms schoolmarm?"

Jack had to slap his back when the old man started coughing. "I do not find it a laughing matter."

Neither did Samuel when Jack told him about the arsonist, the irate marquess, and the pimp. Samuel agreed to keep a watch out and confer with the new guards if he saw anyone suspicious. Then he said, "You always were a one for finding trouble, weren't you?"

Jack did not appreciate the old retainer's opinion—a wrong opinion at that. He had not set out to find Harriet, Miss Silver, or Patsy. All he'd wanted was to run his club, find his sister, and enjoy himself while doing both. After years in the army, he felt he deserved that, not headache piled upon havoc. "Trouble seems to find me, rather."

"It always does. Why, I remember the time when you and the earl went off to that fair, innocent as lambs."

"That was not my fault. The bear was wandering around loose."

"So you always said. A fine to-do that turned out to be."

"Do not mention the bear, or any of my youthful peccadilloes, to Miss Hildebrand. She is enough of a scapegrace as is. Oh, and by the way, has my brother asked you to find a pony for the heir?"

"The heir?" Samuel picked at his teeth with a bit of straw. "Wasn't the little viscount born just a year or so ago?"

"More or less. The new infant should arrive early in the new year. He—or she—will need a pony too."

"Now? No, his lordship said nothing to me about any pony for a babe that can't walk yet and one not even born. Besides, he intends to keep them in the country most of the time."

"But if you just happened to find the perfect mount, not too dull, not too headstrong, you might consider purchasing it for the future, mightn't you?"

"Without the master's orders?"

"Oh, we both know he gives you leave to run the stables as you see fit. And I would not trust that gudgeon at the stables at Cardington to find just the right pony for my nephews. Or my new niece."

Samuel scratched his head. "Then I'd need someone small enough to exercise the beast, wouldn't I?"

"Precisely. Miss Hildebrand would love the job. She accepts. She will be here tomorrow unless I miss my guess, pestering you anyway. If you thought the bear was trouble, you have not met Harriet."

Jack breathed a sigh of relief. Now he could go back to his own affairs. His ward and her warden were safe, sheltered, and scandal-free. Now he could put his mind to making money and finding his lost sister. If he wanted to have a liaison with one of the lovelies who came to his club, that was his business, too. No one was going to frown and chide him for his morals; no one was going to accuse him of corrupting the mind of a minor.

And no one was going to sigh so sweetly when he kissed her.

Oh, hell.

Jack decided he was sick. None of the women appealed to him; none of the games of chance interested him; none of the club's income satisfied him; no one came with information about Lottie to sell him. So he went back to visit Harriet and Miss Silver late the next morning. After all, Harriet was costing him as much as a mistress, and she was a great deal more fun.

The door to the house was closed to him. His own house! Well, his childhood home, anyway, his brother's house, where Jack was always welcome, until he'd installed a shrew there. The guard—his own man, on his own payroll—refused him entry.

Oh, he could come in, of course, to speak with the

architect or inspect the work, but he was not permitted
to interrupt Miss Harriet's lessons in the mornings. No
one was, Lundy reported. Miss Silver felt that strongly
about it, and the others would be embarrassed.

The others? Had the want-wit of a woman taken in
other infants to educate on his time, with his money?

He pushed past his former soldier. Lundy would be
a former employee, too, Jack warned, if he did not
stand aside. Then he squeezed past two men with a
ladder on the stairs, a large wooden crate on the upper
landing, and piles of holland covers in the guest wing.

The door to the sitting room was open, so Jack went
in without knocking, only to be caught up short at the
entry. Half of his employees were there, Darla and
Maisy and Monique and the new maid, Patsy, along
with Calloway, Cook, Mary Crandall, and his other
guard. They sat on the elegant new furniture or on
the floor, slates in their laps, chalk in their hands. Miss
Silver stood at a larger chalkboard, writing letters
from the alphabet and simple words for them to copy.
Harriet was circling the room, correcting a misspelling
here, a curlicue there.

"*Cee* is for cat," Allie was saying, her back to the
door as she wrote. "Cuh, cuh. Cat. Cards."

"Cap'n Jack," one of the girls said.

"Excellent, Maisy."

Jack cleared his throat. Allie turned, and turned
seven shades of scarlet. "Oh, *that* captain."

Jack was the one who was embarrassed. Clunch,
cork-brain, clod. He had not known so many of his
people, people who depended on him, could not read.
How could they find better positions, improve their
lot in life, without a skill he took for granted? Callow,
uncaring, caper-witted, he called himself. "Carry on."

"No, we are almost finished for the day," Allie said,
putting down her chalk. She gave Harriet a stack of

papers to hand to the others, so they could practice on their own.

"Tomorrow at eleven, Miss Silver?" Hawkins asked. "I'll tell Lundy. It's his turn."

Now Jack felt even more of a cur as the rest of them filed past him, their eyes downcast. "I, ah, I think this is a fine thing you are doing, learning to read," he told them. "I am sorry I never thought of it myself."

"That's all right, Cap'n. You were too busy."

When they had left, Harriet racing toward the stables to see if her new pony had arrived, Jack told Allie, "I should have made the time."

"But you are here now, to spend the afternoon with Harriet." Approval shone in her gray eyes, making the blue flecks dance. Jack had not known how much her approval meant to him until he felt warmed by her regard. He'd feel better yet if he had truly come to visit Harriet, and not her governess.

"I thank you for what you are doing," he told her, and meant it. He was still upset that he had neglected those under his care. He tried to explain it, as much for his own benefit as hers. "I, ah, was not raised to be the lord of the manor, you know. That was my brother's job, ruler of his little kingdom, responsible for the well-being of everyone in his domain. I was merely the frippery second son, the afterthought in case of emergency."

"Nonsense. I'd wager that while you were in the army you held more men's lives in your keeping than your brother ever did. Your veterans all sing your praises, saying other officers never looked after their men so carefully. Why, Calloway told me some of the officers did not even ride into battle with their troops, but sent the men ahead on their own. You never did."

"Calloway talks too much." Bless his larcenous heart.

Allie was going on: "And now you are hiring as many former soldiers as you can, to give them an income and self-respect."

"But you are giving them, and the women, hope for a better future and pride in their accomplishments. That is worth a great deal."

Allie straightened the remaining papers. "I like to teach."

Jack surprised himself by saying, "And I like you, Miss Allison Silver," which may have been the most honest, least flirtatious, words he had ever spoken to a female. He waited expectantly.

And waited.

Finally Allie said, "I think you are doing a fine thing, taking in Captain Hildebrand's daughter and trying to give her a decent upbringing."

Away from him and his gambling club. She did not say the words, but Jack heard them anyway.

He cleared his throat. "Yes, well, I shall go see if Samuel in the stables has tendered his resignation yet."

Allie made a tidy stack of the slates and gathered the chalks into a jar for the next day. Still without looking at Jack, she said, "I understand that you promised to visit Harriet, but I wish you would not interfere with her lessons. Mrs. Semple always believed that a regular schedule taught the students discipline and organization."

"What about fun?"

"There is time for play, early in the morning when we shall go to the park and in the afternoon after the classwork. I thought you would be late rising, with the club open until long past midnight. I scheduled the staff's lessons for as late as possible, so as not to disturb their rest. You may come after that."

Jack was dismissed . . . and he was disgusted. Here

he was, paying the woman's salary, keeping her in elegant surroundings, doing his damnedest to protect her reputation, and baring his soul besides. And what did he get? Not a kiss, not a smile, not even a handshake. He bowed and left.

Allie sank onto a chair. There, she had done it. *Ess* was for success and self-preservation and seeing her plan through. She had let Jack go without begging him to stay. Keeping her distance was the only way, she had decided, that she was going to survive working for Captain Endicott. Otherwise, she might be tempted to throw herself into his arms, right in the makeshift classroom. That or throw herself off the freshly shingled roof of Carde House!

What sounded easy enough in the middle of the night while she was alone in her bedroom was a lot harder by day, with Jack standing a few feet away. He looked so handsome this morning, with his hair still damp from his morning wash. He had fresh, healthy color in his cheeks, as if he had walked the distance from the club, instead of a habitual gambler's nighttime pallor. He wore a spotted kerchief around his neck instead of a neck cloth, and fawn breeches that hugged his muscular thighs. And she was going to turn her back on him?

Then he said he liked her. Not enough to want her for his mistress, of course, but he liked her. Allie was glad. She was glad that he respected her, and glad, she told herself, that he was not interested in her for anything but Harriet's sake.

Besides, she had thought long and hard last night—with plenty of time, since she was not sleeping—about these peculiar feelings she had for the man. Lust, that's what they were: a spinster's last gasp at knowing a grand passion. Of course he was attractive and charming and practiced in the art of pleasing a woman.

Well, tempting a woman, at any rate. He was a rake, for pity's sake. Allie pitied herself, because she was all too tempted.

He might be a libertine, but she was no lightskirt. Why, she blushed now to think of how high he had raised her skirts, but that was beside the point. If she behaved like a proper governess, he would treat her like a proper governess. Otherwise, she was lost.

Her virginity was not all she would lose, either. Her very soul would be his to cherish or destroy on a whim, today, tomorrow, next month. Well, a maiden-head and a heart were not all that much to sacrifice, were they, for time in Jack Endicott's arms? Neither one had done her much good for the past twenty-five years.

But what if she had a child? The idea of a babe of her own, an infant to hold and nurture, almost brought tears to Allie's eyes for what she had never thought to have. But although the babe might have Jack's brown hair and eyes, and his authoritative nose, the child would not have Jack's last name. And a man did not marry his mistress, and a rake did not want a female who was breeding. Allie would have her child, but no home, no income, no career. No. She could not do that to her unborn infant, or to her parents' memories.

And he wanted to know if she liked him. Hah! *Bee* was for buffle-headed and bacon-brained, and for biting her tongue to keep from telling him how much.

She did not like him? Jack told himself she would, soon, because gamblers were optimists by nature. After all, why would anyone bet if he did not believe he would win? Jack did not consider himself a true gambler, since he seldom played games he could lose or for more money than he could afford. When the cards were bad, he simply withdrew. He did not depend on luck, only skill and experience.

Like now. He truly believed he could change Miss Silver's mind. She might not approve of him and his chosen vocation, but she already liked his kisses. On reflection, for which he had a great deal of sleepless time, he decided that the kisses were part of the problem. The silly widgeon had enjoyed them too much, he'd bet, to her own surprise and dismay. Lust was not part of the teacher's syllabus, so she was embarrassed and anxious and keeping him at arm's length or farther.

She might even be afraid he would dishonor her. Honest as always, Jack confessed to himself that she might have cause. But he had not, when he could have, so she ought to trust him. Then again, mistrusting gentlemen, known womanizers and wagerers especially, was definitely a lesson learned at every girls' school.

He would simply have to teach Allie otherwise.

All good soldiers planned their campaigns carefully and relied on allies. Jack had a guidebook and Harriet. No child's education was complete, he decided, until he or she had seen all the sights London offered. The history, the architecture, the marvels of modern science, all were laid out as a course of study. Besides, Harriet should know her way around in case she ever got lost.

Miss Silver could not argue with him. He was paying her salary, and he was correct: London was indeed a treasure trove of wondrous knowledge waiting to be discovered. Nor could she argue with Captain Endicott's declaration that the governess had to go along with him and Harriet on their jaunts. How else was she to plan her own lessons around what they had seen? What if Harriet needed to use the necessary? Shouldn't Allie know her way around the city, too?

And she was itching to explore all the sights she had read about.

So they went off most afternoons after schoolwork and riding lessons. They visited the Tower and the port, at least ten churches and cathedrals, Parliament, museums, and art galleries. They went to the gardens at Kew and the maze at Richmond and Covent Garden flower market. They saw balloon ascensions, the new steam engine, and a waxworks. If a spot was listed in the guidebook, they went.

Jack knew Harriet was happy. She would have thrown tantrums otherwise. But she behaved, for the most part, if one discounted the moustache on that portrait, the slightly smaller shard of Roman art, and the organ grinder's missing monkey. Of course now she had a canary, a white rabbit, and a goldfish in a bowl, plus enough sweets for an entire orphanage. But she behaved, and she was learning. The monkey was, too.

Jack was learning how to cope with an inquisitive, mischievous ward, and he was also learning about Miss Silver. He discovered she preferred scenery rather than science, art rather than architecture, books above everything. He found she was a tireless walker, an intelligent conversationalist, and a good listener.

He liked her more every day.

Jack could not discover that she liked him any better, though . . . any better than before, or any better than she liked the organ grinder's monkey.

He was frustrated on a hundred counts. He was running out of places to take the brat and the unbendable governess. He was spending all of his profits on ices at Gunter's, books at Hatchards, toys at Foster's, and tips for every tour guide and gatekeeper in the metropolis. And in return he had hugs and kisses—from Harriet.

Miss Silver made sure they were never alone, and she never favored Jack with more than a polite smile. She never let her hand remain in his when he helped her into a carriage, and she never accepted more than a biscuit from him, not a nosegay of violets, not a book, not a new pair of gloves.

She still wore her ugly bonnet and shapeless gowns, but Jack knew what was beneath both now, and found himself looking at her instead of the artwork, wondering at her mysteries instead of the scientific marvels, licking his lips when she licked her spoon.

Worst of all, he had no interest in any other woman.

So he had a hot wash when he awoke, and a cold bath when he returned from an outing with her.

Lord, he was frustrated.

CHAPTER TWENTY-ONE

Jack's search for his sister was frustrating, too. After a spate of successes, the progress toward finding Lottie had ground to a halt. Mr. Rourke told Jack that Bow Street had hit a dead end. They were not giving up, but they were not close to returning the missing heiress to her home and her half brothers.

At least they had earned their salaries by finally finding Molly Godfrey's direction. The suspected kidnapper's sister had left her seamstress job at Drury Lane within a week of the carriage accident that killed Lady Carde, Lottie's mother. The woman had left no address, and had never returned for a visit. An actress from a traveling troupe, though, had passed on to a wardrobe mistress who'd told an aged Macbeth that she'd seen Molly somewhere, with a child.

Everyone suspected the unmarried Molly had found herself in an interesting condition and left London out of shame, or to find a husband. Bow Street knew she picked up the extortion money from the bank once or

twice a year, using the name Mrs. Molly Godfrey. But
that was all they knew, because she'd stopped coming
for the money before anyone realized she existed. She
might not have been a conspirator in the coach accident, but she was certainly guilty of profiting from it,
so Bow Street concluded the woman must have gone
into hiding. And she must know where Lottie was.

At last, when enough of Jack's blunt had changed
hands and enough pints of ale had been lifted, someone from the theater had recalled that Molly once
spoke of a friend in Manchester.

With that bit of information, and more money to
send a man north, the Runners traced the hired thug's
sister to a small house in Manchester. There Molly
sewed piecework at home for a local dressmaker who
had once designed costumes for the Opera House.
That woman had moved to India. The vicar of the
church where Molly was buried three years ago was
dead. Everyone in the parish recalled a child, a quiet,
polite girl of surpassing beauty who helped her mother
with the sewing. No one knew what had become of
her.

According to the local gossips, Molly had moved to
the industrial city years ago, a war widow and her shy
little girl. She had bought a modest house away from
the city proper, and kept to herself. Molly had no
friends other than the mantua-maker, and the child
did not attend the local school. Their next-door neighbor thought a tutor had come in days, but how could
that be, on a needlewoman's wages? This was no small
town, where everyone knew everyone's business, or
London, where gossip was the prime entertainment of
the idle rich. The citizens of Manchester worked hard
and minded their own business.

Molly Dennis, for such was the name the kidnapper's sister was using, paid her bills on time, spoke

little to the tradespeople, and never let the child go anywhere by herself. When she grew up, the girl did not attend the local assemblies or have any beaux. A few of the mill owners' sons had tried, but Molly kept the girl too close for a flirtation.

Then Molly had died a few years ago, taking her secrets with her. The house was sold and the daughter left, taking her belongings with her. No one knew where. The solicitor handling the sale had passed on.

The older woman must have gone to hell for stealing a child that was not her own, but where the hell had Lottie gone? She had not come to London for the money in the bank, because the ransom price was still there, in the account. So how was she living? Where? With whom? Bow Street had no idea, and Jack had no place to look.

He did have one clue. The Runner reported that Molly always called the little girl Queenie.

Jack put up new reward posters. LADY CHARLOTTE ENDICOTT, they read. ALSO KNOWN AS LOTTIE, OR QUEENIE. That had to be his sister! And she was alive.

Someone kept ripping the posters down. Jack received no more threats against the club, and heard nothing from Fedder or Lord Montford. The card-sharp, Sir Jethro Stevens, was languishing in debtors' prison.

Jack put the posters up again, with extra nails.

His brother was as excited as Jack when he received his copy of the Runner's report, but he could not come to London right now to help. His wife was growing large with the new child and more sickly. Lord Carde was near to panic, afraid of losing the infant or, worse, his darling Nell. Alex wrote that he was sending for accoucheurs from Edinburgh and prayers from on high. Nell's crazy aunt, the earl confided, was consulting her friends, who just happened to be dead.

Alex did not care, if the specters could save his wife and baby.

Alex also wrote to Jack to do everything necessary for the search and for his new ward. He enclosed a bank draft to assist in both, telling Jack to swallow his confounded pride and use the funds. Of course the Grosvenor Square house was the proper place for the girl, Alex agreed, not The Red and the Black. Harriet was to consider Carde House her home.

Alex concluded that he had total confidence in his little brother. Jack would do the right thing by the Hildebrand orphan and by Montford's granddaughter.

Good old Ace, Jack thought, as subtle as a sledge-hammer.

So he did his best. He took the nuisance and the nemesis to Astley's Amphitheatre to see the circus. They both liked the trick horses, the trapeze artists, and the clowns. The manager liked the organ grinder's monkey, thank goodness.

Allie could not remember when she had had such a good time. Life with her father had been pleasant and comfortable. Teaching at Mrs. Semple's had been rewarding. But touring London with Captain Endicott? That was a dream come true. She got to see places and artwork she had merely read about, and she saw them both through the eyes of a child and through the eyes of a knowledgeable man-about-town. Jack was the most patient guide anyone could wish, never seeming bored or in a hurry to move on to the next masterpiece or the next place of historic interest. He knew a great deal about everything, but was not too proud to consult a guidebook when he did not or to pay a docent to conduct a tour. He was generous and courteous and intelligent, and he smiled to show his enjoyment.

In her admittedly limited knowledge of gentlemen, Allie had never come upon one who seemed to take such delight in everyday things. Perhaps, she thought, he had a better awareness of the uncertainties of life, having been in the war. He was savoring what he had, and sharing it with her. And with Harriet, of course. Allie had adored her scholarly father, but he had never actually played games with her, racing, climbing, making up silly stories and outrageous wagers the way Jack did with Harriet.

Harriet was thriving on the attention her guardian paid her, the activities he planned, the fun he made for her. With little time to be idle, she had less time to get into mischief. She was far ahead of her age in schoolwork, eagerly learning everything Allie set in front of her to make Papa Jack proud of her.

Jack was learning, too, to Allie's amusement. He did not let Harriet keep the injured swan, the soup turtle, or the monkey. If he learned to stop wagering with the child, they might not have to find a place for a decrepit old donkey.

Allie's education was also expanding. Now she knew how a steam engine worked and how a female was led astray, not by flattery and flirtation but by kindness and shared laughter. She learned who was buried in Westminster Cathedral and what dreams were buried deep in her heart. She learned her way around town, discovering that the city was bustling and beautiful, which parts to avoid and which parts to savor. She did not have to be afraid of London anymore, thanks to Jack.

Now she only had to be terrified of her own feelings, thanks to Jack.

Jack returned from their latest outing even more dissatisfied than usual. He was not upset about the sticky stains on his waistcoat or the one-eyed cat he seemed to have acquired in lieu of Joker. He did not even mind that Calloway was not at his post by the front door, but was likely at Carde House's back door, with Patsy. This was a deeper discontent.

The Red and the Black suddenly felt small to him, tawdry. Its very air smelled stale, as if too many people had breathed it. He felt no eager anticipation for the night ahead, winning new subscribing members or winning their blunt. Jack realized he enjoyed his time with Harriet and Miss Silver far more than his time at the tables, where he had to joke with the gentlemen, flirt with the ladies. The pleasure of being with Harriet and Allie was natural, not part of his business.

Yet Allie was still distant. She often walked behind him and Harriet, as if she were no more than a servant. She still looked like a frump, although not as thin and pinch-faced. She laughed and she smiled, but she would not take Jack's arm and she would not stroll through Hyde Park with him at the fashionable hour, when members of the *ton* were on the strut.

"That will only give rise to more gossip," she'd said. She was right, but he did not like limits on their friendship.

Friendship? Jack had never had a female friend before. Lovers, employees, flirts, but none he could call a friend. Nell was his sister-in-law, so she did not count. Besides, she was still wary of him for the snakes and spiders he had put down her back when they were children. She liked him for his brother's sake, not his own.

Jack decided he liked having a woman as a friend. Females did not seem to have that sense of competition males shared, always placing wagers, trying to beat each other at cards or fisticuffs, the speed of their horses, or the glamour of their women. Of course he never thought about any of his male companions in their undress, even when they were, in fact, undressed. He thought far too often of Allie out of her clothes.

Allie was an excellent companion and a good listener, he told himself, gathering his straying thoughts. She was the best of mentors for Harriet, firm but caring. She was giving and generous to her other, nonpaying pupils. She was helpful to the workers at Carde House, giving her woman's opinion when asked and staying out of their way otherwise. Damn, why wasn't that enough for him?

Jack wandered through the club, not going to his office to work on the books or upstairs to change into formal wear for the evening. As he went from table to table, from the empty casino to the busy kitchens to the well-stocked wine closet, he realized that he had what he'd set out to accomplish. He'd proved he could run a profitable business on his own, not dependent on his brother's title or his prowess on the battlefield. He was a success. But was not enough: He wanted more.

Downs rescued Jack from facing truths he did not want to name. "There you are. I thought I'd heard you come back, but I couldn't find you anywhere. A young lady is in the interview room—"

"A lady? The one who came before? Not a prospective dealer or doxy?" Jack felt his pulse start to race. That was what he was missing: fulfilling the promise to his father to find Lottie. "Is she blond? Beautiful? How young?"

"Yes, she is fair and pretty, and yes, very young, when she lifts the veil she wears but—"

Jack was gone, straightening his neck cloth as he ran toward the room behind the black door.

A fashionably dressed young woman and her maid were the only occupants of the room, since it was past business hours. The lady's face was indeed covered, but Jack recognized the quality of her clothes and the elegance of her posture as she sat on the wooden bench. He skidded to a halt in front of the lady, then knelt at her feet, taking her hands in his.

"Lottie? Is it really you?"

The maid shrieked and the young woman pulled her hands away and then slapped him.

Jack rose and stepped back. "My pardon. I take it you are not my sister?"

"But you are as much a rake as I heard." The lady pulled back her veil.

She was no one Jack recognized, but he knew few women in their teens. "You cannot be here seeking a position. If you are seeking thrills, go elsewhere. Well-bred misses are not welcome in The Red and the Black. I do not want irate fathers or husbands thundering through my rooms, demanding my blood or my gambling license."

The young lady blushed at his scorn, but she did not leave. "I have come for an introduction to my cousin. Nothing more."

"And your cousin is . . . ?" Where Jack's blood had been coursing, now it sank to his toes. He knew the answer before his unwelcome visitor opened her rosebud mouth.

"Miss Allison Silver. I am Lady Margery Montague. My father is Earl Montjoy and my grandfather is—"

"The Marquess of Montford," Jack finished for her, then groaned. "He'll try to shut my place down if he knows you are here, and he has the power and influence to do it, too."

"He'll lock me in my room for a month if he finds out, but he need not know. My maid is loyal and will never tell, and my driver is her beau."

Jack looked at the maid dubiously, but she stood

and curtsied. He had no choice but to trust her and her mistress for the two minutes more he would permit them to remain. Lord, what if any early gamesters saw them leave and recognized the carriage or her gown? Montford would have his guts for garters.

"Your cousin is not here."

"I know that. Everyone knows you moved her and the little girl to your brother's home. But I promised Grandfather I would not call at Carde House. You must know that I do keep my promises."

"How very honorable of you," he said, thinking that the chit reasoned like Harriet. Were all girls as devious? Heaven help Alex if the next babe was a daughter. "I do not believe it was the actual house your grandfather objected to. And I do think he would consider your coming to a gambling club a great deal worse."

Lady Margery tipped her head in acknowledgment. "Miss Silver is my cousin. I have a right to meet her. Besides, I admire her greatly. Goodness knows *I* would not be able to support myself if my family lost its fortune."

Lady Margery wore a pink gown with frills at the hem. She had on a light pelisse that was all the style but not warm enough for the weather. The silly goose could not last a day on her own, much less make a career the way Allie had done. Jack doubted the debutante could dress herself or heat water for tea. He felt ancient next to her naïveté.

She was going on: "And I also admire her bravery. Everyone at Montford House heard about how she spoke up to the marquess. No one else has ever had the courage to shout at him." She shuddered delicately. "I never have, at any rate."

"She is indeed a fine woman, your cousin," Jack agreed. "But I do not think it is to the advantage of either of you to become acquainted. Your grandfather could make Miss Silver's life more difficult if he chose."

"He is making my life difficult enough," Lady Margery snapped back, showing her age and her temper and her spoiled nature. "The old crosspatch will not let me marry the man I love."

Ah, Jack thought. This was not about Allie at all. "What about your father? Surely Lord Montjoy is the one who has to approve your future husband."

"Not in my family. Grandfather makes all the decisions because he holds all the bank accounts. Besides, my father is in the country where he always is, tending the estate. Not that Grandfather appreciates the work Papa does for him."

According to the word in town, Montjoy stayed in the shires rather than share a home with his martinet father.

Lady Margery went on: "But I am old enough to be presented now, so the marquess sent for me and Mama to come to London."

"I thought coming to London was every girl's dream."

"For the dancing and shopping, perhaps, the balls and the Venetian breakfasts. But Grandfather wishes me to make an advantageous match." She spoke as if he wanted her to eat insects.

"I believe all parents and grandparents wish the same thing for their children."

"But Grandfather only wants what is advantageous to him. A member of Parliament or some duke's son, some fusty old man like him."

Jack shrugged. That was the way marriages were arranged in the upper echelons of English society. "And you wish to wed . . . ?"

"Harold, from home."

"Ah, Harold from home. He is not your groom, is he, or the stable boy?"

"Of course not. I know what is due my name. He is the son of a baron whose land marches with ours. I have known him since the cradle, and have intended to wed him since I was ten."

"Did Harold know that?"

Color flooded her cheeks, making her look even younger. "He has known since last year, when he turned nineteen. I told him." She lowered her brows at Jack's snort. "But he agreed."

"Yet he does not ask for your hand like a man?"

"He would have, if Grandfather would grant him an interview. Instead he called Harold an insolent dog."

A stripling nobody seeking the hand of a marquess's granddaughter? That sounded like a presumptuous puppy to Jack. "Let me ask you this: Would you be happy living in the country with your baron's son?"

"I like the balls here well enough, but Harold promises we can come to town in the spring. But yes, I enjoy country pursuits. We do have assemblies and dinner parties, you know, so it is not as if we are entirely isolated. Besides, I would miss my mama and papa if I had to move far away or stay in London all the time."

She was too young to marry anyone, Jack thought. It was none of his affair, of course, but he said, "You defied your grandfather by coming here. Why do you and Harold not elope to Gretna Green?"

"Harold refuses. He says that would be dishonorable of him, destroying my reputation."

So the peageese had one brain between the two of them. "Harold sounds very, ah, noble. But what are you going to do, then?"

"I intend to ruin myself."

Jack jumped back and looked at the maid, then at the door, ready to run. "Not with me, you are not."

"Don't be silly. I am saving myself for Harold."

"Thank God. That is, of course you are. True love and all that."

Lady Margery ignored him. "But if I meet my cousin and befriend her, Grandfather will consider me fallen. I will be beneath his notice, like Allison's mother was. He won't be able to marry me off to one of his dreary old friends, so he'll have no choice but to let me go home and marry Harold."

"No, I will not help you ruin yourself. It would be bad for my business. Besides, your cousin is respectably established now. There is no gossip and no scandal, so you are wasting your time. Your grandfather might not like your knowing his outcast relation, but he cannot claim you are disgraced by meeting her."

"I would still like to meet her. Perhaps Cousin Allison will show me how to be brave enough to stand up to Grandfather."

Jack was not sure about Lady Margery's motives, but he was pondering the potentials. Allie and her cousin. Allie and Montford's acknowledged granddaughter. Allie and a member of the *ton*. The association could make a real lady out of the governess.

That was Allie's rightful place in society, and Jack owed it to her to help her find it. Even if it tightened the noose around his own neck.

CHAPTER TWENTY-TWO

"We are going to the Egyptian Rooms at the museum tomorrow afternoon."

Lady Margery made a face reminiscent of Harriet's when Miss Silver declared bedtime. Jack added, "It promises to be highly educational for my ward, and your cousin is interested in antiquities."

"We have some Roman ruins near our house. They are well and good for showing to guests, I suppose, but going to look at mummies? Those are dead people! Viewing them is worse than stepping on a grave. And there are supposed to be curses on those who dug them up."

"All of which is why Harriet is thrilled to be going."

"Gracious, has your ward no tender sensibilities?"

Jack laughed. "Nary a one, I am pleased to say. You'll see, if you meet us. Among the dead Egyptians. Did you know the kings buried their wives and their slaves in the pyramids with them? Alive, some say."

Lady Margery's cheeks drained of color, and Jack

was sorry he'd teased the girl, who seemed to have a surfeit of those fragile feelings, unlike Allie or Harriet, thank goodness. Montford's granddaughter was blond and blue-eyed and rounded in society's current ideal— and almost as much a child as Harriet in Jack's jaded eyes. She was a lady, however, so he begged her pardon. "Besides, weren't you the one who just spoke of learning to be brave? Put some starch in your spine, soldier."

She looked at him blankly.

"I beg your pardon. I am used to lecturing raw recruits. What I meant to say was take a lesson from Macbeth and bring your courage to the sticking point."

She looked just as confounded.

"That is, conquer your fears. If you cannot face a dead pharaoh, you will never stand up to Montford. Then you will never wed your *parfit gentil* knight."

"I told you, Harold is the son of a baron, not a knight."

Jack apologized again, his lips twitching.

Lady Margery squared her shoulders and said, "But you are right. I shall do it. What time will you arrive? And will you tell my cousin of my intention to meet her?"

"Gads, yes. You might think that Montford is hard to deal with when crossed. You have not met our Allie yet."

Lady Margery pulled her pelisse closer. "Perhaps I should reconsider if Miss Silver is another like my grandfather. I see no reason to suffer through the gruesome display if my cousin is not agreeable."

"Nonsense. Miss Silver is nothing like the marquess. She is perfect, and you will be proud to call her cousin."

Something in Jack's voice—or his calling Cousin Allison "our Allie" and "perfect"—must have struck a chord in Lady Margery's calculating mind. She smiled up at him and said, "You know, she is as much Montford's granddaughter as I am, and you are an earl's son."

"I am well aware of everyone's ancestry, miss."

"Yes, but even my grandfather would have to admit that yours would be an ideal marr—"

"Shall we say three o'clock?"

Allie said otherwise. "No, I see no reason to meet the young lady." She untied her bonnet, prepared to stay behind when Jack and Harriet went to the museum.

"What, you are not even a little curious?"

"To see the sarcophagi? Yes, but I can go another day. To meet my cousin? You already told me she is a silly, spoiled little minx. I believe those were your exact words. Oh, and conniving, too, I think you said. I taught enough young ladies like that to last me a lifetime." Allie started to remove her precious new York tan gloves, being careful of the soft leather.

Jack refrained from taking her hands in his to help, just barely. He took a step back, away from temptation, and said, "Yes, but she is a friendly minx who wishes to know her relative."

"Those so-called relatives have blithely ignored my existence for my entire life. I can happily ignore them now."

"Surely you are too fair-minded to blame Lady Margery for her elders' antipathy. She is nothing but a girl. Perhaps she is trying to mend the rift."

"Without Lord Montford's approval, I'd swear. I cannot condone disobedience. That would be a poor example for Harriet."

"You think Harriet obeys now?"

"When it suits her. And when certain persons do

not dare her to defy him by praising the trick riding at the circus, yet forbidding an eight-year-old to try standing on her pony's back."

"The surgeon said her arm is not broken."

Allie went back to tugging off her second glove as if he had not spoken. "As you said, Lady Margery is young. She does not understand what trouble a powerful, wealthy, and determined man like Lord Montford can cause. He can disown her and withhold her dowry, as he did my mother. Will my cousin's beau be so eager to wed her then? Or the marquess can send her away from her loved ones altogether, to some distant relative or tropical estate. A woman, especially a young woman, has no control over her future—the head of her household does."

"The girl is very aware of who holds the reins, but she wants to throw over the traces."

"Then she is a selfish miss, besides. Montford cannot disinherit his heir, of course, but he can keep funds from Lady Margery's parents, or force them from their home. Would my cousin be happy knowing her parents were suffering because of her schoolgirl stubbornness?"

"So should she forget about her childhood sweetheart and meekly accept her grandfather's choice of husband for her? Montford is looking for a London politician or a diplomat, while Lady Margery prefers the country."

Allie hesitated, knowing a gently bred female was raised to be a pawn in the dynastic chess game. She also knew young girls—and old maids—had dreams of their own. "But what of you?"

"As a prospective bridegroom? Montford would give the girl to Old Nick himself rather than me. Unless you were asking whether I preferred the country to the city. I much prefer town. Ruralizing is fine for hunt parties and picnics, but not much else that I can see."

"As you very well know, I was speaking about Montford's ability to shut down your club for interfering with his plans. You told me yourself how much influence he has in the government. The magistrates are in his pocket, and half the courts. He can bring trumped-up charges against The Red and the Black, and against me. He can ensure that I never find another position."

"No, he cannot do that. You shall have a place here as long as Harriet needs you. I need you."

"So you say. But if you lose your income? Or decide to send Harriet away to school? What then? Or perhaps her uncle might yet return to claim her, or her grandmother in Bath could recover enough to wish Harriet's company. I would still need to work."

"You are borrowing trouble. The grandmother is too old and the uncle too dissolute to want a poppet underfoot. And recall, my family is not entirely without money or muscle. Alex can and will protect his own."

Allie lowered her voice and twisted the gloves in her hand, showing her anxiety by ignoring the damage she was doing. "But I am not the Earl of Carde's to protect. I am not his family or his employee."

"What, are you thinking I would leave you to the lions? Or that I cannot take care of my responsibilities? I told you I would not let anyone harm you, and I will not, not even Montford." He took the gloves from her before she destroyed them entirely. "I thought you were coming to trust me. You can, you know. Now be as brave as I urged your cousin to be."

"What, is she afraid to meet me?"

"No, she is afraid of dead Egyptians. If that silly twit can rise above her fears, you can spend an hour

with her. Montford will never know a meeting was
planned, so he cannot blame you, me, or Lady Margery. That is, if he hears of our encounter at the museum at all. I cannot imagine he will, for few of his
cronies frequent such places, and town is thin of company at this time of year anyway. Unless Hapworth
from the *London Lookout* is having us followed, no
one will publish our names in the gazettes."

He handed back her gloves, then watched as Allie
pulled them on and straightened the fingers, smoothed
the wrists. A man could endure only so much temptation, though. He brushed her hands aside and retied
the ribbons on her bonnet himself, letting his hand
rest on the side of her cheek for only a minute longer
than necessary. That minute was necessary to him. He
lowered his head toward her lips, telling himself that
one more little kiss could not make him more of a cad.

As she had the other times, Allie met him halfway.
She leaned forward, closed her eyes, and licked her
lips.

"Aren't you ready yet?" Harriet called from the
door. "We'll be late!"

Harriet was excited to be meeting Lady Margery
and made her best curtsey without waiting for a
proper introduction. The young woman was not her
kin, she understood, but the lady might come to be
vaguely related by marriage, if Harriet's hopes and
prayers and wishes came true. For a child who had
known nothing but aged grandparents, a father far
distant, and uncaring instructors, the bigger the family
the better.

"My grandfather was a viscount," she boasted to
Lady Margery, skipping ahead of the older girl and
her maid through the door that led to the exhibits.

Lady Margery did not want to go forward at all,

but she would not be bested by an unmannered orphan with jam on her face. No, those were freckles, the poor thing. "My father is an earl."

"Well, my father was mentioned in the despatches. He was a brave hero."

Lady Margery's father was not brave at all, staying in Nottingham rather than facing his own sire. She sighed, remembering Harold and her hoped-for marriage.

"That's all right," Harriet said, afraid she had hurt Lady Margery's feelings before she could enlist the young woman's help in making those wishes come true. "My uncle is a murderer."

Lady Margery clutched her vinaigrette and looked around for rescue. The captain had arrived in a large party, and was now speaking with Harold near the entrance to the museum. Lady Margery clutched the little container harder when she saw the captain's companions.

Two of the women were dressed in a fashion more often seen on street corners than in select drawing rooms, and one of the men might have been a pugilist or a pirate, he was so large and rough-looking. Maybe, she hoped, those others were simply strangers who had chosen this very afternoon to visit the Egyptian artifacts. Then the large man took the smallest, youngest of the women on his arm and said, "Me and Patsy've got some business of our own, Cap'n Jack. We'll come back in an hour. I'll keep her safe."

Her grandfather would strangle her. Her mother would dampen the dinner table with tears. Her father would wring his hands and go back to his mangel-wurzels. Lady Margery tried to catch Harold's eyes—which were on a pretty redhead—to signal that she wanted to go home. Then she spotted a slightly older woman in dark clothes with an ugly bonnet on her head. She could not be a loose woman, not in that ensemble, not with her back as stiff as a board.

"Cousin Allison?"

Jack made the introductions. Lady Margery firmly put her arm through her cousin's, rather than chance being forced to walk with one of the men or, heaven forbid, one of the other women.

Harriet had already commandeered Harold as her escort, ensuring that the cousins could speak privately. "I bet there's no real body under those windings," she said.

"Of course there is. This is the British Museum."

"Bet you a shilling there's not. They just say there is to scare children and flighty females."

One of the females was hanging on Allie's arm. She kept looking at Allie rather than at the coffins and hieroglyphs.

"You resemble your mother," she said. "I would have recognized you from the portrait we have of her and my father as children."

"I thought all traces of my mother were erased from her ancestral home."

"Grandfather never goes into our family wing at the Mount. He sends for us when he wishes to give a lecture."

"I see. All I have of my mother is a miniature painted when my parents were first married. But thank you for the compliment, whether you meant to make one or not. I considered my mother quite beautiful."

Lady Margery wrinkled her nose, and not at the smells in the room. "I daresay you could look better than you do if you rid yourself of that dreadful bonnet and wore brighter colors."

Allie slipped her arm out of the other woman's clasp and became busy examining a case of scarabs.

Lady Margery glanced into the glass case and shuddered. "Beetles? They thought insects were sacred?"

"*Chacun à son goût,*" Allie said, then translated when Lady Margery declared she did not read Egyptian. "To each his own. I am a governess, nothing more, so I have no need to improve my looks."

"I have met Captain Endicott, Cousin. There is every need."

Allie studied a nearby glass case of jewelry rather than reply.

Lady Margery was interested in the breastplates and arm bands and rings, but then they moved on to a statue of a jackal-headed figure on a pedestal.

"Why would anyone put a dog's head on a man?" she asked. "That's stupid."

"He was a god, Anubis, I believe." Allie looked ahead for Harriet. "I really ought to be with my pupil, seeing that she learns all this."

"Oh, Harold knows almost everything, so he can teach her. He went to university for a year, you know."

"I did not. How, ah, nice."

Lady Margery thought so, and thought the previous conversation ·was not finished. "I might not be as learned as you," she said while Allie admired the statue of a cat. "Well, to be truthful, I had hardly any education to speak of. Mama could not bear to send me away, and Grandfather would not hear of my going to the local school with the tenants' children. The governesses never cared if I did any lessons at all. However, I do know fashion and I do know that Captain Endicott likes you."

"Nonsense. You have a vivid imagination, that is all."

"I tell you I know about these things. I knew Harold and I were the perfect match, didn't I?"

She looked across the large room to catch his eye and gave a small wave. He smiled back, a wealth of silent communication in the simple exchange, and Allie was jealous. She did not envy her cousin's fortune or her clothes or her jewels or her title, and especially not her youth, but, oh, to have a man look at her that way. She was not too old to remember her schoolgirl dreams of a love of her own, a dream that was keeping her awake nights now, when it might be too late.

Allie could understand why Lady Margery would give up the chance for a more advantageous match, why she would risk incurring Montford's wrath. Her Harold, with his one whole year of university, was a pleasant-looking young man, nothing more. He did not wear his clothes with the same casual elegance as Jack—who could?—nor did he have the height, the breadth of shoulder, the easy, confident grace of the former officer. But he obviously loved Lady Margery. That was enough.

Judging from his attitude to Harriet, Harold would be a good father. Judging from the way he watched Lady Margery's every step, he'd be a loyal husband, sharing the same country pleasures. He would not be out of place in the city, either, if Montford received them after their marriage.

Or they could just wait for his demise. Not even the marquess could live forever. Allie admitted that was a terrible thought, but the old man had played puppeteer for so long it was time for someone to cut the strings, even if that someone was Death with his scythe. Waiting was hard for young people, though, especially young people in love.

Allie supposed that's why Lady Margery was here, defying her grandfather. "Aren't you afraid of what

Montford will do if he discovers you made yourself known to me?"

"Oh, he'll never hear about it."

Montford not hear about it? Everyone heard Lady Margery's shrieks when Harriet took off her sling, unwrapped the bandage around her sprained arm, added some rags she found, and wound herself into a miniature mummy, moaning. If Montford did not hear his granddaughter's screams, he certainly heard her mother's when the girl was carried home in a swoon . . . by a nobody from Nottingham and a notorious gambling club owner.

Oh, he heard, all right.

CHAPTER TWENTY-THREE

"You, stop caterwauling," Montford shouted at his daughter-in-law, making her cry harder.

"You, unhand my granddaughter," he ordered Harold, who was supporting Lady Margery in the marble-tiled hallway of Montford House. She had recovered from her faint, but had not recovered from the delight of finding herself in her beloved's arms. Now she found herself dropped so fast she almost fell to the floor again.

"You," her grandfather told her, "go to your room."

"But I—"

"You have interrupted my correspondence, disobeyed my orders, and torn your gown."

Lady Margery looked down, saw that her favorite sprigged muslin was ripped at the scalloped neckline, likely from her swoon at the museum. Now it was gaping like an open oyster, revealing most of one pearly breast. She gasped like a beached fish and dove for the curving staircase, her clamoring mother and her maid in her wake.

"You, out." The Marquess of Montford pointed at Harold, then at the open front door. He completely ignored Allie and Harriet, who were hovering on the front steps outside, on the unlikely chance they were needed, in Allie's case, or had the opportunity to beg pardon, in Harriet's case.

Harold joined them. Jack would have, too, but Montford pointed his gnarled finger in the captain's direction and said, "You, follow me."

If Montford thought Jack would jump to his orders, he was gravely mistaken. Jack walked toward Allie and told her, "I suppose he deserves some explanation. Tell James to drive you home. I'll take a hackney."

"No, we have only to cross the square, while you'll need to go to the club. I . . . I am sorry if Lord Montford's wrath falls on your head."

Jack smiled in reassurance and tapped his skull. "But you must know it is too thick to damage."

"And too empty to avoid the danger in the first place. No good could have come from today's meeting."

"How gracious of you not to say 'I told you so,'" he said, taking her hand in his.

Allie looked to see if Montford noticed, then gave Jack a gentle shove. "Go back and talk to his lordship before he grows even angrier."

But Jack was not ready to march to Montford's drum. He raised Allie's gloved hand to his mouth, but turned her hand over and found the bare spot of her wrist above the glove's edge. He kissed that.

"You must not. Lord Montford, the child . . ."

"I must." He did it again. "Now, go."

Allie took Harriet and started home—in the wrong direction.

Jack's smile grew as he watched her turn around, blushing while Harriet giggled. Then his grin faded as he followed Lord Montford to the marquess's book room.

Montford sat behind his massive desk without inviting Jack to sit. He sat anyway and crossed his legs to be more comfortable. Since every soldier knew the best defense was a strong offense, Jack said, "Nothing happened at the Egyptian Exhibit beyond a childish prank," before Montford could speak. He did not give the older man the chance to accuse him, Allie, or Lady Margery of plotting to circumvent his express orders. "Your granddaughter—your younger granddaughter, that is—is unharmed. And her curiosity is satisfied."

"The peagoose was curious about the ancient artifacts? I'll believe that when pigs fly."

"She was curious about her cousin, quite naturally, in my opinion. And you made Miss Silver more fascinating to her still by banning the acquaintance. You would not permit Miss Silver to call here, and you prohibited Lady Margery from calling at Carde House. It was inevitable that they encounter each other somewhere. Forbidden fruit, and all that."

Montford pushed aside the letter he had been writing before the uproar in his entry hall. "What, you have had Hildebrand's gal in your care for a handful of days and you are already an expert on child-rearing?"

Jack brushed a speck of museum dust off his trousers from where he had knelt at the peagoose's side. "I am something of an expert on females. Young or old, their minds work the same."

"Faugh, they barely have minds enough to decide what gown to wear to which ball. That is why they need a man to guide them. Margery needs a wiser head than a mere stripling she can lead around like a puppy."

"Her beau seems to be a decent chap with a good head on his shoulders. He did not panic when she fainted, and he caught the gold chalice she threw at Harriet when she found out—That is, he was not fazed by her emotional histrionics, nor by being tossed out of the museum. Many a man would have fled the scene, abandoning his inamorata. Young Harold stayed. A female could do worse."

"An earl's daughter can do far better."

"But Harold loves her."

"Faugh," the marquess said again, slamming the cap on his inkwell. "I'll send her to her mother's people in Cornwall."

"Forbidden fruit," was all Jack said.

"She'll forget about him," Lord Montford insisted.

"He'll follow."

"Not when he finds out I won't pay out her dowry, he won't."

"That did not work with your daughter, did it? Miss Silver's mother married her scholar despite your edicts and your financial finagling."

"Thunderation, I only wanted little Margery to get some town bronze before she settled on that bumpkin. She's too young, I say!"

"But she loves him."

"And she can love someone else tomorrow."

"Then test their affection, do not deny it. What say they agree to wait six months to wed, if you do not separate them or stand between them?" At least Jack hoped the nodcocks would agree, since he was bargaining for their future.

"A year, with no formal announcement, so other chaps can court the gal. With what I paid for her wardrobe, she ought to catch the eye of a nabob, at least."

"They are young, in love, and curious. Surely you remember?" The marquess might be too old to recall passion's eager panting, but the nobleman would never forget his family honor. "Six months, unless you wish your great-grandchildren to arrive before the wedding date."

A quill pen snapped in Montford's hands.

Jack went on, certain of victory: "If they are still desirous of wedding after that time, you'll have no call to forbid the marriage, none that will convince Lady Margery, anyway. I'll wager the youngsters will still be in love."

"Now you are an expert on love, too?"

Jack went back to brushing off his trousers.

"Very well, six months. But no anticipating the vows, is that clear?"

"Lud, I cannot answer for two near strangers on that count. You shall have to speak to Harold."

"Bah, the whelp is liable to wet himself if I raise my voice. You tell him. You're the one doing the negotiating, aren't you? You tell the lobcock I'll see him volunteered for the King's army if he dishonors my granddaughter." He pounded the desk. "You tell him he'll never have to worry about begetting an heir if he gets familiar with the gal."

Jack nodded, although he was not looking forward to that conversation. "I'll tell him. What about Miss Silver?"

"What, is he aiming to dishonor her, too?"

Jack knew the old man was stalling. The gapeseed and the governess? The idea was absurd. "You know he is not. What about Lady Margery's friendship with her cousin? Will you still stand in the way of that relationship now that they have met?"

"Will you give your word you have no dishonorable intentions toward her?"

"Good grief, she is just a child, and in love with Harold besides. I never—"

"Not that one. A downy bird like you would never be interested in a silly widgeon like Margery. I would not let you within a mile of her if I thought otherwise. But Margery is a lady."

"As is Miss Silver. Every inch a lady."

Montford studied the younger man, from his steady brown gaze to his relaxed posture. "That's your answer, then? The schoolmaster's daughter is a lady? Albeit she is naught but a teacher, a governess?"

"She is your grandchild as much as Lady Margery is. And she is a gentlewoman in the finest sense of the word."

Montford stood, the interview at an end. "You are playing a deep game, boy."

"Boy? No, my lord. I am no boy. I am a man grown, my own man, answerable to no one but the Crown and the Almighty. I am a gambler, however. We always play deep. And we play to win."

Jack felt ancient, lecturing Harold. He'd given the talk to his raw recruits about diseases and dagger-wielding foreign fathers, but he had never had to address another young English gentleman about proper behavior in a nearly engaged couple. Heaven knew who was more embarrassed, Harold or Jack.

Jack ought to be used to standing in loco parentis, as it were. Aside from Lady Margery's six months' unofficial betrothal, he had told Calloway to wait six weeks before seeking Patsy's hand in marriage, to make certain they both knew their own minds. They already seemed to know every dark corner of Carde

House and the gaming club. Fedder had been firmly discouraged, forever.

The first banns for Darla and Downs would be posted in six days.

Lud, Jack felt as if he were sixty years old instead of twenty and six.

Lady Margery claimed she was *"aux anges"* when she heard the news that she would eventually have both Harold and her cousin. That is, she claimed she was all oranges, but everyone knew she was thrilled. She even hugged Harriet when they met by prearrangement in Grosvenor Square park a few afternoons later.

The debutante credited Allie with all the success. Her joy, Lady Margery decided, was entirely due to her new relation's influence. She was determined to repay Cousin Allison by bringing her into style, seeing that she was accepted in the highest social circles where she might find an eligible *parti* to marry. Margery did not mention that she already had a brave and handsome hero in mind for Allie. She also refused to listen to Allie's demurrals that she was not interested in dressing like a fashion plate, dancing at Almack's, or donning a wedding ring.

"Besides, it was Captain Endicott who carried the day with your grandfather," Allie told her while Harriet tried to convince Joker to wake up and chase a squirrel through the park. "No one else was brave enough to take him on, much less win concessions from the old despot."

"Pooh, the captain is already up to snuff when it comes to fashion, but he is too far beyond the pale for a single female like me to make socially acceptable. Now if his brother the earl were in town to convince the gentlemen— No, they all gamble at the captain's club. They would not want him waltzing with their wives and doing the pretty with their daughters."

Allie could well imagine Jack in a ballroom, flirting with every woman, deb or dowager. He would make them smile, then make them think he hung the stars. He'd be the handsomest man in the room, Allie imagined, and all the other gentlemen would be jealous. Of course they would not want him winning their ladies' hearts. Of course Allie felt ill at the thought of him doing so. "I would not wish to go—"

Lady Margery was going on: "Mama does not like to entertain here in town, or we could enlist her help. She gets in a fidge whenever Grandfather asks her to arrange a supper party for his cronies, though. She would have the vapours at the idea of serving tea to a here-and-thereian."

"Captain Endicott is no—"

Lady Margery patted Allie's hand, acting like an elder auntie. "Of course he is not, Cousin. *We* know that, but the polite world does not. His own sister-in-law might be able to bring the gentleman back into society's good graces, but the Countess of Carde is a mere babe when it comes to the beau monde. She was a country connection herself, you see, not of the *ton*."

"And she is busy filling her nursery."

"So we shall have to leave the captain out of our plans for now."

"We have no plans, Lady Margery. If Captain Endicott wished to be a member of your fashionable world, he would never have opened his gambling club. He would be going there at night to lose his fortune, not make it. As it is, if he, with all his service in the army and noble birth, is not acceptable in your circles, why should I be? I am a governess, nothing else, and that is all I want to be."

"Piffle. Every woman wishes for a home and family of her own. You might dress like a dowdy old spinster, but I have seen the way you look at the captain when you think no one is noticing. You are even nice to Harriet, so you would adore a nicer child, especially if it were yours."

"Harriet is quite enough, thank you. Educating a young mind is a challenge and a responsibility and brings great rewards."

"It brings the Watch running, too," Lady Margery murmured, then went on: "Grandfather will come around once he gets to know you and when he sees what a good influence you are on me. Why, I would never have apologized to that nasty museum curator if you had not told me I should. Although why I had to write a letter when Harriet did not—"

"I told you, her arm is strained."

"Too bad it was not broken," Lady Margery muttered. "Anyway, you can move into Montford House soon. I know, we can tell Grandfather that I need you as my companion, to help plan the wedding. Mama will be delighted to be saved all the shopping and list-making."

"I have to repeat, Lady Margery, that I am a governess, not a lady's—"

"And you must call me Cousin Margery. We can go pay visits together so the best hostesses see you are a respectable woman, a part of Montford's household."

"I must call you a prattlebox if you do not listen to what I have been telling you. I am a governess, Miss Harriet Hildebrand's instructress. I am employed by Captain Jack Endicott, who has turned his back on polite society to open a profitable gambling parlor. I am not fashionable. I am not of your world and have no desire to step foot on that hallowed ground. I shall not live under your grandfather's roof, even if he should deign to invite me, which is not a sure bet, as Harriet and Captain Jack would tell you. Furthermore, I know nothing of weddings and have less desire to learn about them than you have to learn French grammar."

"Fustian. Every girl dreams of her wedding."

"Every pauper dreams of being a prince. That does not mean he knows how to govern. And dreams are for the young, my dear, not old maids like me." Allie was lying, but her cousin did not have to know the truth. Dreams never faded, it seemed, no matter how hard a woman wished them away. Perhaps when she was old and gray she could forget a pair of laughing brown eyes. Or perhaps not. "Harriet, do not throw sticks for the dog. He will not chase them, and you might hit someone else by— Ouch!"

"Then . . . then you won't be my friend?"

The trembling lip, the tear-filled eyes, Allie had seen them all, heard all the pitiful, quavering notes a young girl could dredge from her soul. Still, she could not help herself. Margery was young, and her very own first cousin. She rubbed at her sore shin and said, "Of course I will be your friend, just not on your terms. I will see you occasionally, likely on excursions with Harriet or here in the square. You'll see that is for the best. I have no experience of high society, and no wardrobe suitable to take a place in it."

But experience was meant to be learned, and clothes were meant to be bought. So Lady Margery went to Harold, who would move the moon for her if he could.

Harold spoke to Captain Endicott, who was teaching the lad the fine art of fisticuffs and how not to be fleeced at games of chance.

Jack talked to Mary Crandall, Allie's supposed companion, who in turn visited Mr. Burquist, Harriet's supposed solicitor. The sooner Miss Silver's future was settled, old—but not too old—Mr. Burquist supposed, the sooner his own comfort with the cozy widow could be considered.

Somehow he found a clause in Lord Hildebrand's will. Somehow he convinced the trustees of Lady Hildebrand in Bath that her granddaughter's upkeep was part of their responsibility. How much easier to send some funds than see to a child. She already had a competent foster father, didn't she? Besides, no one wanted the murderous uncle to inherit more of the Hildebrand fortune than necessary.

Jack was guardian of Harriet, and now guardian of her inheritance.

Harriet had a more handsome dowry.

"I'd rather have a dovecote. We could have pigeons and you could send messages to your brother."

Jack ignored her and invested the entire sum in the Funds, under Mr. Burquist's care.

Harriet had an allowance.

"Can I build an ant farm? Where else can they go in the winter?"

That money was designated for her books and her clothes, with a bit left over for sweets and such.

Harriet had a competence, a quarterly income for her education.

Jack redeemed his racing curricle. "No, you cannot take the reins."

"I'd rather have a frog, then."

Jack felt so good he bought her the frog and disappointed a hungry emigré French count. Now that the Hildebrand estate was paying for Harriet's governess and her nursemaid, Patsy, he could put his own profits in the bank. With no more trouble at the club, he could send the hired guards on to his brother, to work at the estate in Cardington. Fedder the Pimp was not going to bother Patsy, not once Calloway made it known he had an interest there. And the cardsharp Sir Jethro Stevens was still in the Fleet.

Jack left Hawkins and Lundy at the London town house to serve Harriet and the women, but with the men's room and board paid, their wages were not high. And someone had to help look after Harriet's menagerie, which was educational. The inheritance paid for the men, too.

Jack was solvent, above oars with the world, feeling far more optimistic about the future.

And Miss Silver had a raise in salary.

CHAPTER TWENTY-FOUR

"**H**arriet needs new clothes," Jack began.

Allie knew that. Harriet had few frocks to start with after the fire at the school. She'd quickly outgrown them with the plentiful meals at The Red and the Black and Carde House, the clothes that she had not ripped, ruined, or stained beyond repair.

"I had not wanted to ask, with your circumstances so strained and our needing the extra staff at the earl's residence." Allie was going to purchase some fabric from her own savings to make Harriet new apparel.

"Ah, but we are in funds again. The Hildebrand trustees have decided that Harriet should have what her father would have inherited, a good education, a—"

"Will you be sending her to school, then?" Allie's breath caught in her throat, and not just because she was riding high in Jack's curricle, clutching the rail on her side as if that might keep the light vehicle from overturning.

Jack took his eyes off his horses for a moment. "What, can she not learn what she must here? I thought we were doing a superior job of it, you with your lessons and me with the guidebooks."

Allie could breathe again. He wasn't sending her away. That is, Jack wasn't sending Harriet away, she told herself. And he was an excellent hand at the ribbons. They were not going all that fast, after all, not in Hyde Park. "No, that is, yes, we can teach her what a proper young female is expected to know, and more. I am proficient at French and Italian, with some German and Spanish, also the globes, the natural sciences, basic artwork, needlework, and a bit of music. And deportment, of course."

"Of course. I never doubted you knew the perfect conduct for every situation." He slowed the pair of chestnuts to a walk so he could organize his thoughts better—and look at his passenger, or what he could see of her beneath her ugly bonnet and blanketing cloak. "I was not asking for your qualifications. I swear you are the most competent woman I know."

Competent was nice. Allie could think of a hundred things she'd rather be, though. Like beautiful, attractive, alluring. Like the women Jack saw every evening. She gripped the railing until her fingers grew numb.

She saw him in the afternoons, with Harriet, at some exhibition or other, or at Carde House, where he inspected the progress of the renovations, with Harriet. The captain took his ward to riding lessons at the indoor ring at a nearby livery stable, and took her to war with his old lead soldiers, unearthed from the nursery. He was teaching her archery and cricket and croquet in the rear gardens of the earl's town house, being a far more competent guardian than Allie had imagined possible. Now he had noticed the child was in too-small tatters. Of course. He noticed the lowered necklines of the women he employed. He'd even briefly ogled Lady Margery's décolletage in the dratted museum.

"Allie? Miss Silver?"

"Oh. I beg your pardon. I must have been wool-gathering." No, she had been wool-smoothing, trying to tug down the collar of her gray wool gown under her cloak with her free hand. Not that pulling would make much of a difference in the prudishly cut gown, or that she had much to ogle beneath it. At least her gloves were new, if they did not rip under the strain of her death grip on the side of the curricle.

She turned to face Jack to show she was paying attention, but that was a mistake. He was so handsome, driving hatless, with the capes of his coat fluttering around his broad shoulders, that she wished she were better at painting, so she could have this image to cherish forever. Jack with the sky behind him and a pleased smile on his lips, above the common ground, all power and pride and manly confidence. Watercolors would never do to capture that strength of body, strength of purpose.

"Oils," she said, unfortunately out loud.

"Excuse me?"

"Nothing. That is, Harriet is not ready to learn oil painting, thank goodness, for I am not as capable at that medium as I might wish. If she shows aptitude, you might consider hiring a—"

"Harriet does not need another instructor. But as I was saying, the Hildebrand estate is going to be paying your salary now, a larger one than I could afford."

"Truly?" Allie was so happy she could have kissed hi—his dog, who was riding at their feet, his ears flapping as the carriage traveled.

Now she could save more of her income for when she could no longer bear to work for Jack. She was

already half-jealous of Harriet, of all the foolish
things! The dealers at the club dealt her the green
sickness, and the women who came to the club to
gamble, or who smiled suggestively at him while viewing statues at the museums, tied her innards in tight
knots. She could not live like this forever, or even the
ten years or so before Harriet was grown.

Why, the captain might marry before then, to start
a nursery of his own. Allie thought she might die
rather than teach a tiny child with his nose and his
eyes—and another woman's blood in him or her.

He'd select a lady like her cousin, Allie decided,
smarter than Lady Margery but fashionable and as
richly dowered. Perhaps the taint of the gambling parlor would eliminate the most finicky of tonnish families from his consideration, but Jack could choose a
bride from the wealthy merchant class, too. Allie
chose not to be around when he did.

"And a clothing allowance."

"I beg your pardon. I was not paying attention."

He frowned. "Are you feeling quite the thing?
Should we turn back?"

"What, and disappoint Harriet?"

Harriet was riding her pony for the first time outside
of the stable training ring, with Samuel from the Carde
House stables mounted on a sturdy cob on one side
of her and a groom on foot on the other. The surgeon
had declared Miss Hildebrand fit for gentle riding,
since Harriet had only used the sling to tie the kitten
onto Joker, so her so far unnamed cat could learn to
ride, too. Now Samuel reprimanded her for waving to
Jack instead of paying attention to her mount. Allie
could understand the child's distraction, too. "I am
fine. I shall try to keep my wits from going begging
again. Harriet has an allowance, you say? Oh, no, she

will fill the house up with bats and badgers and budgie birds."

"Her personal allowance is for minor incidentals. She has a quarterly sum set aside for her books and her clothes, which is what I have been trying to tell you. There are now ample funds for her to dress like the officer's daughter she is. I wish you to see to her wardrobe."

"That will be my pleasure. Lady Margery will know where we can have frocks made up for her and the best places to purchase fabrics. Shopping appears to be my cousin's greatest pleasure in London—aside from being with Harold, naturally."

Jack clucked to the horses to step up their gait to follow the pony and its entourage. "And your own."

"And my own? No, I do not enjoy shopping. Finding the best gloves at the best price was altogether too time-consuming."

"I was speaking of your wardrobe. I wish you to dress like a gentleman's daughter also."

"I do not understand, and I know I have been paying attention this time. You cannot think that I would let you pay for my clothes?" She used her free hand, the one not clutching the rail, to grab at her bonnet as he set the chestnuts to a trot, leaving Harriet and the others behind.

Jack concentrated on his horses, but he spoke to her anyway. "No, but I cannot have one of my employees traveling about London looking worse than a charwoman."

He meant for her to spend her earnings on fancy dress rather than squirreling it away for a rainy day or leaving after his wedding. "Shall I don a uniform in your colors, then? Red and black, so people know where I am truly employed?" She could not keep the bitter sarcasm out of her voice. To dress in his colors would be announcing to the town that she was no better than she ought to be. Riding alone with him in his sporting equipage was forward enough, even if the park was empty of fashionable strollers. In an hour or two the place would be full of the gossips and gadabouts, although many of the elite had left town to spend the Christmas holidays at their country residences. "I refuse."

Jack's mouth was drawn in a fierce line as he maneuvered his horses off the tanbark and onto a grassy knoll where they would have more privacy. "You work at Carde House, not The Red and the Black, and of course I do not want you to dress like a footman or a parlor maid. Furthermore, I am no longer paying your salary, Hildebrand's estate is. I merely wish you to look like a wellborn miss's companion."

"I look like her governess, which I am."

Jack set the brake. He wrapped the ribbons around the rail and turned to face her. "Your cousin would like to invite you and Harriet to go on calls with her. That is important for Harriet, so she meets other young girls, but also so she will be accepted when she comes of age. She has a decent dowry now, so her circumstances are not as dire as they would be were she a poor orphan from a scandal-ridden family, with a, um, an unlikely guardian, not to put too fine a point on it."

"You mean a bachelor owner of a gambling parlor."

He cleared his throat. "I mean that prospective bridegrooms can overlook a great deal in a well-dowered female, especially if she has their mamas' approval."

"You are planning her wedding?"

"A good soldier looks beyond the current battle to the next campaign."

"Very well, I can understand trying to pave Harriet's way, if Lady Margery is willing. But what has that to do with me?"

"You are a, ah, an embarrassment to your cousin. Not you, of course. She admires you greatly. But your clothes . . ."

"My cousin is a worse conniver than Harriet. I see her dainty hand in this. She wants me to act as her companion, thinking I will let her go off with Harold on her own more than her mother would. She also does not wish to have her cousin in service. That is a poor reflection on her own standing, she feels."

"Can you not consider that she wishes better circumstances for you?"

Allie nodded. "She is a minx, but I suppose she has a good heart. Still, I shall not cater to her whims."

Jack sighed. "I have another reason for wishing you to improve your wardrobe. The search for my sister is stalled again. A young woman who was called Queenie left no trace behind when she left Manchester. I believe she might be my half sister, Charlotte. The mystery of Queenie's birth is simply too coincidental with Lottie's disappearance. On the other hand, if this female is not the one I have been seeking, I have to know that, too, so I can look elsewhere, or give up the quest."

Allie was listening attentively now, but Joker jumped down and found a puddle to drink from. Jack frowned, whether at the hound or his failed hunt, Allie could not tell.

He was going on: "I think she might be a certain female who came to the club, perhaps twice. I do not know why she never called again. But that woman is here in London, and I need your help in finding her."

"Mine? Of course I will lend what assistance I can, but what can I do?"

"You can go to the dressmakers. Every one you can locate, no matter how small or how unfashionable. The woman who raised this Queenie was a seamstress. We know she trained the girl in her craft, and Downs says the young female appeared stylishly dressed. It makes sense that if the woman came to London, she would seek a position at a modiste's shop. Don't you agree?"

"Unless she has friends to visit, or a beau in the city, or enough funds to be here on holiday. Then she might not be looking for work."

He did not want to hear that. "But if she is seeking a position, she would look first at the mantua-makers."

Allie had to concur. "Yes, she is too young and unknown to establish a business of her own. Patrons would not come to an untried dressmaker, so she would have to build a reputation first."

"That is what I thought. Mr. Rourke from Bow Street is scouring the shops, but the women will not talk with him. They are suspicious of his red vest, I suppose, or a clumsy male in their midsts. Or else they simply do not wish to reveal the identity of a proficient needlewoman, lest they lose her services. She might be using another name, or selling her sewing piecemeal, without giving a name at all. I do not know. I only know that Bow Street cannot find her."

"But you think I can?"

"I think that if you let your cousin take you and Harriet shopping, you can hear all the chatter in all the fitting rooms, where a man could never go. Rourke has never managed to get past the proprietress of any establishment. You can. You can ask about this Queenie of the assistants who pin up hems or take measurements or whatever they do."

"But Harriet does not need a huge amount of clothes, merely some fresh pinafores and a pretty frock for dinners or visits. And the assistants will not speak without the lure of tips or the promise of larger orders, which I cannot afford."

"That is what I have been trying to explain. You shall have a clothing allowance, the same as Harriet, as part of your increased salary. It is important for her future, and it is important to me."

To have fashionable clothes in soft, silky fabrics and bright colors without spending her tiny hoard? To make a better place in the world for Harriet? To please Captain Endicott? How could she refuse?

"Yes, thank you."

"Blue," he said, getting down from the curricle and holding his arms out, to lift her down.

"Blue?" She looked at the distance from the ground, and then she looked at his strong shoulders and that lopsided smile, and stepped into his waiting arms.

"Yes," he said, swinging her down but leaving his hands at her waist. "That is the color I have been imagining you in. Blue."

He thought about her? Allie smiled from the inside out.

Then he said, "And I have imagined helping you out of it."

He thought about her without her clothes? Oh, my. Of course he must say that to all the women. But no, he could have any of those women, with or without their clothes on, so he need not imagine anything. Yet he was not paying afternoon calls on willing widows or high-fliers; he was here, with her. Rather, she was here, in his embrace, where she'd never felt so desirable.

Allie was giddy with the feeling. The words, the mental image, the touch of his hands at her waist, the scent of his cologne, all combined to make her spirits soar and her knees go weak. She was drunk on love.

Love? No, that could not be! Governesses did not
fall in love with libertines. They were too smart for
such silly infatuations, weren't they? So why was she
letting Jack lead her behind a stand of trees, where
they could not be seen from any of the paths? And
why, for gracious sake, was she letting him kiss her
senseless?

Because she might die if he stopped.

"I am sorry," he was murmuring between kisses. "I
never meant to do this. It isn't right." His hands were
on her back, her neck, her derriere, pulling her closer
to his body. His very hard, in places, body. "I shouldn't.
I told myself I wouldn't."

He was. And Allie was. And they kissed like
parched castaways finding a keg of rum, deep and long
and wet and not worried about tomorrow.

At last he cupped her face in his hands and kissed
her eyelids, first one, then the other. "But I had to.
I've been good for days now, keeping my distance.
But you are like an exotic wine, once tasted, never
forgotten. I cannot get you out of my mind. No other
woman interests me in the slightest since I met you,
confound it. And I know I cannot have you. You are
a respectable woman. My ward's governess. My employee. Every tenet of decent conduct demands I leave
you alone."

His hands were now under her cloak, cupping her
breasts instead of her face, that was how alone he was
leaving her.

Allie's hands were burrowing beneath the capes of
his driving coat, that was how offended she was. "But
if Mr. Burquist is paying my wages through the Hildebrand estate, then I am not technically your retainer."

"Hmm. But you are not a loose woman."

Not usually. Only when he was nearby, or when she
thought about him. Which was far too often for her

peace of mind. Her mind was in pieces anyway. Only he could put it together. She pressed closer to him still, until nothing but a thread could have passed between them.

Perhaps one more kiss . . .

They might be out of sight of the passersby in the park, but they could not hide from the hound. Joker came to find them, his nose quivering. Then he shook mud on both of them.

"There, now you need a new cloak, too."

CHAPTER TWENTY-FIVE

"**H**ow do you know?" Allie asked Patsy, when they walked together toward the next shop on Bond Street.

"Lady Margery's maid, Perkins, told me where we should go to find the best bargains. She wrote it down, and I can read it, Miss Silver, I can!"

"Good for you, Patsy. But that's not what I meant. How do you know that you are in love?" She glanced behind her to where Calloway was following, his thick arms already full of packages. Jack had taken Harriet driving with him to save the child another boring afternoon of shopping. Allie prayed they both came back in one piece, without another piece of the menagerie.

Calloway had offered to accompany the women, instead of one of the footmen/guards. It seemed he did not like Patsy out and about without his protection, not even in London's busy streets in broad daylight.

Calloway was not the man Allie would have chosen

for Patsy, a green girl from the country. The differences in their ages and experience should have kept them apart. And Calloway was still a large, fierce, battle-scarred soldier, no matter that his heart seemed gentle.

"How do you know he is the man you should marry?" Allie asked.

"Do you remember that day you found me in that alley and Mr. Calloway picked me up as if I were naught but a feather? He told me not to cry, else he would drop me in the gutter."

"How, ah, sweet."

"But then he said he wouldn't let anyone hurt me, and he called me a little chick and he rubbed my back so I wouldn't be afraid. And I wasn't, not with him there. And I reckon I'll never be afraid again. He made sure that dreadful man Fedder knew I had friends now. But we're a lot more'n friends," she whispered, blushing. "Do you believe in love at first sight, Miss Silver?"

"I do not know about that, but I believe a successful marriage depends on respect and common interests and trust."

"Maybe that's how swells pick their spouses. But I know I'd rather be with Mr. Calloway than with any other man I've ever met. If that's not love, I don't know what is. And we'll make a new life together, with bairns in common, if I am so blessed."

"Then I wish you the very best. What say we find a special bolt of fabric this time, for your wedding dress?"

"Oh, Cap'n Jack already gave me coins for that. I've been looking, while we picked out dress lengths for you and Miss Harriet."

"Very well, but since I am not paying for my new

clothes, I can easily afford to purchase you a trousseau. What do you think about a pretty nightgown?"

Patsy looked back and Calloway winked at her.

Patsy blushed even redder, but said, "I think that would be a waste, ma'am. But I have always wanted a silk petticoat."

"Then a silk petticoat you shall have, and silk stockings, too. Does that meet with your approval, Calloway?"

His grin, with one gold tooth, said enough.

Allie asked Lady Margery next, when they were at Gunter's having ices and making lists of more dressmakers and more ensembles Allie should commission. Harriet was on her second dish. Joker was on his third.

"Why, I always knew Harold and I were meant to be together. Do you believe in destiny, Cousin?"

"That people were fated to meet, fall in love, and spend their lives together? I am not certain."

"Well, I do. I believe there is one perfect match for everyone. Harold is mine."

Harriet was not interested in talk of love or marriage, especially when the women were not speaking of Cap'n Jack's marriage. "Are you going to finish your lemon ice, Allie? If not, can I bring it home for Kitty?"

"Yes, I am going to finish it. No, you cannot bring one home for the cat." Allie was not finished plumbing her cousin's opinions of the weighty topics. She had not supposed Lady Margery had a deep thought beyond the cut of her gowns, but the young woman did seem to know about romance. "But how do you *know*?"

Margery had to think a moment, which meant she had to put her spoon down and put a finger on her chin. "Have you ever seen a bonnet in a shop window and thought it was absolutely what you had been looking for your entire life? No, I do not suppose you have, not when you wear such atrocious hats."

Allie had decided that visits to the milliners could wait. Jack's sister was not likely to be working at one of those, and until she had selected all the fabric and styles for her gowns, she would not want to chose a bonnet that might not match. "But what if when you enter the shop and try on the bonnet, it does not suit?"

"It must, if it is the right one. It will not only fit perfectly, but it will make you look and feel more beautiful than you are. Just putting it on makes you happy. No, just knowing you own it makes you happy. That's how I feel about Harold."

"Like he's a hat?" Harriet asked. "That's silly."

Lady Margery sniped back: "Not as silly as taking that dumb dog with you on a shopping trip."

"Joker is a big help. He wanders around and I can follow him without anyone thinking anything of it. So I can look in the back rooms and see if there are any pretty young women named Queenie there."

"You are doing an excellent job, Harriet," Allie said, "but please do not let Joker eat any more of the poor seamstresses' meals. They do not earn a great deal and might have gone hungry if I had not carried so much money with me. And I cannot charge that expense to your trustees since it was due to my laxity. Why do you not go see if Hawkins and Lundy want an ice?"

When Harriet left, Margery continued with her favorite subject: Harold. "I know he is not the best-looking beau, or the fittest, or the wisest. And he does not have a title yet, and never will have a great for-

tune. But he loves me. And I love him. He will never
dishonor me or disappoint me."

Allie sighed and pushed her plate away, unfinished
after all because she was full—of envy.

"And he makes me tingle, too. I feel all shivery
whenever he's nearby. How could I ever think about
another man?"

How indeed?

Darla turned philosopher, too. "Me and Downie?"
The moonstruck look on the dealer's face answered
most of Allie's questions, but Darla was all too happy
to talk of her beloved Mr. Downs. "Do you believe
in luck, Miss Silver?"

Allie put away the storybook she was having her
adult students read. "Do you mean like not walking
under ladders and tossing salt over your shoulder?"

"No, that's superstition. I mean like being in the
right place at the right time. You see, I was set to find
myself a protector. I know I shouldn't be talking about
such things to a lady like yourself, but it's true. That's
not what I was raised up to do, but no man I wanted
to marry ever made an offer, and a girl's got to eat,
doesn't she?"

Allie knew how few opportunities existed for a female, so she nodded her understanding.

"Well, then I heard they were hiring here. And
there he was, sitting at his desk. And then Cap'n Jack
told me to start a diversion, and there he was."

"Luck?"

Darla handed her the jar of chalks. "Good luck.
I've known my fair share of men, chaps with more
money and better looks, but they none of them ever
appealed to me. Downie does. I know he limps, but
that makes him easier to love, 'cause he's not perfect,

and my curly hair never stays neat anyway. He's too serious, but I'm too flighty. He's kind of quiet, but I talk too much. You see? We match. It's like he's the other half of me that I never knew I was missing. And it was just luck that made me come here."

Allie had come to The Red and the Black because she had nowhere else to go. Only time would tell if that was good luck or bad luck. She made a neater stack of the chalkboards the students had been using.

Darla straightened the chairs. "Now I want to share everything with him, my dreams, my future, my children. Even the air I breathe. Oh, he's the one for me, all right. And I mean to get him in front of a vicar before he changes his mind. Or some other girl sees what a prize he is. Just a few more weeks now. I can't wait."

She hadn't. Her wedding dress was already having to be let out.

"Do you believe in second chances, Miss Silver?" Mary Crandall asked. "I do." She passed the plate of sweet breakfast rolls across the table in their sitting room. "I never thought I'd find another man, you see. I loved my Joseph, and he was a good husband, when he wasn't being a soldier. But that was a young love, all groping and giddyap. I didn't know anything, not how hard it would be following the drum or waiting for him not to come back from battle."

Allie could not imagine the strength it took to survive both love and war. She poured Mary another cup of chocolate.

"Oh, I know what the others are saying about me and Mr. Burquist. Cream pot love, they're calling it. But they're wrong. I have my pension now, thanks to Cap'n Jack. I don't need the solicitor's money, but I do need him. And he needs me. No, not to run his household, but to keep him from settling into a crabby, cranky old man. No one wants to be alone forever or have nothing but a cat for company. And he's not too old, if you know what I mean."

Allie knew what she meant: tingles, trust, together forever. Too late, Allie realized. She believed she was in love.

Jack was also making inquiries. "Marriage is such a big step, Downs. Are you completely certain, for once the rest of the banns are read, there is no going back without disgrace."

"Are you questioning me because of Darla, Captain?" The former soldier looked ready to take up his pistols again. "Because she is one of the women of the club and you think I could have bedded her without benefit of clergy?"

Jack held up his hands in surrender and apology. "No, no, not at all. It's just that marriage is so permanent."

"And sex isn't. I know, and I would not have it— or Darla—any other way. I know you saw us in a compromising position."

Compromising, hell. The two were copulating in the broom closet. Jack cleared his throat, denying opening the door to see who was moaning inside. "It was too dark."

"But it's not just about sex. I want to be with her forever, even when we are too old and decrepit to sneak around corners and make love in hackney carriages or under the craps table."

Good grief. Jack wondered if he should purchase the pair a special license, but the wedding was soon, and he supposed a few weeks would not make much difference in the appearance of their first child. He hoped they did not name the babe Roulette or something, in commemoration.

"She makes me happy," Downs was saying, "and I want to spend my life making her happy in return. And she'll keep her vows, if that's what has you worried, the same as I will. The idea of lying with another woman leaves me cold. The notion of another man touching my Darla . . ." His hands formed into fists. "Well, I might not be agile enough to take up swords, but I can still shoot. That's another thing. Darla doesn't mind that I will always limp. I can't dance or take her for long walks in the countryside, which bothers me, let me tell you. But she says it makes me more attractive, like that Byron chap. As long as she doesn't expect me to spout poetry, that's fine. And she is learning to read, for me, she says. How could I not love her?"

"I cannot imagine. Just do try for a bit of discretion, will you?"

"We did lock the wine cellar door. How were we to know Calloway and Patsy were already there?"

"It ain't just the sex, Cap'n, I swear. Nor that I feel protective of the little dab of a thing either. She's safe enough now, and I still want to look after her."

"But marriage? At your age?"

"I'm not all that old, begging your pardon. Just had a hard life, is all. And I aim to have an easier one from now on. Not finding a different woman every time I want my itch scratched, not going drinking all night for something to do. Not getting into brawls for the hell of it. No, I aim to be a good husband to my gal. She deserves it."

"I am sure she does. Patsy seems a likable sort, and she is doing an admirable job with Harriet and Miss Silver." Both were looking better by the day, prettier, neater, more like ladies than street sweepers.

Calloway's massive chest puffed out in pride. "She is learning her trade all right and tight. And she'll keep doing it, until she has a bairn of her own."

"Not too soon. Please."

Calloway grinned his gilded smile. "I told you, it ain't just about the sex. My Patsy's as sweet as sugar and soft as a summer shower. As pretty as any of those pictures in those museums you go to, too. And she loves me, crusty old soldier that I am, tattoos and all. Do you know how that makes a man feel? Ten feet tall, Cap'n, ten feet tall."

"Yes, well, carry on, Calloway," Jack said, then hastily added, "but not at Carde House. I wouldn't want Harriet to see anything unfit for her tender eyes."

"Then I guess I can't show her my new tattoo like I promised. It's PATSY, spelled out on my—"

Jack left. He didn't want to know.

Jack felt foolish asking the solicitor his intentions, but he felt he owed it to Sergeant Crandall's memory to make sure Burquist was not playing fast and loose with the dead man's widow.

"That's none of your business, sir," the older man puffed. "But I will tell you that I am not one of you young rakehells, acting the tomcat about town, so you can stop glaring at me that way. I have never kept a mistress, not in all my years. I fully intend to marry Mary Crandall, if she will have me, as soon as I can accustom myself to the idea. I have spent my entire life alone, dining when I wish, visiting my clubs when I feel like it. I never thought of having things any other way until Mary Crandall came by and made me realize how lonely I was when I did not have to be. Changing my ways will be hard, though." He looked down at his lap, speaking of hard, and smiled for something he'd thought he'd lost. "But Mary is worth it. Not that this is about sex, of course."

Of course not.

Jack felt even more foolish asking young Harold about his coming leap into parson's mousetrap. The boy barely shaved. What did he know about life and loyalty and regard for the same woman lasting for the rest of your life?

Not for the first time, Jack wished his older brother were in town, or that he lived closer. Ace would understand Jack's confusion, for he'd fought off the matchmaking mamas for years before deciding to marry Nell. She was the ideal match for him, of course, despite their differences, but how had Alex known that?

Harold barely understood Jack's question. "What do you mean, why am I marrying Margery? I love her. Why wouldn't I marry her?"

Why, indeed?

CHAPTER TWENTY-SIX

No one asked Harriet what she thought. What, consult an eight-year-old about the nature of love? Seek a little girl's opinion of matrimony? She couldn't even know anything about the physical attraction between two adults, much less whether it would last, to build a permanent relationship upon it.

They should have asked her. Harriet knew plenty. More important, she knew what she wanted.

Harriet wanted a family, with two parents who were going to stay together. Not a governess who could be dismissed or who might take another position; not a guardian who could marry a wicked witch who believed in sending children away to school or keeping pets in the barn. She wanted her beloved Papa Jack and her dear Allie to get married so she did not have to worry about them moving apart, leaving her homeless again.

They loved each other. Harriet knew it. She could tell by how Allie went all rosy when Papa Jack came to call for them, and how she pretended not to notice how smooth his shave or how tight his pantaloons. She noticed, Harriet knew, because she blushed even redder.

And the captain watched the teacher all the time, and smiled to himself when no one was watching. Harriet was watching, to make sure he noticed how Allie's new clothes were in style, with lower necks and higher waists. He noticed, Harriet knew, because he licked his lips as if his mouth were dry. Besides, he called her a goose, which meant he liked her, all right.

They had to be in love, and they *had* to want her.

They had to want each other, too. Who said Harriet did not know about physical attraction? Harriet knew that Patsy and Snake were always sneaking off for cuddles, and Darla and Mr. Downs were forever stealing kisses. No, she could not believe that babies came from the broom closet, because she checked, but she'd overheard Mrs. Crandall say that Darla had found one there.

Harriet wanted a baby. A brother or sister. Maybe one of both. Dressing the dog was all well and good, but Joker couldn't talk or play skittles or giggle under the covers at night like some of the girls at school had done.

Everyone knew only married people could have babies, which was why Darla and Mr. Downs were hurrying through the reading of the banns. But Allie and Papa Jack did not seem to be in any hurry at all.

Allie did not want to marry a gambler. And Jack did not want to marry anyone. Besides, the captain was trying to find his sister. He was spending all his money on that, so he couldn't afford to keep a wife. Harriet hadn't found anything about Queenie at any of the dressmakers they went to, and neither had Allie, but they kept trying.

Meantime, both of them were as stubborn as Joker. And as silly as the kitten.

They needed help.

Lady Margery had agreed to lend her assistance toward making the match, but so far all she'd done was drag them off to meet this dowager or that dragon—and advise Allie to lower her necklines another inch. Harriet could not see where that did any good. If a gentleman only looked at a lady's bosom, he wouldn't notice her nice eyes and her friendly smile. And, Harriet feared, Allie's bosom could not compete with the dealers' at the club or even the fancy ladies whose front shelves acted as crumb-catchers during those everlasting teas.

Besides, if Papa Jack only liked Allie because her clothes were in the latest styles, his liking wouldn't last. Allie was pretty inside, where it mattered, but Lady Margery was too addlepated to understand. She was too happy with her Harold to bother about Harriet's problems anyway.

So Harriet decided to pay a call.

She was used to doing this by now, sitting through boring conversations in her best new frocks that she was supposed to keep clean. She was supposed to mind her manners, too, which meant not speaking unless she was addressed, sitting straight in a chair without swinging her legs, and not putting any of the silverware in her pockets with the macaroons for Joker.

Harriet decided that she almost liked shopping better, where she could wander off and talk to the seamstresses. She wanted to help Jack find his sister, but the measurements were tedious and the fittings were painful if she wriggled.

She wrinkled her nose. She'd rather be in the park or the stables or in the kitchens at The Red and the

Black or playing games with the workmen at Carde House than either ladylike pursuit. But today she was tired of waiting. She had bigger game in mind.

She doubted she'd be welcome at her destination, so Harriet decided to bring a gift. That was proper and polite, wasn't it? Allie would approve.

When Harriet announced to Hawkins that she was going to the stables, he thought nothing of it. She frequently visited her pony and the rest of her menagerie in another one of the box stalls. He went back to throwing the dice with Lundy. Harriet went to the back of the house and across the gardens to the rear gate. The mews were on the other side of the fence, guarded by Samuel. But Samuel was out driving Allie and Patsy on their latest shopping expedition, as Harriet knew full well.

Would her host prefer the white rat or the fish in its bowl? The rat was not precisely housebroken, especially when one first picked it up, and the fish's water might slosh on Harriet's new coat. She took a tin bucket that had a mesh lid instead.

Then she walked across to the road to Grosvenor Park, waving to all the nannies and the flower seller and the old man who fed the squirrels. They all waved back, assuming Miss Silver or one of the other Carde House residents was nearby as usual.

"Hey, where's yer dog?" the newsboy called out.

"Home sleeping," Harriet replied. "The lazy thing."

"I guess you don't have any treats in yer pockets, then."

Of course Harriet did, in case her host made her wait or did not offer her tea. She shared her toast fingers and butter with the boy, who grinned and wished her a happy afternoon.

It would be, if Harriet had her way.

*　　*　　*

When Allie returned from her shopping trip, laden with packages, Jack was waiting in the hallway, conferring with the architect. Allie started to hand her bundles to Hawkins and asked him to help Patsy upstairs with the rest.

Jack took a hatbox from Allie, tempted to look inside, curious about her taste now that she was not restricted to plain and dull. So far the gowns and accessories she had purchased were tasteful without being flamboyant. They suited her. And one at least she swore was blue, although he had not seen it yet. The gown she wore today was a soft, light brown that made her hair look more golden—and made Jack want to see how silky it felt. The dark honey curls were now allowed to trail around her face and down her neck from a top knot, instead of being plaited so severely at the back of her head. Jack's fingers twitched to take the pins out and let her hair fall altogether down her shoulders.

Now she looked more like a lady of stature than a spinster of strained circumstances. She did not resemble a fashion doll, either, thank goodness, all ruffles and ribbons and lace, so she must not be listening to her cousin. He handed the hatbox to the footman and tried not to stare at Allie.

"I wanted to speak with you."

"And I wished to speak with you."

He led her past two workers chipping at paint flakes on the ornamental plaster work in the hall. He opened the door to the breakfast parlor, which was almost completed. Allie knew, because she had selected the wallpaper when the countess's choice was unavailable, and had checked on the progress and the results. It was bad enough she was living in the Lady Carde's house without inflicting her suspect tastes on the other woman.

The wall covering of tiny flowers in a diamond pattern was cheerful and bright, perfect, she'd thought, for the first thing in the morning. Who could resent getting out of bed in such a springtime, sunny room? The round table and sideboard and chairs were all pushed against one wall, covered in holland cloth so they looked like miniature icebergs amid the garden. No one was working there.

"Good," Jack said. "Now we can talk." But suddenly he did not have the right words to say.

Neither did Allie, although she had been rehearsing a speech for hours, it seemed. "Do you think your sister-in-law will like the wallpaper?" was the best she could do.

"Bother the wallpaper! We need to talk about this . . . thing between us."

There was nothing but a broom and a dustpan between them, as far as she could see. Then she looked back at him, which was a mistake. Jack's eyes were full of heat and hunger, and suddenly there was nothing between them at all except a few layers of clothing. His mouth was on hers, coaxing and caressing.

Allie knew she should not permit such liberties, of course. And of course she knew that Jack would let her go instantly if she protested. She also knew she wouldn't be able to make that protest, to tell him *no*, to step out of his arms and forgo the pleasure he offered. She never had been able to resist Jack, so why bother now, when she had already decided to give herself to him?

Instead she wrapped her arms around him, pressed her body closer to his, and kissed him back. This was exactly what she wanted, what her body had been craving, what her mind had been imagining, what she'd convinced herself was meant to be.

Allie let her tongue touch his in tentative exploration, to be rewarded with a deep sigh. Or was that hers? She breathed in the spiced scent he wore and tasted the wine he'd been drinking and felt a pressure against her that was matched by a pressure inside her. Both were growing, it appeared.

"Oh, Jack," she murmured into his ear when he bent to trail kisses down her neck, now that her gown did not button to her chin. "I should tell you to stop."

"Oh, Allie, I will die if you do." He was bending lower, to kiss her collarbone, and then the soft flesh that rose from her lowered décolletage. His tongue flicked out to lick that sensitive, satiny skin, and she sighed. Or was that him?

"This is wrong, but it feels so right."

"We can make it right, sweetheart."

He was already making her wish her precepts to perdition.

"I should leave, but I couldn't bear to miss this."

"You will never have to."

Never? But mistresses did not last forever. No, Allie refused to think about that now. She refused to do anything but feel, and float on his desire for her. And hers for him.

"This," he said, his fingers trying to tug the gown lower so his mouth could taste more of her. "This is what is between us. I cannot keep my hands off you."

Her hands were busy, too, loosening his neckcloth so she could kiss his neck and feel the difference between his shaved cheek and his chin. Her mouth just happened to be next to his ear, so she tasted that, too, and he groaned, which was precisely how she felt.

She was not in pain, but she was aching. She did not have a fever, but she was burning. "And I cannot refuse you."

"Good. Then you will?"

Despite the steam inside Allie's skull where her

brain used to be, she knew she was crossing a boundary that she could not recross. Once she became Jack's lover, there was no going back to being the prim and proper Miss Silver.

To hell with Miss Silver. The person that she was here, now, in his arms, had never felt so alive, so needed, so much a woman. "I will."

Then she was in Jack's arms, her feet off the ground, and being carried toward the table. He swept away the dusty cloth covering and sat her on the bare wood, with her legs dangling over the edge. He stepped between them, raising her skirts to make a wider space. "You have made me very happy, my love."

Already? Allie intended to make him—and her—a great deal happier. She was not quite sure how, but she had an expert to show her. She pulled Jack toward her. Now he had both hands free to stroke her while he kissed her and whispered words of endearment: He'd never met a woman like her, he could not stand to be without her, Harold had told him how it would be.

"Harold? You talked about this with Harold?"

Since his hand had raised her skirts even higher and was inching up her thigh, he could honestly say, "Not this, exactly."

Then his hand was exactly where he wanted it to be, and where Allie had never dared imagine it being. She was feeling sensations swirling through her and leaving her gasping and glowing and grabbing at Jack's shirt front to pull it up, so she could feel his chest and the soft hair that grew there and try to reach what was below the waist of his trousers.

He moved his hand, to stop hers. "Not yet, my love. Let me lock the door. It would be just like Harriet to walk in."

"Harriet who?"

He laughed and left. Allie suddenly felt cold. No fire burned in the empty room, and no heat coursed through her blood without Jack to keep her warm. The thought of Harriet was like an Arctic blast.

Harriet was a child, her pupil, the girl she was supposed to be teaching ladylike conduct. Allie was meant to set an example, a moral paradigm of virtue. On the breakfast table?

Good grief, she'd been about to let herself be served up like a rasher of bacon, a bowl of eggs, a stack of toast! No poor dead kipper could feel as wretched as she did at that moment. Allie jumped off the table, her cheeks flaming scarlet to think that she had been such a willing accomplice in her own seduction. She shook down her skirts and tugged up her bodice, and passed Jack on the way to the door.

"Where is Harriet, by the way?" she asked as she started to turn the key in the lock again. "You said she might stay behind with you rather than sit through another fitting."

Jack was mentally kicking himself for destroying the moment. But there would be more moments, thank the gods of fertility, now that she had said yes. He ran his fingers through his disordered curls, wishing he could do the same for Allie's hair, but then she would look more wanton and well loved. He sighed for lost opportunities and lustful longings, and said, "That was earlier. I had to speak with the foreman here about the roof tiles, so I brought her home after an hour of feeding the ducks on the Serpentine. Joker ate most of the bread."

"Ah, then she must be in the kitchen looking for more, or out in the stable, feeding her pets."

"No, she said she was tired and was going to take a nap."

"A nap? Harriet? And you believed her? You are even more a fool than I am, thinking I could become your—"

Jack was already halfway up the stairs to the guest wing. Allie flew after him. She was just in time to see him fling back the covers over a small figure in a lacy white nightcap.

Joker growled, angry at being disturbed.

"Damnation!" Jack cursed, and the dog jumped off the bed, crawling under it.

Allie looked there, but saw only a missing stocking. "Why would she have lied?"

Allie looked in her room and the dressing room, then across the hall in Mary Crandall's room. "Because she is Harriet. It is second nature to her. But I wonder where she would have gone?"

"Better yet, why?"

Allie looked in the clothes press. Only one of Harriet's new gowns was missing, and her cloak and the new chip-straw bonnet. "She did not pack up her belongings."

"So she did not run away from home."

"She wouldn't. She loves it here and loves you. She most likely wanted to spend the afternoon in the stables with her pony and the rest of her menagerie and knew you would not let her, with Samuel gone driving me and Patsy. I think she was concerned about that hedgehog's cough."

Jack was already striding out of the door and down the stairs, shouting for the guards and the workers. No one had seen the girl since she went to the stable, hours ago. Hawkins had assumed she'd come in through the kitchen door, as she often did.

Samuel was still rubbing down the carriage horses. He hadn't seen Harriet since the morning.

The boxes and bowls and cages of Harriet's collection seemed undisturbed, and the pony was placidly munching its grain.

The footmen were sent to scour the rear gardens. Jack checked the kitchens and the cellars while the workmen searched the renovation area. Patsy and Allie opened every door on every one of the upper floors and the attics, calling Harriet's name.

Allie met Jack back in the entry foyer, worried now. Harriet was willful and wily, but she would not miss tea, or time with her Papa Jack. "I cannot understand why she would leave."

"Or where she would go." He sent a messenger to The Red and the Black, just in case Harriet had decided to visit one of her friends there, although she was never supposed to travel anywhere on her own. "She intends to come back," he reassured Allie. "She would never abandon her pets. Or you, of course."

Allie was not comforted. "But heaven alone knows what could happen. London is such a big, crowded place. She does not know her way around all that well and might get lost. And I doubt she has a full purse after purchasing that goat."

"We have a goat?"

Allie ignored him and went on: "What if someone sees a nicely dressed child out on her own? She could even be abducted, now that she looks as if she comes from a prosperous home."

"Lud, some poor chap will be sending us money to take her back."

Allie could not laugh at Jack's effort to relieve her anxieties. This was London, and Harriet might be alone, frightened, hungry, and friendless.

That was Allie's worst nightmare, and Harriet could be living it.

"Find her, Jack!"

CHAPTER TWENTY-SEVEN

"You know I will," Jack said.

But Allie was weeping, so he took her in his arms. "It is all my fault," she wailed against his chest.

"Hush, sweetheart. It is none of your fault. I should have known the little she-devil was lying."

"But she is my responsibility. That is what you are paying me so handsomely for, to look after her. And her grandparents, to keep her safe. But there I was, fussing over foolish clothes like some vain debutante in her first season."

"No, you were asking after that Queenie woman for me."

"But I was enjoying myself picking out styles and colors and feeling the luxurious fabrics. I had no business neglecting my true duties."

"I asked you to, as a favor, remember? And you deserve pretty things, too. What woman would not enjoy them?"

"Then I should have taken her with me. We all

know how Harriet gets into mischief if she is left to her own devices. I should have stayed here with Harriet, teaching her to play the harp. I saw one in the music room under wraps. Harriet's musical education has been neglected too long."

Jack released her from his arms long enough to reach for his handkerchief. As she blew her nose, he said, "Her musical education has not been neglected long enough if it means I have to sit through another harp recital. I swore off the plaguey things when I joined the army. Try the pianoforte if you must—I'll make sure it is in tune—but not the harp."

Allie sniffled and agreed.

"Besides," he went on, wishing he had another excuse to take Allie back into his arms where she fit perfectly, "you left her for what, a few hours? Even the lowest scullery maid is entitled to her half day off. A week with Harriet ought to count as a month of battle time, so you deserve more holidays. We'll hire another woman, a real nanny, for those times, and so we can go out in the evenings without worrying."

"What, now my negligence shall cost you an additional expense?"

"Cease blaming yourself, Allie. It was my fault for believing the little vixen in the first place—and for letting her out of my sight while you were gone. I trusted the brat when she said she was taking a nap. I knew she had Joker and the kitten, and the new book we just bought. I expected her to obey me when I told her to be good, as if she were one of my soldiers. Lud, I wouldn't be surprised if Burquist tries to overset my guardianship. Now that there is money involved, he can find any number of families willing to take the snippet. I guess I just proved I am no fit trustee. After all, what do I know about being a father?"

"You know everything you need to know."

"Except where Harriet is."

The messenger came back from The Red and the Black with Downs and Calloway, Darla and the cook, but no Harriet. They had not seen her. Nor had Lady Margery, when Allie and Jack hurried across the park square to Montford House. The nannies were all gone, taking their charges home for supper. The flower girl had sold her final bouquet ages ago, and the newspaper boy had taken his last issues to a busier section of town. The man who fed the squirrels was asleep on his bench, and no one else had seen a small red-haired girl.

The butler at Montford House was at the vintner, selecting wines, but a footman quickly summoned Margery from the orangery. The young lady was out of breath and Harold was out of his cravat, but they had not seen Harriet. Margery ran upstairs to her room, thinking Harriet might have been waiting for her there, but no, all of her face creams and lotions were intact. Harriet had not been in the bedchamber. The others looked in all the rooms off the entry hall, in case Harriet had fallen asleep until Lady Margery returned. The only place they did not check, of course, was the marquess's book room.

They met up again near the front door and hurried back to Carde House, hoping the child had returned on her own. Mrs. Crandall was wringing her hands, while Darla was weeping in Downs's arms. Well, she was in Downs's arms, anyway.

Jack sent for the Watch and Bow Street.

"I'd wager she just went for a walk and forgot the time," the young Runner, Mr. Rourke, suggested, taking notes in his Occurrence book. "You know children."

Actually, Jack did not. "But I do know Harriet. If

she had been for a mere walk, she'd have returned hours ago, with a giraffe in tow."

"And she would not be missing her afternoon tea," Allie added, "leaving Joker to fend for himself."

"Maybe she went to Hyde Park to view the toffs in their finery?" Calloway asked, his beefy arm around Patsy. "She likes to look at the horses."

Allie shook her head, still clutching Jack's handkerchief. "No, she promised never to go so far on her own, and Harriet would not go back on her word."

The others looked uncertain about the brat's sense of honor, but they did not speak their doubts aloud.

Allie did. "Someone must have stolen her from between the stables and here or else she would have returned."

Jack cursed. Someone had stolen his sister, and they never got her back. "No, that cannot be," he insisted. "Harriet is no infant. She knows her way around. She climbs trees and drainpipes and rides horses twice the size of her pony."

"She does?" Allie went two shades paler.

The Bow Street officer made more notes.

"And she never goes anywhere without her slingshot," Jack concluded. "So she is fine. And will be until I get my hands on her for causing us this worry."

"But she is just a child!" Allie cried.

Jack put his arms around her, not caring that the Carde House hallway was filled with interested spectators. "Get any thoughts of foul play out of your mind. No one has abducted Harriet. No one."

Just to make certain, he sent Calloway to make sure the pimp Fedder was not getting his revenge, and he sent Rourke to see that the card cheat was still in debtor's prison. He deployed everyone else to search again, to knock on each front door and kitchen door in the neighborhood, all the grand houses and the smaller ones, too. "Ask if anyone has kittens or puppies she might have gone to visit, or if they saw her speaking with a peddler, especially if someone was selling live chickens or piglets. Talk to everyone!"

Dealers, doormen, and decorators all scattered throughout Grosvenor Square, with Harold and Lady Margery calling on the owners of the houses, the others asking the servants if they had seen a red-haired child. Samuel volunteered to ask at all the stables.

Mrs. Crandall and Patsy stayed behind. They were to recall the searchers by beating the fire gong when she was found, because those two were the least likely to beat the missing girl.

Jack could not swear he wouldn't throttle the brat, just for that haunted look in Allie's eyes. As he led her away from the front of the house, wondering where to look, he grasped Allie's hand and said, "We'll find her, I promise."

"But you promised to find your sister and you have not!"

When Jack dropped her hand Allie brought it to her mouth. "Oh, I am so sorry. I should never have said that. It is just that I am frightened and—"

"You need not apologize. Do you think I do not live with the truth that I have not fulfilled my vow to my own father?"

"But you were a boy when you swore that oath, and you have been trying ever since. And your brother, who has all the resources in the world, made the same vow, and he has not succeeded either."

"No, but we shall find Lottie. And we shall find Harriet. And heaven help anyone who has harmed either of them."

Allie took up his hand again and squeezed it. "We will find them. Together, we will."

But no one rang the gong and none of the searchers had any news.

"Damn, I wish I knew where else to look," Jack said. "If that chit thinks this is some kind of joke, hiding—"

"Joker! That's it! The dog can find her! He's a hound. That is what he is meant to do, isn't it?"

"Joker believes he is meant to find lamb chops and a soft bed. I doubt he could trail a rabbit if it bolted in front of him, unless it was carrying a tray of strawberry tarts."

"But we can try!"

So they went back to the house and up to Harriet's room, where the dog was looking disgruntled, his wrinkled brows and baggy eyes giving him a pitiful look. He'd been shut in, with no treats or tea.

With the promise of a meaty bone or a macaroon, the old dog followed Jack and Allie down the stairs. Allie waved one of Harriet's stockings, from her darning basket, under his nose. "Find Harriet, Joker. Find your friend. She'll find you food."

Joker ambled down the front steps and across the wide street to Grosvenor Park with Allie eagerly following, offering encouragement and the promise of steak.

"You see?" Jack held the gate open for the dog and Allie. "He just had to relieve himself."

Harriet had to, also. She'd been waiting hours, it seemed. And she'd been good. Well, she'd been good after lying to the Montford House butler about waiting in Lady Margery's chamber, that is. But the sneering old stick was too full of himself anyway, so he did not count. Once she'd found the marquess's book room, though, once the butler went about his duties, she had not touched any of his lordship's papers or sampled any of the interesting contents in the nearby decanters. She couldn't help it if the frog got out, though. Or that a table had fallen over when she tried to catch him. The jade horse was not in all that many pieces. Allie could fix it.

But Allie was not here. She ought to be, though. She'd like all the books in their leather bindings. Thinking of the injustice done her beloved teacher, Harriet was resolved to stay, no matter how hungry she grew, no matter how loudly nature called. She ignored the other calls, too. The door was so thick here that she could not make out the words, and did not care. No one knew where she was, so no one would be looking for her.

She would have been gratified to think that she mattered to so many people. For most of her life Harriet had mattered to no one. Now she had to make sure that never happened again.

The country was going to hell in a handbasket, and the idiots in Parliament would do nothing but argue about how fast it was rolling. Lord Montford was weary, aggravated, and irate. He did not care about any crisis in Grosvenor Square or that his granddaughter had gone off with hapless Harold to help. The marquess did care that his dinner would be late, deuce take it. He decided to wait in his blessedly quiet private sanctuary, with a bottle of cognac.

And a frog?

His beloved book room was in a shambles, the end table overturned, a priceless jade sculpture in pieces. Worst of all, a small red-haired gremlin was hopping from foot to foot in the center of the room in some pagan dance. As the marquess stood there, his mouth hanging open, the imp thrust the slimy creature into his hands.

"This is for you. I've got to piss. And Allie needs her dowry."

Great gods, he'd lost his mind! Pointing—with a frog, by Jupiter!—Montford directed his unwelcome but now identified visitor to the water closet through a hidden door. The frog could wait. Allison Silver's doubtful dowry could wait. Hildebrand's brat could not wait, it appeared.

Montford wanted his cognac more than ever. And more of it. But his hand was shaking—no, that was the blasted frog. The Marquess of Montford was holding an anxious amphibian, and which of them was the more appalled he could not begin to guess. Damn, if the little witch wasn't using the chamber pot, he could put the frog there. Instead he set the beast in a cut-crystal goblet, and used a second one to better purpose as he sank onto the chair behind his desk.

"I do not suppose you know anything about a disaster in Grosvenor Square, do you?" he asked when the moppet reappeared, looking much more cheerful.

"No. Did I miss something interesting? Drat! But I have been waiting for you for an age." Her voice sounded accusatory, as if running the country was less important than an interview with an impossible infant.

Montford was too exhausted to argue the point, or to point out that he had not invited her. "I would not be surprised if people were looking for you. Run along now. And take your familiar—that is, your friend—home with you."

Harriet crossed her spindly arms over her chest. "Not until you listen to what I came to say."

Montford could have rung for his butler. He could have shouted for a footman. For that matter, he could have picked up the chit and tossed her out the door himself. But he was tired, old and tired, and no one had brought him a gift in years. He looked at the frog in his heirloom crystal, gulping, then he looked at the freckle-faced girl with flyaway curls, glaring, and he laughed.

His butler would have called for the doctor. His daughter-in-law would have fainted, and his grand-daughter would have turned into a watering pot. Harriet Hildebrand laughed with him.

"There," she said. "I knew you couldn't be such an ogre. So you have to see that Allie—"

"That should be 'Miss Silver' to you, missy."

"Oh, Allie isn't stuffy at all, sir. And she loves me. She says it every night, although she always adds that it's against her better judgment, but that is all right. And she loves Papa Jack, too."

"That would be Jonathan Endicott?"

"Cap'n Jack, that's my new papa."

"And does he love him against her better judgment, too?"

"Oh, no, everyone loves him. But, you see, he can't really afford a wife and a family, and Allie's afraid he might lose what he has, because his business is gambling."

"Does he love her, too?"

"Of course. He'd never get married if he didn't. That's what Mrs. Crandall says, that a bachelor won't budge unless his heart kicks him in the . . . that is, he needs a good reason. Allie's the best reason he could have, and the best wife he could find, except that she's poor. If she had a dowry, they would get hitched, like Samuel says, I just know it."

"And then your guardian could gamble with my money instead of his own. No thank you. I could feed my bank notes to the hogs. At least I might get some bacon out of the investment."

"Oh, Cap'n Jack would never wager with Allie's money. He is a gentleman."

"And half the members of the House of Lords, gentlemen all, are in debt to the cents-per-centers while their well-dowered wives go without new frocks. There is no guarantee what a hardened gamester will do."

"But Papa Jack isn't like that. He hardly wagers at all, except when he has to, to pay the bills. And he always wins."

Of course, Montford reasoned, he could make so many stipulations in the settlements that the former officer could never touch a groat of the money. That is, if the marquess decided to grant the child her favor, which was by no means a foregone conclusion, except in Harriet's mind.

She pressed on. "But if he had funds, maybe he would start a new business, one Allie could like better, so she'll marry him faster."

The marquess looked at the child over the top of his glass. "What makes you think I care whether those two get wed or not?"

"You care about Lady Margery and Harold being happy, don't you? And you are going to pay her dowry, they say, and they don't even need it, 'cause they can live at home in the country or here with you."

"Heaven forfend," his lordship muttered.

"Allie and the captain need the money, and she is your granddaughter, too. It's only fair that you give her the same amount, like what you would have given her mother."

"I would have given Miss Silver's mother far more, if she had married the man of my choice."

"But she had to choose the man she loved, like Lady Margery and Darla and Patsy and Mrs. Crandall."

"Am I supposed to dower them, too, whoever they might be?"

"No, only Allie. It's only fair," Harriet repeated.

The marquess's views had not been changed by wiser heads and better orators. He set his glass down and stood. The conversation was at an end. "I am sorry, young lady, but the world is not fair. You will have to learn that lesson sooner or later. Now go on home before someone comes searching for you here. I have had enough botheration for one day. I owe nothing to your guardian or your governess."

Harriet's lip started trembling and her eyes filled with tears. "My lord," she said, her voice not much louder than a whisper, "my mother was killed by my uncle when I was three. My father died in the army, and my grandmother is too addled to care for me. Don't you think I know that the world is not fair?"

Montford stared at the frog, rather than the child.

"Don't you think I deserve a family, sir?"

CHAPTER TWENTY-EIGHT

Jack was pacing in the street in front of Carde House. Allie was standing in the carriage drive. He was waiting for Harriet to come home; she was waiting for a ransom note. Neither wanted to think about someone carrying back a small broken body or, almost worse, no news whatsoever.

Then there she was, skipping through the nearly empty park, merry as a grig.

"I'll kill her," Jack growled.

"There will not be enough of her left when I am done," Allie said when she saw whose hand Harriet was holding. The Marquess of Montford was holding a tin bucket in his other hand.

Harriet saw them waiting and rushed forward, her arms opened wide. She raced past Jack, who knelt to scoop her up, and she rushed past Allie, who held her own arms out, despite her fury.

Harriet hugged the dog.

Patsy and Mrs. Crandall had been watching through

the windows, so now they ran out and beat the fire gong as hard as they could and as long as their arms could stand. Servants and searchers came tearing out of houses all along the street, cheering and laughing, and patting one another on the back.

"Ale for everyone, in the kitchen," Jack called out, winning another cheer. "And thank you, my friends."

"A fine welcome, eh, Miss Hildebrand?" Montford asked, his lip curling in a sneer at the spectacle.

"The best! Oh, Allie, you were wrong! His lordship isn't a mean old dastard at all! He is giving you a dowry and letting me keep Hubert."

Jack looked at the older man, who had kept his distance. "Why is the marquess suddenly recognizing his elder granddaughter, snip, and who the devil is Hubert?"

Now Montford stepped forward. "Hubert is the frog. Miss Hildebrand says I might come visit him whenever I wish. With your permission, of course," he added dryly. "As for the dower money, you might say Miss Hildebrand and I had a small wager."

"About how far, ah, Hubert can leap?" Jack had thought about making a few bets on the frog's jumping himself. He set the bucket down.

"No, rather about how many tears it takes to bring an old man around to her way of thinking and under her thumb. The puff-guts in Parliament ought to take lessons from the child in manipulation."

Jack grinned. "I'll wager it did not take many tears at all."

"Oh, but you cannot bet anymore, Papa Jack. I promised so Grandfather Montford would give you the money and you and Allie can get married."

"What?" Jack swore. "You have gone beyond the line this time, my girl. Going to Montford and playing your tricks off him behind my back? Making promises in my name? Sticking your nose into matters that do not concern you? Just for that you cannot come to the wedding!"

"Wedding?" Allie asked.

No one answered.

Jack turned to Montford. "Did you think I would live off my wife's money? That I needed your gold to sweeten the deal to restore your granddaughter's good name? Then you are an old fool, and I won't invite you either." He reached into his inner coat pocket and pulled out an official-looking paper. "I purchased a special license this very morning, with my own money, thank you. And I asked Allie to marry me without any of your meddling, miss, or your sudden consideration for Miss Silver's reputation, my lord. And she agreed."

Allie tugged on his arm. "I did? I thought I agreed that I would be your lover."

Jack clamped his hand over her mouth, a bit too late. "Damn, I am tempted not to ask you to the wedding either!"

"No wedding, no dowry," the Marquess declared. "I won't have my family name dragged through the muck and the mire, I say."

Jack was not paying attention to his future in-law. "What kind of man do you take me for, to dishonor the woman I love?"

"You love me?"

"Of course I do! Why else would I ask you to marry me?"

"Good, then that is settled and I can go home to my supper." Montford turned to go. "Have your man of business call on my solicitor in the morning to discuss settlements and draw up papers."

"Wait, my lord," Allie called to him from Jack's arms, where she thought she might stay forever. "What makes you think I will take your money?"

"Because Miss Hildebrand says you are no fool, that is why. What, would you let pride rule your life like I did mine, costing me my only daughter? I wouldn't be surprised, for your mother was just as obstinate. I thought you were more intelligent, though, than to give up your best chance for respectability because you were too mulish to forgive a stubborn old man."

"I have decided that respectability is not all it is cracked up to be, especially as you in Society define it. Being with the one you love is more important, as my mother decided before me."

"Yes, but now you can have both. Think of how much better your life—and Endicott's and your future children's lives—can be with a share of my fortune. Would you turn it down and condemn them to a life of chance? Would you gamble on their futures at the outskirts of acceptance, when all you have to do is accept what should have been your mother's portion?"

Allie looked at Jack, then at Harriet, who was starting to look forlorn, even though she had used up her quota of tears at the marquess's house. Jack shrugged his broad shoulders. "I can support my own family, but not as comfortably as I would wish."

Allie swallowed, then said, "In that case, I accept, my lord."

"Grandfather."

"Grandfather," she acknowledged, stepping out of Jack's embrace and holding her hand out. Montford placed Hubert's bucket's handle in it. "I'll come by to see how you go on tomorrow, what? And you, sir," he said to Jack. "I have a few ideas of what you can do so that my great-grandchildren will not be social pariahs."

After he left, Jack sent Harriet to her room, promising a few words about disobedience, disappearing, and deceiving a nobleman. And about dealing him a heart attack when he could not find her.

Then he took Allie's hand and led her through the house, past the grinning workmen and the smiling servants. He kept going, out through the French doors to the terraced gardens behind his brother's house.

"I have a few ideas of my own, Miss Silver."

"Do you?"

So he showed her, starting where they had left off that afternoon, but a cold concrete bench was not conducive to lovemaking. It was perfect for love-pledging, however.

Jack reluctantly took his arms from around Allie—where they had been to keep her warm, naturally—and knelt at her feet. "I realize I did not ask you properly before. But now I am begging you to make me the happiest of men. Will you marry me, my dear Miss Silver? My life, my love?"

"Are you sure you love me?"

"Sure? I am kneeling in damp dirt for you, aren't I? Ruining a perfectly good pair of trousers."

She pulled him up to sit beside her again, keeping his hand in both of hers. "But are you sure about staying married? What if you decide next year that you'd prefer to be a bachelor again?"

"I am sure that I want to change my life, become a better man for you. I cannot promise forever. Look at Hildebrand, dead so young. But yes, as long as there is breath in my body, I will love you, and only you. That's the family motto, you know, 'Ever true.' You are the only woman I have wanted since I first laid eyes on you. You are the only woman I will ever want."

Which called for another heated celebration.

"But what of you, my dear? You have not said yes. For that matter, you have not said you love me."

"Of course I do. I would have left the day I arrived, otherwise. And I was ready to be your lover, because I cannot think of anything I would rather be, except your wife. You have made me the happiest woman on earth, my own true love."

"No matter that I am a gambler?"

She patted his chest, where his heart was beating madly. "It is not what you are but who you are. Inside, you are the man I love."

"Then you won't mind if I change the club into a school? I have been thinking, you see, about finding a new occupation. The club has not brought my sister back, but maybe a school would. What do you think about opening an academy for young women of limited means, so they can learn skills and not have to take to the streets? My brother will help set up an endowment. He already finances orphanages and hospitals, so I am sure he will contribute. That way I can keep a place for information to come and rewards to be offered. We will not be wealthy, but neither will we be in need."

"You would really start a school? That has been my dream for years. Oh, Jack, I think that is the best idea you've ever had, other than marrying me, of course."

"Of course. And I do have a bit of property in the country, and some funds of my own and—"

She patted his chest again. "You have everything I need, right here."

"The special license?"

"My heart, in your keeping. Forever."

"You can bet on it."

While Jack and Allie were planning their wedding and their future, a young woman was also looking forward. A beautiful blond-haired girl was at the docks in Dover, waiting to board a packet boat headed for France. She wasn't safe in London, with people looking for her, people threatening her about old secrets. But in France, she could study with one of the grand couturiers, learn to design exquisite gowns for exquisite, wealthy women. She had names, letters of reference, and enough funds to live on while she learned. When she was done, she could return to England with money and prestige.

Then Queenie could unravel the secrets of her past herself.

Read on for a peek at

Queen of Diamonds

the exciting conclusion to the

House of Cards trilogy,

coming from Signet Eclipse

in June 2006.

Harlan Harkness, Lord Harking, hated London. Oh, the viscount liked the camaraderie of the clubs, the lectures at the Agricultural Society, the bookshops, and Tattersall's. Harry, as he was universally called, appreciated having his tailor, his bootmaker, and his hatter all close by, and all knowing his preferences. What he disliked were the dirt and the smell, the crowds and the crime. And the matchmaking mamas.

The whole society business irritated Harry: the wearing of uncomfortable formal dress to make uncomfortable conversations with young females who would be more comfortable in the schoolroom—while their Machiavellian, maneuvering mothers tried to snabble every available bachelor.

What was wrong with a chap of twenty and nine staying unwed? Harry had plenty of time to create an heir, and if he did not, his cousin would make an admirable viscount. Leonard already had two sons and a shrewish wife. Besides, Harry was no prize on the matrimonial market that he could see. His face would not frighten dogs or small children, but he was no Adonis. His hair was an ordinary brown, his eyes an ordinary brown, and his cheeks took on a silly schoolboy blush in the cold, the heat, or in ballrooms. His physique was nothing out of the ordinary for a big man who worked along with his tenant farmers. He was not slim and graceful like the Town tulips—not when he had to help repair bridges and fix roofs after storms. In fact, he was clumsy on the dance floor, clumsier at light flirtation, and an outright clod when it came to courtship—to which it had not yet come, thank goodness. His fortune was not even large enough to raise eyebrows or expectations, although Harking Hall was a handsome pile, if he had to say so himself. The Hall was attractively set amid parks and profitable farmland with a racing stable, oval course, and paddocks all in sight. He loved the place. He wished he was there now.

The London ladies did not care about fine horses or fertile farms or fine old architecture. They cared about filling their dance cards, being fit for their fancy clothes, being seen at the right parties, catching the best *parti*. The most advantageous match, the highest title, and the deepest pockets seemed to matter more to the misses than affection, respect, or mutual interests.

They sure as the devil could not be interested in a plain country lumpkin like him. Yet they were setting out lures everywhere he went. Hell, they were digging mantraps for Harry—in Town less than a week.

He was staying at the Grand Hotel, rebuilt after the fire, where at least he could see Green Park from his suite's windows and imagine himself back in Lincolnshire. Invitations somehow found their way to him, for everything from Venetian breakfasts—after noon—to waltzing parties. Hah! Were the wallflowers so desperate they were willing to sacrifice their toes for his minor viscountcy? Then there were the invites to six dinners, routs, debutante balls, and theater parties—each and every night, even now in late winter before the height of the Season, with half of Society at their country homes, where Harry longed to be.

Then he entered his friend's nearly empty gambling establishment. Trust Mad Jack Endicott to attract the most beautiful ladybirds in London.

The smaller woman was a rounded dumpling of a brunette who flashed him a saucy smile while her friend spoke to the clerk. It was the friend who stole Harry's breath away. No, that was the fast walk here and the cold. No bird of paradise was going to distract him from his mission, attract him to indiscretion. But, lord, the black-clad female was stunning. The color of her clothes might be somber, but the cut was anything but, delineating her tall, slim figure under a velvet cape. The velvet did not look half as soft as her skin, either. He could not see her eyes, but he could glimpse a halo of shiny ebony curls under a scrap of ruffled black lace, with a plumed black feather held with a bright blue ribbon. Style, grace, and beauty all in one woman—and didn't she just know it? Hell, the woman had a dog that matched.

Harry admired the dog too.

BARBARA METZGER

Ace of Hearts

Book One of the House of Cards Trilogy

Never did Alexander "Ace" Endicott,
the Earl of Cards, imagine himself to be
thrice-betrothed against his will by the
doings of three desperate debutantes.
So he escapes London for his property in
the country, where he follows through
with his father's last wish—to find his
long-lost step-sister.

But the search takes a detour, leading him
to Nell, and forcing him to wonder if two
mismatched lovers can make a royal pair.

0-451-21626-1

Available wherever books are sold or at
penguin.com

S028/Metzger

BARBARA METZGER

"Barbara Metzger deliciously mixes love
and laughter." —*Romantic Times*

Wedded Bliss
0-451-20859-5

A Perfect Gentleman
0-451-21041-7

The Duel
0-451-21389-0

Available wherever books are sold or at
penguin.com

S026/Metzger

All your favorite romance writers are
coming together.

SIGNET ECLIPSE